STRANGE BEDFELLOWS

The Hot Blood Series

HOT BLOOD

HOTTER BLOOD

HOTTEST BLOOD

HOT BLOOD XI:
FATAL ATTRACTIONS

STRANGE BEDFELLOWS

Published by Kensington Publishing Corporation

STRANGE BEDFELLOWS

THE HOT BLOOD SERIES

EDITED BY JEFF GELB AND
MICHAEL GARRETT

KENSINGTON BOOKS
http://www.kensingtonbooks.com

KENSINGTON BOOKS are published by

Kensington Publishing Corp.
850 Third Avenue
New York, NY 10022

All Kensington titles, imprints and distributed lines are available at special quantity discounts for bulk purchases for sales promotion, premiums, fund-raising, educational or institutional use.

Special book excerpts or customized printings can also be created to fit specific needs. For details, write or phone the office of the Kensington Special Sales Manager: Kensington Publishing Corp., 850 Third Avenue, New York, NY 10022. Attn. Special Sales Department. Phone: 1-800-221-2647.

ISBN 0-7582-0692-5

First Kensington Trade Paperback Printing: November 2004
10 9 8 7 6 5 4 3 2 1

Printed in the United States of America

Dedicated to our legion of fans, without whom the Hot Blood series would have experienced its last orgasmic shudder years ago.

Contents

INTRODUCTION	ix
ABOMINATION by Greg Kihn	1
DRIVING BLIND by Ilsa J. Bick	23
THIRTY MINUTES by Lonn Friend	41
THE LOST HERD by Del Howison	55
DANCE: THE DEVIL'S ORGASM by Michael Laimo	69
RAGNALL REDUX by Abbie Bernstein	81
FOREVER AND EVER by Dave Zeltserman	97
FADING MEMORIES by Michael Bracken	109
TIGHTER by Christa Faust	119
WHERE NO ONE EVER DIES GOOD by Stephen Gresham	133

DESIRE 161
by J. F. Gonzalez

THE LAST ROMANCE 179
by Catherine Dain

LOVE CONNECTION 195
by Alan Ormsby

STRIP SEARCH 205
by Elle Frazier

COMMITTED 231
by Jeff Gelb

THE LAST MAN ON EARTH 247
by Marv Wolfman

HYPOEROTICA 267
by Dana Solomon

THE NEXT-BEST THING 275
by Michael Garrett

CAMELOT 287
by Graham Masterton

ABOUT THE AUTHORS 317

Introduction

How hot can Hot Blood get?

After eleven volumes of the world-renowned Hot Blood books, what was left to say? That was our challenge in collecting stories for our twelfth edition of the series. Your enthusiastic response to the return of the Hot Blood books from Kensington was gratifying, so when we got the nod for another volume, we put the word out, hoping that our favorite writers could pluck one more erotic, horrific tale out of their twisted subconscious minds. As always, we also spread the word to authors new to the series to get their take on the subject.

What's the allure of sex and shocks anyway? Why does the mere flash of cleavage, the curve of a breast, the sight of a bra strap make men shiver? Why are guys mesmerized by the sight of a bare navel under a tight, short T-shirt? Or a tattoo that starts visibly at midhip and travels south to regions unseen by all but a lucky few? Why are men driven crazy by low-slung jeans?

And what about you ladies? Why does the sight of unbuttoned jeans on a bare-chested hottie get your juices flowing? What is it about watching a man bend over the hood of a car in tight, faded Levi's and a white muscle shirt that turns you on? And then there's the silhouette of your man behind glass shower doors washing himself, letting the deluge of water bathe his suntanned skin.

Just what is the secret of sex? And why are we even more fascinated when sensual situations go wrong? Terribly, horribly awry, in a way that we couldn't even create in our worst nightmares? It's the stuff of which movie classics like *Fatal Attraction*, *Basic Instinct* and *Body Heat* are made.

What's more, we had to ask: What constitutes erotic horror fiction in this new millennium? What are the boundaries? Are there any boundaries? What is horrific? Do vampires and werewolves still thrill, or is horror now real-world stuff like terrorists and serial killers? When we cast our wide author net, we sat back and awaited their stories with great interest.

We were amazed and surprised by what today's best authors had to say on the subject. And now you're about to find out just how hot Hot Blood can get. Join us on another journey of all-new depraved discoveries as we tear back the curtains and reveal some of the most stunning stories yet, from the minds of the world's most imaginative authors of horror fiction.

Is the darker side of sex to be found here? Answers await on the forthcoming pages!

Abomination

Greg Kihn

A stranger story has never been told than that of the world-famous Siamese twins Kang and Chen. In the year 1889, in the city of New York, the bizarre events I am about to describe occurred. My involvement began with the visit of Cecil R. Putnam, entrepreneur and showman, to my law office. I knew of him, as his oddities exhibitions were widely covered in the press.

He walked up to me and shook my hand forcefully. He was a big fellow with a large, florid face, made even more prominent by prodigious sideburns. Forceful and direct, he came right to the point.

His voice boomed like a carnival barker. "Mr. Ruebach, I am in need of your services, sir."

I smiled, curious. "Well, in that case, please have a seat and make yourself comfortable. It's quite an honor to have such a celebrated individual within these humble walls."

I motioned for him to sit and he did so, instantly producing a cigar from his waistcoat.

"What is the nature of your business?"

Putnam fixed his eyes on me. "Let me come right to the point. This is not in regards to me, sir, but rather, one, or perhaps I should say two, of my clients. They appear to be in a terrible fix. I took the liberty of approaching you directly in this rather delicate matter."

"Of course."

He lit his cigar and puffed a great billow of smoke into the air. It hung around his head like a storm cloud.

"You have no doubt heard of the Siamese twins Kang and Chen?"

I nodded. Their appearances at Putnam's National Museum and Oddities Exhibition Hall were the talk of the town.

"As you may know, I am their exclusive promoter." He leaned forward and his voice modulated down a half step. "I can assure you, sir, that they are one of the great box office attractions in the world. They've toured Europe, been the guest of kings and queens, made vast fortunes, but more than that, these men are husbands and fathers."

"They're married? But how is that possible?"

Putnam chuckled. "There are more things in this world than you can imagine. Why, at this very moment I have on exhibition not five blocks from here a twenty-five-inch man who happens to be married to a thirty-inch-woman. Have you seen the presentation?"

"No."

"Be my guest."

He handed me a pair of tickets, which I accepted with mild trepidation. Human oddities were not my cup of tea.

"As it happens, Kang and Chen married sisters in Wheeling, West Virginia, and have fathered, between the two of them, nineteen children."

I was astonished. "How is that possible?"

Putnam waved a hand. "Kang and Chen are joined at the hip by a fleshy ligature, five-and-a-half inches in length, Mr. Ruebach. One can only conjecture as to the arrangements they made regarding sexual matters. But, as in every other facet of life, these remarkable men have found a way."

"What is their legal problem?"

Putnam folded his hands. His cigar was clutched between powerful jaws.

"Last night, at eleven-forty-five, Kang and Chen were arrested by the New York City Police Department on charges of murder."

"I see."

"The police say they have evidence to show that the brother known as Chen is responsible for the murder of a woman named Cassandra Billets, a streetwalker by all accounts."

"I see. They charged Chen, but not Kang?"

"That is correct," Putnam said. "As to your fee, I am authorized to prepare a bank draft to serve as your retainer. These men are quite wealthy; money shouldn't be a concern. I'm told you're the finest criminal lawyer in the country, perhaps the only man capable of defending these poor creatures. I can't begin to tell you the unique nature of their situation, and the attendant problems. The public interest in such matters is ravenous. I dare say that the publicity surrounding this trial could prove to be a major distraction. Already my office has been besieged by reporters. They can't be more than a few steps behind me even now."

I stood, walked to the window and looked out. Below, carriages traversed the rutted street; the pulse of New York City flowed. On this crisp October day, I saw no reporters.

Putnam's voice rumbled behind me. "We're dealing with freaks of nature, Mr. Ruebach. *Abominations.* Most people are repulsed, but also strangely attracted. I know the phenomena. I trade in it."

I turned away from the window, facing him again. "How much do you know of the crime itself?"

"Only what the police allege: that Chen contracted favor with Miss Billets and, once alone with her, pierced her heart. Of course, the term 'alone' doesn't really apply here in the usual sense."

"Of course, because the other brother saw it all. You say these two men, though conjoined, are completely different people? Independent of mind, and, as far as possible, of body?"

Putnam's cigar smoke made fascinating patterns in the slanting light. I stared at it as he spoke.

"Yes. As far as the ligature allows, of course. Their personalities differ vastly. Kang is a scholar, a philosopher, while Chen manifests a more licentious deportment. Two men couldn't be more contrasting. When one considers that they are bound together for life, well, one can get a sense for their predicament."

I nodded. "What do you know of Miss Billets?"

"Only that she knew both brothers, that they had frequented her room on several occasions."

"It must have been difficult for Chen to find a willing sexual partner, even among prostitutes."

"Miss Billets may have been a specialist."

I pondered the situation for a moment. "I would like to meet these men, straightaway."

"Then you accept the case?"

"Most definitely."

My first glimpse of the brothers was at their jail cell in the central facility. Except for a disquieting closeness, one brother to the other, they appeared as two normal Asian men in their thirties, and it was only upon closer examination that I could discern they were indeed joined in the manner described by Mr. Putnam. The ligature was barely visible through the folds of their shirts, and I tried not to stare. No other abnormalities did I observe at first glance. They sat side by side, angled slightly inward, their heads turned away from each other. Four legs crowded the floor before them.

"Good day, gentlemen," I said, tentatively extending my hand, to which brother I knew not. I was hoping it would be Kang.

The brother on the right took my hand and grasped it firmly. "I am Kang, Mr. Ruebach. This is my brother Chen."

Chen grunted and remained still, declining to take my hand.

"Thank you for coming. I'm afraid we are in a dire predicament." Kang spoke with a slight accent unfamiliar to me, but I found his manner educated and refined.

"Yes, so Mr. Putnam has told me. May I ask the circumstances of last evening and the events that led to your arrest?"

Kang nodded and withdrew an envelope from his pocket. "Yes, of course. But first, I have written a letter to my wife. I wonder if you could see that she gets it."

I took the letter he offered. It came from the jacket of his suit, and I noticed for the first time his custom-made clothes. They were of the finest quality.

"The news of my arrest will grieve her," he said.

I nodded. "And what of Chen's wife?"

"I have included a message to his wife as well. She is the sister of my wonderful Betsy."

"Of course."

Cecil R. Putnam took Kang's hand. "Please, my friend, tell Mr. Ruebach your story."

Chen had not yet spoken. He seemed sullen and uninterested.

"My brother and I have different interests. We divide our time equally between us. One night he chooses our activity, the next I do, and so on. On his nights, we, from time to time, enjoy the city's nightlife. I allow him his liberties, Mr. Ruebach, and he allows me mine. It's the least we can do under the circumstances."

"Did you know this woman, Cassandra Billets?"

Kang became silent, his eyes downcast.

"Kang, you must tell me the entire truth, not only for your sake, but your brother's, too. There is no way I can represent you in court without full disclosure."

Kang lowered his head. "Of course. Yes. Forgive me, Mr. Ruebach, but what I have to say is painful to both of us."

"You'll not say a thing!" Chen suddenly shouted.

Kang reacted to his brother's outburst instantly. He swiveled his head to face him and brought his outside arm to bear in a threatening manner.

"You can't silence me!" Kang barked at him. "I won't pay the price for your transgressions. I told you that, so keep your tongue."

With that, Chen balled his fists and actually struck his brother a glancing blow on the jaw. Kang reacted by sliding his inner arm up around Chen's throat. They fell off the chair and went rolling across the floor.

"Gentlemen! Please!" Putnam and one of the guards fell upon the unlikely combatants and, not being able to separate them, held their arms down until hostilities ceased. Such a show of spontaneous animosity, delivered with such venom, unnerved me.

"Perhaps we can do this another time."

Putnam shook his head. "There is no other time. Chen will have to curb his protestations, even if we are forced to hold him down."

"I don't care!" Chen shouted. "I don't care what happens to me!"

Putnam placed a hand on the hostile brother's shoulder.

"This man is here to help you. He is, in my estimation, the only man who can help. My God, man, don't you realize what's at stake here?"

Chen said, "Very well, let Kang speak. As for my own defense, I have nothing to say. If he wants to try to save his hide, let him."

Kang nodded. "Thank you, brother."

"Be damned, Kang."

The two brothers locked eyes. The look that passed between them was something I think I shall never see again. I saw hatred so pure and venal as to have weight and substance, yet also a profound sadness, the resigned acceptance of their symbiotic suffering.

Kang turned toward me and smiled weakly. "Then you may consider yourself to be my lawyer alone, and Chen will have to fend for himself. If, in the course of your duties you also find yourself defending Chen, then we would be in your debt."

I put out my hand, and Kang shook it. "Agreed. Now, the entire story. Leave nothing out."

"Last night at nine o'clock, we entered the pump room of our hotel, the Excelsior, and Chen had several drinks. At ten-thirty we exited the saloon and hired a carriage to take us to an address on Houston Street. We arrived during a rainstorm and there were few people on the street at that hour."

"What time was that?"

"Oh, it must have been around eleven. We knocked at the door and a man answered and admitted us. The atmosphere inside was something like a men's club. There was a bar, a smoking room, and a salon. We were approached by Miss Billets. My brother negotiated with her."

"So you were in a house of assignation?"

Kang nodded gravely. "I'm afraid so."

"May I assume that Miss Billets was a prostitute?"

"You may. We had contracted her services before, on several occasions."

"Was it Chen who hired her, or did you both?"

Kang sighed. "Originally it was Chen. But to be in such close proximity to the sexual act and not become aroused is quite difficult, I discovered. You can only imagine what I went through. At first I felt repulsed at sharing a woman with my brother, but Miss Billets encouraged me."

"Encouraged you?"

"Yes, she was quite demonstrative. She actually seemed to take some kind of pleasure in it."

"So you both had sex with her?"

"Yes, several times." Kang blushed.

I glanced at Putnam. He fidgeted in his chair, a light sheen of perspiration across his brow.

I cleared my throat. "How did Chen come to stab her?"

"While in the act of copulation, Cassandra often became quite vocal. She said all sorts of provocative things to both Chen and me. It seemed to stimulate her strange desires. I can say that it had a great effect on Chen, and he became more and more forceful in his actions. She goaded him on, calling him filthy names, insulting him until he became violent. The more violent the exchange became, the more she seemed to enjoy it. He strangled her neck, but she cried for more. He struck her and she moaned with pleasure. She cried out the one word that has always stabbed our hearts. She called us an *abomination*."

Kang paused, his voice dropped to a whisper. "Chen pulled a dagger out and held it to her breast. She laughed in his face."

Kang began to sob. "She wouldn't stop laughing. She was capable of astonishing cruelty. She dared him to kill her. She actually demanded it. I knew Chen would break."

Chen sat motionless throughout Kang's testimony. I glanced at him and saw anger in his face.

"All the while he was pumping her like a machine, and she met each thrust with one of her own, matching him every step of the way. Her eyes were on fire. She growled like an animal. At the height of their passion, he stabbed her and ejaculated into her limp body."

"You witnessed this?"

"I was there."

"Good God," Putnam groaned. "This is dreadful."

I turned to Chen, who glared at me. "Did you stab Miss Billets in the manner described by your brother?"

Chen said nothing.

"I strongly advise you to cooperate with me, sir. For your own good, I need to hear it from you. Did you stab her?"

Chen shook his fist in my face. "You're a fool," he hissed. "Ask me no more."

I turned to Kang. "With which hand did he stab her?"

Kang looked at me strangely. I think the question surprised him. "Why, I believe it was the left hand."

"You believe it was the left hand?" I asked. "You were a witness—didn't you see it? Was it the left hand or the right?"

Kang nodded. "Yes, yes, the left hand. It would have to be the outside hand, to get the proper leverage and keep it away from me."

I pondered his statement. "Yes, of course. Otherwise you could have grabbed the hand and stopped him."

"Probably, had I the chance."

"What happened next?"

"We rushed out of the room. Downstairs in the salon, we called for our carriage. The proprietor noticed blood on Chen's hands and sent someone to check on Miss Billets. When her body was discovered, we were detained. The police came shortly thereafter and arrested us."

I turned to Chen and asked, "Do you have anything to add?"

Chen scowled and said nothing.

"Those are the facts, sir," Kang said softly.

Chen chuckled.

I stood and looked at Putnam. "I would like to speak with the police captain at this time."

Putnam looked dazed. "Yes, yes, of course."

I said my good-byes to Kang and Chen and, as I shook Kang's hand (for Chen would not extend his), I had the most overwhelming sense of pity. These men, for some reason chosen by God, had been made to endure the unendurable and were absolutely helpless to do anything about it. Fate had carried them as far as this, but now what?

Captain Ellis Hagen, an officious man with a huge gray beard, greeted me in his office. He looked tired and uncomfortable in his uniform.

"I would like to know what evidence you have against my clients, Kang and Chen."

Hagen looked me over. "I have witnesses who saw them go into the room and come out of the room. The girl was alone with them; God knows what kind of perversions she was involved with. The place is a notorious house of assignation, with a thriving opium business going on the side. We've shut them down again, hopefully for good this time. Frankly, I'm surprised they were admitted, considering the prospect of having sex with those monsters."

"Is that what you consider them? Monsters?"

Hagen looked perplexed. "What else would a good Christian man call them?"

"I believe the term is human beings."

Hagen snorted. "Hardly."

"In the eyes of the law," I said slowly, "they are human beings. I think that's what's important here."

Hagen bristled. "That creature is one entity, joined at the hip. If one hangs, the other dies anyway, so I say hang 'em both and be done with it. I'm sure the judge will see things quite the same way."

"I suggest we have them examined by a doctor, Captain Hagen. I understand that a noted surgeon, Dr. Wilmont Hardison, is familiar with their condition and would be qualified to act as an expert witness. He has an office here in Manhattan."

"The thing is—they're guilty. I have the murder weapon and an eyewitness."

"Eyewitness? You mean the other brother? Kang?"

"Precisely," Hagen nodded.

"But surely you can't make him testify against his own brother," I said.

"Regardless, we have them, hands down, and my job is clear. I'll let the doctor in, as you suggest, but the fact remains that *abomination* killed somebody, and that whatever it is, whether it's two men or one, the guilty party will be brought to justice."

"I'd like to see the body," I said.

"The body? That's most irregular."

"But hasn't the coroner done with it?"

"Sir, there was a coroner's inquest this morning at the site of the murder. He is finished. The coroner corroborated what I already believed to be true, that your client, excuse me, I mean *clients*, did her in. We will both testify in court that she died of a knife wound in the chest. I find your request to view the body repugnant."

"I need to check something. It will only take a minute. I would also like to see a copy of the coroner's report."

Hagen rolled his eyes. "Very well, counselor. As long as the undertaker hasn't been round to claim it, we'll play your ghoulish game. Come with me."

He led me to the morgue, where I viewed the remains of Miss Billets. She had been a good-looking woman in her twenties, with long brown hair and prominent breasts. As the sheet was drawn back, I held my breath and leaned forward to examine the wound, and noticed immediately that the cut marks left by the knife went from right to left. I ascertained this given the angle and depth of the cut. The knife seemed to penetrate from a starting point on the right, and as it passed through her flesh, reached the maximum depth on the left side.

Hagen let me gaze for a few moments before drawing the draping down a few inches more, revealing the rest of her torso.

"What about these?" I asked, pointing to a pair of cuts, one on each breast.

"What about them? They're of little consequence. The fatal wound was in the heart."

I examined the cuts closer. "Mutilations. They appear to be deliberate mutilations. Have you taken a look at these, Hagen?"

He shrugged and leaned over the cold, white body. "Curious."

"See how shallow they are, almost delicate? It occurs to me that they were inflicted after she was dead."

Hagen frowned. "That's preposterous. Why would anybody stab somebody after they'd already killed them? It's ridiculous. You lawyers amuse me. Anything but the obvious truth, eh? I suppose next you'll tell me that the last thing she saw, the image of the killer, is still on her retina, like a daguerreotype, or some such nonsense."

He was referring to a recently published report in the *New York Herald* speculating that the last image seen by a murder victim was preserved on the eye of the deceased. This unproven theory was quite controversial and the object of ridicule by certain groups.

Hagen said, "These wounds mean nothing. It's the death blow that matters. Those scratches on her breasts could have occurred when she fell."

"I would like to talk to the proprietor of the house."

"You mean Madame LaFlore. I can easily arrange for an interview with her. As a matter of fact, she is currently our guest here at the City Jail."

* * *

Madame LaFlore sat on a chair, her chin up and her breasts thrust out, a proud woman of commodious size. She stared defiantly at me.

"Did you know the accused?"

"I most certainly did. They were regular clients."

"Did they always see Miss Billets?"

"Yes. She specialized in grotesques."

I blinked. Madame LaFlore saw my discomfort and seemed amused.

"Ahh, that Cassie was a wild one. She'd do anything for money. We once had a Polish count with a hunchback. He was absolutely repulsive. None of the girls would touch him. Then, here comes Cassie and lays him out as pretty as you please. Later, she told me how she'd enjoyed it. You see, the more disgusting her sexual partner, the more she relished it. She had a client list of peculiars that would frighten anyone. And it didn't stop with just physical infirmities, mind you. She eagerly bedded psychopaths, criminals, even the diseased."

"The diseased?" I croaked, my mouth as dry as chalk.

Madame LaFlore nodded. "Men with horrible afflictions and severed limbs. It was quite remarkable."

"But why?"

Madame sighed. "Who can tell? In this business I have seen enough of the human condition to not be surprised, or repulsed, by anything. There's always the money, of course, but Cassie was different. I knew very little of her past except that she'd had a tough life and started selling her body while still a child. A more hardened, streetwise soul you'll never meet. She'd been with us off and on for three years."

"She would willingly submit herself to these indignities?"

"Eagerly. I think Cassie sought to cheapen and degrade herself because she was, at her core, greatly troubled and unhappy. She would offer herself up to sadists as a willing victim. Now, why would she do that? Because she wanted to be punished, that's why. I think she actually loved the pain."

I scratched my head. "So, it was only natural for her to gravitate to Kang and Chen."

"She looked forward to their visits. Sometimes they came every night, asking only for her. She was paid handsomely, of course."

"Did she reveal anything to you regarding their sexual relationships?"

Madame LaFlore smiled wickedly. "Curious? Of course you are. Who wouldn't be? It was the talk of the salon. She would emerge from the bedroom bruised and disheveled, and, on one occasion, bleeding. Oftentimes, screams could be heard, then moans. One of the other girls told me that Cassie once bragged to her about taking both men simultaneously, one in front, the other behind. She said the climax nearly made her faint. As for the rough stuff, well, that was Cassie's stock-in-trade."

"Did Chen exhibit any hostility to her?"

Madame LaFlore shrugged. "I couldn't tell them apart."

Dr. Hardison examined the brothers early the next day and reported his findings to me.

"They are two healthy male adults, conjoined, unfortunately, in one of nature's cruelest tricks."

"I am particularly interested in their physical relationship. They share no organs?"

"Each man has his own heart, lungs, and brain. They seem to function independently of each other, but it is impossible to say in what way they are the same. The blood that flows through their veins is, I believe, for the most part separate. But I can't be sure. There appear to be no veins in the ligature, but without actually operating on them, it's impossible to tell."

"I understand."

"I think the medical problems are only part of the picture here." He handed me a card. "There is a young doctor in Vienna whose name is Sigmund Freud who has some revolutionary theories." I glanced at the card. Printed on it were the words DR. SIGMUND FREUD, NEUROPATHOLOGIST, PSYCHOANALYST.

I was surprised. "Psychoanalysis? He's an alienist?"

"Yes. I know that you're considering the link between the brothers' minds. You need to establish the individualism, the independence of thought, of each of the brothers. That is the terrain of the psychoanalyst, and Freud is the father of this form of therapy. He's your man if you want an expert opinion on the matter."

"Can they be separated?"

Hardison shook his head. "The surgical procedure would be very dangerous, even with Lister's marvelous new antiseptic techniques. It just can't be done safely."

"How can I contact Dr. Freud?"

"He is in New York for a lecture at the Academy of Medicine. He departs for Boston in two days to speak at Clark University. He is accompanied by two other giants in the field, Jung and Ferenczi. Perhaps we could persuade Dr. Freud to examine the brothers before he leaves."

Sigmund Freud sat patiently taking notes in a brown leather journal as he interviewed the brothers.

After an hour, Kang broke down. "Why do you insist on asking me about my mother? What does she have to do with it? If you must know, my mother hated me! She hated *us.* She cast us out, cast *me* out, called me a demon. She lived in shame for the rest of her life."

"She sold us into slavery," Chen said unexpectedly.

Freud nodded and acted as if he heard such discussions every day. "Did you hate her?"

Chen laughed. "Of course I hated her. She brought us into this world."

Freud constantly took notes. "And you, Kang, did you feel the same way?"

"No," Kang whispered. "She was my mother. I loved her."

"Your brother seems to disagree," Freud said firmly. He closed his journal.

Later, Dr. Freud addressed Mr. Putnam and me. "Gentlemen, it is my published theory that man is the logical product of his environment. We react to events when we are young that shape our lives. The mind represses painful and unhappy memories, pushing them from the ego into the id, causing subconscious changes in our behavior."

"The id?"

"Our mind works on two levels, the ego and the id, the id being the subconscious."

"So," I said, "it should stand to reason that the id of both men should be the same, full of the same repressed memories, since they both experienced the same traumas at the same times."

"Yet they're entirely different," Putnam said.

Freud nodded. "It would appear so. However, in medicine, as in life, things are not always as they appear."

The trial was held at the recently constructed Criminal Court of the City of New York at 52 Chambers Street, which had quickly come to be known as the "Tweed Ring Courthouse," a dubious moniker, since the building, like the man, was in a constant state of construction. Though unfinished, it nevertheless was crowded the day of the trial. Reporters from the *Times,* the *World,* the *Tribune* and the popular *Leslie's Illustrated Weekly* elbowed into the great room to observe the proceedings.

I advanced with the first line of my defense, which was simply that the law can't punish the innocent brother for the crimes of the guilty. It was an impossible situation. The prosecution took the approach that it didn't matter; the two were really only one in the eyes of the law.

The climax of the trial came with the testimony of Kang.

The court sat hushed as he described a life of terrible hardship, citing their various tribulations and how they had turned Chen bitter and him philosophical.

Kang's voice was thin and had a singsong quality to it, causing everyone in the room to listen carefully. "After the monks had raised us to the age of thirteen, we were purchased by a carnival and put on display. An Australian named Robert Wells paid the carnival to take us away to England."

"He bought you as slaves?"

"Essentially, yes, but it was better than the slavery we already had endured at the carnival. There we had been kept with the animals, chained and mistreated. We were beaten often. It was a very hard and painful life there."

Kang sighed. "On the boat to England, we were shown kindness for the first time, and it was a revelation. We were allowed to walk the deck, have our own room, and even a special bed. It was much better than the carnival. Once in England, we were put on display. We became famous and toured Europe and met several kings. In fact, because of my love for books I was given a royal tutor by Prince Leopold of Romania. It was a marvelous opportunity. I learned to read and write and study the arts. Eventually an agent for Mr. Putnam approached us about coming to New York. We accepted the offer."

"Can you describe the events leading up to the death of Miss Billets?"

Kang told the same story he had told me.

"Did Chen touch Miss Billets after she was dead?"

"No."

I considered the additional wounds I'd observed on Miss Billets and thought it best to not reveal them to the court. I thanked Kang and he stepped down.

I called Dr. Hardison to the stand to testify as to the medical danger of separating the two brothers.

The judge asked, "But is it even remotely possible?"

"Yes, remotely. I would advise against it, however."

I called Dr. Freud to testify that the brothers were indeed two distinct individuals.

When, at last, I reached my closing statement on the final day of the trial, I spoke with as much force and dignity as I could muster.

"This man should not be sentenced. He has already been sentenced by God, sentenced to live a life beyond our scope of suffering. He is a victim of circumstance, nothing more. If you condemn one, you condemn the other."

When the jury returned and the foreman read their decision, the attention of the world seemed focused on his words.

Kang and Chen rose to their feet. Kang stood stone-faced and Chen remained, as he had throughout the trial, despondent.

The foreman spoke without emotion. "We find the defendant Chen guilty of murder in the first degree."

The room exploded. Several newspapermen rushed from the room, a shouting man was ejected by the bailiff, and a large, severely dressed woman fainted.

The judge cleared the court and summoned me to his chambers.

"Mr. Ruebach, I cannot let Chen go free. He has been found guilty and will hang, as prescribed by law. It is what to do about Kang that is the problem. It's a devilish situation. In the interest of justice, I am advising Dr. Hardison to attempt to separate the two by surgically severing the ligature exactly halfway, giving each an equal chance to survive. If Kang lives, he will be set free. At least this way he has a chance."

The twins were moved to the Bellevue Hospital in preparation for Dr. Hardison's operation. The night before the surgery, as they lay in their bed, Chen was overcome with grief and depression. He committed suicide by drinking a solution of tincture of heroin which he purloined from a nurse. He had been brooding since the trial, refusing to eat, and feeling ill. His brother did not notice him slip the bottle from the table into the covers. Later, when he drank it, Kang had been asleep.

When Kang woke up the next morning and found his brother dead, he gave out a great wail. Dr. Hardison rushed to his side.

Kang was frantic. "I am attached to a dead thing! It will decay next to me and rot me from the inside! For God's sake, perform the operation now, before his body begins to decompose."

Hardison took pity on Kang and the operation was performed immediately. Even with Chen dead, it was an extremely risky procedure. After ten hours in the surgical theater, with the finest medical doctors in the country watching, Hardison looked up and nodded.

The twins were finally separated.

After a lengthy and delicate recovery period, Kang began to improve. When at last he was allowed visitors, I went to his hospital room and found him awake and lucid.

"I'm free at last, but what a cost."

"I grieve for your brother, Kang, and I am truly sorry for the way this whole affair has turned out."

I paused and took a deep breath, reluctant to continue, for my next words were difficult to say. "But I must talk to you about something that has been bothering me."

Kang looked at me, his eyes watery and sad. "What is it?"

"Well, in the course of my investigation, I happened to examine the body of Miss Billets, and the wounds I observed were not as you described."

Kang frowned. "What do you mean?"

"I mean that the wounds went counter to the way they should have, if Chen did indeed kill Cassandra Billets in the way you said he did. In point of fact, the wounds suggest exactly the opposite, that it was someone using the knife on the other side. The cut marks went from right to left. You see, that would have been unnatural, perhaps nearly impossible, for your brother."

Kang replied quickly, "The knife could have been in an odd position. His hand could have jerked in any direction. In the heat of the moment, anything is possible. The appearance of the wound means nothing."

I nodded. "Perhaps. But something Freud said intrigued me. He insisted that since both of you experienced the same things at the same time, your mental condition should be similar, if not exactly the same. The repressed memories responsible for the rage that killed Miss Billets must have been shared by both."

"What does that prove?"

"In and of itself, nothing. There was something else, though, something about the body that I didn't reveal at the trial because I was defending you, and I am too good a lawyer to turn my back on that sacred trust. It placed me in a very difficult position. I made up my mind to defend you as best I could, and then, when a verdict had been reached and my job was through, I would come forward with my evidence. Your testimony was damning to Chen, and I wondered why you said it. Then it dawned on me that it was because you were trying to shift the blame from yourself. I decided to try to save Chen's life and bring the real killer to justice. But then the same situation would arise, wouldn't it? They would have the same problem with the sentence, don't you see?"

"You're mad," Kang hissed.

"I think that at the moment of Miss Billets's death, you were engaged in a sex act so vile and intrusive that I would not utter it in private, much less in a court of law. I think you had both penetrated her. Judging from the wounds, I think she was between the two of you and you reached around from behind and stabbed her heart."

"Ridiculous."

I paused. "The body had been mutilated, postmortem, in a curious, deliberate way. I sketched the pattern of the wounds. They were more like deep scratches actually. I showed that drawing to a professor of Asian languages at Columbia University and he recognized them. They were Chinese ideographs representing your name, Kang."

Kang's mouth dropped open. "Impossible."

"Didn't you see what Chen was doing with the knife after you killed her?"

"No . . . I mean . . . this is preposterous!"

"He carved your name, Kang. He carved the name of the killer in the dead flesh of the victim's body."

Kang threw his head back into the pillow and moaned. "Oh God, when will this end? How much suffering must I endure?"

Then, suddenly, his eyes flashed and he shouted, "You! You don't know what it was like! You can't *begin* to know what it was like! It wasn't just me; Chen was bad, too, don't you see? He wanted her dead as much as I did."

"Chen remained silent through the trial while you testified against him. He sacrificed himself for you."

"Chen wanted to die! I wanted to live!"

"What you did was unspeakable, Kang."

He began to wail. "I knew she would destroy us! I told Chen, but he didn't believe me! I saw the danger of our unnatural obsession with her. When we were with her, we felt alive, we felt free. Once we saw that she was not repulsed, but rather attracted to us, the perverted lovemaking became addictive. She was the devil. So beautiful, yet so absolutely corrupt. She called me an abomination, but, in truth, *she* was the abomination."

I shook my head. "I'm going to see to it that your brother's name is cleared and that you are brought to justice, sir."

Kang died before he could be brought to trial.

An infection started at the site of the incision and quickly spread through his body. The effects of the operation had ultimately proved fatal to both brothers.

As Dr. Hardison believed, they could not survive on their own. They were meant to be together in death as in life. The brothers were buried, side by side, in West Virginia. Cassandra Billets rests in an unmarked pauper's grave in New York City.

A fire destroyed Putnam's National Museum and Oddities Exhibition Hall the following spring. To his credit, he never rebuilt.

Driving Blind

Ilsa J. Bick

The nightmare oozed into the cracks of Sylvia's brain like black ink leaking from an overturned well onto clean, white paper.

The car is close and hot with the smell of a man's sweat and old sex. She's driving, her hands gripping the wheel so hard they cramp. The hum of tires against asphalt is very loud, and her pulse bangs in her temples because she knows, He's *there, hunched in the backseat, just out of sight. Her skin prickles, the tiny hairs standing on end. She can't take her eyes off the road because she'll crash, but her* longing *is unbearable and knifes at her thighs. She throws her head back.* Fuck me. *She's still driving, straight-arming the wheel now, her vision blacking, glazed with lust.* Fuck me, please, please, please.

And then, suddenly, he's covered her face, and she can't breathe. She can't see. She's driving blind, and she can't stop, and in another second, she'll crash, and there's nothing she can do. . . .

With a jolt, her consciousness contracted the way a supernova explodes then collapses under its own gravity. Sylvia bucked, shivered, and nearly broke the link. The images and sensations of the virtual reality rig being piped into her brain shimmied and rippled, and she had the eerie sensation—a memory, actually, from that very morning—of the way she'd felt when her car sluiced and fishtailed on the long winding curl of gravel that led from her house to the main road.

Sylvia fought hard to stay in the link because Ben was there, and she was hungry for Ben. She wanted him. But the nightmare was there, too, bumping against her awareness like an amorphous crowd of angry bystanders milling at the margins of a barricade.

Ben. Jerking her mind free, she pushed the threads of the nightmare back into the world of her black dreams where they belonged. *Ben.* Focusing her thoughts into a bright sliver, her mind screamed, *Ben, Ben, I'm here, take me....*

She kept her eyes shut tight, focusing now on the sensations that came to her in sinuous threads, bleeding into her brain on a stream of electrical impulses the way clouds cohere and break apart and then coalesce into recognizable shapes.

There.

His hands on her body. Cool fingers trailing over the smooth domes of her breasts. His tongue tasting the sweat beaded along the hollow of her throat, then teasing her nipples until they were so hard they ached. He smelled of olives and warm bread, an all-encompassing aroma that drew her in like an embrace. Her back arched, and she moaned, reached for him, felt the hard edge of his shoulders under her hands, and then, an instant later, his knee forcing her legs apart. And then he was there—hard, insistent—pushing his way in, and then he was moving with long, slow strokes that got harder and faster, and she felt her orgasm build with each thrust, the feeling like overlapping waves that swelled and grew and—

The shrill of her office intercom, sharp as a policeman's whistle. And then her receptionist's voice, flat and atonal through the speaker, "Dr. Steiner, your two o'clock is here."

"Thanks," Sylvia managed, her eyes still shut tight. "Just a minute." She lay on her office floor, her naked heels digging into a rough, nubbly carpet. Her skirt was hiked up around her waist, and she'd tugged her blouse free. Stifling a moan, she writhed and bucked; her hips jerked, and the stippled electrodes of her interface dug into her scalp, but the link held, and she was close, so close, and Ben was still there, hard and throbbing, and the sensation of his sweat-slicked chest—electrically generated until she couldn't distinguish fact from fiction, or the dream from the nightmare—crushed against her breasts.

"Yes," she hissed. "Yes, yes!" And a few seconds later, the orgasm roared from her pelvis and shuddered into her throat, and Sylvia clapped her hand over her mouth and screamed, the sound muffled, her body heaving and straining under the touch of a phantom.

"And then before I knew what he was doing, he hit me." The patient, a pale woman with tousled mousy brown hair and a lower lip so puffy the lump looked like a fleshy pink tumor, tweezed a Kleenex from a box squatting on a round glass table with bronze legs. The tissue came free with a ripping sound, and the patient, Mary, slouched back into a plush, upholstered cream-colored chair. The cushions gave way with a low moan, and the seat was so low Mary had to look up at Sylvia who sat just across. "I must've made him mad."

"How did you do that?" Sylvia's mouth was dry, and her lower lip was so parched the skin had split in the middle, right down the center. She desperately wanted a glass of water. "What did you do to deserve getting hit?"

"I don't know." Mary hiked a shoulder. Her restless fingers played with the Kleenex, tearing away white bits that fluttered to the nubbly carpet. "With him, you never know. He can be real calm one second, and the next . . . like some kind of crazy animal."

Crouching in a car that smelled of old sex . . . Sylvia blinked away from the nightmare. "What about your daughter?"

Mary's gaze flickered up to Sylvia then back to the carpet. She'd made a mess of the Kleenex, the remains mounded around the tips of her shoes like snow. "She saw what he did."

"Did he hit her, too?"

A pause. "No."

"Listen." Sylvia leaned forward in her chair until her eyes were level with Mary's. "You're a grown woman. You're free to make choices, even bad ones. But I can't let you choose against your daughter."

Mary's eyes were a very pale blue and looked a little washed out. Now they fixed on Sylvia, and Sylvia thought of the underbelly of a dead fish.

"What do you mean?" Mary asked.

"I mean that I'll make a call. A child's in danger; I have to call Protective Services. I'm a psychiatrist, and that's the law. I don't have a choice." She waited, let that sink in, and then saw, by the rabbit's look of fear that chased across the woman's features, it had.

"Don't call," said Mary. Her Adam's apple worked in her throat. "Please."

"I think," Sylvia began, and then, at her hip, her pager *brrred* to life. Glancing down, she saw the number flashing, and her pulse jumped.

She blew out, thinking fast. "Look, this is the deal. You have until tomorrow to file a restraining order. And I want to see it, understand?" She smoothed her palms, suddenly damp, on her thighs. Abruptly, she stood. "Your daughter's who I have to worry about now. So I'll see you tomorrow. Stop by the receptionist's desk and she'll squeeze you in."

Mary just sat there, her eyelids shuttering up and down over those milky, dead-looking eyes. "Okay."

Sylvia's pager hummed again. *Move, you idiot! Can't you hear I've got a page?* Sylvia took a step, then put a hand on the woman's arm and tugged firmly enough to pull the woman out of her slouch and steer her to the door.

"Tomorrow," Sylvia said, almost pushing the woman through. She pulled the door shut with a crisp *snick*, then locked it. She threw a glance at her clock. Half an hour left before the next session and more than enough time . . . She went to her desk, pulled open the top drawer, and dug out her rig. For a few moments, she stared at the device, the curled black wires, the stippled cap of electrodes that would feed impulses into her temporal lobes, amygdala, and hippocampus. The device that would bring Ben swimming into her consciousness.

And the nightmare, right on his heels.

Stop. There's Ben, there's only Ben. She jerked the cord for the blinds, and the metal slats came down with a *brrraccck*, like the clatter of bones. Kicking off her shoes, she settled into her chair, slipped the cap over her hair, and in another moment, Ben was there, his hungry mouth on her throat.

Moaning, she slid down. Her knees sagged apart. "Ben . . ."

She sensed the nightmare, black and organic, teetering at the knife edge of her awareness.

Go away. Her mind flinched. *Not real, there's only Ben.* Her hands tugged at her blouse until her fingers crawled over her flesh and found her breasts. "Ben."

She felt bruised.

Three hours later, she was done with her last patient. Ben paged her once more just as she was set to leave, and she almost ignored him. Almost. She watched that flashing number, resolved not to answer. Then she remembered that morning and the day before, and the three weeks before that, and a sudden flash of desire stabbed at her groin and left her weak. So she thought that, probably, one more time with the rig couldn't hurt. And it hadn't, although Ben was rough, punishing, maybe angry that she'd taken so long to respond, and she'd stoppered her mouth with her fist to keep the scream bottled up.

But there was something strangely good about the pain, too.

Now Sylvia drove home. The drive went slowly, and not because she wanted it that way, but Washington rush hour traffic was a bitch, the beltway an endless lash of cars that undulated like the tail of a metallic serpent. Still, the traffic was a blessing, because she had time to calm down, collect her fragmented thoughts.

Become herself. Her lips curled into a wry smile. Time for Sylvia again, wife to David, mother to Katie. The good doctor. She drove like an automaton, taking the turns, making the ramps, feeling the vibrations of the road shudder into her legs and up her thighs.

Crouching just behind, in a car that smelled of old sex . . . and then she's driving blind . . .

What *was* that? She worried the thought the way a dog noses an old bone. The nightmares had started a month ago and were getting worse. The same one over and over again, and what could it mean? She was a psychiatrist; she specialized in things like this, but the nightmare made no sense. All right, *yes*, she was little obsessed. Okay, all right, *yes*, maybe she was a little addicted. But it was under control. Her hands closed over leather-wrapped metal. She was in the driver's seat.

Still, maybe too much input over too short a period of time . . . She'd have to read up on this, see if the medical journals had anything useful to say. Yes, she'd do that. Her mouth was still dry, and she ran her tongue over her lips and tasted something brackish.

Bit myself. She worried the clot, felt the stipples of gnawed flesh with her tongue, and realized that she hadn't felt the pain at all. She'd been focused on Ben filling her, and then he'd rammed his . . .

Off to her right, a car horn blatted. Gasping, Sylvia swerved, felt the car sway. Heart pounding, she drove, perfectly focused, until the adrenaline rush trickled away, and her pulse slowed.

Get a grip. She shouldn't do so much. But she couldn't help herself. Ben was there. She'd never seen him. They'd never *really* spoken. He was a man reduced to shared brain waves, distilled to sensation. But that didn't matter, because when her pager went off, she ran for her rig—and because she was a doctor, she always had an excuse to leave the house. Last week, once, she'd been out until three. David hadn't said anything.

And David . . . A twinge of annoyance tweaked her gut. If she sat herself down the way she would a patient, she'd have to ask, *So,* nu, *what's so wrong with David?*

Answer, nothing. Nothing so wonderful either. Just . . . David. A good man. Steady, dependable. Married twenty years, and next month, she'll turn forty. . . .

Forty. She barked a laugh, the sound harsh in the empty car. That reminded her of a patient, what he'd said about his wife, "I don't know, Doc, but she turned forty, and she just went apeshit nuts. . . ."

No, not nuts. Textbook. Happened to everyone, the same need that drove women to devour romance novels for vicarious thrills and sex on demand. Her rig was as easy as turning a page for something racy enough so a woman could close her eyes and imagine that the sweating, panting body with its shoulder jammed under her chin wasn't her husband.

Nothing wrong. Sylvia hit the blinker to signal a turn and eased the car into the right lane. She wasn't hurting a soul.

Still. She angled into the turnoff. If Ben paged her that evening, she wouldn't answer. Probably.

Their house, a two-story colonial with white pillars and black shutters, perched on the crest of a rise at the top of a winding gravel drive, a quarter-mile back from the road from which the steep gravel drive curled left, then right, then left again. She always took the gravel road slow because they lived in the country and, once, she'd nearly hit a deer.

As she came around the first bend, she saw Katie wobbling down the gravel drive on her bicycle, coming toward her. The bicycle was pink with white grips on the handlebars and glittery tassels that flowed like streamers when Katie, a risk taker at eight years old, really got going. Now Sylvia watched as the handlebars jittered back and forth from the gravel, and Katie lurched left.

Sylvia braked, lowered her window. The glass hummed into the slot. "You should be wearing your helmet. And where's your headlamp? It's getting dark out."

"It's not *that* dark." Katie wore glasses that made her brown eyes look very big, and now she widened them until she looked like a wounded fawn. "Besides, no one ever comes up here."

"Still," said Sylvia. "Wear the helmet. And dinner in a half hour, okay?" Then she left her daughter to shimmy her way up and down the drive.

Dinner: Spaghetti. A salad. Something Sylvia threw together because she was late. *Because you let Ben make you late*. She stabbed lettuce and swirled it in a gob of vinaigrette. *You've got to cut that out*. She forked the bite into her mouth and chewed. Stopped.

She thought, *There's nothing there. In my mouth*.

She let the wad of lettuce and vinaigrette sit in a puddle of saliva at the floor of her mouth. She concentrated. *Vinegar's sour, but I don't taste anything. It's like eating air*.

Her gaze traveled to her husband, her daughter, then clicked back to her plate. Strange, how the plate, her food, her family were . . . vague. Like ghosts. Oh, they were *there*; they moved and chewed and swallowed, but— And now she felt her heart flutter in her chest, the sensation like a bird beating its wings against a cage. Compared to Ben, they were flat outlines, drained of color. Cardboard cutouts. And the nightmare . . .

And then there's blackness over her eyes, her mouth and she can't breathe, she can't see. . . .

"Sylvia?"

She looked up and saw her husband staring at her. "Yes?"

"Are you all right?" he said. David had blue eyes, but she

had to focus to see the blue, and then the honey-wheat of his hair trickled in, like straw-colored water dribbled into an empty glass. "You look sick."

My God, what's happening? "No." Sylvia forced back her salad. She forked up another mouthful. "I'm fine."

"You don't look fine." The skin of David's forehead folded in a frown. "You look . . . washed out, tired."

"I'm fine," said Sylvia. She scraped her chair back from the table and began gathering up dishes. "Really."

He dropped it. Later, she read to Katie, kissed her good night, and delayed bed until she heard David turn on the shower. Then she undressed, slipped into a nightgown, and slid into bed. Arms rigid, she lay under the sheet, her nerves jumping. Her ears honed in on the drum of water battering tile and then that high squeak of the spigot. Quickly, she reached over, flipped off the light, and turned on her side, her back to his side of the bed.

A low creak of hinges, and her nose twitched with the scent of mint toothpaste and fresh soap. The bed dipped and sagged as he climbed in.

He'll touch me. She was stiff, her eyes wide open, staring into the dense, gathering blackness. . . .

A flash of the nightmare: *Hunched out of sight, in the back seat . . .*

A light brush of his fingers on her neck, and the tiny hairs on her neck rose. "Are you awake?" he asked.

She knew that he knew she was, so she only told one lie. "Yes. But I'm tired."

He was so still she heard the whistle of his breath streaming from his nostrils. "We haven't made love for a while."

"I'm sorry," she said. Another lie.

"Let's try," he said, and now his fingers stroked the angle of her jaw.

Her pager hummed, and she was rolling away, clicking on the light, sweeping the pager up from the nightstand. She squinted at the number. "Damn." She threw the sheet aside and swung her legs over the edge of the bed. She stood, looked back over her shoulder at her husband. "The hospital."

"A page?" David frowned. "But I didn't hear . . ."

"In a sec," she said, picking up the phone, punching in numbers. Then she listened to a recording of her own voice inform her that the office was closed, and please leave a message. She said, "Yes, this is Dr. Steiner. . . . She is? When did she . . . I see." She sighed, and then she heard the high-pitched beep of her message clicking off. "All right, I'll be right in," she said, and killed the phone.

Starting for the dresser, she yanked open a drawer, tugged out a pair of slacks, a blouse. "I've got to go," she said, peeling out of her nightgown. "It might be a long time. Don't wait up." He might've said something, but she was already moving out the door and didn't hear.

The car rocked down the gravel road. She heard the sound of small rocks spewing to either side, and a plume of gray dust billowed in her headlights. She took the last curve a little too fast, and the car fishtailed, but she fought it, and in another moment, she was on pavement, heading for her office, the lancing beams of the car's headlights skewering the darkness.

For some reason, at the last possible second, she looked back, over her right shoulder. There was blackness and a rush of trees, and then the house appeared, the solitary square of yellow light from their bedroom like a beacon. But then the light winked out, and Sylvia's house went black.

The car is close and hot with the smell of a man's sweat and old sex. She's driving . . . the hum of tires is loud and her pulse bangs. . . .

Sylvia jerked awake. For a second, she was disoriented, but then she felt the prickle of carpet on her cheek. She'd fallen asleep, on her side, her rig still attached. Groaning, she straightened her legs. She was stiff, and her joints complained. When she pushed up on her arms, she felt a trail of tacky saliva on her left cheek.

Staggering, she made her way to her desk, then slid into her chair. With a weary gesture, she dragged the interface cap from her head. Her hair was wet, and her scalp itched. Her vision was foggy, and her eyes so gritty she had to blink a few times to get the numbers on her office clock to make sense.

Seven. Her breath left her mouth in a *hah*, as if she'd been punched in the gut. All night? My God, what would she tell David?

Stop. Stay calm. She shook her head to clear her thoughts. She'd stayed out last week, and David never asked. Besides, she couldn't think about that now. She had to get cleaned up, make her rounds, then get back for her first patient at nine.

Her pager *brrred*.

"No," she said, out loud. Her throat felt as if she'd swallowed knives. Had she screamed? And she watched the number flash on and off, on and off. "No, you can't be serious. I can't do this again, not now, no matter how good, I can't. . . ."

She thumbed the pager off then dropped it into her purse. On an afterthought, she crammed her rig in, too.

The medical office building had a shower downstairs for people who went jogging at lunch. Sylvia didn't jog, but she had a small cache of toiletries she saved for emergencies. *Though I wasn't exactly expecting this.* She stood under the water, feeling the fine hot needles sting her flesh. *I've got to take some time off; no more Ben, not today.* There was no help for her clothes; she'd have to make do. She brushed her hair and teeth, applied makeup, and smoothed down her blouse.

She was about to head out the door for the hospital when she remembered her purse, still in her office. She trudged upstairs, and as she pushed into the inner office, her phone rang.

Too early for a patient. Sylvia hesitated. *Maybe David.* She picked up the handset. "Dr. Steiner."

"Hello." The voice was deep and male. "Why aren't you there?"

Sylvia frowned. "Pardon me?"

"I said why aren't you there? I paged you; you're not there."

Ben. How . . .? For some reason, the pit of her stomach iced. "I . . . I have to get to the hospital. . . ."

"But I want you." Ben's voice was insistent, seductive. "I want you *now*."

"But I told you . . ."

"I don't care."

"Listen," she said, gripping the handset until she felt the skin of her knuckles draw and tighten. "You're great, it's been wonderful, but I need a breather, I need . . ."

"No," and now she heard an undercurrent of fury surging just under the smooth surface of his voice. "You need me. You *want* me. I do things you've only let yourself imagine."

She swallowed. "Look . . . yes, you're right. But . . ."

"Now," he said. "Right now."

Her gaze flicked to her office clock, and she felt her resolve crumble. "Okay," she said, her voice breathy. "But it's got to be fast. Ten minutes." She reached for her purse. "Just let me get my rig, and . . ."

"No. Right now. On the phone. Listen to me and do exactly what I say."

Despite everything—how she felt, the way her common sense screamed that things were going too far, they were going out of control—she felt herself get wet. "Now?" she asked, faintly, even as she slid into her chair. "Here?"

"Now," and then he told her what to do and how to do it.

And she did everything he said.

This is nuts. What's wrong with you? Are you crazy?

Mary was talking, and Sylvia tried to focus, but her mind skipped like a needle stuck in a groove, back to that morning, the night before. Something wrong with the rig. Had to be, because her vision was odd at the margins, as if the light and color were draining away like runny chalk on a wet sidewalk. She blinked, winced as a sparkle of sharp pain shot into the space between her eyes. Her brain felt pulped.

But the rig didn't explain everything. Her teeth caught at her lower lip, and she bit down until it hurt. For God's sake, she was a doctor, not some helpless sex slave. This was ridiculous, this was insane; no man was going to bully . . .

"Do you want to see it, Doctor?"

I can't see anything! Leave me alone! "What?" Sylvia looked up. "What did you say?"

Mary held a piece of paper, white, with black letters and an official-looking stamp. "The restraining order. Do you want to read it?"

"Yes, of course. Good." Sylvia covered by plucking the document from Mary's fingers. But she couldn't read. The letters blurred to mush. "Excellent," she said, handing the paper back.

"And I called the women's group." Mary carefully folded the paper in half once, and then again before tucking it into her purse. "They're sending someone over this . . ."

The woman's prattling drilled a burr hole into her brain, and Sylvia had a strange, wild urge to scream and throw a chair. Her fists bunched, the nails biting her palm. Smash her head, until the brains and black blood and nightmare gushed . . .

Suddenly, Sylvia lurched to her feet. "You have to go. I'm sorry. We'll reschedule."

Startled, Mary opened her mouth, closed it, then opened it again, the fish-like motion matching her eyes. "But what . . . ?"

"Please," Sylvia said, her teeth clenched. A hot rush of blood flooded into her face. "*Please*."

There must've been something in the way she looked that got Mary's attention, because she got up so quickly her elbow knocked against the Kleenex box, and it thudded against the carpet.

"Leave it!" said Sylvia as Mary bent. She took Mary by the elbow and propelled her to the door. "Just . . . just go."

She leaned her weight against the door when Mary was gone, and sagged. Her chest was tight, and she had to work to catch her breath. Her head ached, and she couldn't see well. . . .

The phone rang.

"No!" She took the distance to her desk in two strides and wrenched the handset from the cradle. "No, no, *no!*"

"Sylvia?" It was David. "Sylvia, what's wrong?"

Somehow—*how*?—she managed to lie. No, nothing was wrong. Yes, she'd be home soon. And, no, things hadn't gone well at the hospital, not at all.

Before she left the office, she fished out her pager, thumbed it to life, and slapped it on her hip. *Why*? Her heels clattered on concrete as she crossed the parking lot to her car. *Why are you doing this*?

The pager didn't go off all the way home. For some reason, that made her angry, and she banged the wheel a few times with her hands. "Damn you," she said. The inside of the car smelled sour and was very hot. "Goddamn you."

As she turned up the road, she saw Katie bumping up and down the gravel drive. It was getting dark, the sky to the west smeared with a ribbon of burnt orange. Katie's bicycle headlight was on, winking as the bike bounced over gravel. Katie waved and pointed at her head, and Sylvia saw something bulbous and white there and she thought that Katie had a rig, and no, no, not *Katie* . . .

Sylvia blinked twice. Not a rig. A helmet.

You're losing it. Sylvia stopped, and she watched Katie skitter up, her back tire skidding out to one side as she braked on the slick gravel.

Sylvia pushed a button, and the driver's side window scrolled down. "Good girl," she said, in a rote monotone. "Good about the helmet. Dinner in a half hour, hon." She gunned the engine, the tires crunched gravel, and she sputtered up the drive before Katie could respond.

When she pushed open the garage door into the kitchen, she saw that David was waiting. "I called the hospital last night," he said.

Her heart slammed against her ribs, but she nodded, turned away. Dumped her purse on a kitchen chair as she shrugged out of her coat. "Oh," was all she said.

David waited a beat. He cleared his throat. "The page operator said she hadn't paged you. The emergency room hadn't either. And neither had the ward."

She stood, the throat of her coat crumpled in one hand, the rest dragging on the white-and-yellow ceramic tile floor, like the limp tail of a dead cat. "All right," she said. Her head felt airy and unreal, and the space before her eyes was grainy and gray the way it is at sunset when everything loses definition and melds into shadows. She pulled back a chair from the kitchen table. The legs gave a loud screech. She dropped into the seat. "Okay."

"Are you going to tell me?"

"Tell you what?" Then when he only stared, she said, "In my purse." She waved a listless hand. "Go and see."

His fingers dipped into the leather pouch, and she heard the rattle of keys. Then he pulled out the rig, the cap bristling with electrodes, the enhancer pack.

"What is this?" The rig's wires curled over his fingers like a ball of black yarn that's come undone. "What the hell is this?"

So, she told him. Everything. Why, she didn't know. No, that was a lie. She did know. *No more secrets. David will go away, and Ben and I . . . in the flesh . . . there's nothing more, nothing . . .*

When she'd done talking, David didn't say anything for a few seconds. Then he moved to the table, sliding into a chair like an old man. He put her rig on the table and, for an instant, the thing looked ridiculous, a floppy white bathing cap studded with prongs and curled black springs.

David propped his head in his hands and dug his fingers into his hair. "You've met him?" His voice was hoarse. He stared at the table. "You've *been* with him?"

"Yes," and then she stopped, confused. "No, no, I've never . . . but I've been . . . I've *slept* . . ."

"He's not real," said David, fiercely. He swung his head up, and she saw his features were contorted with grief and rage. His lips trembled. "Jesus fucking Christ, Sylvia, he's just . . . he's something you've built up in your mind. You don't even know what he looks like. . . ."

Then the pager on her hip went off with a whirr, and she jumped.

David's eyes narrowed. "Sylvia?" When she didn't answer, he said, "Sylvia, what's wrong?"

"I . . ." Her pager went off again, and she snatched it up. The display was flashing; she saw the numbers. *Have to answer*! She held out the pager. "I . . . he . . . I have to . . . he *wants* . . ."

She saw his eyes flick to the pager then back to her face, and now there was something else in his eyes, but not anger. Fear. "Sylvia," said David, carefully. He reached to take the pager. "Darling, your pager hasn't gone off. There's nothing there. No one's calling."

"No!" She snatched her hand away, clutching the little black square so tightly she felt the bite of plastic into her flesh. "He's there. He wants me. I have to . . ." She gave a short scream as David's hand shot forward and grabbed her wrist. *Have to answer, have to get away*! "No, no, no! I'm going, David, I'm going, and you can't stop me!"

"Sylvia," he said again, only his voice was strangled. His fingers tightened around her wrist. "Sylvia, please, there's nothing there. The pager's not going off, don't you see? Sylvia, he's not real. He's just a . . . a thing in your mind, something you can't even touch. He's not *real*."

"No, no, he *is*." Her blood roared in her ears, and she was so frantic, she felt dizzy. "He will be. I just . . . have to *go*. I have to *get out*!"

"Sylvia, no, listen to me! It's in your mind, but I'm here, Sylvia, I'm real," and then his voice broke. "For God's sake, I'm right in front of you!"

Her pager went off again, the vibrations rippling up her arm. Twisting free, she jolted from her chair. Her chair crashed to the tile floor, and as David reached for her again, she stumbled back out of reach. "No! No, no, I have to leave, I have to . . ."

And then she grabbed her purse, swept up her rig, and spun around, digging for her keys even as she banged out of the kitchen. She heard David call her name, but then the door slammed, slicing his voice like a ribbon of sound snipped in two.

"Ben," she said. Her fingers were clumsy, and she had to work to shove the key home into the ignition. She gave the key a twist, and her car roared to life. "Ben, Ben, Ben."

Sylvia jacked the car into reverse, backed out, spun the wheel hard right. The car skidded, the rear careering to the right. She looked up as the kitchen door opened, and then there was David, framed in a wedge of light, and he was out the door, running.

"No!" she cried, and threw the car into drive. She spun the wheel hard left and in another moment, she was hurtling down the road. Gravel sluiced in a spray and pinged off the bumpers, the windshield. She took the first curve right, then looped left, and then she roared into the straightaway, shooting for the last turn. The car barreled down the drive, and she hit that last sharp curve at the end, going much too fast, so that when she saw the wink of a bicycle headlight, flickering like an orphaned firefly, it was much too late.

"Katie!" Screaming, Sylvia hit the brake. "No, no, *Katie*!" The rear of the car fishtailed, and she fought it, feeling the car whirl out of control, and then there was a sickening thud as the car struck something that was first hard, then soft, and then seemed to be nothing at all. But the car kept sliding sideways all the way down the drive and spun into the street, and Sylvia heard gravel scour the underside of the car and the scrape of something dragging, and a shriek of metal grating against metal.

Then, just as suddenly, she stopped. The engine died. The chassis rocked forward on its shocks, back, forward. Silence.

Sylvia sat, stunned. Then she let her breath go, and her mouth was open, but no sound came out. She saw a dense, white cloud of dust slowly settle over the car, and her ears caught the soft, dull, *pock-pock* sounds of dirt raining against the hood, the fenders, the trunk. The inside of the car stank of her sweat—only that, and nothing else.

Her pager *brrred*. Dumbly, she stared at the flashing light. The pager *brrred* once, twice more. And then the light winked out and the screen went black. Moving in a kind of trance, Sylvia thumbed through the pager's memory, looking for the number—and finding none. *But all those pages, I saw the numbers, and then he called my office, he did, I* heard *him, Ben can't have been* nothing, *Ben was* there, *he* was . . .

She looked up, back toward the house, and there was David, running—no, *charging* down the gravel road, and even inside a locked car with the windows up, she heard his scream.

Oh, God, God! Flinging the pager aside, she clawed at the door handle. The door popped open with a wrenching, metallic scream, and David's wild cry burst over her like a solid wave of sound. He rushed past and dropped to his knees on the opposite side of the car, and then she heard him, "Katie?" Then, a raw, agonized wail, "*Katie*? *Katie? KatieKatie*Katie?"

And now she's driving blind, and she can't stop, and in another second, she'll crash, and there's nothing . . .

"Oh, God," she moaned. "Now, there's nothing. *Now* . . ." Blindly, she put her hand on her husband. He lifted his face, and she saw his tears and felt the keen edge of her grief. Crying out, she sagged. Gravel bit her knees, and as she reached for her daughter's broken body, Sylvia knew that she would remember this instant and what she'd made of their lives for as long as she lived, a ruin of devastation and despair.

Thirty Minutes

Lonn Friend

"Come, let us take our fill of love until the morning: let us solace ourselves with love. For the god man is not at home, he is gone on a long journey: He hath taken a bag of money with him and will come home at the day appointed. With her much fair speech, she caused him to yield, with the flattering of her lips, she forced him." —Proverbs 7

The same thought ran through Jack Offenbach's mind every time he stepped through the door of the unassuming gray building with the sign ACUPRESSURE above the front window. "This is absolutely the last time," he'd say to himself. "One more half-hour of erotic entertainment and volcanic orgasm and that's it. End of the addiction. This is it." God, he felt good about himself tonight. Just like he had the thousand other times he'd floated the same lie into his psyche over the past fifteen years.

He knew all the spots in town. There was the little place on Sepulveda where Helen worked Mondays, Tuesdays and Saturdays. She was so sweet, loved to talk about golf in her broken Korean-tinged English, before diving onto his manhood with vim, vigor and delightfully anonymous abandon. That establishment had his weekly number for more than five years until he was greeted one evening by a FOR LEASE sign. Jack gazed in the dirty window of the abandoned stucco box and recalled the cheesy middle-of-the-road Muzak that would mysteriously start playing as soon as he was deposited in Room One.

He recalled the nights when the elderly lady who ran the place would be cooking up Oriental dishes, the aromas always mixing nicely with the scents of baby powder, alcohol and Tiger Balm back rub. And he wondered where Helen went. Her ass was so tight. She sucked his cock without a rubber. She told him that he was the only one who warranted such special attention. She trusted him and he believed her. The empty bungalow held a hundred cum-drenched memories. Jack stayed in the quiet parking lot just long enough to feel both relief and excitement. *Thank you, Lord, for closing this place,* he thought. That revelation lasted but an instant. *Guess I'll have to find a new haunt,* he pondered. He knew he was hopelessly addicted.

Jack tasted the proverbial apple the first time he walked into that tiny West Hollywood massage parlor a decade and a half ago. He happened on the place by accident while driving south down La Cienga Boulevard one evening after work, where he was paid to help people plan their trips. He loved being a travel agent. He fantasized about visiting the exotic places around the globe. He could speak so intelligently and colorfully, you'd think he'd actually been there. But he hadn't. He hadn't been anywhere save the streets and back alleys of Los Angeles, a city choking with demonic, delicious distractions.

Wow, where did that place come from? he thought, never conscious of its existence before. Jack had heard about massage parlors but he'd never actually seen or walked into one. Even after three years of a sexually healthy and happy marriage, Jack's eye still wandered, though he'd never messed around with any other girl but Elaine. He loved her deeply.

"Thirty minutes?" the elderly woman at the counter asked.

She didn't feign kindness but she wasn't entirely cold either. Jack was nervous, but he did his best to hide it. "You been here before, yes?" she said. He paused, responded affirmatively, an instinctive lie, and slid two $20 bills from his wallet as instructed by the cardboard sign on the counter. "You see Tina," she said. "She very nice." The pumping in Jack's chest was only superseded by the throbbing in his pants. She escorted him to a room down a narrow hallway. It was dimly lit, dominated by an elevated table that stood firmly against the far wall with slickly tucked white sheets. A sign above the table instructed Jack to remove his clothes and cover up with a towel. He followed orders.

"Hello." The girl was smiling, almost bubbly. "My name is Tina," she said. It was his virgin voyage, but he knew that wasn't her real name.

"Hello, Tina," he replied, now more excited than nervous. He wasn't sure how the game was played or what he was supposed to do. Should he come right out and ask for a hand job? That's all he'd expected. But he didn't have to take the lead. This was Tina's turf. She knew what to do.

For the first fifteen minutes, Tina rubbed his back, legs, feet and then, as she got to his buttocks, she shifted gears. From the deliberate, high-pressured, firm hand movements, her motion softened. She began to stoke his buttocks ever so gently, her fingertips strategically grazing the crack of his ass. He was instantly aroused. Then, as she slid her right hand underneath his frame and grabbed hold of his ball sack, his cock sprang to attention before you could say, "Me love you long time."

The Korean masseuse moaned lightly as Jack purred in complete surrender. When he felt the moment was ripe, he rolled over onto his back, exposing to his new friend a concrete pillar begging for embrace. She tickled his nuts, which made him nuts, and then, as if perfectly scripted, she floated her right hand over to the nightstand, filled it with baby oil, and returned to Jack's manhood.

Tina's oily hands encased Jack's cock and began to stroke it lovingly up and down. He closed his eyes and drifted headlong into the sensation that was quickly reaching a point of glorious no return. As she quickened the pace, the shaft engorged with blood and the head glistened like a florescent bulb. With her left hand, she pinched and tweaked his balls. That was all she wrote, as Jack's eyes rolled back into his head and he exploded into her hands.

The next few seconds were somewhat surreal. For the travel agent who had never traveled, this was an adventure he had not anticipated. He lay there on his back and processed the moment. He felt warm, empty, satisfied; yet almost immediately, a sense of guilt and anxiety cloaked him like a dark blanket. *What am I doing here?* he thought to himself. *This is wrong.* What felt so good an instant ago had morphed into nothing but bad. Or was it? Jack ruminated for the next three minutes while Tina prepped for the customary post-cum cleanup.

She returned with a hot bath towel, swabbed down his privates, and rolled him back over for a brief, moist rub. But he didn't really enjoy it, because immediately following orgasm, all he could think about was getting out of there and back home to his wife and two children. After slipping Tina a $10 tip (he figured that was a generous gratuity), Jack slinked out the back door and into his car. On the ride home, he uttered to himself, "God, that was amazing: so easy, quick, painless and anonymous. I am never doing that again."

Fifteen years, thousands of dollars and hundreds of massage experiences later, Jack was at the outer limits of his addiction. He had visited these institutions in twenty states and a dozen foreign countries. The phony names and Oriental faces blended into the landscape of his memory like an ongoing dream sequence. From that initial hand job so long ago, he had elevated the massage experience to a place of near reverence. For years, it was just about getting in, getting off, and getting out, but that ethos ended long, long ago. In the past couple of years, it had become more like performance art, due in large part to one particularly animated young lady. Her name was Happy, the archetype embodiment of angel and devil, a massaging succubus unafraid to test the boundaries of paid, private pleasuring. She was the most engaging and wild partner he'd ever encountered.

When he met Happy at that tiny spot just minutes west of where he'd first bit the addictive apple years and years ago, he was a man in the throes of midlife, questioning all, enjoying little. Sex in his home was virtually nonexistent, commonplace to the veteran married man and the bread and butter of these prurient institutions. Jack was lonely, not just sexually but emotionally. He and his wife rarely talked anymore about anything but the day's events, like the kids' schooling or what movie to see on Friday night. His job had become a nine-to-five grind. Fulfilling other people's fantasies no longer fed his own growing sense of boredom and frustration. He still hadn't been anywhere really exciting, romantic, passionate, anywhere except the parlors. They remained his sole destination for erotic escape and dreamy departure. And now there was Happy, an insatiable pornographic pirate with a snapping pussy and disarming, delightful demeanor that elevated the thirty minutes to almost cosmic significance.

Here was a man now fully exposed, naked to the lust and the lie that had become his life. He used to be so careful, never entering places that required identification for fear of being "discovered." He'd lost that concern sometime ago. There were piles of slips bearing his driver's license number scattered about the city of angels and devils. It was almost as if he wanted to be caught. That was the only way, he mused, the addiction would end. He required some divine intervention, especially with Happy in the house now.

As he navigated the asphalt River Styx on this particular spring day, nothing seemed askew. The sky was its usual clear powder blue; the day had been just another end to just another week of booking trips for the not-so-rich-and-completely-infamous. And above all else, he was horny—horny for Happy. He knew she would be there, Friday afternoon. "This is going to be the last time." He said it over and over, like a mantra; it floated into the folds of his awareness. Jack prayed that this time, it would take hold. Or perhaps, he prayed that things would always stay this way. He was on autopilot. The neon sign beckoned as it always had. Inside, wet dreams and no questions asked.

He walked inside as he had countless times before, but his eye caught something completely new. There was another man in the waiting area. This was unprecedented. In fifteen years, Jack had never had to wait, not ever. He had never come face-to-face with someone else, another man, another addict, a kindred lost soul in search of a few minutes of release. This was always his private space, just him and the girl. No onlookers, no voyeurs, no competitors, no witnesses. He gazed at the man and thought for a second about leaving, but the mamasan pounced on her favorite customer. He altered his glance from the stranger to the counter.

"*Com ba wa*," she said with a smile. "Happy here!" He hesitated for a second, turning around to face the stranger, who was staring straight back at him. There was something odd about this man. He was normal height and build, unshaven for a couple days, but his eyes went right through Jack. It was not an anonymous glare, but rather one beholding a message or warning. Jack felt anxious. Time stood still. Who was this guy and why was he here? Why today? He gathered himself and turned back to face Mamasan.

"Thirty minutes?" the proprietor asked rhetorically. She acted as if the stranger weren't even there, as if Jack was the only one in the room.

"Yes," he answered nervously, slapping his driver's license on the counter and peeling three twenties off for payment. The fee had risen to $50 for a half hour. She rolled $10 change off the wad nestled in her front apron pocket.

"Come this way." Jack turned around again. The stranger was staring right at him, his eyes emanating an almost menacing presence. *What the fuck is wrong with me?* Jack thought. *What am I afraid of? He's just here to get off, like me, like everyone else who's ever walked into this place. It's nothing.*

He bounced down the long hallway past three other rooms to the big room in the back where a nice-sized bed rested against a mirrored wall. The moment he removed his clothes and took his place on his familiar spot, his mind left the man in the foyer and turned to Happy and what was coming. He could feel the fire burn in his loins, laying ash to all fears, all illusion. He stared at himself in the wall mirror and pictured Happy's hungry mouth on his hard cock. This was his sacred space. He took some deep breaths and waited for salvation.

"Happy here in ten minutes." Mamasan popped her head through the door and delivered the news. This was very unusual. Once Jack had paid and been escorted to his room, Happy was always there in an instant unless she was finishing up another client, another "john," but Mamasan would always tell him that at the counter. "Happy busy. You wait few minutes," she'd say and Jack would go to his room and wait. He never sat in the lobby. No one ever did. No one until today.

With the pause in the proceedings, Jack's mind wandered back to the stranger with the eerie eyes. *Is he still out there?* he wondered. *Is he getting a massage? Is Happy with him? No, she couldn't be. He would have been in his room before I arrived. Is he with another girl?* Jack's mind hopped about like a rabbit. There were always at least three girls working at any given time. *Sure, he was getting a massage from another girl. Happy's finishing up someone else. That's it. Mamasan just forgot to tell me that when I got here.*

A few moments passed and he heard the toilet flush in the bathroom and the sound of washing hands and gargling throat. Happy was the cleanest girl Jack had ever met within the confines of the massage world. She smelled fresh, from the top of her mildly punk haircut head to the tight, squeaky-clean gash of her immaculate pussy. For the first time in his long addiction, he had discovered the perfect masseuse, the adoring whore. This fact both intrigued and terrified him. It was never supposed to get this good, nor this bad.

The second he saw her, he forgot about the stranger. He forgot about everything, as he always did. For the next thirty minutes, there was no reality except this room, this girl, this escalation to ejaculation. "My favorite man look good today," she cooed. The scent and proximity of her being escalated his breath. She approached the table, his naked body spread out facedown on the horizontal platform. He could smell her a step in front of him. She leaned over and began nibbling at his right ear lobe. "Happy very horny today. Happy very horny every day." Her laugh broke his concentration and he slowly opened his eyes, catching her gaze. She reached around his torso and grabbed his cock, already rock-hard.

Jack didn't rush anymore. He used to get the massage first and let the buff job come at the end. That was an old routine, long dissipated into the ether of sinful moments passed. Now, each time he entered the room with Happy, he had no idea where it was going. She was a totally free spirit, up for anything. She resisted no gesture. Her body was a temple of extraordinary sensation, a lightning rod for touch and taste.

He took her breasts in his mouth and gobbled them hungrily. She moaned as her nipples hardened from the stimulation. He loved sucking Happy's tits. They were a perfect mouthful, tender, sweet, like twin papayas. Once into the carnal parade, all doubts and self-loathing evaporated. Subconsciously, he knew he shouldn't be there, doing this, violating his vows for the multihundredth time, a victim of addiction. But in the Zen moment of this special sexual enclave, reality ebbed and Jack leapt on the fantasy train bound for the Promised Land.

It was considered hygienically reckless to eat a masseuse's pussy, and Jack almost never partook in such fare. That is, until Happy. Her crotch and asshole were so pristine and inviting, he lost all sense of decency. He leapt into her dual gashes like an Olympic diver, lapping up the wonderland like a love-starved puppy. Happy's pussy was so wet it drenched his face. His dick pointed skyward like a noble redwood.

Jack reclined back into sexual surrender position "A," for it was time for Happy to do her magic. She secretly grabbed a condom from under the towel at the foot of the bed and popped it into her mouth. Then she lowered her head over his smoldering staff and slipped the raincoat over its head. Her mouth and hands worked in tandem, bringing him to near-climax. But she paused for a second because she knew what he liked best. He was blind, deaf and dumb to the divine Universe.

Moistening her middle finger with a gob of saliva, Happy inserted the digit slowly and gently into his asshole, as her mouth never broke stride on his cock. The harder she sucked, the deeper her finger probed. Pleasure and pain battled for supremacy as climax approached. It was the most decadent yet incredible feeling. As the cum rose from his sack up the shaft of his cock toward the head, he felt as if he would blow a wad so hard and fierce that it would take the back of her head off.

"Oh my, oh my, oh my," she uttered, sucking the milky fluid through the rubber and kneading his balls with her thumb as his ass bucked. Jack was gone. He'd checked out for this apocalyptic instant. It was pure evil that brought him to this place of unholy ecstasy. He knew the dynamic at work in this passion play. It became clear thirty seconds after he lost his load.

"*Choai yo*," he whimpered, breathless, a lame attempt at "I like it" in Korean. Happy got a towel, cleaned him up, cracked his back by walking expertly up and down his spine, and helped him dress. What was forty bucks fifteen years ago was now fifty, but the money was the least of his concerns. "I have to stop coming here, Happy," he said.

She looked at him knowingly. "You have good cock and Happy like that. Married men don't have sex. They come to massage for fun. It always like that."

Jack put his clothes on. Happy always did his socks and shoes. As she walked him back down the hall, past Mamasan and toward the black, iron mesh-gated front door, he paused at the waiting room. The stranger was gone. Or was he? "Ma-masan," he said nervously. "Where is the man who was here earlier? Is he with one of the girls?"

She looked at him curiously and responded with a half-grin, "What man? There no other man here but you for over an hour."

"What?" But that was it. He couldn't muster an argument, not with the madame of a massage brothel who barely spoke English.

While his brain attempted to process what was or was not happening, Happy took his hand, opened the front door and lightly sent him back into the real world. "See you next time!"

Jack pulled his keys from his pocket and looked up and down the street. Nothing. No stranger, just the usual collection of neighborhood peeps moving to and fro, ignorant to all but his or her own existence.

Upon reaching his car, however, he observed something on the windshield. A note. He again looked around. Nothing. Lifting up the wiper blade, he removed the note, took a deep breath, and read it. The words were boldface, inscribed with a strong hand, evidenced by the indentations in the paper. The ink was black.

> *Let not thy heart decline to her ways, go not astray in her paths. For she hath cast down many wounded: yea, many strong men have been slain by her. Her house is the way to hell, going down to the chambers of death.* —Proverbs 7

He stared at the note and a cold chill came over him. It was terror, authentic in its manifestation. His heart began beating fast, but his mind—his mind was at light-speed. *The stranger. This was his doing. But no one saw him? Who wrote this? What's happening to me? I need to get home. Someplace familiar. Someplace safe. It's a sign. Yes, that's it. It's a sign from God. Or Satan. I must stop this. Now and forever. I need to see my wife, hold my wife, hold my children; I must get right with the world, get right with myself. I'm not a religious man. Or am I? What the fuck is going on? Who am*

I? Where am I? Why *am I?* In thirty minutes, Jack Offenbach's entire world had changed, or at least that part of the world that involved his demon self. A man not given to great spiritual insights or religious education, he was now questioning everything.

Driving his car east toward his home, toward his foundation, his sanctuary, away from the parlor, the brothel, away from temptation, the mantra began, almost deafening him: *The last time. The last time. The last time.* "Yes," he whispered to himself. "This was the last time. Absolutely, the last time."

For the next several weeks, Jack felt a sense of peace about his home, his family, even his job. The fire that had burned so long and so hot dwindled. He passed Happy's parlor several times but didn't stop. He recalled the incredible sex and the ecstatic moments where his cock exploded like St. Helen's. The memories were wicked and fun and nasty. He missed Happy but not enough to tempt fate. Since the day of the stranger, he had begun reading the Bible before bed. His wife had about the same interest in scripture as she did in sex, but she liked having him home at night. So did the kids. Life was good—until one summer evening when temptation resurrected.

Jack was having a good week, booking vacations. July was blazing across America and everyone wanted to get away. When he looked at his commissions on Friday afternoon, Jack realized he'd just experienced the best five days of his career.

Tony was his best friend in the office. They shared stories, both public and private. Jack had confessed many tales about his "parlor days" as he came to call them. Tony had never partaken. He was single, Italian, handsome, and always getting laid. He didn't need to pay for it.

"Wanna have a drink after work?" asked Jack. "I've had a record week, Tone. Feel a bit like celebrating."

"Sure, buddy," came the response via interoffice e-mail. "How 'bout El Cholo? Great margaritas!"

At a little after six P.M., Jack and Tony were swilling frothy tequila sundaes and munching chips and guacamole at one of the west side's busiest Mexican eateries. It was happy hour and the restaurant was crawling with gorgeous girls, letting their hair down after a long week's toil. It was hot, so the outfits were scant. Jack and Tony were feeling the buzz. And the happier Jack got, the more he started to think about . . . Happy.

"Hey, Tony, you wanna do something crazy with me?" he suggested, the tequila doing its thing to drop the fear of expression.

"What's that, buddy?" Tony responded, eyes slightly glazing from the Cuervo Gold.

"Go with me to my old massage parlor," Jack fired back. "I've been good for a long time. I owe myself a treat. I don't think God will mind if I hop on the bike for one more ride, for old time's sake."

Tony smiled and said, "Buddy, I love ya, but I'm meeting Samantha at eight o'clock at her place. She's cookin' for me tonight. My sack will empty and it won't cost me a dime. Ain't love beautiful?"

"Okay, okay," surrendered Jack. "Guess I'll go it alone. One more time. Just one. Happy, baby, here I . . . come."

The tequila was working its black magic. Jack had all but erased from memory his last visit to the parlor. As he pointed his car toward perceived Providence, he didn't flash on the stranger or the note or the blinding terror of that day three months ago, the day he vowed to change course away from the dark and toward the light. All he could imagine now was the touch of Happy's fingers on his ass, the taste of her perfect pussy, the resonance of her wail as he fucked her hard, long and sweet.

Parking his car in the usual spot on the street, he glanced in the rearview mirror and looked himself in the eyes. "Last time, Lord," he said aloud to the reflection. "Last time."

"Ahh, long time no see!" Mamasan greeted Jack with a welcoming smile. He closed the gate behind him and stepped through the waiting room to the counter, unconscious of his surroundings or the last time he walked through that door. All he could think about was Happy and the swelling member in his pants. "Thirty minutes?" she asked.

"Of course," he responded. "Is Happy here?" Mamasan paused as she scribbled down Jack's driver's license number on the tiny white slip. "Happy not work here no more. I give you new girl. Candy. You like her. She very nice."

Jack's face flushed. "Happy's gone?" he slurred, the booze revealing itself.

"She move away. But Candy, you like Candy. Try Candy."

Through the alcoholic haze, Jack attempted to define what was happening. He was so horny for Happy. She was the one, the best there ever was. She was his last roll in the devil's hay. And now she was gone. But he was here. And the sex, the promise of orgasmic release, was here, in a different package, but here just the same. Here for the taking. "Fifty dollars," said Mamasan, waiting for the cash. Jack stood frozen in thought.

What am I supposed to do? he pondered. *Is this another sign? Am I being tested? Do I walk away? Happy's gone. I should go! But I'm so fucking horny. I need to get off. Just one more time. I promise. Just one more time.* He pulled three $20 bills from his wallet and waited for his change. Something made him look over his shoulder, but the room was empty. He followed Mamasan down the hall to the room he knew as well as his own bedroom at home.

"Candy be in soon," she said.

Jack began to undress, a slight unease mixed with the buzz that was doing everything in its inanimate power to keep his cock hard, his fire lit, his demon engaged. The time crept like a snail across a sidewalk.

Then came a light tap on the door. "Hello," she said, entering the room. "I'm Candy." She was stunning, an Oriental jade sculpture, absolutely perfect in form. He had never seen a body so exquisite. He forgot about Happy the moment Candy kissed his neck with her soft, wanting lips. She smelled like puppy's breath. Both the booze and the muse intoxicated him. Candy was an Eastern goddess so divine, she eradicated all past and brought him to the absolute, immaculate present. Her slightest movement made him quiver, the shape of her breasts made him weak, her eyes . . . her eyes, so dark, so piercing, made him forget. As he dove into her waiting mound, time and space collided and the fabric that kept Jack Offenbach on the corporeal plane . . . ripped.

Tony's girlfriend called around 7:30 and said she wasn't feeling well. Migraine or something. Feeling the buzz from happy hour, he wasn't ready to call it a night. He thought about his friend Jack and headed for that place he'd heard about but never visited. Why not? he thought. Just one time.

As he walked through the front gate, Mamasan greeted him with a smile. "Hello," she said. "Thirty minutes?"

"Uh, yeah, sure," Tony replied, new to the game. "Say listen, my friend, Jack, he's been coming here for years. He said he was on his way over. Is he here?"

Mamasan looked blankly at Tony. "No one here for over an hour," she replied. "Fifty dollars. I got nice girl for you. Her name is Happy."

"Happy, huh? Sounds like fun."

Just before entering the hallway to his room, Tony felt a strange urge to turn around and shoot a glance at the waiting area, like an invisible tap on the shoulder. For a second, he thought he saw Jack sitting there. Then he blinked, and the image was gone.

Huh, must be the tequila. He laughed to himself. Happy, here I . . . come.

The Lost Herd

Del Howison

The rain moved like sheets across the open spaces of the landscape, flowing with the wind, like breakers across a beach. It allowed the men to look up between waves to see where they were riding, had they only known exactly where they were in the first place. The brims of their hats acted like gutters, funneling the rain to shoot off in minifalls and splash against the bodies of the horses they rode. The beasts themselves plodded, heads down, sightless in the downpour, but not wanting to stop for fear of drowning while standing up. Shelter, any shelter against the weather, would be a welcome sight.

They had picked up the herd of cows three days south of the normal trail, but had never made it back to familiar surroundings. Then the men had lost the herd when, stupid and panic-stricken from flashes of lightning, the cows had run into the darkness, mooing and screaming. The men had tried to keep them calm, lest they lose a season's livelihood, but to no avail. The terrain was unfamiliar to them. Now they were lost as well, looking for somewhere to stop to save the rain from beating them into mush.

On each side, the rocks jutted and rose in angular slabs, and the muddy trail they rode seemed to be the only way between them. For all they knew, it could all end in a boxed canyon or a cliff's edge in the darkness. The point rider moved carefully between the jagged stones. As point man he was known for having cat's eyes, but even those served him little in the rain. Water gushed through the canyon's opening as they worked their way up the incline, almost forcing them to turn and swim back down the river of mud and tumbling stone they were maneuvering. Gray light told them they had been riding all night and morning was arriving, with no relief in sight from the relentless downpour. Nobody spoke, despite the fact that the thunder had ceased some time ago. The downpour splashing against the rocks, combined with the rushing of the water through the cut, was too loud for conversation, and they were too sullen for talk. There was nothing to say that each of them wasn't thinking anyway.

As the point man reached the top of the climb, the rocks seemed to open up on a plateau where all five of the riders could gather side by side. The point man turned to the big man riding just behind him and pointed into the distance. There, through the weak light of the new day, were the dark shadowy shapes of what appeared to be buildings. The other three pulled up alongside their leader.

"Could just be some more rock sides. Hard to tell from here," said the big man who'd been riding second.

"Hope not." Point turned and looked at one of the other riders. "Joplin is getting pretty weak. We might have lost him if he hadn't been tied to his horse."

"Only one way to find out," returned the big man. "I just hope we're not riding out of Hell and into Hades."

He gave his mount a quick nudge with his heels and a cluck, riding ahead in the direction of the shapes. The point man followed, and the other three, with nothing to lose at this juncture, followed suit. Joplin was slumped forward more than the others. As they picked their way down the slope, the rain began to lighten up, along with their mood. Rounding a boulder, the trail dropped into some trees, and the buildings disappeared into the misty forest in the distance. Bushes and foliage indicated the steep drop in elevation they were taking on the trail. Even the smells changed as the greenery surrounded them on all sides, giving the feel of a living cave as the forest's throat swallowed them.

The rain, though it was lessening, seemed harder as it dripped from the leaves and branches. But it was uneven, sporadic in its fall, splashing off the horses and men and, at times, seeming to move in an almost horizontal direction. The darkness of the woods seemed to close out sound as well as light, like the earth itself was swallowing them deep into its bowels. The big man pulled up and waited for the others behind him to stop. He was peering straight ahead, as if somebody could squint for sound.

Point broke the silence.

"What is it, Ray?"

"Nothin'," the big man said, almost in awe. "Absolutely nothin'."

Point looked ahead and then glanced back at the others. Lemon shrugged. Justin spit, and his horse pawed the ground impatiently. He looked back up at Point.

"I've stopped for a lot of things in my life, Ray," said Point. "But I ain't never stopped for nothin'. I'm telling you it's gonna be somethin' if we don't get movin'."

As if on cue, Joplin suddenly slid to one side of his saddle, his rope catching him from falling off his mount. He screamed out in pain, and Lemon moved up alongside him, helping to straighten him up. Justin grabbed Joplin from the other side and pulled him up. Lemon looked to Ray.

"We gotta get him off this horse, Ray! The bleeding is getting worse. This shirt is soaked through and it ain't just rainwater."

"Well, we can't do it here." Ray looked back at the injured rider. "Let's keep movin'. Maybe we'll run into those buildings up ahead. Ain't but one trail down so far as I can tell. If those were buildings, we gotta run into 'em."

"Yeah, and if they weren't buildings we may have a dead man on our hands. We gotta get inside."

"Lemon!" Ray glared at the rider. "You got a better idea? Because if you don't then shut the hell up! Joplin ain't dead yet." His voice softened hopefully. "It can't be too much further."

Ray kicked his horse back into action and continued on. Justin looked at Lemon who shrugged again, and then joined the single-file line down the trail. Point stood off to one side and let the line pass. He looked backward into the darkness they'd come from. There was nothing. No sound. No light. No good. No good at all. He shook the reins of his horse to join the others, and moved after them in the direction of the lightening morn.

They had just broken through the tunnel of trees when Point called out, "Ho, Ray!" The line of horses stopped and turned back towards Point. Joplin sat slumped forward on his horse. His arms dangled against his mount. Point jumped off his horse and ran up to Joplin, raising his head by grabbing a handful of hair.

Ray came riding up. "Is he still with us?"

"Hard to tell," Point said, lifting Joplin's eyelids and then letting his head drop back down. "He's either out cold from the pain or he's dead."

Ray took his rope off his saddle and handed it down to Point.

"Here, tie his hands around the horse's neck. He'll stay mounted." He looked up in the direction they'd been headed. "It can't be far now. At least that will keep him on top until we get there."

Point took Joplin's arms and wrapped them around the horse's neck. Then he coupled his hands together like a prisoner and tied them. Point walked back to his horse and took down his rope. He tied one end to the reins of Joplin's horse, then jumped up on his horse and tied the other end to his horse. He looked up at Ray.

"Best we'll get. Let's go."

Ray swung his mount around and continued past the men in the direction they had been going. Point followed with Joplin's horse in tow. The other two followed them in case Joplin could figure out another way to drop off his saddle. They shot a look at the sky. No sun today. Overcast and rain seemed like the forecast, even though it kept getting lighter as the new day forced itself past the darkness.

Through the thinning line of trees, the gray structures stood before them like washed-out monuments from another era. They sat in a flattened area at the edge of the mountain. They were mining buildings, weathered and long since out of use—a mining camp from a dead vein. From what must have been the workers' boarding house on the far side of the camp came the sound of the front door opening. A female in what had once been a white slip and undershirt stepped out onto the wooden porch. The shirt had been slit in a long vee-shape and her breasts threatened to slip sideways into view with every movement. She held a shotgun in her hands, pulled diagonally across her chest. It wasn't threatening, but it was available. She smiled as the group slowly rode toward her. Her teeth were so white they seemed to reflect what little light was available.

"Hello, boys. Kinda off the beaten path, aren't you?"

Ray pulled his horse to a stop in front of the porch and looked her over. He would have guessed her at about thirty. Her underwear, which had once been white, showed a lot of dirt up close. It could have been her work outfit. Her everyday wear. There were torn edges and frayed threads. Her arms were dirty from what Ray figured must have been digging. She was thin but still gave off an aura of sexuality. She was a girl with the experience of a woman. When she smiled, they could feel it in their groins. Her eyes took them all in. The men shifted self-consciously in their saddles. Justin wrapped his hand around his saddle horn. Ray looked up at the smoke rising from the boarding house's chimney.

"I take it you live here?"

"Yep." She shifted her body weight. "If you call this living. It gets a little lonely out here."

"You live here alone?"

Point rode up beside Ray to get a better look.

"Not really!" The voice came from the far end of the porch as another girl stepped from around the corner. She also held a shotgun.

"Boys, this is my sister Virginia. I'm Chelsea."

Virginia nodded at the men and licked her lips. She swiped the back of her hand across her mouth, wiping what appeared to be blood from her face. Her hands were wet and stained. The nail on her index finger extended well beyond her fingertip, but the other nails were black and broken off at different lengths, some down to the quick.

"You boys will have to excuse me. Wasn't expectin' no company. I just finished eatin' but I'm sure we could rustle up a little grub for you if you're hungry."

She carried a little more weight than her sister. Her clothes hid more curves and roundness. She wasn't much cleaner than her partner, but she smiled the same toothy grin. Point realized they hadn't crossed any running water on the way in. Maybe there was none. Maybe all they had was a well for drinking. Joplin groaned and Ray shot him a look.

"I need to get my man inside. He's very ill."

"Follow me," Chelsea said with a crook of her finger. "You can lay him down inside."

Justin and Lemon jumped down from their horses while Point held the lead steady. They untied Joplin and lowered him gently from his mount. Justin slipped his arms underneath Joplin's, while Lemon grabbed his feet. Joplin moaned again, on the edge of consciousness. It was a good sign. He was still with them. They carried him up the porch and inside.

"Go ahead, Ray," Point said. "I'll tie up the horses and be right in."

"Yeah, go ahead, Ray," a sultry voice behind them said.

They turned and saw a third woman standing back aways. She wore jeans, a torn long underwear shirt and a pair of pistols slung just below her navel. Her hands rested on the gun butts. Unlike the other two, she seemed built for speed instead of just comfort.

Ray grinned at Point. "Don't be too long. I want to make sure Joplin's taken care of."

Ray walked up the porch and into the boarding house. Point took the reins to his horse and looped them around the hitching post. After doing the same with Ray's horse, he picked up the reins of the other two and turned to the girl.

"You got a stable here?"

She took a few steps toward him. Her sexuality was as palpable as heat. There was an old hunger present.

"Sure do." She flashed him her pearlies. "Doesn't get used as much as it should, I mean with just our three horses. Lots of nice clean hay just waiting for somebody like you. Some nice straw in there for bedding also. Follow me."

"I don't see a problem with that," said Point.

He watched her turn and walk toward the outbuildings across the way. Her ass pitched from side to side under her pants. It was a good, tight butt and it moved well in time with her body. He was beginning to feel his own heat rising. All that riding in the rain, in the dark, had created an appetite growing within him, and it wasn't just for food. He clucked once and led the horses after her. His eyes were glued to the earthquake movements of her body. Virginia watched them cross the square and smiled to herself. She walked down the long porch and into the front door of the boarding house.

Someone cleared off the top of a table, scattering the contents about the floor. Joplin was laid on it and they ripped his shirt open. Chelsea stood with Ray at Joplin's side. Her breasts heaved against the light material of the top she was wearing as she watched with concern the darkened material being pulled away from where it was sticking to his chest. Despite the dirt and sweat that coated her chest, there was a feeling of animal yearning that swirled someplace deep in Ray's body. She kept glancing up at him. He suddenly wasn't as tired as he had been.

"What happened to him?" Chelsea looked up at Ray in concern. He thought about how nice it would be to touch her. He could see the shape her nipples made against the material.

"We got separated from the herd when it scattered in fright from the thunder and lightning," Ray started. "This is unfamiliar country to us, never having been this far south. We knew we couldn't catch them all and we knew we needed shelter. We kicked our horses and started running after what we thought was the largest group of the cattle, figuring they'd naturally find safe shelter from the storm. We entered the woods running at top speed. I guess a branch was low and stickin' out. It caught Joplin in the chest like a spear. It nearly ran through him, lifting him off his saddle."

"Oh, shit," Virginia cursed and shuddered visibly, hugging her arms tight against her chest. It was like she was feeling that pain herself. She turned and walked away from the group. Chelsea shot her a look of agitation and then turned back to Ray.

"Lemon and I pulled him off," Ray continued. "And Justin was lucky enough to pick up his horse, which had pulled up in the trees. We tied him to the saddle and somehow picked our way through the darkness to here."

Chelsea was breathing heavily as she bent over Joplin to examine the wound. She ran her fingers slowly along the edges where some of the blood had dried, causing him to moan in his stupor. She held up her blood-coated fingers to the light, examining them closely, her tongue sticking out slightly from between her lips. She picked some small dark pieces of bark off them.

"This wound will need to be cleaned out. If you boys can move him to the bed in that first room there, Virginia and I will see what we can do." She turned in the direction where Virginia had gone. "Virginia, bring in a bowl of fresh water."

Chelsea threw her leg up on a chair seat and began ripping a piece of cloth from the bottom of her filthy slip. Ray looked at her leg and began to feel the heat again. He had the overwhelming desire to slowly run his hand up the inside of her knee and thigh until he felt the soft slit of skin he knew waited. His large hand could wrap itself almost completely around the soft top of her leg. He knew how nice that would feel. She looked up at him as she tore the cloth and smiled with those magnificent teeth. He felt as if she could read his thoughts and a small pang of embarrassment flashed through him. She let the garb rise higher than needed as she worked it. Its edge was high enough that, from his angle, he could see a tuft of hair edging its way out from under the cloth. She finished tearing and followed the two men carrying Joplin into the bedroom. Then she shooed them out.

"You send Virginia in with the water as soon as she gets here," she said. She gave Ray one last smile and shut the door. Virginia followed a minute later and also shut the door behind them.

Ray shook his head at his own feelings. He couldn't remember getting a rise that quickly before. Suddenly it was as if the exhaustion covered him in a cloud, and he plopped himself down in the nearest straight chair. The other two had already slid down the wall to sit on the bare floor. The spartan furnishings really didn't offer them much choice.

Point entered the barn with the horses. It was clean and utilitarian. No extras. The girl pointed to a couple of empty stalls next to what he assumed were the ladies' horses.

"Take your pick," she said of the stalls. "I'll get some hay for them."

He watched her walk away and shook his head to himself about the upcoming prospect of bedding her right there in the fresh new straw.

"Thank you."

Point placed the horses in the stall, then fetched the other two and put them in the adjoining bin. By then she had returned with a wheelbarrow full of hay.

"Here, let me take that for you." Point awkwardly moved his arms around her to grab the handles. His crotch rubbed against that fabulous ass of hers, and he immediately began to grow hard. She spun around inside his arms so that her breasts were pressed against his chest. She hummed a little guttural noise deep in her throat, then ducked out from under his arms.

"Thank you for helping with the hay," she cooed. "We don't get many visitors out here, you know."

He wheeled the barrow to the stalls and began pitching the hay to the horses. "I can imagine. How do you make it here?"

She sashayed over to him, twirling a strand of hair with her fingers as she spoke.

"Oh, we got a few head of beef and some chickens out back. We grow some of our own food, and we barter with folks like yourself who may happen to come by."

Point threw the last bunch of hay into the stall and turned to her. "You grow enough to barter with?"

Somehow she just didn't strike him as the farmer type.

"Not really," she said.

"So what do you trade with?" he asked.

She smiled and walked toward him.

The bedroom door creaked open, and the two girls stepped out. There was blood splattered on both of them, and Chelsea was wiping her hands with the bloodied piece of cloth she had torn from her clothes. Virginia absentmindedly brushed a wisp of hair off her face, leaving a trail of blood meandering across her cheek. Ray stood up to go into Joplin's room, but Chelsea placed a bloody hand on his chest.

"It's best you leave him alone right now. He's got a fever, but he's sleeping. I cleaned out the wound as best I could, but I don't have much to work with."

She smiled up into Ray's face, then grabbed his hand and started leading him away.

"Maybe you'd be kind enough to help me get cleaned up. Virginia, see if the other two boys there can help you out with your problem."

She led Ray down the hall to a door at the end, while Virginia stood before the two cowboys with her bloody hands on her hips. She began pulling her top off.

"How about some help, boys?" she said. "I'm real dirty."

Point stood against a pile of straw in the corner of an unused stall. The girl stood before him and began unbuckling his belt. She licked her lips and looked into his eyes. His internal temperature rose perceptibly, as the anticipation of what was about to happen engulfed his body with a pulsating eagerness. She reached down inside the front of his pants and grasped his enlarging member with her cool hand.

"If you loosen my pistols, I'll loosen yours," she whispered.

Ray grabbed both sides of Chelsea's shirt and ripped it open, revealing her soft breasts and large nipples. Her skin was cleaner under the clothes line, as if the material had protected her from the dirt. Ray placed his mouth over her breast and tickled at the nipple with his tongue. She moaned deep in her throat and tossed her head back.

"It's been too long," she said. "You are in for quite a night."

He looked up from his prize and smiled at her.

"I believe that goes for both of us."

He pulled her slip up over her head, leaving her naked before him. He laid her back on the bed and ran his dirt-caked hand over her downy belly, stopping as his fingers entwined with the top of her pubic hair. She nuzzled at his neck, making small animal noises. She began licking, tasting his skin. With his palm flat against her pubic bone, he reached down further, feeling the damp heat of her anticipation. She had worked his pants down past the top of his legs and was cupping his balls with one hand while stroking his manhood with the other. It seemed to bob and weave with her every touch, and she worked carefully to be sure he didn't waste himself prior to her getting exactly what she wanted. Slowly, he spread her vaginal lips and slid two fingers inside to meet her moist excitement. His fingers played rhythms inside her. He paid equal attention to both breasts with his mouth, while he squeezed and kneaded her ass cheeks with his other hand. He paused and looked up at her.

"You know how you can tell if a cowboy's had sex?"

"No. How?" Her voice came out in little breaths.

He slid his hand out of her and held it up so that she could see. "Clean fingers," he said.

She squealed in mock anger. "Oh, you're terrible!"

"I get worse."

He slid his hand back down and this time slid three fingers inside her. He looked directly into her eyes, only inches from his. "Bye-bye baby," he said.

With catlike speed he pulled upward and out, tearing her pelvic bone completely away from her body, opening up a long slab of skin and flesh all the way to her breasts. She was able to give out one quick scream and look down to see her insides spilling out on the mattress before she was silent. He buried his face in her belly and ate his fill.

Point lay on top of the girl, jabbing his cock into her with the ferocity of a beast. She clawed at his ass, digging pieces of skin away from his cheeks, ignoring the rancid smell around them. She swung her head from side to side with the tidal rhythms of her approaching orgasm. Suddenly she began screaming, "Ooh! Ooh!" over and over again. As she hit her stride, Point opened his mouth and two canine-like fangs elongated themselves from the roof of his mouth. They were beautiful, magnificent saber teeth, and he sunk them deep into her neck. She died in the spasms of orgasm, and he drank the highly agitated blood. It was his favorite and filled him with his own kind of sexual completion.

Ray walked out of the bedroom, carrying Chelsea like a tray that he was being careful not to spill. He passed Lemon and Justin on the floor, feeding upon Virginia, who was still awake and staring up at him. Her vacant eyes managed to follow him as he passed. Her mouth opened and closed, but no noise came out other than the gurgle of some blood bubbles. Ray walked into the bedroom and laid Chelsea on the bed next to Joplin. He took out a bloody piece of internal organ and ran it across Joplin's lips.

"Here, taste this," he said as he squeezed it to make some of the liquid fall into Joplin's mouth. "The ladies of the house prepared a medicinal feast to help you get better. You'll be strong in no time. But I don't want you to get sick from gorging on these delicacies. Take your time."

It was only a moment before he had to stop forcing it upon Joplin. He was soon eating and drinking on his own, making the slurping sounds of a hungry dog. Ray stood up. "She's all yours, buddy."

Point walked into the bedroom. Looking like somebody had tossed a bucket of blood over him, he pointed at Joplin. "So how's he doin'?"

"Oh, he'll be fine," Ray said. "All he needed was a little nourishment. It truly beats that beef we've been havin' to survive on. We'll lay low tonight and head out tomorrow night, when the food's finished and the daylight has sunk away. His strength will be back by then. He should be mostly healed."

Ray smiled at the carnage before him. "Damn, that was easy. Too rarely is it offered to you."

Point sighed. "Loneliness can do that to you."

Ray slapped Point on the shoulder. "It sure can. So can

horniness. It's every man's fantasy and every woman's nightmare."

"Ray, nobody wants to lose control unless they feel safe."

"Don't worry," Ray said. "I'm feeling pretty safe."

They both laughed and walked out of the room, toward the sounds of feasting.

Dance: The Devil's Orgasm

Michael Laimo

"Man, the Strip bustles every night. Ain't one no different from the rest."

Leslie feigned interest in the cab driver's monologue. *Doesn't he realize I'm a local?* "Sure does," she answered. She looked at her wristwatch, then added, "Could you please hurry a bit? I'm running late." She dug into her purse for a compact, checked her makeup, then smoothed the black velvet of her size-three miniskirt against her thighs. The lace G-string she bought at the Forum Shops this afternoon sought something of value deep inside her buttocks, and she did her best cheek-to-cheek shift in an effort to deny it entry. *It's always the new ones that do this,* she thought, finally opting to exercise a manicured nail to wedge it free.

"Something bothering you, ma'am?"

Ma'am? I'm twenty-one years old. "No, I'm fine," she lied.

"I'm from Philly," the cabbie said. "Just moved to Vegas last week. Only my third day on the job."

A sick burning sensation welled inside Leslie's gut. It rose into her throat in the form of a knot. She ran the fuzzy cotton ball that had skillfully replaced her tongue across the roof of her dry mouth, wondering if this man would live to see the world tomorrow. Passing the Venetian and its Grand Canal complete with gondolas captained by knickers-wearing Italian tenors, she gazed over the blurring hordes of tourists holding hands, clutched in groups, and pointing in the direction of the exploding volcano at the Mirage Hotel across the street.

Fire and brimstone, she thought. *The world just may come to know no other means of existence.*

The cab made its way down Sin City's famed Strip, gargantuan hotel resorts giving way to the smaller and less popular—but no less crowded—hotels and motels at the south end.

"Where ya from?" the cabbie asked. "I mean, originally."

Her thoughts traveled back in time, to her years growing up an only child on Long Island. Back then, life had been simpler, more pleasant, from her toddler years all the way through high school and then beyond, as her devoted parents ultimately supported her decision to attend UNLV. Unable to acquire financial aid, she'd had to pay her way through college, and used her comely looks and feline sexuality to extract her earnings at the Olympic Garden Cabaret, Vegas's most popular strip club. It hadn't been a poor decision at the time; working only part time, the money more than sufficiently covered her needs.

She'd never been ashamed of her body, and at the time enjoyed the exhibitionistic nature that came with the territory. She could pick and choose her customers, skillfully hunt down the thick-pocketed ones, clued in by their Rolex watches and gold chains, their Armani suits and Joseph Abboud shoes.

The night she spotted the dark, handsome man in the black suit striding into the club and parading all those urbane attributes, the dollar signs flew across her mind like a flock of crows. She approached him before he managed to find a place to sit—before one of the other temptresses sank her talons into this prime piece of walking real estate.

For the millionth time, she cursed herself for being near the door at the very moment he'd arrived. He'd immediately locked eyes with her, smiled. She'd smiled back, at once enraptured by his piercing gaze, his chiseled profile, his *Esquire* looks. Without a word, they'd settled down together on a high, rounded sofa . . . and instantly connected, once and forever.

A hollow sickness filled Leslie's stomach. It quickly melted into a hot, pulsing fear. Tears of indignation welled in her eyes, and she did her best to quell them before they caused her heavily applied mascara to run.

"Ma'am?"

She shook away the living nightmare, feeling giddy, disjointed from reality. *But what is real? The world is a cloaked facade, and beneath lies the harsh reality of it all.* "I'm sorry?"

"I was wondering where you're from, originally, that is."

"New York," she answered abruptly, gazing down at her toned thighs, at once wishing she could trade places with someone lacking of looks and charm for a life far away from the one she knew.

The cab crossed over Paradise, where the glitz and glamour of the Strip gave way to the darker, less populated environs of Vegas. A half mile of wedding chapels, liquor stores, dingy motels, and peeking streetwalkers decorated the street—the membrane of Vegas's iniquity—until the cab crawled into the fenced-in lot of the Olympic Garden Cabaret.

She paid her fare, then exited the cab, careful not to get her purse caught on the door. A cement canopy and two large wooden doors welcomed her, granting her access into the dark smoky habitat of the OG's interior. Fixing a loose strap on her high heel, she scurried inside toward the left of the red velvet rope. To the right, four men in cheap suits paid a fifteen-dollar cover, grins as wide as the open flaps on their wallets. Door maid Samantha, a dancer now past her prime, collected their admissions and handed them tickets good for two free drinks.

Ralphie, five feet shoulder-to-shoulder and six feet from the ground up, buttoned his tuxedo jacket and left his post alongside Samantha to meet Leslie. Despite the cool environment, a sheen of sweat had formed on his brow.

"You're late," he said.

"I know . . ."

"Your customer is here."

Of course he was. He was *always* here . . . he came in every night at the same precise time, at six minutes after six. And she guessed that if she'd made an effort to time his exact arrival, it would've been six seconds after the minute, too.

"In the VIP room?"

Ralphie nodded. "As usual."

Leslie hurried across the club, weaving in and out of the leopard-spotted couches and gem-lighted hexagonal stages that showcased the dancers of the moment. Men of distinct persuasion sat solemnly atop pink vinyl barstools, hunched over their spirits of choice, eyes turned yearnfully toward the money-grabbing seductresses in no-win plights for intimacy. She climbed the small spiral staircase leading up to the deejay's booth.

"Rico . . ."

Rico lowered the headphones from his ears. His thin black moustache was as manicured as his eyebrows were tweezed. "You're late today," he said, eyelids fluttering.

"I know, I know," she replied, feeling that hollow sickness in her stomach again. Something like lava seared her esophagus. "Next song, okay?"

"You got it, baby cakes. Nothing over six minutes."

"Thanks." She rushed down the steps, back across the club, mindfully aware of the hungry eyes sizing her up like a piece of prey. Behind those eyes, dirty little minds drummed up images of what it must be like to have her grind one out for them. The whole scene was a common example of man's primordial urges. It came with the territory . . . but so did the money. She wondered what level of income the dancers of ten years ago made when the physical contact between dancer and customer had been limited to three feet of airspace. A marginal amount, she'd always assumed—at least enough to afford the groceries and pay the rent.

But then, everything changed. Someone, somewhere, decided to push the envelope, and the no-contact gap in the clubs promptly vanished (along with the ten-dollar dance), turning the now obsolete table dance into the expensive and somewhat exploited lap dance. Soon, strip clubs were opening up everywhere, offering UP CLOSE AND PERSONAL dances with the sexiest girls in town, and men of all shapes and sizes were flocking to them by the millions, shelling out the bucks for dry sex with the seminaked woman of their choice. It all seemed to have happened overnight. The cabaret business had flourished from an outlet for temporary entertainment to a lifestyle geared not only to men but to women and couples as well. It became a monster that would never go away as long as there were those willing to feed it.

Her thoughts proved a viable distraction to the act she was about to perform. At first the anticipatory anxiety had made the daily ritual seem undoable; each time she'd nearly swooned by the time it was over. But she soon found that providing herself with thoughts and images outside the bounds of her obligation to society—to the *world*—made committing the deed something she could get through and still leave with her sanity intact.

Just six minutes . . . and then you can go home.

Until tomorrow . . .

She passed the front door, catching concerned glares from Samantha and Ralphie and two bikini-clad dancers whose names she did not know. She turned away from them, then reached into her purse and spritzed herself with his favorite perfume, Red. The glass doors of the VIP room loomed, a large script "OG" etched in snowflake-white purposefully obscuring the personal activity about to take place within.

Leslie took a deep breath.

She entered the VIP room.

And there he sat, legs crossed, wearing his signature black suit. His hair was slicked straight back, face tan and clean shaven. He provided her with a smug grin, making her feel even less comfortable with the now all-too-familiar situation.

"Hello, Leslie," he said, his voice dry and intense. "Are you ready to play?"

Leslie hesitated, feeling nauseous at the sound of his voice, then looked away in an effort to avoid his hypnotizing gaze. Quickly, she paced to the sofa alongside the far wall, placed her purse down, then stood there unmoving, staring at the carpeted floor and listening to the seductive groove of Rico's current selection.

"I'm looking forward to our dance," he said.

"Of course you are," she answered angrily, removing her shirt. She could feel his gaze running along the lace edges of her bra.

"I wonder what scourges you'll impart tonight?" He always asked her that—his actions never strayed from the habitual nature of his routine.

The soft beat faded from the sound system's speakers, distorted guitars and booming drums quickly eating it up like a sudden storm smashing a window, stirring the VIP room into action.

Time for today's dance.

Leslie slinked over, setting the curve of her hips into motion. She hooked her manicured thumbs beneath the silky fabric of her miniskirt and slid it down over the smooth bronze skin of her thighs. It landed on the carpet in a feminine drift. She used the toe of one heeled shoe to gently shake it away.

Leaning forward, she placed her hands on his shoulders. She could feel the alarming heat of his skin through the European fabric, and it nearly burned her palms. She closed her eyes, sucked in a deep breath and held it, mindful of the pain.

"Look at me," he demanded.

She obeyed his command, hips swaying seductively to the song's heavy rhythm. As the vocalist began to plead a tale of love long lost, the man's large brown eyes pinned her and took her to yet another vile place, one she'd never visited before, where rivers of lava flowed boundlessly over the undying bodies of those caught in its flow. She witnessed great agonies, of flesh sloughing away in blistering slabs, leaving behind tattered tendons, stark bones, and the rictus grins of a million immortal sufferers. He grinned lecherously at her clear awareness of the images imparted upon her, and the whites of his eyes went red with blood. She pulled her horrified eyes to her swaying legs, trying desperately to wash the wretched imagery from her mind.

"You look wonderful tonight, my dear," he said, his voice a low hush. "Perhaps tonight's the night? The be-all and end-all?"

Forcing a smile, she reached behind her back and unclasped her bra. Her enhanced breasts stood firm upon their release, the sundrenched flow of her skin uninterrupted by tan lines. Nipples, dark and petite, stood perkily under the cool blow of the air conditioner. She leancd forward and pressed herself against his muscular chest, retracting slightly from the scorching heat emanating from his body. She could feel his breathing quicken, hot tempered breaths embracing her cheek, the slight odor of sulfur reaching into her nostrils.

His hands ran along her waistline—

She jerked back. "The rules," she chided playfully. "No hands. Just like everyone else."

Like a child told not to touch, he quickly returned his hands to the sofa's armrests. "Then you too must play like everyone else."

Leslie raised her arms in the air. Her all-over tan reached perfectly across her smoothly shaven underarms. In rhythm with the music, she pirouetted and stopped, facing away from him, arching over to exhibit the muscular roundness of her buttocks, the unblemished drift of skin leading from her ass cheeks to her hamstrings, the black lace G-string accentuating the peachy blonde hairs riding finely up the small of her back. Placing her hands on her knees, she pressed her backside into his crotch and, keeping pace with the music, began to grind.

A low growl resulted, the odor of sulfur rising even further from his lungs. The heat from his crotch surged, nearly scorching her skin. With each downward grind, his hips pressed forcefully up against her in waves of unbridled lust. Turning her head to the left, she could see his hand grasping the sofa, pointed nails now protruding from his angular fingers, clutching the already damaged leather.

She could feel his erection growing, rubbing against her, the thin fabric of his pants marrying the heated lace of her panties.

"Yes, Leslie, that's it . . . just like that. There are so many evils longing to make their way out."

No . . .

She pulled away, twisted around . . .

. . . and shuddered at the sight of him. She'd witnessed his transformation dozens of times, yet still hadn't found a way to accept it—to deem it a common circumstance in this ungodly routine. She swallowed hard, seeing his grin—a mouth rife with dark yellow points for teeth—green smoke seeping from his nostrils like a firecracker's aftermath, eyes widening to twice their normal size, fully coated with blood. She stood motionless, shuttering her eyes, trembling uncontrollably as the song played on.

"The dance, Leslie," he growled, his voice deep and unholy, "continue the dance."

Obeying the house rules by keeping one foot on the floor at all times, she leaned forward and wedged a gentle knee into his crotch, feeling out his full erection while keeping a hand against the back of the couch. Her breasts fell upon his waiting face, her knee dancing back and forth against the front of his burning staff.

"Oh, Leslie . . . that's it," he said, flicking his forked tongue out against the side of her right breast. She closed her eyes in pain, in disgust, hot wet heat sending fear through her body. "The seeds of evil are starting to spill."

He said that every time. It was a sick, twisted analogy, yet so very real in its denotation. As a young adult entering womanhood, she'd always remembered from school that a woman could get pregnant from a man even if he didn't ejaculate in her, because the penis would leak a substance called "pre-emission." There'd be millions of sperm swimming around in this tiny drop of clear liquid, and all it took was one of those sperm to make a baby. Eventually, Leslie discovered that most men were perpetually horny and could leak this stuff even if the wind blew against them the right way.

The seeds of evil, he called them. His sperm. When she danced for him, he would become aroused and would leak his vile semen, filled with millions of sperm, each single damned one manifesting itself into a unique evil act, released into the world to wreak havoc amongst the human race, be it small or large, fatal or not. A rape, a murder, a kidnapping, a deadly fire, a car crash, or a building collapse. Plane crashes, fatal accidents, even acts of domestic violence like spousal battery and child abuse. Each instance would occur as a direct result of the release of a single seed loosed from the genitals of the man in black.

She pulled away, careful not to allow the act to carry too far. The song blared through the speakers, reaching a crescendo. He arched his head back in ecstasy, his Adam's apple jerking up and down like a pogo stick. Thick green smoke oozed from his mouth, the skin on his face growing coarse and scaly, cheeks red and swelling, eyebrows extending out into a chiseled ridge. His tongue, now eight inches in length, slithered from his mouth like an eel, lapping the fiery saliva pooling on his lips.

"The song's not over, Leslie. Dance!"

Careful not to touch him, she turned around, unable to watch anymore. She pressed her rear back into his crotch, feeling the ferocity of his burning spade, the searing throb within, the sharp point digging into her, the mottled bumps filled with venomous blood. She cursed herself for permitting this to happen . . . to be the one responsible for allowing evil into the world. Yet, if she refused his nightly demand, then *she'd* end up swimming the lavas of hell, suffering eternally in its sweltering flows, and some other dancer would become his regular channel for release—he'd promised her that.

Once she'd found the temerity to ask him, "Why not do it yourself?", and he'd smiled and said, "Evil only exists through the lure of immorality. Without it, I am nothing."

And what better place, she thought, *for evil to thrive than Las Vegas?*

The music began to fade from the speakers. Leslie pulled away in relief, staggering to the couch where she'd placed her purse. She collapsed there, knowing that for another day the world would continue on as it was, with only its fair share of evil making itself known across the globe, and nothing more.

The man gazed tiredly at her, now composed, appearance as neat and normal as when he first arrived. "Short song tonight."

"It'll never reach your required length. I'll make sure of that."

He grinned at her, laughing derisively. "Someday . . . oh, yes, someday it will."

Yes. Someday. It probably would. And she prayed it wouldn't be her dancing for him when the song reached a total length of six minutes and sixty-six seconds, because that's how long it would take for him to release his entire flow of corruption upon the world. There were enough evil seeds inside him to conquer every last drop of good on earth, and if they came out, the world would quickly fall to unceasing evils, wars and fires and plagues and genocide and—

He stood up and walked over to her. He handed her a wad of bills.

Her tip for the dance. Six hundred and sixty-six dollars.

"See you tomorrow?" he asked.

She nodded, pocketing the cash. "Same time, same place."

He paced away from her and exited the VIP room, leaving a soft trail of green vapor behind. Leslie gathered her things, and stood to leave, wondering if tomorrow would be the day the Devil finally reached his orgasm.

He won't, she thought, *as long as the song is shorter than six minutes and sixty-six seconds.*

Leslie exited the VIP room. Out on the main floor, the dancers, in the midst of their lap dances, were looking around the club, seemingly confused. Their customers remained patiently seated in position: universally slumped, open-mouthed, and legs spread. Ralphie and Samantha were looking up toward the deejay booth. Rico was there, hands held up in question.

The CD was skipping. And he couldn't stop it.

Across the club, Leslie spotted the man in black seated by the bar. He held up his drink toward her. And grinned.

And the dancers kept on dancing.

Ragnall Redux

Abbie Bernstein

Curse notwithstanding, Tony Caudell thought ecstatically, *who says you can't have it all?* He lifted his arms, acknowledging the applause from the three thousand banquet attendees, loving the way his custom-tailored tux jacket continued to drape flatteringly. He loved still more the way his carefully cut tux pants effortlessly held their place around his hips, even though—below the rim of the dais, where none of the cheering three thousand could see—the belt was undone, the fly was unzipped and the contents were in motion.

Kelly, Tony's incomparable wife (*and she* is *incomparable*, he told himself, *there's no one like her—well, okay, one other, sort of*), seated beside him to his left on the dais, gazed up at him adoringly, the grip of her silky palm so artful and her arm movement so subtle that no one in the crowd could detect what she was doing for her husband. Well, perhaps *some* could. Tony surveyed the faces of a number of men in the Hilton ballroom and happily detected an envy bordering on despair in their eyes. Even if they couldn't guess what Kelly was doing in those firm short strokes, grip tightening, loosening a fraction of a fraction of an inch, then tightening again, every male in this room wanted to get next to the blonde vision in the silver sheath, to be just where Tony was now.

The knowledge contributed as much to Tony's hardness as his wife's skilled efforts did. Kelly Ragnall Caudell was beautiful—five-nine, much of it in the long legs she liked to expose in Band-Aid skirts or gowns, like the one she was wearing now, slit to the hip. Her breasts were high and prominent, yet firm enough that they held up the front of the strapless silver number all on their own, without any support. The dress's back was cut so low that it almost revealed her likewise taut rear. Her eyes were a startling off-turquoise, and her poreless skin was a smooth tan without even one freckle. Oh, and the hair—silky dark gold that fell straight to the tops of her breasts. Even men who liked (or used to think they liked) their women smaller or rounder or darker took one look at Tony's Kelly and made up their minds right then to do anything they could to be anywhere in her orbit.

It was a fact of nature—Kelly's nature—and Tony knew that it benefited him greatly. Everyone, from the lowliest geeks in accounting to Grant Maulding, CEO, just one step on the rung up from Tony at Phoenix Pharmaceuticals, wondered what it was that Tony was doing to get and keep such a goddess. Whatever it was, Tony Caudell's employers and competitors reasoned, he must be good at it, which meant they could pay him even more to come work for them.

The first time Tony had been seen in public with Kelly after they got engaged, by the next morning, he had three potential new clients, who in no time at all signed up with him and then wanted to socialize in foursomes, client and wife, Tony and Kelly (because there was no way the horny bastards could ask to be alone with Kelly—which would have been a bad idea, anyway). It was exactly how Kelly had told Tony it would be once they got serious about each other.

Tony inhaled deeply—"It's so *great* of you, honoring me this way"—convincing some of his listeners that he was genuinely emotional and not just talking around a moan on the way to orgasm. Well, actually, Kelly had told him how it *could* be. There were a few other ways it could be. For instance, not that he'd ever get himself into such a trap in a million years, but Tony could have wound up like that loser Jim Reardon, married to Kelly's sister Kath. Jim was just a cop, so his world was one where appearances didn't matter that much, but Tony would have bet every dollar he had that Jim's career would hit a ceiling, if it hadn't already. Jim's superiors were bound to wonder what was wrong with a man who'd be faithful to a woman like Kath, and there was no way in hell Jim would ever get promoted to any job that called for photos of him and his spouse at a social event. The insane part was, Jim had had the same choice Tony had had, only Jim had blown it. . . .

Wondering what had put his in-laws in his mind at a moment like this, Tony realized Kelly had *paused*, damn it, and then Tony smiled fondly at his wife, because she knew he had to finish his speech, bring it to a climax, as it were, so he could sit down. He ended his thank-yous with a sincere, "And of course, I couldn't have done it without Kelly here." It was an excuse to lean down and kiss Kelly, who slipped the edge of her tongue between his lips and resumed her grip as he eased back down onto his seat, settling right back into her stroking him, harder, faster now under the table. A toast had begun, and some of the women (their husbands knew better, Tony would bet) thought it was sweet that Tony looked so moved.

Arthur at the Round Table couldn't have felt more like a king than this, Tony thought, and he only had twelve knights. I've got three thousand—and Kelly. . . .

Goddamn fucking curse, Jim Reardon thought, so furious and worried, trying to get his own front door open—the damn thing was sticking in the summer heat—that he kicked it and sent it banging open into the entryway wall.

"Jeez, Officer," Kath said, amused, "should we freeze, put our hands in the air maybe?"

"Sorry, baby," Jim murmured, shutting the door gently before he crossed the living room and knelt next to Kath. His wife was sitting on the couch, holding a sandwich bag filled with ice cubes to her cheek.

Jim couldn't immediately tell exactly where or how bad the wound was, but he saw that Kath's friend Naomi was holding a dish towel that had overlapping bloodstains on it. Naomi was a 250-pound emergency room nurse who was an ace at taking care of other bodies even if she wasn't doing so great with her own. She'd called Jim and told him there'd been an incident and he should come home, even though Kath was insisting in the background that it was no big deal. Jim knew Naomi had made sure to disinfect and soothe and do everything possible to make Kath comfortable, and a part of him wanted to leave his wife in Naomi's very capable hands while he tracked down the son of a bitch who'd tossed a bottle at Kath and then break every bone from spine to little toe in the asshole's body.

Mostly, though, Jim just wanted to make sure Kath was okay. He put his hand on her wrist, which was blotched white and red with dead flaking skin and the angry bared flesh underneath, the texture meeting his fingers a mixture of brittle and sticky. Jim still noticed the uncomfortable feel of it after all this time, but he'd learned not to mind it much. "Now lemme see," he coaxed.

Kath started to protest but then gave up and let Jim lower the ice pack so he could see the bloody gash interrupting her cheek.

It was hard to tell what other damage had been done, because the wound wasn't the only interruption in Kath's face. Bruises tended to get lost in the red and purple mottling of her sallow, leathery complexion, which was in turn marred on cheeks, chin and jaw by a series of little black hairs that looked like randomly planted insect legs sticking out of a hive and felt like bits of barbed wire when touched. There was hair on Kath's upper lip as well, though it was overshadowed—literally—by the bulbous, dipped end of her nose. Her teeth, which didn't take to whitener any better than her skin took to moisturizer, were yellowed and just that much too big for her mouth.

Kath's shapeless clothes suggested but did not absolutely reveal breasts that had to be stuffed into support garments to at least hold their mass at approximately the right level instead of hanging like long, empty sacks. Her belly protruded over legs that were bony, yet lumpy with cellulite. Some people felt so strongly about Kath's overall appearance that they made their objections known by hurling insults or, say, broken bottles in her direction.

Jim Reardon believed in the law, but at this moment, he wanted to do murder. Not just plain old whip-out-the-service-pistol murder either, but tying the fucker down and punching sand-grain-sized bits of ground glass into every pore, to see how the glass-hurler liked it.

He must have *some* expression on his face, Jim realized, judging by the worried looks he was getting from Kath and Naomi. He brushed limp, colorless hair off Kath's forehead and kissed her there.

"She needs stitches," Naomi said, as if she'd been repeating herself on the subject for hours (which Jim didn't doubt). "I told her, but you know how she gets."

If Naomi only knew about the curse . . . but she didn't, so she thought Jim was being a prick for not dragging Kath to the hospital. Then again, maybe if she knew, she'd think he was an even bigger prick. "If it doesn't stop bleeding, we're going straight to the E.R.," he vowed. "You see who did this?"

"White kid, maybe twelve, on a green bicycle," Naomi replied, when Kath didn't speak up. "Least the little bastard deserves is a good scare from a cop. *Very* least."

Jim nodded emphatically. "Glad somebody around here sees the big picture."

Kath moaned. "He's a kid. How're you gonna find him? And what're you gonna do if you do find him? It's *my* goddamn face, okay?" Kath's protest was quiet, but her shoulders hunched forward protectively. Naomi probably thought Kath just looked really tired; Jim knew Kath might start crying and thought, *what am I putting you through?*

He said in a voice so soft that Kath knew he wasn't arguing further, "We know, babe. It's just . . . throwing glass isn't . . . normal. Not even with the . . ." He stopped, because the curse wasn't to be talked about in front of other people.

Jim knew he had a tendency to practically throw Kath's friends out when he wanted to be alone with his wife, so he compensated by inviting Naomi out to supper with him and Kath for Thursday, listened to Naomi's sensible advice on wound care, watched her go, then closed the door so he and Kath were alone in the living room with no one able to see in. Then Jim turned around.

The gash on Kath's cheek looked more livid now that it contrasted with fair, smooth skin, worse than he'd imagined when he came in.

"I'm fine," Kath insisted. "It'll heal right up, it always does."

"Yeah, always." Jim could hear his voice thickening a little. He couldn't help it. As soon as they were alone together . . . well, yeah, a lot of it was that mane of dark gold, not straight and fine like Kelly's but thick as lion's fur, framing Kath's oval face. A lot of it was the lithe body, lean and muscled and high-breasted under clothes that now fit her about as well as draped tent fabric. The lips, wide and dark pink over even white teeth, definitely had something to do with it, too. And sure, the shock of the magic, the change, never failed to impress, even when it happened a few times a day.

But mostly it was Kath's eyes. The beautiful hazel color, equal green and brown, was the one feature that remained constant, even when she was around other people (though in public, the whites were yellow and bloodshot). Kath looked at Jim with absolute trust and absolute need. That, more than anything, never failed to get his blood rushing straight down, making him so hard so fast that it was tough to think straight, let alone talk.

But a decent man would concern himself with the fact that his wife was being repeatedly injured, so Jim strove mightily against his desire. "This keeps happening, Kath. We could stop it if—do you want a divorce?"

Kath then flung the ice pack at Jim. It bounced off his shoulder to the floor.

"Ow!" he protested.

"That is the single stupidest thing you have ever said."

"I don't want you to keep getting hit and cut and hurt!" Jim flung back. "Is that stupid?"

Kath started to say something sharp and stopped. It wasn't just her looks that changed in an instant, her moods did sometimes, too, though they weren't subject to anything as clear-cut as whether she and Jim were alone together or with others. "'Course not. We'll talk about it after, but right now . . . just make me feel better, okay?"

It all felt like the same movement, crossing the room, bending down and putting his arms around her. Their tongues lapped together and they kissed, eyes open. Jim knew that was how Kath liked it best. She loved to be looked at when they were with each other like this. He grabbed a handful of the shapeless, drab garment that covered her body. Kath gave a sexy little wriggle and was free in less time than it would have taken Houdini, leaving her stark naked.

It seemed like they started lovemaking the same way every time, not due to any lack of imagination—that always surfaced later—but because each knew what the other liked best and aimed to please. So Jim cupped his right hand over Kath's left breast, its swell filling his palm, and teased her nipple. His tongue ran down the side of her long neck until his mouth reached the valley between shoulder and collarbone, while her teeth and tongue played with his earlobe, both her hands busy undoing his belt.

Jim reached his left hand between her legs, where it was as wet as her mouth. He slid two fingers in and out and Kath clenched herself around them, promising so much that Jim wondered if he was going to either come or pass out from trying to restrain himself before Kath got him free of his pants and then, thank God, the belt was open and his zipper was undone. He withdrew the two fingers, letting Kath guide his cock into her.

"God, you're so beautiful," he said, and meant it every time.

They rocked together, his hands holding her up so she was in his lap, moving vertically on him, clenching and relaxing, her breasts molding to his chest, and Kath said what she always said, "You're safe, love. I wouldn't ever hurt you."

It scared Jim to think that he probably knew what she was talking about, though nothing could have scared him enough to make him stop.

Four years earlier, Jim had met Kath Ragnall through work. She was a social worker, good at her job, smart, funny and turned out to be interested in English mythology, just like he was. She didn't think there was anything laughable about the way Jim drew parallels between medieval knights and modern police officers. At some point, Jim had asked Kath out. And a funny thing happened. Jim could remember they'd had a great time, what they'd had for supper and how good it felt when they kissed, but damned if he could remember what Kath Ragnall actually looked like. It happened again on the second date. By the third date, he thought he was going crazy, but felt he owed it to Kath to let her know he had developed some kind of psychiatric problem. "I know this is gonna sound weird, but . . ."

"You can't remember what I look like, even when you're looking straight at me?" she'd offered.

"Yeah"—Jim heaved a sigh of relief that she was so understanding—"that's exactly—wait, how do you know that?"

Kath blushed (and it was also weird Jim could tell that about her without knowing what she looked like). "I think it means . . . we're getting serious here."

"It does?" Jim was very pleased, then realized, "But why

would how *you* feel affect *my* memory? This can't be a sign of good mental health."

"No," Kath said matter-of-factly, "it's a curse. You know the Arthurian legend about Sir Gawain and Lady Ragnall?"

"Sure." Jim loved Arthurian myth; he could practically quote Tennyson backward. "King Arthur tells Sir Gawain to marry Lady Ragnall, who's under a curse. She can either be beautiful in public and hideous in private, or hideous in public and beautiful in private. Sir Gawain leaves the choice up to her, and that breaks the curse, so she's beautiful all the time." He smiled expectantly into the instantly forgettable face of his otherwise wonderful date.

"Shit," said Kath miserably.

"Shit?" Jim echoed, surprised.

"You can only get around the curse if you don't know how to get around the curse. Now you really do have to pick one—if we're gonna be together, I mean."

"Well, then, you choose—wait, this can't be for real."

"No?" Kath arched an eyebrow. "Why do you think you can't tell what I look like even when you're staring straight at me?"

Jim had to admit she had a point there, although it took a lot more discussion before he was ready to accept that Kath really was descended from *that* Lady Ragnall, that the curse was real and that all the women in the family line had it. But once he did believe it, he repeated, "*You* choose."

"If I was hideous in private, would you be able to get it up?" Kath asked cautiously. "Be honest."

"Um." Jim tried to be honest with himself. "How hideous are we talking? I mean, I like to think I make love to a girl for who she is, but past a certain point . . . I guess the choice is either everybody envies me but at home we're really just best friends, or everybody wonders why I'm with you, but I know what you really look like."

"That's about it," Kath agreed.

"Well," Jim had said, "I know what I want, then, but it's still up to you."

"Well," Kath said, her tone both shy and sly, "I'm kind of hoping we're gonna have sex."

Jim grinned. "Well, so I guess let's go with the pretty in private—Jesus H. Christ!" he blurted involuntarily as the curse promptly took effect and he saw what Kath looked like in public.

"Hideous?" she surmised.

"Surprising," he replied gallantly. "Let's go home."

It turned out that they only needed to go as far as Jim's car. As soon as no one else was looking, Kath was the most beautiful thing Jim had ever seen. It didn't take them long to get married, partly because Jim truly loved Kath and partly because after sex with her even once, he knew that being with another woman would just feel like jerking off into a cut cantaloupe.

Kelly Ragnall didn't make any particular impression on her brother-in-law until she got involved with Tony Caudell. Jim had always seen Kelly as an okay-looking young and well-off widow, but when Jim and Kath had been married a little over a year, Kelly and Tony had their engagement party. Kelly walked into the room, suddenly so stunning that Jim had a moment where he thought his heart might literally stop, and Jim was a faithful guy. God only knew what was going through the minds of men who couldn't come home to his Kath. Kelly caught his gaping expression and winked at him. He was the only man at the party she didn't flirt with, out of loyalty to her sister. Her intended didn't mind Kelly's behavior at all; in fact, Tony looked like he enjoyed seeing other men so openly want what he had.

Nobody said anything, but Jim could see the guests sneak looks from one sister to the other and wonder how the goddess and the hag could possibly be related. He could see Kath notice those looks, too. She grinned at him, a what-do-they-know grin with those cracked lips and yellowed teeth, and he found he was grinning back, because he realized he was part of the best secret in the world.

When they left the party, Jim asked Kath as soon as they were alone in the car, "Does Tony know about the curse?"

"Mm-hmm. She can't marry him otherwise."

"But Kelly's . . . she's, uh, pretty," Jim finished mildly.

"Well, yeah, but you haven't seen her in private. They just chose differently than we did."

"But—I mean, if it was us, I'd lose it, seeing you like this all the time around other people and then not being able to . . . I mean," Jim amended, "you think he doesn't mind that she doesn't look like that when they do it?"

"Well . . ." Kath giggled nervously, sounding like a high schooler with a lewd secret. "I mean, he's rich, right? He could pay people."

"You think he'd screw around on your sister with hookers?" As a cop, a married man and Kelly's brother-in-law, Jim found this disgusting on any number of levels.

"Oh, no, I mean hire people to watch him and Kelly. You know, so they're not alone when they do it."

Jim was so astonished that he came within two inches of swerving into an SUV in the next lane. The driver honked, glared and, for a minute, Kath had on her public face.

"Uh, and Kelly likes that?" Jim asked dubiously.

Kath looked pretty dubious herself. "Well, Kelly likes being rich. I just hope he makes *some* time to be alone with her, that's all."

That had been three years ago, but the conversation came into Jim's mind as he lay naked on his back on the couch, his wife resting her full weight on him. He fondly stroked her breasts as she gently rubbed a finger along his cock, urging his spent erection to recover so they could go again. "Is it just us," he mused, "or the curse?"

She looked up at him curiously, her hand keeping its pace. "Is what us?"

"Every time we're alone together, we just go at it like crazed weasels."

Kath laughed, her hand gripping now. "Crazed weasels don't have opposable thumbs." She kissed his belly. "It's more romantic if it's just us, but . . . does it matter?"

Jim stopped her hand with his. He wanted to talk, now, before his brain fogged up with wanting and needing and doing again. "That kid who threw the bottle—"

"It'll heal," Kath assured him again.

"Yeah, but there's always a next time," he said, touching her cheek where the blood was drying. "Do you wish we'd chosen differently?" he asked quietly.

"Oh, hell, no," Kath said emphatically. "Baby, for the five-hundredth time, people who don't want to have sex with me don't care what I look like, or they shouldn't, anyway. If they do care, hell with 'em. I just want you to like how I look. And I know you do." She punctuated her words with a playful nip.

"Yeah," he persisted, "but Kelly doesn't get cut up just walking down the street."

Kath sighed in exasperation and sat up, abandoning foreplay for argument. "What Kelly does—I'd rather *eat* the broken glass than be married to Tony Caudell. Do you know he hasn't been alone with her at all, in six months at least? You know what that's doing to her?"

And Jim realized, no, he didn't know, because somehow this exact subject hadn't come up in quite this way before. "I guess . . . she's lonely?" he ventured.

"Well, yeah," Kath agreed, but Jim could see that hadn't been where she was going with this. "The thing is, I don't know if Kelly could be happy the way I'm happy, you know?" She stopped talking for a moment and brought her mouth to Jim's, emphasizing her own enjoyment of her husband and her life. "I mean, she likes everybody to look at her and she likes—she calls it 'financial latitude.' "

Jim thought Kath looked wistful, but he couldn't tell if it was for herself or her sister.

"But—I mean, I know she was hoping Tony would figure things out on his own, but he didn't, and now she's in one of her 'If you really loved me, you'd ask the right question' moods. Which can last . . . a really long time. She acts like everything's fine, and he thinks everything is just great the way it is."

Jim was now completely lost. Hoping it was the right question, he asked, "What should Tony have figured out?"

"That he's supposed to be alone with her once in awhile!" Kath burst out. "It's a curse. It's *supposed* to have a little bit of a downside. And sometimes, whatever she looks like . . . I mean, if he loved her, he'd want to be alone with her sometimes and just talk, right?"

Jim nodded, shifting so that his arms were around Kath, drawing her closer as she explained further, "He's been trying to trick the curse, have Kelly gorgeous in public and still be able to have sex with her all the time and . . . I'm getting worried about the buildup."

And Jim, who could never be accused of lack of curiosity, asked, "What do you mean 'buildup'?"

The luncheon had gone better than even Tony could have hoped, lasting on into the evening. The last hand had been shaken on the last deal of the day—not counting Kelly's several delightful, surreptitious handshakes throughout the afternoon—and now the Caudells were in the executive suite upstairs. Jessica St. Clair, of Clarendon Escort Service, sat in a chair, stockinged legs crossed, waiting for instructions.

"You're new," Kelly observed. "Where's Brenda?"

"Client took her to Paris for a week," Jessica reported.

Tony waved an unconcerned hand as he shrugged out of the tux jacket while Kelly undid his tie. "She just sits there anyway."

Kelly planted a precise kiss on Tony's lips. "Don't be rude, darling." She addressed Jessica over her shoulder. "Would you like some champagne?"

Jessica nodded. "Thanks. I just watch, right?"

"That's right." Tony didn't look at the girl. She wasn't his type at all, but if he didn't pay attention to her, she wouldn't actively turn him off, either. "Watch, stay there, and keep quiet."

Tony ran a hand down the bodice of Kelly's silver dress and the fabric rolled down easily, exposing her erect nipples. Tony put his mouth on one, then the other, then detected movement and saw that the girl from the escort service had turned away. "Hey, what're you doing?"

Jessica held up her half-filled champagne flute. "She said I could," she said defensively.

"Fine," Tony sighed, then returned his attention to Kelly's breasts and repeated the word with an entirely different inflection.

The dress peeled away at a touch. Kelly was naked underneath except for sheer stockings and silver garters at the thighs. Tony undid the garters, loving how Kelly's stiletto heels showed off her splendid calves. Tony put a hand on her blonde pubic hair and pushed, not too hard, just enough to ease her back onto the bedspread. He undid his shirt, breathing hard as he watched her undo her ankle straps, then lay back again, legs spread for his delectation.

Tony lay atop her, kissing her mouth as she peeled down his trousers, his tongue probing as she sucked on it. Down below, she was just the way he liked her, moist without being soaking. Kelly clenched around him, magnificent thigh muscles making themselves felt over his buttocks and her cunt tightening on him like a fist. "Oh, yeah," Tony breathed.

Jessica's tightly crossed legs failed to register with Tony as a sign of bladder distress; he thought she was aroused by the display, or at least being a good pro and faking it admirably. He didn't notice the girl's mouth moving silently as she counted to ten, then twenty, looked longingly at the open bathroom doorway that was on the other side of the bed, then gritted her teeth. Finally, Tony had a loud, guttural orgasm and withdrew, rolling over next to his wife, eyes closed.

In his state of momentary relaxation, Tony did not see Jessica catch Kelly's eye. The escort pointed to the bathroom door, made a gesture indicating that she didn't want to disturb Tony by moving too near to him, held up a forefinger indicating she'd only be gone for a moment, and darted out into the hallway to seek the public restroom, even as Kelly said, "Wait—"

This left Tony and Kelly Caudell alone in the room.

Although Tony heard his wife speak and the click of the door closing behind Jessica, his first real clue that something was out of the ordinary was tactile. Rubbing his hand along Kelly's hip, he felt something wet, then slid his fingers down farther. His hand touched something soft and damp and papery, but while it yielded, it was more or less smooth.

Tony opened his eyes and looked down. For a moment, he thought that Kelly's labia had shifted into the path of his fingers, but that was not it. There was a soft, dusky purple-pink mass of flesh between Kelly's legs, as though it had simply fused shut.

Too confused at first to react, Tony looked at his wife. The tan was gone, as was most of what Tony would normally consider skin. Sticky, raw, red patches covered everything—face, neck, arms—furrowed by rows of flaked white skin so hard and dry they could and did cut into what they encountered, both the bedspread beneath and Tony's flesh above.

Tony gawked. Kelly's fingernails had turned to raptor talons, thick and yellow and curved like short scimitars. Her slender torso was suddenly skeletal and wood-hard, rib cage protruding through the angry peeling skin.

Kelly's face was the worst, though. Her turquoise irises were unchanged, but the surrounding whites were bloodied saffron. The skin around them was cracked like old paper, and her lips had vanished. Upper lip and lower jaw now simply *stopped* in an "O" around a black, empty-gummed maw.

Kelly's teeth, meanwhile, had surfaced elsewhere. Her breasts had imploded into two fleshy caves that seemed like mockeries of her now-distorted genitalia. The dark, wet, new orifices on her chest had teeth set in rings that looked like something one might find in the maw of a barracuda.

Tony fought down a scream. "What did you *do*?"

"We're alone," the Kelly thing rasped. "Told you how the curse worked."

Tony's gaze whipped round. The hooker's handbag was next to the now-empty chair, and he belatedly recalled the sound of the door closing. "Bullshit!" he yelled. "Kath doesn't turn into this!"

"Kath changes back and forth every day," the Kelly thing croaked. Then it added, "Move carefully."

Carefully? Tony thought incredulously. He did not want to be in the same building as this horror, much less naked in bed beside it, and he was getting the hell away.

Tony tried to spring up off the bed, but in his panic, he lost his balance and fell against Kelly.

Kelly's chest contracted. The teeth in the orifices where her breasts had previously been clamped shut, biting deep into both sides of his chest.

Tony's scream rose to a squeal as agony matched terror. He tore free and rolled with a thump to the floor. Dizzy and weak, he looked down. What was that, pulsing under all the blood and torn flesh? *Oh, Christ,* he realized, *my heart. The bitch bit away so much of my chest, I can see my heart through my rib cage.*

Tony tried to speak, even as he was fainting from the blood loss that was about to kill him. No one would believe that his about-to-be-nondescript-again wife, or indeed any human at all, could possibly have caused such damage. "I didn't know you'd become . . ."

It was hard to tell, but Tony thought Kelly sounded sad. "Sorry, baby, you never asked."

Forever and Ever

Dave Zeltserman

I noticed Morrisey eyeing the fudge brownies Luanne had sent me. "Anything I can help you with?" I asked.

Morrisey, the weasel, tried to give me a friendly smile, showing off badly formed, yellowed teeth. He scratched behind his ear and asked if he could have one.

"Of course." I held the box out to him. "Three dollars. Cash up front."

He kept the smile going. "Come on, be decent, man. You're not going to eat them all anyway."

"Probably not," I agreed.

"You'll end up throwing them out."

"No, I won't," I corrected him. "Not after waking up a few nights ago and watching you pick through the garbage for my last leftovers. When I'm done with these, one way or another, they get flushed down the toilet."

The smile drained from his face. He shrugged and moved back to his bunk. I put the brownies down and picked up Luanne's folder and took out her picture. It had been sprayed with a flowery sweet five-buck perfume. I felt a lump form in my throat as I studied it. She was a doll. Big brown eyes, long flowing black hair, soft full lips. I knew her lips had to be soft. I tried to imagine how they would feel.

Morrisey said something. I carefully put Luanne's picture back in her folder and turned and stared at my cellmate.

"I'll pay you fifty bucks if you let me use your photo," he said, repeating what he'd said.

I kept staring at him.

He shifted his small black eyes away from me. "Seventy-five," he offered weakly.

I shook my head. "I'd like to take your money," I said. "I really hate to pass it up, especially how my picture wouldn't help you one damn bit. But I got a reputation to think of."

"Come on, man, you don't need it anymore. You're out of here in three weeks."

"That's not the point."

Morrisey started to argue. The way he saw it, the only reason I brought in the money from the personal ads was because of my looks, and if he had my picture he could do just as well.

I tried to explain the obvious to him. "No matter what you convinced the ladies you looked like," I told him, "you still wouldn't be able to squeeze a dime out of them. You want to know why?"

A shadow seemed to fall over his small black eyes, darkening his features. For some reason, it annoyed the hell of me.

"Because it comes down to intelligence," I continued. "You should quit deluding yourself and stick with what you do best—sniveling and sneaking through the trash."

Morrisey's eyes glazed over as he looked at me. Then he lay down on his back, hands clasped behind his greasy little head. I had to fight back the impulse to get up and kick the crap out of him. Most of the cons in the joint regarded my accomplishments with awe, but there were a few, like Morrisey, who acted as if it were all nothing but luck. Like they could do the same thing.

I pulled the cardboard box I use as a file cabinet out from

under my bunk and put Luanne's folder back with the others. Morrisey wouldn't have a prayer of running the type of operation I run, juggling thirty-seven women at once. My success was partly due to treating it like a business instead of just a quick score. Being organized, keeping folders on each "client," running credit checks over the phone on them. But again, that's only part of it. The way I played them was the key. Squeezing every last dime out of them. Having them all hocked up to their lonely little necks. All but Luanne . . .

I found Marge Henke's folder and took out her picture. She was blond, a little overweight, plain. For the most part, a typical patsy—except for one little thing. A credit check showed she was worth three million, and I had her hook, line, and sinker and dangling from the end of my line.

A low convulsing sound came from Morrisey. His black eyes sparkled as he stared at me. I watched as he shook uncontrollably and his Adam's apple bobbed up and down.

"And what do you find so funny?" I asked.

"A joke," he said. "Ha ha."

He was smirking at Marge Henke's picture. I felt a hotness flushing my cheeks. "She certainly isn't much to look at, is she?" I asked, forcing a smile.

He didn't say anything. He just kept laughing. A soft, raspy, wheezing laugh.

"I guess not," I admitted. "But three weeks from now, I'll be marrying her and thanks to California's community property laws I'll be worth a million and a half. And we both know what you'll be doing in three weeks. Same as usual. Rotting away. And you'll still be ugly as a stillborn weasel."

"I'll be laughing my ass off," he snickered, "because it's a pretty funny joke. Ha ha ha."

He kept laughing. I felt the hotness spreading, tightening the veins in my throat. I closed my eyes. I had two choices—ignore Morrisey or kick his teeth in—and I knew if I started I wouldn't be able to stop. And if that were to happen, I wouldn't be marrying Marge and her three million net worth. I squeezed my eyes shut, squeezing tighter until I could hear the blood rushing through my head. Until the sound drowned out Morrisey's soft, convulsing laughter. After a while, I was able to ignore him completely.

Luanne visited me twice during the next three weeks. My heart ached just to look at her. She was so young and sweet and fresh. So damn beautiful. She knew I was getting out, but the way I explained it to her was I needed time alone on the outside to find myself, but we would continue to write, and after no more than a year we would be together. She pleaded with me to live with her right away. I almost broke down and agreed. I had eighty-two thousand in a bank account thanks to my enterprises, and I weighed it and Luanne against the million and a half Marge Henke offered. Watching Luanne's soft brown eyes moisten with tears almost did it for me. I came within a hair's breadth of throwing away Henke's money when common sense kicked in. After all, it would only be a year, maybe less. Then Luanne and I would have all the time in the world together. And we'd have the money to enjoy it.

I thought about Luanne a lot my last three weeks. About whether I could go a year without seeing her. Of all of them, she was the only one to have ever visited me. Twice a month, as allowed by prison policy, for the last two and a half years. None of the others had ever seen me except for the photos I sent, not even Marge Henke. At times, some of them would suggest coming to the prison, but it would be easy enough to talk them out of it. Deep down inside, they wanted me to talk them out of it. It was safer that way than to risk having their fragile make-believe worlds shattered by the hard cold truths of a con.

After Luanne's last visit, I lay awake that night trying to imagine what it would be like to make love to her. I tried to picture her lying naked with her legs open, her eyes and arms inviting me to join her. I tried to picture myself entering her and her hips moving rhythmically with mine, but the image kept shifting on me and Luanne kept changing into different girls I've fucked over the years. And there were a lot of them. Maybe hundreds of them. All different types: white, black, Asian, Hispanic. The only things I ever cared about were that they looked good with their clothes off and I could get something out of them. Money, sex, it didn't matter. But now that I wanted to think of Luanne, I couldn't do it. I just kept seeing all the others, all with their pussies wide open for me. Sometimes with their asses waving at me as they were on their knees doggie-style, sometimes with them riding me from on top, sometimes with them flat on their backs with their legs straight in the air. I wanted so badly to think of Luanne, but I couldn't hold onto her. I just kept seeing all the others.

On my last day, as I was being led out of my cell, Morrisey made some crack to me about kissing my new bride for him, and then he broke out laughing. When I told him to go to hell, he just laughed harder, his ugly face twisted in mirth.

When I was let out the front gate, I found Marge standing there waiting for me. As I first saw her, I instinctively took a step back toward the prison. The picture she had sent me was a bigger fraud than anything I'd ever attempted. It had to have been taken decades earlier and still had to have been doctored. She was blond, or at least the stuff on her head had been dyed blond, but that was about all she had in common with that picture. The woman in it was plain, slightly overweight, somewhere in her thirties. What was standing before me was closer to fifty and more than double the size.

It was the expression on her face that freaked me, though. Like I had caught her in the act of twisting the heads off puppies. And I don't know how I could've possibly been prepared for that smell. There was nothing in the pen like it.

"Marge, darling," I said and forced myself forward. I caught a stronger whiff of her and somehow kept from gagging.

"Honey pie," she offered demurely. She was caked in makeup. A heavy glob of bloodred lipstick had been smeared across her lips, and thick pinkish rouge was layered over her cheeks. She tilted her cheek toward me, expecting a kiss.

As I pulled away, I couldn't help tasting the rancid sweetness that came off her. My breakfast started to come up. I lunged forward, grabbing my duffel bag and hurrying away. "Let's go, darling," I murmured, trying to keep the sickness down. "Let's get married."

I ran through the parking lot with her trotting behind me. By the time we got to her car, a battered 1978 Chevy Chevette, she was out of breath, gasping for air. When we got in the car, I rolled the passenger window completely down. Her smell had saturated the cloth seats. After six years of prison life, I thought I could deal with anything, but not that. It was like onions and garlic and dirt and sewage and sweat all mixed together. Like sickness and rotting flesh. I could barely stand it.

She drove the three-hour trip to Sacramento. Every few minutes, I'd catch her sneaking a peek at me. As we approached the city, she pulled into a fleabag motel off the highway, telling me she had booked a room there and that she needed to freshen up before the wedding.

After we checked in, Marge again tilted her cheek toward me for a kiss. "Honey pie," she offered coyly, "after we legally marry, I'll let you do more than just that." And then she disappeared into the bathroom.

As I sat on the bed waiting, a feeling of longing for Luanne overwhelmed me. All I wanted was to be with her. I wanted it more than I ever wanted anything. I closed my eyes, and could see her the way she was during our last visit. In my mind's eye, I could see her standing in the same yellow sundress she had worn. The way her hair fell past her bare shoulders, how slender her hips looked, the way the dress outlined her thighs and then ended a few inches above her knees . . .

Marge Henke's monotone humming filtered in from the bathroom and knocked Luanne's beautiful image out of my head. I got up, found some paper, and wrote Luanne a letter expressing how much I needed her and how it was only a matter of time before we would be together and, when we were, that it would be forever. All the pain inside drained out of me and onto that letter.

The bathroom door creaked open. I folded Luanne's letter and slipped it into my inside jacket pocket. Marge Henke stepped out. I noticed all she had done in there was apply more makeup. Her stench was as strong as ever.

"I have to put on my dress," she announced irritably.

I told her that I would go take a shower. Inside the bathroom, I put the water on full and scrubbed myself, trying to get her smell off me. After a half hour, I could still smell faint traces of her on my skin.

When I got out of the shower, I yelled out to her about what a lucky man I was going to be. She didn't answer. I dried myself off, dressed, and yelled out before leaving the bathroom that she'd better be decent.

The motel room was empty. Her suitcase was still on the floor, but she was gone. I looked out the window and saw her car was gone.

I sat on the bed, took out a pack of cigarettes and turned on the TV. At first I was sort of relieved, but after an hour I started to get annoyed. As I stared at the TV set, I decided I was going to take more than a million and a half from Marge Henke. By the time I was through bleeding her, she was going to be one anemic fat broad.

I finished the pack of cigarettes and then walked over to the front office and bought a couple more packs. The girl working the desk couldn't tell me anything about where Marge had gone. There was a liquor store next to the motel. I bought a six-pack of beer and a quart of bourbon from it and then went back to my room to wait.

I woke up at four A.M. with my head pounding and the TV blaring away. Marge Henke still hadn't come back. I finished off what was left of the bourbon and then paced the room and kicked at the bed. I couldn't understand what had happened. Then it came to me. I got up and checked my suit jacket's inside pocket. Luanne's letter was still there, but I could also pick up Marge's smell on it. There was nothing else to do so, I turned off the TV and went to bed.

I was woken up the next morning by her smell. It was stronger than ever. I lifted my head and saw Marge Henke standing over me, hands on her hips.

"Look at the mess you made!" she exclaimed. Her eyes were bloodshot and her skin looked paler than ever.

"Where were you, darling?"

"I don't know what you're talking about!"

I sat up slowly, trying not to move too fast. I had gone six years without touching any alcohol, and the bourbon and six-pack had hit me hard.

"You don't have to talk about it," I said, squinting against the light. "I guess you needed time alone to think things over."

"I still don't know what you're talking about." She narrowed her eyes and peered at me, her large, doughy face expressionless. "My Lord," she cried out as she glanced at the clock. "It's eight-thirty already. You better get up if we're going to get married!"

We drove into Sacramento, found City Hall, and a half hour later were man and wife. The J.P. involuntarily grimaced as he told me I could kiss the bride. I managed to give her a little peck on the lips, and fortunately only tasted the lipstick that had been smeared over them.

Marge had a house in Davis, about a two-hour ride from

Sacramento. During the trip I dozed off. At some point I started dreaming of Luanne. We were alone together, and she was wearing the same yellow sundress. She moved over to me and lifted her arms so I could pull the dress over her. I did, and all she was wearing underneath were white cotton panties. Her eyes glistened as she took hold of my hands and placed them on her small but perfect breasts. I felt her nipples hardening under the light pressure of my thumbs, and then I let my hands slowly fall, tracing her body, feeling the outline of her ribs, and then down to her stomach. It was mostly flat with only a small curvature to it. She moved my hands so they were on her hips. I could feel her trembling as I lowered her panties. My mouth felt dry. I could barely swallow as I looked at her. I wanted her so badly. I let my hand slide gently between her legs, first feeling the softness of the slight patch of hair she had, then her wet pussy, and finally her small but firm ass. She started to undo my pants. I stopped her and got down on my knees, putting my nose against her soft pubic area and moving my tongue under it. As I tasted her, the smell stopped me. It was overwhelming. At first I thought it was coming from inside her, but it had hit her also. That rotten, putrid stench was all around us, engulfing us, staining us. I looked up and saw that she was making a face as if she was about to be sick.

"What's that smell?" she asked me. "It's horrible."

And then I was jostled awake by Marge.

"You must've gotten letters from a lot of girls," she said, a sly look on her face.

It took me a few seconds to get used to that smell again. "I guess so," I muttered.

"Why don't you tell me about them?"

I looked over at her. She still had that sly look on her face, like she knew something I didn't. "There's not much to tell. It took a lot of letters before I found the right person."

"I bet some of the girls were real pretty."

"One, anyway." I smiled at her and squeezed her knee. I got no reaction, just the same sly, calculating look. "Most of the ladies were lonely and pathetic. A couple were nuts."

She didn't talk after that, and I went back to sleep. I think after that I dreamt about being trapped in a sewer.

When she woke me up and I caught sight of her house, I almost broke out laughing. The car was bad enough for a woman with three million dollars, but that house? It was nothing but an ugly little clapboard shack.

"We're home, honey pie!" she announced.

Inside was worse than anything I could've ever imagined. The smell almost knocked me over. There was dirt and clutter and garbage everywhere. And that smell! Gawd, it was worse than her car.

Marge pushed me aside and went straight to the telephone. I overheard her talking to someone named Henrietta, telling her about how we got married this morning instead of yesterday. "He just took off yesterday afternoon," she said. "That's right, he left me waiting in the motel room all day and night. I don't know where he went. But he came back this morning and we got married." After that she called someone named Irma and gave the same story.

"Why'd you say that?" I asked.

"I don't know what you're talking about." She stood up, made a sour face, and ran her hands against her rumpled dress. "I have to go to the bathroom."

As I stood alone, a sickish feeling began to work its way into my stomach. I called my credit agency and asked for another credit check on Marge Henke, giving them her address and phone number. I then took my duffel bag into the kitchen and found Marge's folder.

As I read it, a cold chill ran through me. Her file had been tampered with, mixed with the file of another woman, Mary Henderson. The numbers I had scribbled from my credit service had been switched. I pulled Henderson's file and found

Marge's earlier letters hidden in it. They were the ramblings of a deranged mind.

In my mind's eye I could picture Morrisey rearranging the two folders, mixing papers between Henderson's folder and Marge's. I could picture him laughing hysterically over what he had done. I could almost hear it.

The phone rang. It was the credit agency, letting me know that Marge Henke was a bad risk with less than three hundred dollars in savings.

Marge walked out of the bathroom, peering at me expressionlessly. "What you doing, honey pie?" she asked.

I didn't bother to answer. I walked back to the kitchen and packed away my folders, then grabbed my duffel bag and started past her. "A big mistake was made, lady," I said. "Don't wait up for me."

"You ain't leaving me!"

"Oh no?" I started laughing. "What do they use to get rid of a skunk's scent, tomato juice? Well, as soon as I'm out of here I'm buying a case of it. Wish me luck."

"You heard me tell my friends about how you went away yesterday. Unless you want to end up in big trouble, you better just read that copy of the *San Jose Examiner* I brought back with me. Page fourteen."

As I stared at her, I felt a weakness in my knees. Luanne was from San Jose. "What the hell are you talking about?"

"You just better read it!"

I found the newspaper lying on the sofa. On page fourteen was a story about a young, pretty girl who had been strangled to death in her apartment. The girl was Luanne Williams.

"You killed her," I heard myself saying.

"I don't know what you're talking about."

As I looked at her, her large bloated body dissolved into a sea of redness. Before I knew it I was clawing at her, pushing her face into the wall, choking her. There was a surprising hardness to her flesh as she fought back. Her face inched its way toward mine. The harsh, fetid smell of her breath assaulted me. My senses were reeling. The ground seemed to be slipping sideways away from me.

I collapsed onto the floor, weeping uncontrollably. "You killed her," I sobbed.

"Look at the marks you left on my neck," she said in a calm, almost indifferent voice. "I'm going to show Irma and Henrietta these marks." As she stood over me, a horrible smile formed on her face. Like when I first saw her.

"Who do you think the police are going to believe, an ex-convict or a woman like me who's never had any problems with anybody? Especially after I show Irma and Henrietta what you did to my neck. Now, honey pie," she added softly. "Why don't you get up and lie down with me? You might as well, because we're going to be together for a long time. Forever and ever."

Somewhere in the distance I could hear Morrisey laughing his head off. Laughing like there was no tomorrow.

Fading Memories

Michael Bracken

Soft, moist lips gently covered hers, slowly drawing Ashley from sleep. The kiss began gently, grew firm as she returned it, sucking the other's lips into her mouth and nipping at them with her pearly white teeth. Then tongues met, insistent and thrusting.

One hand slipped between her thighs and cupped her pubic mound, one finger stroking the length of her slit. Ashley drew her knees up, parting her thighs and opening herself.

She reached up and took the other's head in her hands, her fingers wrapping around hair fine as silk, and for the first time her eyes fluttered open.

And saw nothing.

Ashley blinked, then blinked again.

She rolled over and glanced at the clock. She had been asleep less than an hour. After switching on the bedside lamp, she pushed aside the covers and sat up. Her reflection stared back at her from the mirror above her dresser.

The bedroom door stood ajar, even though she'd closed it before retiring, and she hesitated before swinging her legs out of bed. Wearing only a Cowboys T-shirt her ex-boyfriend had given her, Ashley felt a chill creep up the inside of her thighs. She pulled on a floor-length terry-cloth robe before venturing into the hall.

"Steven?" she said. He had given her the T-shirt, but he had not returned her house key. "Is that you?"

She switched on the hall light, then the living room, kitchen, bathroom, and second bedroom lights. She opened every closet and assured herself that every window remained securely locked. Even the dead bolts and the chains remained fastened on the doors.

She didn't return to bed until 3:00 A.M.

After work the next evening, Ashley curled up on her sofa with a glass of wine, a bowl of microwave popcorn, and the television remote. The doorbell interrupted her channel surfing. She pushed herself from the couch and walked to the open door.

Steven stood on the front porch. He wore tight jeans, a sleeveless blue sweatshirt, and a lopsided grin.

"What do you want?" she asked through the screen.

He held up her house key. "To return this."

"You could have mailed it."

"And get my Robert Earl Keen CD."

"You should have called first."

"I knew you'd be home."

She stared at him. "Doesn't matter. You still should have called."

He just stood on the porch, grinning his grin.

"I'll get your CD."

She turned away, walked to the entertainment center, and sorted through a stack of CDs until she found *West Textures*. When she returned, she pushed the door open and handed Steven the CD. He held out her key. When she reached for it, he caught her wrist and held it.

"Miss me?"

"Not even in your dreams." She snatched the key, jerked her arm from Steven's grip, and stepped back.

"You will," Steven said.

Ashley slammed the door and leaned against it. She knew her ex-boyfriend would remain on the porch for a full minute, maybe even two, waiting for her to change her mind and ask him in.

She wouldn't give him the satisfaction, and she forced herself not to look through the window for nearly five minutes.

By then, he had gone.

Ashley told no one about her nocturnal visitor and within a few days had convinced herself that it had been nothing more than a vivid dream brought on by an emotional breakup with her former boyfriend, a lack of sleep caused by overwork, and too many glasses of wine before bed.

Mostly she blamed the breakup. At first, she'd been intoxicated by Steven's muscular good looks and his attentiveness in the bedroom. She slowly realized they had nothing else in common and that he had grown increasingly demanding of her time and attention. When she ended their relationship during dinner at an Italian restaurant downtown, he'd reacted poorly, dumping chicken primavera into her lap and swearing that she would regret her decision.

Ashley had yet to regret her decision . . . except when she fell asleep alone, clutching a body pillow. She didn't miss Steven, but she missed having him in bed with her, his weight balancing out the mattress, his warmth often forcing her to cast aside the covers. She missed falling asleep in his arms after sex, missed waking in the morning to find his tongue teasing her nipple, his hand caressing the curve of her hip.

Steven found Ashley sitting alone at her favorite Mexican restaurant, the one he'd taken her to on their second date. They had consumed too many margaritas that night and had sex for the first time against the trunk of his car in the restaurant's darkened parking lot.

He slipped into the booth across the table from her.

"I've been thinking about you," he said. "About us."

"It's over," Ashley said. "We never had anything."

"We had sex," he said. "Don't you miss the sex?"

"Not as much as you'd think."

"I'll bet you dream about me."

Her eyes narrowed to slits and she glared at Steven until he slipped from the booth.

He leaned over and whispered in her ear. His warm breath tickled. "Call me when it gets to be too much, when you're all alone and you want someone inside you."

Ashley shivered.

The following Saturday evening, after a long day spent caring for her yard, Ashley stood half-asleep in the shower, her eyes closed and the hot, pulsing water cascading over her body.

She felt a pair of hands—large and slick with soap—slide around her from behind and cup her heavy breasts. Then fingers stroked her rapidly stiffening nipples, and she felt a man's body pressing against her, the thick tube of an erection nestling between her ass cheeks.

Ashley's eyes snapped open and she spun around, nearly falling and barely catching herself by grabbing the towel rod inside the shower door.

She remained alone, yet her tightly constricted nipples still tingled.

Ashley quickly finished her shower, then wrapped a terrycloth robe around her still-wet body. She checked every room. The windows remained closed, the doors remained locked.

She returned to the bathroom and finished preparing for bed. A few minutes later, alone under the covers and wearing only a green-and-gold T-shirt her parents had given her the Christmas before graduation, Ashley stared at the ceiling.

Her nipples had remained painfully tight ever since her shower, and they created twin dimples against the thin cotton T-shirt. Ashley closed her eyes and remembered how she had felt when the hands slid around her in the shower, cupping her heavy breasts and teasing her nipples. She wet her lips with the tip of her tongue, then touched her own breasts, feeling the nubbly surface of her constricted areolas and painfully tight nipples through the T-shirt.

She knew she'd been alone in the shower, but she remembered the feeling of a man pressed hard against her as if it had really happened. Ashley spread her legs apart and let her free hand drift lower. She pulled up the hem of her T-shirt, revealing her still-damp muff of blond pubic hair. Her fingers slipped through the silky hair and she stroked herself with one slim finger. Within moments, Ashley had grown moist with desire and her finger slipped between her swollen pussy lips. She moaned softly as she pushed her finger deep inside herself.

Then she pushed aside the delicate folds of skin guarding her clit and slid one slick finger over the tight bud. She moaned again and arched her back, stroking herself in slow circles, stroking faster and faster and faster.

Just when she felt herself on the verge of orgasm, she felt her hand pushed aside, replaced by the spongy-soft head of a man's erect cock. She struggled to open her eyes, but couldn't. And then the cock slid into her, deeper and deeper and deeper, filling every bit of her.

She felt her T-shirt tear away. Hands grabbed her heavy breasts, and thumbs teased her thick nipples. A mouth covered hers and a tongue thrust into her mouth. She sucked on it, sucked on it hard.

And then she was crushed against the mattress as a man's body covered hers, flattening her breasts against her chest. She felt his chest hair rough against her nipples as his hips drew back and he pushed forward. She wrapped her legs around his and arched herself up to meet each of his powerful thrusts.

He drove her to orgasm after orgasm before he finally shuddered, and stopped, and she felt herself filled with warmth.

Ashley woke in the middle of the night. The sheets beneath her were still damp, and her shredded T-shirt had been kicked to the foot of the bed. She sat up, switched on the lamp, and looked around.

Then she caught her reflection in the mirror and saw the bruises on her breasts. She stood and walked to the mirror, then walked into the bathroom and turned on the bright lights. She remembered stroking herself before falling asleep, using her own hands to tease her nipples and stroke her clit, but she knew she hadn't been rough. Each of her breasts had fingertip-sized bruises. She held her hands up to them, turning this way and that before realizing she could not have bruised herself.

Nor could she have caused the rough patch on her cheek, a patch that looked like it had been rubbed raw with sandpaper, but that she knew could only have been caused by a man's five o'clock shadow.

Her eyes widened in surprise as she remembered being pinned to the mattress by a man's weight, a familiar weight. She ran through the house, checking every door and every window. No matter how many times she checked and rechecked, the results were the same.

She remained alone in the house, securely alone. Every door remained locked, every window fastened.

Ashley returned to her bedroom and closed the door. She propped a chair under the handle to keep it from being forced open. Then she sat in the middle of her bed with all the lights on and remained there until overcome with fatigue.

He returned the next night and again two nights after that. Soon, Ashley began to look forward to his visits. She stopped waking in fear, stopped searching the house after each encounter, stopped opening her eyes to see what couldn't be seen.

Steven caught Ashley by the arm as she exited the Alico building where she worked. She hadn't seen him in two weeks. A wife-beater that had once fit snugly across his muscular chest and six-pack abdomen now hung loosely on his gaunt frame.

Ashley shook off Steven's grip.

"Don't you want me back?"

"Why?" Ashley asked. "I have the best part of you, and I don't have to clean up afterward."

"The best part?"

"Memories." She turned and walked away.

A few nights later, her dream lover visited her early and Ashley welcomed him, keeping her eyes closed as his lips kissed her eyelids, his warm breath tickled her ear, his hands explored every nook and cranny of her body. She opened herself to him and felt him enter her, cover her with his weight, and drive her to orgasm before she fell asleep.

She awoke to a ringing telephone.

"You asked me to call first," said the voice on the other end of the line when she answered.

"Steven?"

"Yeah," he said. "I'm coming over."

"Now? But it's—" She glanced at her alarm clock, saw that midnight was rapidly disappearing, and didn't finish her sentence.

"I'll be there in fifteen minutes."

"Why?" Ashley asked. "What do you want now?"

"Fifteen minutes." He disconnected the line.

Ashley stared at the phone for a moment, then pushed herself off the bed and pulled on panties, jeans, and a blouse. She didn't bother with a bra.

She stood at the door and waited until his Mustang slid to a halt at the curb. She stepped onto the porch as he hurried up the walk.

He'd barely dressed himself. His shirt had been misbuttoned and hung loose on his painfully thin frame. His running shoes remained unlaced. His black hair jutted from his head in greasy clumps, and he hadn't shaved in two or three days. His lopsided grin had been replaced with . . . nothing at all.

"I'm sorry," he said. "I didn't mean for this to happen."

He wrapped his arm around Ashley and forced her into her bungalow. As soon as they were inside, she quickly stepped away. Steven hadn't bathed in days.

"Hadn't meant for what to happen?"

"This," he said. He sank onto the couch. "Any of this. I just wanted you to miss me. To want me back."

"Why would I want you back?"

"The sex," he said. "You said I was the best you ever had."

He had been.

Until . . .

"You were the best I ever had and I didn't want to lose it . . . lose *you*." Steven leaned forward and buried his face in his hands. "I don't know how much longer I can go on."

"You're talking crazy, Steven. It's time for you to leave."

He looked up then, and she saw the haunted look in his eyes. "I can't keep up. You're insatiable. You take more than I can give. You always did . . . but this . . . this—"

"Go now, Steven." She stood on the porch and held the door open.

"You don't—"

"*Now!*"

He stood and shuffled out the door and across the porch. He stopped on the bottom step and looked back. "Stop thinking about me," he insisted. "Forget me. Forget you ever knew me."

Ashley turned her back on her ex-boyfriend and stepped inside. She closed the door and locked it. She stripped off her clothes as she walked down the hall, leaving each item where it fell to the floor. Then she lay on her bed and took her heavy breasts in her hands, massaging the soft skin and bringing her thick nipples to erection. She wet her lips with the tip of her tongue, then closed her eyes and this time she called out her lover's name.

"Steven," she whispered. "Steven."

And he came to her one last time, filling her with his desire and driving her to orgasm after orgasm after orgasm until he had nothing left and he slowly faded from her thoughts and from her memories.

Fighter

Christa Faust

Vegas at night—all glitter and neon like smashed candy scattered across the desert's endless dark. Visual cacophony of a thousand billboards, all competing for the mayfly attention span of feckless tourist hoards. A thousand entertainers, a thousand hustles. Comedians and singers, wanna-bes and used-to-bes. Animal acts and acrobats. Strippers and showgirls and drag queens. And Persephone.

In one of the older casinos, a tarnished relic from the days when Vegas was still strictly for grown-ups, Persephone does Monday, Wednesday, and Friday, two shows on Saturday. In the dimly lit lounge, she appears as flashpots explode, clad only in a golden G-string and tiny star-shaped pasties. Her makeup is theatrical, all eyes and lips, and her body is fiercely muscled, slicked with oil and dusted with glitter. Over the aging PA system, a honey-voiced announcer speaks.

"Ladies and gentlemen, prepare yourselves for the most daring, death-defying escape ever witnessed. Just as her ancient namesake descended into the underworld and returned unscathed, so will our modern-day goddess kiss death on the cheek before your very eyes!"

A curtain is parted to reveal a large water-filled tank, hypnotically backlit by hidden green and blue spotlights. Then a single golden light washes over Persephone as a pair of young men, nearly identical in their forgettable perfection, approach her from either side. They are oiled and glittered like Persephone and just as close to naked. Each bears an armful of heavy steel chains and thick, locking cuffs. The audience watches in uncomfortable silence as Persephone is meticulously bound, arms locked behind her back, torso wrapped in unyielding steel, legs woven together, and ankles locked and fastened to a heavy hook lowered from the ceiling. Her face is serene, but her eyes glisten with some manic ecstasy in the seconds before she is blindfolded by a gold silk scarf. One of the boys lifts her in his arms as the other turns a large, theatrical crank to raise the hook higher and higher, until she dangles upside down, suspended above the audience's expectant heads. The tank rolls forward automatically until it is positioned directly beneath her.

"Now as we all know, it takes only three minutes for the human brain to die from lack of oxygen. But in as little as two short minutes . . ."—a dramatic pause—". . . irreversible damage may be sustained."

An oversize stopwatch is unveiled. The space on the clock between two and three is painted bloodred, and the number three has been replaced with a skull and crossbones.

"In 1953, the Great Gambini attempted this very stunt. They pulled him out after two and a half minutes . . ."—another dramatic pause, stretching out to infinity in the hot space above the audience's expectant heads—"but it was too late. Will the lovely Persephone make the history books, or will she just be history?"

A drum roll and Persephone plunges, headfirst, into the water.

The clock starts, a sharp, metronomic ticking like a nervous heartbeat, while a subtle web of low, disquieting music insinuates itself between the seconds.

All around her, video screens light up. Each screen shows a close-up of a different body part. Her narrow, elegant hands.

Her chain-wrapped midriff. Her sculpted ankles and delicate feet. Her lips, spangled with tiny silver bubbles.

Persephone struggles beneath the water. Her skin is pale, gleaming, and her blond hair floats, weightless around her face. The chains that bind her glint and flash. Time continues to pass, and she seems to tire. The audience is on the edge of their seats. It is as if no one dares to breathe until she can breathe with them. Inside the tank, she has gone completely still. Her attendants sell it with nervous faces and hands tightly clenched, one eye on her motionless form and one eye on the ever-advancing clock. The ticking hand hits the red, and the audience's hearts are pounding, palms sweating. A full thirty seconds pass. One of the boys starts toward the tank as if to free her, but his companion restrains him. Then, in a single serpent-smooth move, her muscles flex and ripple and the chains fall away, sinking to the bottom of the tank. She bursts upward in a rush of bubbles and frantic applause as she rips off the blindfold, triumphant.

In the front row to her left is a young man. Hard eyes set in a rough, ugly-sexy face. Bald head and thick sinewy arms end in blunt wrestler's hands. From the stage, Persephone fixes him with a gaze resonant with hunger and frank invitation, and he holds it, doesn't look away. She gives him a small, suggestive smile and slips behind the curtain.

Backstage, Persephone sits before a mirrored vanity, burning. An insistent heat boils beneath her skin, radiating outward from the deep pink grooves left behind by the cold steel chains. Desire pounds its fists between her legs, and she has to clutch the edges of the vanity, stealthy sparkles dancing at the corners of her vision. It is always like this, has been since the first time young Persephone—just plain old Peggy back then—wound a piece of oil-stained rope around her wrists in her father's tool shed, heavy, honey-thick sunlight pouring in through the dusty windows to caress her sweat-glossed flesh as she strained against her bonds, pretending. Pretending that she was captured, pretending that she could not escape, that her bones could not fold up and flatten like the bones of a weasel sliding under the henhouse door. She would wind the fraying rope around her hips, down between her legs, and lie on the cold and filthy cement, struggling, straining against the rope, until the friction brought its own fierce release.

But it was never enough. Sitting here now in her sad little dressing room with desire devouring her from the inside out, she knows that pretending will never be enough. The sharp firecracker orgasms that hit her like rabbit punches as she struggled against the cruel chains on stage only made it worse. She pulls her gold satin kimono tighter around her body. It seems to take far too long for her assistant to fetch the man from the front row.

When he arrives, she does not let him speak. A glitter-nailed finger against his thin lips, and then her own hungry mouth, and he responds with harsh strength, sledgehammer-hard against her belly. There is an impatient wrenching of clothing, and then his chest is bare and her kimono is pooled like golden water around her feet. A touch of glitter remains on her skin, flashing under his rough, clutching hands. She sighs and grips his wrist, moving his hand from her breast to the grooves the chain has left across her ribs. When he runs his fingertips experimentally over the corrugated surface, she shudders, a thick sound welling up like blood in her throat. Her heart is pounding between her legs as her hand flashes out like a cat's paw, nails raking across his chest, across the face of a grinning tattooed demon.

"Bitch!" He grabs her wrist, grip vice-tight, but not tight enough. She slips loose, too easily. Showing her teeth, she lashes out at his face.

He is fast, catches both hands and wrenches them behind her back. She is faint with desire, a wet flush of heat between her legs.

"Tighter," she whispers, grinding her hips against his muscular thigh.

His fingers dig into her flesh, forcing her arms up higher behind her back.

"More," she breathes, nearly begging.

"Are you crazy?" He frowns. "You want me to break your wrists?"

"You can't," she says, and before he knows what is happening, she is free again, slipping away to dig through a drawer in her vanity. When she turns back, she is holding a length of rope.

"Tie me up," she says.

His frown deepens, and she is afraid that she is losing him. She pulls him close and kisses him again, deliberate fingers teasing him back to full erection.

"Don't you want to fuck me?" This a throaty whisper punctuated by a flick of her tongue over the curve of his ear.

"Hell, yeah." His voice is thick with lust, his dark eyes mean and hungry.

She holds the rope out to him. Breathing like a bull about to charge, he takes it in one hand, gripping her upper arm with the other. He turns her away from him and begins winding the rope around her wrists.

"Tight," she says between clenched teeth.

His fingers are clumsy with the knots. She slips loose as if shrugging off a too-big jacket.

"Come on!" she says. There is an edge of desperation in her voice. "Do it tighter."

He tries again, but she can tell his patience is rapidly eroding. Frustration like broken glass in her throat as she finds the rope slipping off like water, even though she was willing to hold on, to pretend.

He is angry now. He throws the rope away.

"Fuck this," he spits. "I don't have time for this bullshit."

"Please." She is begging now, hating herself for it but begging anyway. "Please. I need it."

He shakes his head.

"You need help," he says, grabbing his rumpled T-shirt and

buttoning his jeans. "How can you want to be tied up when so many women are abused for real? It's crazy."

"What does that have to do with anything?" She knows she has already lost, but she's angry now. Angry at him for making her feel like some kind of pervert. "I like to be tied up because it makes me feel good. It's that simple. How can it be wrong to make somebody feel good?" She steps closer, giving it one last shot. Still naked, she pitches her voice low and seductive. "We're both consenting adults. How can it be wrong if we both want it?"

"You want it, not me." He turns away. "I'm outta here."

She wraps her kimono around her body and rushes after him.

"Wait, please . . ."

But he is gone, down the long dim corridor, and she is yelling after him, cursing, and then fighting tears as she leans her forehead against the wall.

"Your clock is fast," a voice says and Persephone turns, startled to see a man leaning against the wall beside her. He is not handsome, strange green eyes amplified by clunky glasses and a body too thin beneath unfashionable clothes. She can see a long, shiny scar inside his left wrist, a suicide ghost peeking out from the cuff of his ugly jacket. He holds what appears to be an artist's portfolio.

"What?" She frowns and looks away from him, wondering how much of the scene he witnessed, feeling the thin heat of shame crawling under her skin.

"Your clock, in the show. It says three minutes, but it was really only two minutes and forty-one seconds." He smiles, and she creases her brows, annoyed.

"Yeah, well, I can hold my breath for much longer than that," she says. "It's just that these days, three minutes is a long time for the marks to sit there waiting. I want to make it long enough for them to think it's dangerous, but not long enough for them to get bored. What's it to you, anyway?"

He shrugs. She notices that his eyes are not just green, as they seemed at first glance, but actually a strange kaleidoscopic cluster of emerald and pale gray. Fascinating, but she looks away, still shrouded in her own frustration and shame.

"My name is Kevin," he says shyly, looking down and away. "I really enjoyed your act, and I wanted to show you some of my work."

He starts unzipping the portfolio when one of her security guys shows up.

"What the fuck?" The muscle takes Kevin's elbow. "I thought I told you to get lost, pal."

Persephone isn't sure how to feel about this, but hey, it's just as well since he's probably some kind of weirdo stalker. Then the unzipped portfolio spills photos out onto the ground between them, and everything changes.

Each photo shows a naked woman bound. But more than bound, they are works of art, sculptures in the medium of glossy red rope and tender flesh. The designs and patterns formed by the complex knotwork flows over their skins like the symmetrical characters of some exotic forgotten language. She kneels down and touches the image of a particularly intricate design, heart gunning in her chest and between her legs. Although she doesn't know what she was expecting, she is disappointed when her fingertips find only the flat, slick texture of a photograph.

"Leave him," she tells the guard.

The guard's eyes ask her if she's sure, but she dismisses him with a quick nod of her head. When they are alone, Kevin kneels down beside her and starts gathering up the photos.

"Did you do this?" She licks her lips.

He nods.

"The knots, I mean . . ."

He nods again. His quick green eyes have not missed her reaction, but he seems nervous, blushing.

"Can you . . .?"

He reaches out and takes her hand, running his thumb over the ligature marks across her wrist and looking into her eyes.

"Is there somewhere we can go?" he asks.

Her apartment is small but meticulously neat, generic, like a hotel room. Posters for her act are the only personal touch.

He has a tightly woven lidded basket, like the sort a charmed snake might rise out of. When he sets it down on her bed and lifts the lid, she sees that it is full of rope. Not the cheap cotton clothesline that she keeps hidden in a drawer beside her bed, but an amazingly rich, reddish purple cord like something an eighteenth-century madam might use to tie back her velvet curtains. She plunges her fingers into the neat coils, their texture fine as satin, as the tender skin inside her mouth.

"Undress," he tells her.

She obeys, stripping down in seconds and standing naked and trembling as he lifts the rope from the basket, seeming to test its weight in his hand and draw strength from its heft. She is amazed to see that it is all one length.

His shyness seems to have evaporated as he assesses her body with a speculative eye. She can see the possible knots mating and combining in his head. Long minutes pass, and she grows restless, impatient, until finally he pulls her to him and begins to weave a complex web across her torso. She loses herself in the beauty of the design, hypnotized by his nimble fingers.

The rope caresses her, squeezing her breasts and her waist and tormenting her swollen clit with a single fat knot that grinds against her with the slightest movement. He wraps a tight cinch around her elbows, pulling them together behind her back until they touch and she gasps, shamelessly working her hips against the rope. Her wrists are last, tighter than ever, and as he steps away from her, there is a moment of explosive joy, a moment where she strains and struggles and cannot get free. But it is a fleeting moment, as her rubber joints twist and shift beneath her skin, and she can feel it slipping away as she pulls, pulls, pulls and then the ropes around her wrists fall away and a thick spike of disappointment slams through her as tears fill her eyes, the beautiful design gone to useless slack around her. She wants to scream, to smash everything. She wants to tear into her own flesh and rip out her flexible, treacherous bones. But then something happens, something that makes her scalp crawl and her eyes go wide.

The rope is moving, flexing and tensing, gliding over her with amazing speed, faster than his fingers, wrapping her up like a constrictor's prey. The knots twist and reform into exquisite designs and haunting symmetry like the blueprints for some profane cathedral. Tighter, too. Tighter than ever, and she is breathless, burning. The final knot winds itself, macramé perfection against her pounding heart, and she is caught again. There are scant inches for struggle, but as she strains and pulls and thrashes, the rope moves with her, seeming to anticipate every escape, only to wind her tighter. For the first time, after a lifetime of escape, she is really, truly caught, and it feels so good, safe somehow, like a lover's arms. Her heart and her pussy and her soul open wide as the most exquisite surrender washes over her, washing her clean like the tears that he kisses from her cheeks. She is in love. She is his.

Later, she is sleeping beside him, and although his arm is going numb beneath her, he doesn't want to move. Like when a beautiful and arrogant cat curls up in your lap, he is afraid to disturb her for fear that she will go away and never return. He still can't believe that she is here at all, his beautiful golden goddess, the woman whose insatiable hunger for restraint had drawn him to her like a plant growing toward the sun. She was everything he ever wanted, as if his own missing half had sprung fully formed, Venus-like, from the chaos of his darkest fantasies. After a lifetime of women who laughed at him, horrified women who called him a freak and a monster, here was Persephone, now and forever. She is curled against him, satiated and smelling of sweat and sex and honey, and he knows that all the years of deprivation and shame really have been worth it. When he'd been spent but still inside her and tasting her tears on his lips, she had told him that she loved him. Now, looking into her sleeping face, he is finally able to answer.

"I love you, too, Persephone," he tells her, the words sounding so small and awkward, barely audible in the hot space between them.

"Again," she says, eyes too bright, breathless.

Kevin looks down at the basket, frowning. He sets it aside. They have been together for three months, and her desperate need for the rope's embrace has increased exponentially until she is not satisfied with less than seven or eight times a day. Her hunger is a black hole, desire that is never satiated. Of all the women he has been with, all the women that he has tied, she is the only one who can never get enough. At first, it was perfect, true love. But now, it is as if she doesn't even see him. She only sees the knots.

"Do we have to?" He reaches out as if to take her into his arms, and she steps back, wary. "Please. I just want to hold you for a while."

"After, okay?" She is acting like a junkie, desperate. It makes him feel invisible, and he is overwhelmed with a desire to hit her, to keep on hitting her until she really sees him. He still loves her so much, and the love feels like its own kind of crushing bondage.

"Persephone," he says. "I can't do this anymore."

Her head swivels sharply.

"What?"

He looks away, pain and resignation in the corners of his mouth.

"Look, you don't love me." His voice is soft and hopeless. "You never did. You love the rope."

There is a moment of anger flashing hot and fierce across her features, then it submerges and she slides her arms around him, all cooing and seductive lies.

"That's not true, baby," she whispers. "You know how much I love you."

She guides him to the bed, takes him down. He knows that she is lying, but her touch, her mouth feels so good, and he lets himself pretend, knowing inside that it really is over.

After, she slips out of his embrace. Moving cat-burglar silent, she pulls on her clothes and takes the basket. He lies in the bed with his back to her, eyes wide and glinting with angry tears. He does not stop her.

In her dim dressing room, she strips naked and opens the basket. The rope is coiled inside like a sleeping cobra, but when she lifts it out, it lies inert in her hands, lifeless. She winds it around her wrists, but it is as limp as the bunched-up cotton clothesline in her vanity drawer.

"Come on," she whispers through clenched teeth, frustration a nest of angry hornets in her belly. "Come on, come on, come on."

Nothing. Just a length of fancy satin rope. She flings it away, furious. So it only works with him. No problem. He's probably still sleeping. She could sneak back in and be there to lovey-dovey him into making it work for her.

"It's dead."

She turns and sees Kevin poking the rope with the toe of his boot.

"Dead?" Fear ignites in her throat. "It can't be . . ."

"Oh, don't worry, baby." His voice is cruel, caustic. He pulls out a stubby little pocket knife and thumbs it open. "There's plenty more where that came from."

He plunges the knife into the inside of his scarred wrist.

"Jesus, Kevin!"

She rushes to him, filled with a sudden terrible fear that he will die bleeding on her carpet and the rope's secret will die with him. But it is not blood that oozes from the quivering slit in his flesh. It is something more solid, stealthy, glistening like a newborn snake. A wet length of the gore-red rope struggles free from the wound, fat as a vital artery and pulsing and Persephone backs away, nausea churning in her belly. Its blind head elongates like an earthworm, straining toward her, and she screams, clawing through her vanity drawer until her shaking fingers close over the cold grip of her .38.

"Keep it away from me," she says, drawing a bead first on the languidly flexing rope, then up to Kevin's forehead. The idea that she allowed one of those things to touch her skin, to wind down between the lips of her pussy, sickens her and brings a cold crawling sweat to the back of her neck. But her fear is underscored by the stealthy flush of desire, her body's memory of that inescapable embrace.

"Come on, baby," Kevin says, his too-green eyes narrow and hot with anger. "What's wrong? I thought you loved this."

The ropelike creature finally wriggles free, plopping with a dull smack onto the floor between them and humping, sidewinder-swift, toward her feet. With a shriek of disgust, she fires at it, cutting it smartly in half. The halves flop noiselessly around, thick sluggish blood splattering the carpet.

Kevin takes another step and she stumbles backward against her vanity.

"Stay the fuck away from me," she hisses. "Freak!"

The anger in his eyes flares into bright, killing hatred, and when he takes that last step, she shoots him, again, and then three times.

He crumples and she instantly regrets her actions, rushing to take him in her arms. It is not love that wrenches high wailing sobs from her twisting belly, but the realization that she has killed the golden goose, that she will never feel that ultimate surrender again.

When a hundred slick ropy tentacles boil up from the bullet holes and seize her, she is almost grateful. As they wind around her throat, crushing her esophagus and cutting off her air, she fights against them, twisting. She cannot break loose. Every time she moves, they move with her, the complex constrictor embrace shifting and tightening, and she begins to gray out, world going red and muddy around the edges. In her mind, she sees a clock ticking relentlessly into the red, red like the pulsing spots that obscure her vision, red like they are, those horrible wormy things that cinch tighter, tighter around her, and she wonders how long it's been. Has it been three minutes? Longer? Is she dying? She imagines a vast, dark, blank-faced audience waiting in excruciating expectation while the clock inches closer and closer to the oversized, cartoony skull that marks the number three. Black starts to swallow the pulsing red and she feels sure that it is really over, when the coils around her begin to slacken, subtly at first, then relaxing exponentially around her. One by one they begin to fall away like the chains in her act, and she tries to hold on, teeth digging into the raw flesh inside her mouth and realization filling her like the blood rushing back into her numb extremities. Her vision returns in slow, gauzy stages and she becomes aware of her cheek pressed against the cold floor, inches from her dead lover's face. The fleshy ropes that still connect them like a dozen corrupt umbilici are slowly liquefying around her. She clutches frantically at them, trying to wrap them back around her wrists, but her desperate fingers punch through their slick, disintegrating skins. She was willing to hold on, to pretend, but in the end she has escaped again, just like always.

Where No One Ever Dies Good

Stephen Gresham

I'm sitting at the Seaside Bar in Placencia, Belize, and I'm drinking cold Belikins with my friend, Sammy, and I'm telling him about it.

Here is what I tell him.

That the Morpho River jungle tour lifted me out of myself. Nothing like I expected: a sweet ending. Lives can have sweet endings. I've learned that, and I pass it along to Sammy, and he belches, nods and smiles a half-goofy, half-serious smile. If Sammy hadn't been ill—some bad conch ceviche, we think—he could have gone with me. Gone to Eden. But at least he can hear what happened.

The Morpho River dumps its primitive muddiness into the Caribbean where Morpho River Village clings to a shifting shoreline in the Toledo district of southern Belize. The setting got its hooks into me right away. They say a trip isn't worth taking if it doesn't generate some fear, if it doesn't seduce with all the inscrutable possibilities of a new experience. Amen to that.

I had tour mates: a young, nondescript couple from Fresno.

I think the guy was maybe an accountant, maybe a lawyer—he looked soft and pale and timid—and his wife was mousy and not pretty or sexy, and she doused herself with bug spray. DEET, she called it. But they had a super little kid. Ten or so. Smart. Small. Pale. Just all kid. Even had freckles, big ears and a gap between his front teeth. I liked him instantly. Don't remember his name. Then there was this older couple—birdwatchers, festooned with heavy binoculars, cameras and well-thumbed avian guidebooks. Both had magnificent mops of white hair, and when they moved they reminded me of large, white, wading birds.

And then there was Rosario.

My God, what a feast for the eyes. That's what I say to Sammy, and he smiles lazily and licks his top lip and pants kind of like a dog you're about to reach down and pet. Sammy presses for me to describe Rosario, so that's what I do. She had a dark complexion, like maybe she was Latina, and brown hair with auburn dancing through it, and creamy milk chocolate skin and pouty naturally red lips, and a body that switched on all my switches. Sweet endings. Around her, I experienced the ardent bewilderment of my senses. But what I really noticed was this: in her red bikini top she had tucked a white, lacy handkerchief between generous breasts (it nested there in the cleavage), and over her heart was a tattoo of a black scorpion, stinger-tailed, packed with poison and viciously clawed. I knew it had to be an optical illusion, but I swear to God that whenever I stared at that scorpion it seemed to move.

Silvio, our tour leader, a taut-bodied, handsome Garifuna with suspicious eyes and an encyclopedic knowledge of the Morpho River jungle, perched like a giant hood ornament at the prow of our long, covered outboard, while his muscular not-so-handsome brother, Manuel, beefy and stoic, steered and never once changed his expression. He never even sweated, a remarkable feat given that it was around ninety with suffocating humidity.

Those of us on tour sat on hard side benches and tried to listen to Silvio's nonstop account of creatures in and around the water: "See, dare . . . snowy egret. Blue heron. Kingfisher. Over dare, see mon, turtle sunnin' hisself, and dare, see, do you see? Morelet's crocodile, jus' a baby. He get bigger—six, eight feet. Bwa-a-h!" About the time my eyes would adjust, another of Silvio's calls would ring out: "Up dare, see mon, iguana. Dey good eatin'. Suc-cu-lent!" A big smile oozed across Silvio's face.

But I did not have the right eyes for the jungle. Not like before.

I never saw the insect bats or half the turtles and mud-gray crocs. I did, however, see the fountains of blue morpho butterflies taking flight as if mechanically staged at Disney World, and I did see plenty of Rosario, an erotic, natural wonder. I was staring at her (and she was pretending that she didn't know I was doing so) when the kid I liked raised his head from some book on the flora and fauna of Belize and said, "Were you in Vietnam?"

I guess he figured since there was this older guy with a camouflage shirt and hat and khaki pants that I had been in that awful conflict, but I shook my head. "No. How 'bout you?"

He grinned and his tongue lolled over his bottom lip—and that's when I started to remember the days I had tried so long to forget. I glanced out at the river because the kid suddenly looked so familiar, so like all I wanted to escape. I could hear Silvio saying something about jaguar tracks on the muddy bank; Rosario asked him a question that I couldn't hear over the chug-chug of the outboard. Words began to do funny things in my head. I looked in the other direction, and the old bird-watcher guy was chuckling as he met my eyes. It was a creepy chuckle.

Sammy interrupts me to ask why it was creepy.

I'll tell you, I say. But I'm not sure I even knew. You see, the old guy was speaking nonsense words for a second or two, and then I heard a few words distinctly: "The dead don't think about us. But we're always thinking about them."

Jesus Christ, maybe I misheard him. That's what I tell Sammy. He nods.

I swung around and stared into the jungle. Somewhere, in another lifetime, a darker one, I once read that the jungle either accepts you or rejects you. And I thought, *I'm too old to be scared.* But not too old to lust after Rosario. Unnerved by how I translated the bird-watcher's words, I slipped into an odd review of myself: late 50s, retired, itching to travel, maybe start up a new career as a travel writer. What did I want? This: to find what had been missing. To recognize the scintilla, the spark that gives life to everything. To be a new me. To draw a new circle—isn't that what Emerson recommended?

Foolish?

When I turned back from the lush, green oblivion of the jungle as it leaned close to the hip of the river like a fat and drunken friend, Rosario was smiling at me. I tried to smile like I was thirty years younger. My smile became a mask, and Rosario's smile flickered mischievously—like she knew things about me she couldn't know—and my eyes couldn't resist drifting down over her body. Seeing her, so desirable, made me think of how women's bodies over the years had become like sandbags, forming a protective barrier between myself and the rising, threatening flood of the past. And yet women like Rosario are different.

Sammy understands, or pretends that he does.

I change the subject. I tell him that on the way to the Morpho River Village we had taken a nerve-shattering boat ride through the narrow, labyrinthian passages of a mangrove swamp—like passing through a portal into another dimension—the mangrove roots all knees and elbows, and that at the village we ate a marvelous lunch of snook balls, beans and rice at Angel's Restaurant. The eponymous Angel, mother of Silvio and Manuel, lived up to her name—a sweetly heavyset maternal goddess of the village, a guardian force that bathed one in protective bliss. On one wall of the restaurant was a display of the beautiful blue morpho butterfly in its various stages of development. I gave it a long look. Metamorphosis became the good word for the day.

Sammy listens, but is impatient to learn more details of the actual tour.

Silvio and Manuel pushed the boat onto a spit, and while Manuel stayed behind, Silvio, wielding not one but two machetes, struck off into the jungle, magically disappearing down the first of many paths that intrigued me. The rest of us scrambled out of the boat and caught up. It was the kind of tour in which you follow the leader meekly, like sheep, like lambs to slaughter, though, of course, that's just an expression.

The jungle closed its fist of heat and humidity around us.

In no time I could see sweat spreading across the backs of my tour mates' clothing like Rorschach inkblots. Not so with Rosario, except for a few beads above her lip and between her breasts. She dabbed at those beads with that white handkerchief, flourished it as if it were more than just an object. I was fascinated by her. I wanted her. We volleyed small talk. Nothing worth reporting.

But mostly everyone listened to Silvio, our beastmaster. He knew the jungle. Was intimate with it. He knew it precisely—the way most of us know important numbers in our lives: birthday, telephone number, social security number—and he flashed one of the machetes as he walked and talked, urging us to see this hot, dappled world of sunlight and shadows as living more livingly than anything else we had ever experienced. He wanted us to notice that the vegetation didn't merely grow there, it leaped, it pulsed, it was predatory, attacking air, water and earth.

"You got to know where to look, my friends," he said. "De jungle, hit know how to hide tings. Yes, mon. Bwa-a-h! The jungle, hit be watchin' you."

Silvio was priest in this realm, celebrating mass. I almost found myself wanting to confess. I needed to confess. Deep in the jungle, I realized it as Silvio's litany encompassed a variety of birds, fungus, termite nests, ants, vines, trees, tracks. At one point, a brief, hard shower slowed us (everyone snickered as if Silvio had deliberately surprised us with it) and the path muddied and felt primordial. I took off my shoes and began to feel different. I wanted to feel the squish of mud that had been there since the beginning of time. I wanted to feel it between my toes. I wanted to sweat furiously and let some new part of myself be in charge—some part of myself beyond death and deaf to eager whisperings generating images of things you cannot see and making you something the jungle would hunt down to claim as its own.

We walked on.

The unreality of the walking. The silence just beneath a scattering of birdcalls. But inside a growing cacophony. Weird music of the soul. Atonal. I looked down at my bare feet. I wondered what it would feel like to step upon a deadly snake.

And that's when I imagined that things passed beneath us. I wouldn't allow myself to glance at the jungle floor again.

Silvio hacked free a pale vine as big around as my arm. It dripped water, and he drank from it and invited each of us to drink from it, but then he cut another that closely resembled the other, and yet this one was filled with ants. Hundreds of them. Thousands, maybe. I was shaken. I would not have known the difference between those vines. I felt a rising panic. Little electrical shocks of panic.

At one point, Rosario slipped and lost her balance and reached out to catch herself. The thorn-covered, haul-back vine cut her, and I stood at her side and examined the blood spotting up in her palm, and I anticipated that she was going to lick herself seductively, but instead she wiped a smear of blood across the scorpion tattoo, and I blinked several times rapidly because the creature was momentarily animated. Her protector.

My God, I could feel myself changing, and more so than just the fact that I had an erection.

"Where are you from?" I asked Rosario.

She smirked. Eyes squinted as if she were looking through smoke. "Out of the everywhere."

She had me. Bitch.

"And so where are you headed from here?"

"Punta Gorda," she said.

"Me too."

"Are you married? Any kids?" she asked.

"Yes," I said. "Two kids. One grandchild."

My heart fluttered like a butterfly.

"You're a grandpa?"

"Yes."

"I've never had sex with a grandpa," she teased.

"Me neither," I said.

She laughed, and it was the most erotic laughter I could imagine.

But there's this: everything I said about being married, having a family, was a lie.

And earlier I had lied to the kid when I said I'd never been to Vietnam.

When Rosario bent down to observe a parade of leaf-cutter ants, I strode on ahead to put the lies behind me. I passed the others. The kid flashed me a survivor's smile. He knew me. I struggled on until I reached Silvio. I sensed that he was a spectacular young man. I imagined him as someone who could sleep beneath the floor of the jungle, his sole nourishment the blood of the earth. He turned as if he knew I was going to ask him something.

"Silvio," I said, fighting to contain my excitement, "how long would I make it out here on my own? I mean, if I got myself lost, how long would I last?"

I knew he wouldn't lie to me.

That smile of his: simple, playful, wise. Brutal. The bright white teeth. He paused dramatically for effect.

"Longer than you like, my friend. Bwa-a-h! Yes, mon. Longer than you like."

Now that's part of it. I think that's really part of it.

I tell Sammy it's what I needed to hear.

The truth was as easy to Silvio as breathing.

We all kept following; we were like beads on a string of silence. I began to notice that all the others seemed calm, but an indefinable fear out of the dim reaches of instinct was making me short of breath, as though my lungs had shrunk. I was feeling trapped. I was nearing a point of surrender.

But to what?

Things kept passing beneath us. Was I the only one who noticed?

Below us, a river of nowhere, never, not . . . something flowing, flowing, flowing . . . I was jetsam and flotsam. I began to connect with what daytime in the jungle meant. I understood that things had retreated, ghosts had been confounded, evil had been confined. That's the way it's supposed to work. The jungle: a world of appearances masking reality, diminishing many truths. The vines seemed snakes. And the snakes spoke to me of the jungle as a world of deceit, subterfuge, duplicity; everything in that green eternity is disguise, stratagem, artifice, metamorphosis.

I kept looking down at my hands as if I expected them to morph into claws.

The snakes grew quiet.

I was sloughing off the skin of my persona, molting—becoming what?

Was that the key?

The bird-watchers remained always the same. At one point, the woman recognized the call of the great tinamou, and then she and her husband argued gently over another call, this one belonging to a parrot of some kind. I heard it too, and it sounded so at home in the jungle. The eyes of the bird-watcher woman twinkled. Then she echoed the call, translating it as well: "Who cooked the food? Who cooked the food?" I think I laughed because she was, comically, right on the nose. But when her husband rendered his translation, my mood shifted. His words kaleidoscoped before I finally made out something: "Who took the blood? Who took the blood?" he cried out.

I shivered.

Again, I must have misheard him.

And that phrase—"Who took the blood?"—became an "ear worm," like an old lyric, endlessly repeating itself. As I walked along, it jangled maniacally in my thoughts: "Who took the blood? Who took the blood?" Tree frogs sang on cue. I suddenly felt paranoid, felt that the frogs knew something about me. My past. I was afraid someone might translate what they were saying.

For twenty yards or so, I pressed fingertips into my ears to keep from hearing.

The heat was a gasping, sucking, life-depleting parasite. Swarms of bugs formed fuzzy domes around our heads. The one above Rosario's head looked like an animated halo—it made her look holy. I sweated, and the sweat left slug trails down my back and across my ribs. I walked behind Rosario and tried to focus on her gorgeous ass.

But she moved in a place almost beyond desire. I followed. She was entirely there, living in the present, in the moment. Hers was a sexy saintliness without possession (except for her erotic armor). And something more. She turned once to smile encouragingly at me and that white handkerchief between her breasts captured my eye again. Was it some vestige of her soul? How did she get the way she was, without the chains of yesterday, without thinking of tomorrow? To me, she seemed amazing.

When I caught up with her, I asked her about the black scorpion tattoo.

"It guards my heart," she explained.

"I have a tattoo," I said, "but it's in a place where you can't see it."

She cocked an eyebrow saucily.

"I'll remember that."

I've never been good at lying.

But I think I would have been okay were it not for the path and the howlers—and that kid.

* * *

The mysterious witchery of the jungle held me spellbound.

So as not to lose my way, I concentrated on Silvio as he blazed a trail between walls of impenetrable vegetation. Magnificent trees—ceiba and strangler figs, quamwood, quanacaste and mahogany—loomed over us as if the jungle had posted sentinels. It seemed there was a creeping ferocity that could wipe out a trail or a path in one night.

I sweated deeper into the passing minutes. We drank bottled water, and Silvio urged us on until we reached what appeared to be a natural fork in the remnants of the main path, and there, erupting from the floor of the jungle, was an incredible stand of bamboo, individual plants nearly a foot in diameter and thirty feet or more in height. There was a quick sucking of the sun by all the nearby vegetation, leaving me to wonder whether one's brain could be sucked as readily.

The bamboo provided a photo op for my tour mates to pose with Silvio against the monstrous sprouting, but something else seized my attention: the other path. I threaded down it in my imagination; I wondered almost desperately where it led. It frightened me—and I don't know why. And I was reminded of an ageless question: Does the path you wish to follow have a heart?

We were in the bloodstream of the jungle. And that path was like an artery into the heart of the living dark, for the area that fascinated me did not let the sun penetrate it. When all the photos had been taken, Silvio noticed that I was staring at that alternative path. I saw a flicker of reaction in his eyes. I think it was fear, but not the same kind that I had experienced moments earlier.

I thought: *there's no place for a human being in a pathless world.*

Maybe it was a silly thought. Sammy doesn't think so.

Silvio left one of his machetes sunk deeply in a thick, bamboo shoot.

And we trudged on.

I lagged back and so did Rosario. God, she became more beautiful, more desirable with each step. Sweet endings. We talked as mud sucked at our feet. At one point in the conversation she said, "My family has lost track of where I am." And those two words, *lost track*, throbbed in my thoughts in a neon coalescence: they sounded sad. Tragic. Then she caught me staring at a small scar at one corner of her mouth.

"A car accident?" I ventured.

The faintest of nods in return.

"Isn't a woman allowed one flaw?" she added.

"But only one," I followed.

I wanted to tell her that I could make that scar disappear if I kissed her hard.

She reminded me of so many other gorgeous, erotic, untouchable women I had seen and known from a distance. There was no way to keep from wanting her. She knew it—it seemed her eyes were telling me to wait. Did she know that I wanted her in a way no one else possibly could have?

Odd sensation: her head dancing off to one side of her body.

I guess it was the heat.

Be patient, I told myself. Patience is everything.

But Rosario frightened me. The jungle frightened me. That's what I tell Sammy. He nods. Sammy understands.

Then I tell him what Silvio did—how Silvio nearly scared the shit out of me.

I wasn't ready for our beastmaster to call the howlers. Life has moments that beat with a sinister heart. The next thing I narrate to Sammy is one of them. It began when Silvio slowed, scanned the canopy, seemed satisfied by what he saw or sensed, and then gestured for us to gather in a clueless circle near him.

"I gwan ta call de howlers," he explained, pausing as always between sentences. Flicking his eyes at each of us. "De black howler monkeys. Dey be close, my friends. A troop of dem. Dis troop, hit gots a new male leader, yes. An' when de new male howler take over, he kill all de babies from de old male. Bloody. Bwa-a-h! Very, very bloody!"

I think we collectively squirmed.

The wife of the wussy guy asked some question. I didn't hear because I was drawn to the canopy. *Who took the blood*? sing-songed in my head. I couldn't see anything up there. I didn't know what I was looking for. But before I could brace myself, Silvio cupped one hand at the corner of his mouth and delivered an astonishingly deep-throated *whup-whup*, *wa-a-a-h*! Then several more. My tour mates and I laughed softly, nervously. We didn't know what was coming. Out of the corner of my eye I saw the kid. He was looking right through me. Grinning.

I had seen him before.

I wheeled away, and there was Rosario: sexy and earthy. She seemed to belong here.

Silvio banged on a tree with the other machete and *whupped* again.

And then we began to hear something approach high above us.

My God, it was like a rustle of wind, only it had more definite substance, force. A rushing, roaring, demonic insistence.

Like mystery on feet of thunder.

Whup-whup, wa-a-a-h!

The jungle was suddenly filled with long, raspy, vibrating exhalations. A crescendo building to a sustained roar. Rosario sought out my arms like in a scene from a hokey jungle movie. A Tarzan film, maybe. Layers of deeper sounds spread over falsetto trillings. I had never heard anything like it in my life.

No, that's not true.

But I momentarily deflected the memory because the troop of howlers—maybe seven or eight—with the big male leading the way, shook with black fury over our heads, perhaps ninety to a hundred feet. The big male was obviously very upset.

"Duck your heads!" Silvio exclaimed. "Don't be lookin' up, my friends!"

I did gaze upward, though soon enough I understood the grounds for the warning. Before we all got showered by monkey piss and shit, I saw something. I saw the black, violent smear of the big male. And then I concentrated, and I saw something more: a face more original than my own.

That's the only way I can say it. And I don't precisely know what I mean.

We dashed for cover. My tour mates and Silvio were whispering together or maybe the jungle was whispering through them. I edged closer, and it seemed to me that they were speaking in a foreign language—and the crazy thing was . . . I could understand them.

They were talking about the place where no one dies good.

Silvio broke apart from them and banged a tree and *whupped* some more.

All I could do was remember. I couldn't help it.

I cringed, steeled myself for gunfire.

I heard the young marines whooping and grunting and roaring at the enemy.

I was terrified, and so I did the only thing I could: I screamed "*Bao Chi! Bao Chi!*"

I left my body, rose up with the howlers, and if I could have I also would have rained down piss and shit. Up there in a pathless world, I found words I never thought to speak in a green introcosm I never thought I should revisit. I never wanted to.

Back in my body, I trembled.

The kid's father put a hand on my shoulder and pushed a puzzled expression into my face. "What did you mean? What do those words you called out mean? *Bao Chi*—what is that?"

I shook my head. "I don't know," I said. "Nothing. Just nonsense, you know."

But that was a lie, too.

At this point, nothing around me was real. My body was foreign to me. But I wasn't dreaming. Things emerged, blotches opaque and nebulous—stuff that lacked the shape of a dream. *I wasn't dreaming*. The world of the jungle had dizzy corners, gauzy dimensions. I breathed hard, breathed pure life from some place insubstantial. I was alive—oh, man, I was alive. And

I was inside the breath of the jungle. My blood streamed through me, sensuous and flood-tide strong. I slowed my breathing, willed it to slow, and then, as if by magic, I was no longer moving *through* the jungle.

I was moving perfectly in sync with it.

And I told no one about this metamorphosis.

I was edgy when a voice yanked me out of that changed world.

It was the old bird-watcher pointing at a blur of feathers. He repeated that line: "The dead don't think about us. But we're always thinking about them." His face swung gently toward me so that I could not avoid those words . . . and I thought of body bags . . . I remembered the smell. I recalled empty pairs of combat boots lined up on the baking tarmac of a landing strip.

God damn it, I wasn't going back there.

So I glared at the old fucker and I shouted, "Sometimes you have to wade far, far into dying just to be able to go on living."

No. I didn't shout those curious words. I didn't say anything. But I wanted to. The rise of inexplicable fear and memory spun the world around, and I just stood there and watched it and tried to stay at one with it. I watched and I waited for what wanted to come, and as I'm telling him about it, I ask Sammy: Isn't that what life is? You wait for what wants to come.

Sammy frowns. I see him swallow. He looks puzzled. He nods ever so slightly.

I remember that the freckle-faced kid was gazing at me—like maybe he felt sorry for me.

With stabbing suddenness, I was reminded of 'Nam.

What started to come was memory—no, more than memory. I couldn't meet the eyes of that kid. I turned and stumbled into a shaft of sunlight, and I was gone. Back to a green hell. That's what everybody called it. I know now that Hell is a Very Green Place. I've been there.

One of the denizens of that hell was a young marine everybody called "AE." He liked to polish the combat boots of the dead for final review, final rites. And he always used to say: "The dead don't think about us. But we're always thinking about them."

He was a super kid. That name, "AE," stuck like Velcro to him because of his remarkable resemblance to the iconic Alfred E (no period after the "E") Newman of *Mad* magazine. The kid was even fond of saying "Quote me on it" whenever he delivered some jungle-inspired battle wisdom. AE: he had wild talents; he lived a weird combination of fear and holiness. He could empty the war out of himself like water out of a pitcher. He could make the sky darken at noon. He taught me how to do it. One day at Khe Sanh I pulled it off. Like a fucking eclipse. AE taught me so much that I desperately hoped one day I would forget.

The first time I met him, he leaned in conspiratorially and said, "You got a shitty job, you know that?"

"How so?"

That Alfred E Newman grin, the tongue straying over his bottom lip. "Because you don't get to kill."

Took me years and years to see the wisdom in his words.

AE claimed that the jungle could haunt you. But whoever heard of a piece of dead, wild, wet ground haunting someone?

"See what it done to me?" he said. "Sucked the fun out. Sucked all the boy out. Like a big ole leech. That's what the jungle does—it ain't ole fuckin' Charlie doin' it. It's the jungle. Quote me on it."

Sometimes I slept in the same makeshift barracks with AE and other marines. He insisted on my being next to him. At night, he heard a terrible, insistent calling, and he taught me how to hear it, too . . . and, God damn it, he made me think I heard impossible things: rain talking to the night, roots and vines singing, insects breathing miles away, and the heartbeats of the enemy sneaking afoot where you couldn't possibly see them. He got me to thinking I had extrasensory capacity, that I could read the mind of the enemy. He claimed the jungle was in his genes. War in the jungle was stamped on every one of his cells. As a boy, he had hungered for the horror. Vietnam was every Christmas and birthday rolled into one.

One night I jogged awake, and in the dim light I could see that he was staring right at me. Jesus, it was spooky. It was as if his stare had somehow woken me. And he began to whisper: "You get out in the jungle where no one ever dies good and you develop a taste for it. You think that's crazy? No, man . . . it's way past crazy."

I shook my head. My brain was cobwebs. "I'm just a reporter," I said. "I don't have a right to call anyone crazy."

"Damn straight. 'Sides that, *you're* the only really crazy fucker here."

"Why you say that?"

"Because you don't have to be here."

He was right, of course.

Sammy and I order another Belikin.

My hands are shaking. That's what memory can do to you.

I remember seeing a young woman one day in Saigon who was so beautiful, had such an erotic aura about her, that I could barely look at her, and yet I could barely stop looking at her. Something unspeakably erotic about her. I remember thinking that maybe someone with that much eroticism about her should be destroyed. After seeing her, I stayed in my hotel the rest of the day. I wanted that woman. If I couldn't have her, I wanted to destroy her.

My eyes were always open in 'Nam simply because I hardly ever slept. You saw a lot of others whose eyes were also always open. Maybe we were seeing the same absurdist play far inside our heads. Or maybe we were talking to ourselves about what we were missing . . . or what we had always missed. Sometimes I got so far inside my head that I grew scared I wouldn't find my way out. I told AE about it, and he laughed and said, "Don't worry, man . . . I'll come get ya."

I got to thinking I would be captured, not by Charlie but by the howling demons in my subconscious. I would be captured and held there against my will and never be able to escape. Escape was everything. Bigger than survival. Do you understand?

Sammy nods that he does. He's a good friend.

I tell him that in 'Nam Conrad's Inscrutable Immutable was always out there. You fought to get through it, an existential wrestling match of take down and slam and pin. Going crazy was, every second, a possibility. Maybe a necessity.

I tell him the Morpho River jungle and that other jungle far, far away—they're both scary, unimaginably scary, scary beyond belief: kingdoms of ghosts. *Bwa-a-a.* I didn't realize I had so many memories of that other jungle.

Then they came flooding back. . . .

One day, four soldiers who looked like they'd been fed upon by vampires crept out of the jungle. Seeing them was a primitive kind of moment in which my fear took directions so wild that I had to stop and watch the many-angled whirl. The jungle was worse at night—a dark room full of deadly threats. Things waited for you there. You never knew what you might bump into. At times, you could feel your eyes go bigger than a full moon.

I learned this quickly in 'Nam: everyone of us from across the ocean was a trespasser. The great sin of the war or "police action" or whatever the fuck you want to call it was trespassing. *We didn't belong there.* The jungle passed a simple judgment upon you: *One day, sorry ass, you're going to die for what you have witnessed.* The jungle and all its denizens of mystery would make you pay.

Because you'd seen shit you weren't supposed to see. Ever.

In 'Nam, I tried to be a writer, but I was never more than a trespasser.

At Morpho River, I began to feel the same way: stranger in a strange land.

One dusk, I was out on patrol with AE and company; ghostly mists were steaming up from the valley floor, eating,

eating, eating light with a ravenous hunger. We got hit. Snap. Crackle. Pop. The jungle breathing fire from the mouth of a hidden dragon.

That day, I learned that at the farthest recess of fear your only possible response is laughter. But if you started laughing, you might just keep at it until you died, until all that's really you died. I could hear my laughter start down in my balls, and I would grit my teeth and not let it snake up to my mouth. And the fire returned. And the good kids around me (most of them) dodging death . . . and then came the hooting . . . *whup-whup, wa-a-a-a* . . . and roaring and black howler fury long before I even knew black howlers existed. The young men hooted, I think, because they had "claimed" the territory. They had defeated, momentarily, the dark powers of the jungle. Or they had kept themselves from laughing to death.

Sometimes the dark powers claimed them.

But I kept asking myself: what dark powers claim me?

I had a chance to get to know some of those young howlers. They were killers—killing obsessed them, absorbed them, lived under their skin and behind their eyes, made them strong in the same way that all predators are strong. They lived more livingly, like things in the jungle.

AE taught me that if you showed proper obeisance, if you were diligently reverent, the jungle would give back some of the boy it had siphoned out of you—"'Cause you got to understand that the jungle is just one big, fuckin' vampire. Quote me on that"—and would allow you to reconnect with your childlike awe. At first, I thought AE was full of shit, bugshit crazy, but he was right. In the jungle over there, I began to reconnect with stuff in my mind that everybody had told me not to touch—like sex and horror—and I made a point not to leave it alone. I shouted down the inner voices that had said *Don't you know better than to leave it alone?*

When I got back to the States, I began to realize all that I had missed.

For years and years, I felt empty: incomplete.

Sammy understands. You do, don't you, Sammy?

And I tell Sammy to indulge me because I have to ramble on some—I have to let memory take me where it must—and then I'll finish the story. Sammy: he's got a lot of patience.

I start to talk again and out of nowhere I choke up, tears threaten. Sammy, he reaches over and touches my shoulder. I'm embarrassed, and Sammy's embarrassed that I'm embarrassed and, oh, shit, this is difficult.

'Nam and AE and the jungle taught me to trust what was difficult.

So I continue.

I tell Sammy how much I hated and feared Saigon. Being in that city was like sitting with a cobra in your lap, like being trapped in a phone booth with hundreds of black scorpions. In that city, poisonous things I never understood were *too close*.

You were warned, especially those of us who were reporters, not to get *too close* to things: Don't get too close to plumes of napalm smoke because they'll burn out the membranes of your lungs. Don't get too close to the spirits of the jungle because they'll take things from you and never give them back. The jungle takes, takes, takes. You couldn't defeat it. The U.S. military tried.

You couldn't control the jungle. In 'Nam, I never felt that I could control anything around me, and I yearned to do so. Most of the time I just reacted, reacted in a way that made me admit to myself I really didn't know what I was doing. I was master of nothing.

Many of the soldiers were the same way, but, my God, in a perverse way I grew fond of them. Some were death-stalkers, some wound-worshipers. In their eyes, I saw a lot of wasted horror. The war claimed them. The enemy claimed them. But at times, simply the jungle claimed them. I remember how they sweated—how fear and the jungle made it so they couldn't stop spitting. The jungle made you think about the dead. So did empty boots. I still can't look at a pair of empty boots without thinking of the dead.

I learned the soldier's mantra and often repeated it to myself: "Just bring your ass out alive." They gave me stories, sure. Lots of them. They needed to give me stories. Made me their confessor. They handed me stories that still had fangs and poison in them. They told me how tired they were and how fucking scared. It was common knowledge that the only time you weren't scared was when you were too tired to be scared.

Exhaustion was a narcotic. You might even get hooked on it.

From the stacks of body bags, I heard the same whisper time and time again: "Hey, buddy, wanna trade places?" You can't imagine how dark your thoughts got. Because nothing made sense.

I never met a soldier for whom killing made sense except for one thing: Better to kill that bastard than for that bastard to kill you. For some, killing was as routine as tying the laces of your boots.

I never got used to spooky sounds. Like, for example, the kind of deep quiet that seized the moment before going out on patrol, quiet like I imagined would surround a firing squad. Spooky sounds in the jungle—one day I began to hear a voice calling my name. Like it was calling from the next room. I almost got seduced off the trail, off the path.

I always wondered what would happen if I got off the path.

How long would I last?

Longer than you like, my friend. . . .

AE kept me sane. It must be odd to hear me say that, but it's true. He was what they called a "charmed grunt." He was lucky. Other soldiers wanted to be around him, and yet he didn't really have friends. He was just too weird. Once I saw him bayonet a dead gook and then lick the blade clean. Like a little boy licking the remains of cake frosting from a mixing bowl.

AE and I talked a lot about the dead. "The only good corpse is the one you'll never have to see," he said. Maybe AE was more of a hunter than a soldier. He had that bitter survivor's smile. I guess that's where I got mine. AE infected me. Around him, I developed the kind of moral awe one might have for a Gandhi or a Mother Teresa. The arrow of his deadly, sacred vision of reality went right through me.

Then one day he said, "Hemingway,"—that was his nickname for me—"one of these days you're gonna explode. Can't you hear yourself tickin'? Tick . . . tick . . . tick. I hear you tickin'. Some day you'll fuckin' come out of that jungle in your head and you'll have claws."

My God, I hoped against hope he was wrong.

AE, that look of innocence destroyed, had transcended the war in an almost spiritual way. He knew I couldn't, and I think, finally, he hated me. I think he thought I was a monster or a freak. Sometimes when he'd see me, those clear blue eyes would take on the eerie gleam of pearls and his freckles would dance and those shell-shaped ears would twitch and he'd cluck his tongue: "Tick . . . tick . . . tick."

AE, like a lot of others, hoarded battle treasures—grisly keepsakes. He had a necklace made of Viet Cong fingers. I brought back pieces of myself stuffed inside my ragged, weary, broken soul. I survived the terrible beauty of firefights, but I did not survive the jungle, despite everything that AE taught me about it.

I thought that in time I would recover myself. Time was another of those obsessions. Every soldier asked the same question: "How much time you got?"

I never had an answer, and I came to fear something more complicated than death.

Not AE—he lost touch with fear. He said he would never go back to the States. He would stay and live in the jungle, because the jungle had made it impossible to return to civilization. I think he had become something leprous to himself . . . and yet he was, if anyone ever can be, at home with his madness.

I never saw him again after the war.

I don't know whether I was a very good reporter. Like most other reporters, I think I became addicted to the war. Don't ask me to explain that. I was an independent stringer, under my own orders. Still am. "You got balls," young marines would say to those of us who didn't have to be there, but they would usually add, "and you're deep-shit crazy." Reporters: yeah, there was drinking, drugs, rock music, an occasional woman, pointless press conferences with the brass, and lots of lies. Mostly there were stories. Nothing like sharing a good story.

The toughest time was May of '68 when the Viet Cong staged a bloody offensive against Saigon. I can't remember which it was, but in one week there were more Americans killed than in any other single week in the war. Some of them were reporters. Some of them I knew. Colleagues.

The first time I got shot at, I didn't even know what had occurred. Green, surrealistic noise. I wasn't even scared. In fact, I got angry before I got scared. Why? Because I couldn't fire back. There was killing, and I didn't get to kill. Funny how in those frustrating moments I thought a lot about women . . . about intensely erotic women. It wasn't merely sex I wanted, it was the admixture of the erotic and the horrific. *Who took the blood?*

I wanted something immense, gigantic, astounding—like some yearning character in a Chekhov tale.

Sammy has a question: he wants to know what "*Bao Chi*" means.

So I tell him. Here is what I tell him: those were Vietnamese words for "journalist." Those were the words written on my tag. But they didn't mean shit. I don't know that they ever saved anyone's life.

Sammy has another question: what happened to Rosario?

So I tell him. Sexy women, I say, I have to kill them because I can't collect them.

* * *

Sammy wants to hear more.

So I tell him.

I guess you could say the tour group lost track of us—Rosario and me. She took my hand just as I hoped she would, and we wandered back to the stand of bamboo and she said, "Won't you need the machete?"

I nodded.

We got off the main path.

"I want to see your tattoo," she said. She thought she was in control.

I nodded. We angled down the path I had noticed before. It was dark. I could have made it even darker. But I was afraid. It was so dark I needed for God to strike a match in the sky. I needed for God to stop me.

I hacked at the riot of vegetation.

"Where does this take us to?" said Rosario, smiling at the path that was no path.

Saliva was thick in the back of my mouth.

"To a place where no one ever dies good," I said.

It must have sounded like bullshit to her.

In Rosario, I recognized beauty and the erotic as easily as I recognized lightning. When she began to strip, it felt like the first time I'd ever been with a girl—so eagerly meaningful—but also like the first time I entered the jungle. In both cases I had to relearn how to breathe. In both cases I heard ticking.

Her breasts were indescribable.

"Isn't this what you've been wanting?" she said.

"All my life," I said. "You see, I've missed out on some things," I muttered through gluey saliva. "I had a shitty job." She looked puzzled. Then I said, "It's all about what you haven't experienced." Then I laughed, and maybe the laugh unsettled her. "No," I said, "it's about knowing how to keep things hidden. The jungle has taught me that."

She was intrigued. Maybe frightened, I don't know. Something she couldn't resist—no, not me. I touched her face. It was not as warm as I had expected. "Imagine," I said, "that your scar has disappeared. Imagine that you are perfect. You're Eve before the Fall."

She giggled. "You are very, very strange."

"Yes," I said. "Yes, I am."

And that's when we heard the singing.

We came upon an extraordinary sight; we were drawn there by a chorus of nasal humming. Rosario screamed, and I stared down at the path—at the thing in the path—and I grabbed Rosario's hand, and I felt the white, lacy handkerchief wadded up there, and I told her not to scream, though it wouldn't have mattered. No one could have heard her—no one human, that is.

The black howler's mouth moved as if in a lip sync. The song was not its own. The swarm of flies and ants and maggots had filled the creature; it was animated by them. Music wafted from it. It looked to be singing. There was no doubt that the nature surrounding us was implacable, terrible, in spite of its beauty. In spite of Rosario's beauty.

Then I think she went around the bend—the horrid sight of the dead, singing howler, and she, like Eve, needing to call upon her serpent. She wrenched the machete from my hand and beat upon the nearest tree. She laughed, a laughter on the edge of sanity, like a moth on the lip of a waterfall. Morpho butterflies falling, fluttering all around us, incongruously, like blue snow flurries in a steamy jungle.

The howlers came, roaring, then echoing Rosario's laughter. And then they began to speak—the big male. I understood his language. I knew what he was urging me to do. I couldn't stop myself.

I took Rosario sexually . . . and then I took her blood.

When I put the machete to her throat, she stuck out her tongue playfully. But not for long. As I took her blood and her hands relaxed, the white handkerchief yanked itself free like a magician's trick. It escaped her hand and fluttered off like a giant butterfly only to return, and I think her dead eyes glimpsed it. I was afraid she was going to scream again, and so I snared the handkerchief and stuffed it in her mouth. Maybe that handkerchief was her soul.

And then I took more blood.

The darkness I generated trembled with fears and slithers, but the only sound worth hearing was the drumming of my heart and my raspy, satisfied . . . very satisfied breathing.

AE had taught me how to use a machete to acquire trophies.

But suddenly I wanted more.

I stared down at Rosario. Being dead, could she tell me things the living have no speech for? I tried to converse with her. But I didn't know whether to talk to her once-sexy body or to her head, no longer attached.

"So beautiful," I whispered.

Then movement. The black scorpion tattoo came alive, stinger and claws aimed at me in evident revenge. I wasn't fazed. I was taking part in so much that I had missed. I crushed the scorpion.

And then I ate it.

Rain began to fall.

Afterward, everything smelled of water, everything had the sound of water, the hand encountered water everywhere.

I buried her head in a special place.

Then I had to rejoin my tour group. Had to tell them the bad news—how I got separated from Rosario—not exactly a lie. They'll never find her.

AE showed me how to hide a body in the jungle.

It began to rain harder. The howlers disappeared. The jungle grew consummately silent.

What else? asks Sammy. He seems very interested. He knows me. He's not shocked. Not really. Not surprised.

Fortunately.

That's it, I say.

* * *

But Sammy presses for more. You know Sammy, he's that way.

So I tell him more. How upset everyone was. The search party. All the stuff you would expect. But I also tell him how I made that machete sing. Jungle song. How I took the blood and talked to the dead. How the howlers knew and the birds knew, and how things slithered. How insects started in on her body even before I could bury it. How, for a short while, she was mine in the way no beautiful woman had ever been. Every sexually desirable inch of her was mine.

How I was tender as well as terrible.

I tell Sammy that the philosopher Bertrand Russell once wrote that he wanted to stand at the rim of the world and peer into the darkness beyond and see the strange shapes of mystery that inhabit the unknown night. That's not good enough for me, I say.

I wanna do more than watch.

But here's the thing: Sammy stops listening.

Of course, no one in his right mind could keep listening.

They say the best kind of story is a story of escape. But in my story, the protagonist does not escape. Neither does his prey. Truth is, in my story the protagonist does not *want* to escape. I like it here, deep in my genesial darkness.

I order another Belikin and stare out at the Caribbean. Nearby, a man and a woman are playing Ring Ting, delicately shoving that ring in a gentle arc so that it will successfully settle onto the nail. The woman stirs me. Breasts about to spill out of an ineffectual tank top. I wonder if they'll be going on an adventure tour tomorrow. But then I remind myself that I shouldn't stay. I look out at the sea. It's incredible what storms through a man's mind when he's just sitting, gazing out at that hard, perfect line of the horizon. Perfect.

Oh, the things you imagine yourself doing.

I return to my conversation with Sammy. He looks worried. So I decide to tell him the truth. Here is what I tell him: that I lied about having sex with Rosario and about killing her. I laugh. But Sammy doesn't.

Then it happens: Sammy disappears like jungle mist at midday. Because, you see, there is no Sammy. I made him up.

But now I'm ready. Tick . . . tick . . . tick. I can do it. I can pull it off.

I'm thinking about taking another trip. Seeing another jungle. And another beautiful, erotic woman. I might even get good at this. *Bwa-a-h*!

Getting off on a different path. Should have done this long ago.

Where should I go? Maybe the Tuichi River in Bolivia or Angel Falls in Venezuela or, of course, the Amazon—*adentro*, the land within, hidden and dangerous. Maybe Africa will call. A place like the Congo or Gabon.

I'll go where no one ever dies good.

I'll get on the Internet and search for a dark place. A place that's primitive, terrible, horrible, spooky, a place so potentially dangerous that it's a living nightmare.

Like me.

Desire

J. F. Gonzalez

I recently had sex with Gloria, my wife of forty years. I never thought we'd have a physical relationship ever again.

After all, she's been dead for five years.

This seems like an unlikely method of writing down the events that have recently taken place in my life, but I want whoever reads this—homicide detectives and the forensic guys—to understand what has happened.

I want it made known that I loved my family. I loved my wife, Gloria. I desired her above all other women; I never once cheated on her, never once had amorous thoughts toward another woman throughout our marriage. I loved the two wonderful children we produced and raised together. I loved my grandchildren. Just know this, okay?

Know one other thing, too. If you do read this document, go into my office and find a file in the right-hand drawer of my desk with the label "Haynes Vs. State of California, 1998" on it. Read the material in that file and the one after that, which is labeled "Related Cases."

Don't even bother trying to find the black box. You won't find it. As I write this, I can see it now on the living room floor, but I'll be willing to bet it will be gone when you read this. You won't find it in the trash, either. It'll simply be gone. I've gone ahead and shot a photo of it on the digital camera (which I'll leave on the table), but I'm willing to bet it won't show up in the photos. Likewise, I'm willing to bet the clerk at Bill's Video and Books on Harbor Boulevard in Santa Ana will have no knowledge of ever selling me a sex doll called "Dream Girl."

Nor will you find any other adult video and book merchant in the country who will claim to stock it.

And if you probe further like I did, you might hear the stories, which might tempt you into exploring even further.

You probably won't get anywhere.

Then again, you might come across it somewhere.

That might validate what I'm about to write here.

However, if you do find the doll and are tempted to purchase it, this might lead you to where I'm at now.

Contemplating.

God, what did I get into?

Already the smell is starting to get to me. If I'm found like this, dead by my own hand, with Gloria here . . . well, they'll think I've been sleeping with the dead, and I want to confess right here and now that is *not* the case. I'm not a necrophile. You'll find that hard to believe if I win this battle, but at least my children and grandchildren will be safe, even if they have to live with knowing that the physical evidence points to that perversity, as well as my implied madness.

But I'm getting ahead of myself. Let me start at the beginning. First, I'm going to get the bottle of Jack Daniel's I have at the bar and I'm going to get the .45-caliber Colt. I'll need both of them.

If I win, I'll save the Colt for the end.

I retired from the Pasadena Police Department in August 1998 with a full pension and a nice 401k plan. I had joined the LAPD in October 1959 and saw a lot during my service. Gloria and I had only been married for two years and had a one-year-old son when the Watts riots broke out. I was on duty when that happened, and Gloria had been frantic throughout that troubling week of unrest. I don't know how I made it through myself, but somehow I did. I quickly rose up the ranks from beat cop to homicide detective in 1969. I was made chief of homicide in 1975, and in 1982 I took a job with the Pasadena Police Department as a homicide detective. I took the job because I wanted to be back in the field again. Being chief of homicide was nice, but it meant staying behind a desk most of the time. I enjoyed the hunt too much.

One of my last cases seemed pretty open-and-shut at first glance. You may remember it: in April 1998, a middle-aged man named Martin Haynes gunned down his wife in the bedroom of their sprawling ranch house in Pasadena with a .22-caliber pistol he had bought fifteen years before. He had lain in wait for her on a Sunday afternoon and picked her off when she entered their bedroom. He shot her five times, killing her instantly. Then he waited for the police to show up.

I was the lead detective on the case and questioned him later at the station. He claimed that he never sat down to wait for the police, which is what it appeared when the first officers arrived. He had been waiting for his girlfriend—some woman named Brandy—to show up. He claimed that he had met this woman two nights before, and that she had promised him that they could go away together . . . only he had to kill his wife and children first.

Here's what eventually got him sent to the Atascadero State Hospital rather than being put on trial for first-degree murder: When he was asked where he met this woman Brandy, he said she had come out of the black box that was in his bedroom. He had bought her at an establishment called Le Sexx Shoppe in Old Town Pasadena.

The funny thing was that we found no black box in his bedroom or anywhere on the property.

Mr. Haynes insisted on this story, though, and he didn't deviate from it under intense questioning. In fact, the psychiatrists we brought in to question him and determine whether he was really delusional or merely faking it reported unanimously that Martin Haynes bore all the signs and symptoms of schizophrenia and paranoid delusions. A conviction would be impossible.

That's where we were by the time my retirement rolled around. In a way, I was glad to be rid of the case.

Of course, we checked Martin Haynes's story completely, or at least the part of it that was rooted in reality. He had checked into a hotel on Foothill Boulevard in La Crescenta on a Friday evening in April. He was very much into sex dolls—you know, the blowup dolls that are sold in porno shops and in the backs of magazines like *Hustler* and *Swank*. Martin had bought a new doll prior to showing up at the hotel, which he claimed was called "Dream Girl," and according to him it was the most realistic sex doll he had ever had. He claimed he inflated the doll and fucked it or whatever the hell else guys like him do to sex dolls. The way Martin talked about that in his interrogations with the psychiatrists and I, you would think he was talking about having sex with a real woman, because that's what it had been like with him. Only after he fucked this doll, he claimed, she became a real woman—a real flesh and blood woman—and that he and this woman had screwed like bunnies all weekend.

So of course I think the guy is making this up to cop an insanity plea. That's the direction our questioning began to go toward: trying to get the subject to contradict himself or trip up. Nothing worked. Martin Haynes stuck with this story and didn't deviate from it at all. It was creepy listening to him. The guy actually believed a blowup doll had become a real-life human being, that it had become a woman with long black hair, dark eyes, a perfect body and beautiful full breasts, and that she was willing to do anything sexually with him. Well, no wonder he called the doll a Dream Girl, right? The physical description of the woman was one of the first things we tried to go on as a way to dismantle his defense, but that didn't work. We had a sketch artist do a composite of her and put that over the wire. We never did locate her.

Once the psychiatrists began questioning him, they agreed he wasn't just making the stuff up. He really believed what he told us, and it was their professional opinion that he was suffering from various delusions.

Much of the evidence supported this fact. The clerk at the adult video store didn't remember Martin, but the store's security video camera showed Martin making a purchase. In the video, Martin was seen purchasing something in a large black box. A search through the store's records showed that the store had received a novelty called "Dream Girl" from a company called Eros, Ltd., based in a small town in Massachusetts. Inquiries to the company were in vain; the firm had dissolved shortly after they shipped the doll to Le Sexx Shoppe. I was still trying to trace their shareholders and owners when my retirement came up.

Other aspects of the investigation went nowhere. I spoke to the desk clerk at the motel Martin had checked into, and several guests who'd stayed on the premises that weekend, as well as a waitress who served Martin and several patrons of the coffee shop where Martin claimed he had breakfasted one morning with Brandy. The witnesses unanimously agreed that Martin had been alone at the restaurant. In fact, the waitress related that Martin had been carrying on a conversation with himself and acted like he was actually talking to somebody across the table from him.

So that's where we were when my retirement came up. Open-and-shut, right? My superiors seemed to think so, as well as the DA. Martin Haynes was whisked quietly away to the Atascadero State Hospital.

But for some reason this case nagged at me.

It shouldn't have. Martin's kids related that their father was not a violent man, that he never would have done something like this. Likewise, his colleagues at the HMO he worked at all had high praise for him and were shocked by the allegations. Everybody we talked to—family, friends, neighbors—unanimously agreed that, even though some of them were aware of strain in the marriage, Martin was not a violent person and never would have harmed his wife. His children were shocked to learn from Martin's confession that he had planned to kill them that afternoon after killing his wife.

On the week before I officially retired, I tapped into the VICAP network and submitted a query to find out if anything similar to the Martin case had happened elsewhere. The data I included in my query was too broad for the system, and so I got thousands of results. I asked an analyst at the office to comb through the spreadsheet containing the information that I sent to him. "Humor me," I said. "In your spare time, see if you can find a pattern in these cases." I gave him some rather general outlines of what I was looking for, gave him my home number, and then tried to forget about the case as I embarked on my retirement.

Howard called me at home five days later with the news that a man in Nebraska named Warren Douglas had killed his wife about two weeks after Martin Haynes killed his wife, Vicky.

He, too, claimed to have been ordered to kill his wife by his lover, a ravishing blond woman he had met that weekend.

A woman he claimed had transformed from a sex doll into a real-life woman.

That's what grabbed my attention. That's what started the obsession.

I contacted the Grand Island police. The case was eerily similar. The perpetrator was a middle manager at a textile firm and had been having marital problems. He claimed his wife no longer wanted to have sex with him, so he had developed a fetish with sex dolls because he was afraid of the consequences that might befall him if he sought pleasure with prostitutes. He claimed that Cheryl (the blond woman) had come out of the Dream Girl box he had bought at a Grand Island adult novelty shop, that he had had the best sex with her he ever had, and that Cheryl told him she loved him, that she wanted to be with him forever, and that all he had to do for them to be together was for him to kill his wife.

The police in Grand Island had made the same inquiries we had and gotten about as far. The establishment that sold Warren Douglas the box had no record of the transaction, and when I questioned them a few weeks later they claimed they had never heard of an outfit called Eros, Ltd. The perpetrator in this case was also judged a paranoid schizophrenic by the psychiatrists who examined and committed him.

Even though I was retired, I couldn't help feeling obsessed by both cases. It drove Gloria a little nuts. We had planned our retirements to coincide with each other's and do nothing but relax and travel the country. But with this newfound information, I began to devote much of my free time to chasing down leads and investigating more fully, even though both cases were officially closed. I stalled when I ran into the same dead end with the Nebraska case.

For the next two years, I kept in touch with my old colleagues at the station, and whenever I had a moment I would do some research on my own. Gloria and I bought a Winnebago, and every few months we would take off on a jaunt. Sometimes we would board a plane and visit other parts of the country. When we were at home, we found plenty to do: gardening, home improvements, catching up on our reading, taking long walks around the neighborhood. We spent every evening making love, and our physical relationship was rekindled to the heat it had when we first met in 1961, when she was a young college girl. She had been beautiful then, and had blossomed into a mature beauty who was natural and radiant. I didn't lie when I said earlier that I never desired another woman throughout our marriage. Gloria remained beautiful and desirable to me from the moment I laid eyes on her. Each time we made love, it was like joining with her in the flesh for the first time. When her heat enclosed me, I could never contain myself, and she would urge me on in a voice that drove me wild. And when I released myself, it was like being young again. Gloria satisfied me in so many ways, and she continued to do so even in our retirement. Our appetite for sex never waned; in fact, it seemed to grow stronger.

Perhaps it was our growing contentment with each other, with our lives, that allowed Gloria to tolerate my fascination with the Haynes case. Sometimes I would do research on the Internet at home, typing "Eros, Ltd." into a search engine to see what came up. Nothing ever did. Or I would stop at one of the many sex shops along Harbor Boulevard in Orange County, or Sunset or Hollywood Boulevard in Los Angeles and browse, noting the novelties, especially the sex dolls. I would ask the proprietors if they had ever heard of a doll called "Dream Girl" or an outfit called Eros, Ltd., and they would shake their heads. Likewise, sometimes I would purchase the raunchiest of the adult magazines by the bundle and go through each one carefully in the privacy of my office, while Gloria was engaged in another household activity, looking for any mention of the company or the doll. I saw neither. And on a few occasions I'd sit at my desk, an issue of *Chic* or *D-Cup* lying on my desk, feeling I was chasing a legend, the paranoid fantasy of a genuine schizophrenic, and Gloria would come in, approaching me from behind to kiss the top of my head, and she'd see the open magazines. "Still obsessed with that case, Jose?"

I would nod. "Yeah, I don't know why I keep doing this, but—"

"It doesn't bother me," Gloria would say, looking at the graphic photos. Her hand would stray down to my crotch or slide beneath my shirt, her fingers tracing lightly over my nipples. "In fact, looking at these magazines gives me some ideas of what we should do for the rest of the day."

And that's how it went for almost two years. Gloria and I enjoyed our retirement. We went through a sexual rebirth in which it felt like we were rediscovering each other, and in my spare time whenever I thought of my last case I did a little research.

Then the nightmare arrived: Gloria was diagnosed with pancreatic cancer.

Our world collapsed.

The pains had actually started a week or so before we left for a trip to Colorado and had persisted throughout our little vacation. Gloria had called her doctor to arrange an appointment at my urging, but she was already dismissing the pains as indigestion. She had her appointment the day after our return, and the test results came back a day later.

All my focus centered on Gloria at that moment.

I tried to make her as comfortable as possible. She took the news like a trouper. She refused to let the cancer thwart her lifestyle, and she continued her social life and gardening, but I could tell that the strain was working on her. The doctors tried everything. The chemotherapy zapped much of her energy, and there were days when she could barely move. I waited on her hand and foot, tending to her every need. Our children—Frank and Jessica—stopped by more frequently and spent every weekend with us, either at the house or the hospital where Gloria was undergoing treatment. I tried to remain strong, but it was difficult. Many times I couldn't take it and collapsed in a crying fit, the sudden emotion overwhelming me. I was losing the only woman I had ever loved, the woman I desired over all others. I did not know what I would do without her, and during the few moments of lucidity we had together I would tell her this, and she would smile and whisper, "You'll do fine without me, Jose. You are a strong man. You will get through this."

Meaningless words meant to soothe my troubled soul, but they were of no use. I clung to their false sense of hope to no avail. On the morning of June 16, 2000, on the fifth floor of the Kaiser Permanente Hospital in Baldwin Park, with our children and grandchildren gathered around her bedside, my beloved wife slipped away quietly and peacefully.

I fell apart.

For the first time in my life, I was lonely. Sure, I had my children, my grandchildren, and my many friends. But I was missing my soul's mate, my best friend, my lover and companion. Gloria was such an important piece of my life that with her gone it was like I was missing something.

I kept her alive in my dreams, in my heart. . . .

In my desire for her . . .

I coped the best I could. I joined support groups for widowers; I became active in my church. My friends and family kept me busy. But there was still something missing. Things just weren't the same without Gloria.

I suppose that's how I got through it. I coped; I continued living. And eventually, I wandered back to that old case, the last one I worked on before I retired.

I must admit it didn't fascinate me the way it had before. One night, I found the files on my computer and read through them, trying to rekindle that old spark. I still found the case interesting, still thought there was something unexplainable worth looking into, but I couldn't get motivated enough to go chasing down leads.

I suppose in a way the only reason I continued my research was that it was something to do, something to occupy my time so I wouldn't have to think about Gloria. Before I knew it, I was back where I had started. I began delving deeper into some of the underground sex clubs on the Internet and made inquiries to the people I met there. I asked them about the doll and struck out every time.

I had better luck with the adult novelty stores. I found twenty-eight cases across the country dating back some twenty-odd years in which a sex doll was sold to a customer and the customer eventually committed murder. Coincidence? Perhaps. In all the cases, a motive was always explained, usually a crime of passion or a murder-for-profit scheme. In only a few instances was the perpetrator judged to be mentally unfit. There was no common thread to connect any of these cases except for their possession of a sex doll, which was always dismissed by the original investigators.

I backtracked through the cases and found out that the doll

purchased was one not normally kept in inventory, or the proprietors could not remember stocking it, or they did remember stocking it but could not find it again due to the manufacturer going out of business. I tracked down all these leads relentlessly. I found as many of the witnesses, victims' families, and investigators who would talk to me as I could. Most of them couldn't tell me much; the passing of time had eroded many memories. Others told me pretty much what I've already related here. When I put all this together I saw a pattern, but it was a pattern of a sinister sort.

The more I pursued this, the more obsessed I became. I began hearing rumors of the object of my search in whispered terms, like it was an urban legend. The stories were the same everywhere: The doll was known as "Dream Girl," or "Fantasy Girl." It came in a black box from an East Coast company that remained elusive. The people who bought the dolls were mostly men, but there had been a few women who bought it and later killed unsuspecting boyfriends or husbands and, in one case, an entire family. And when I spread the data I had uncovered out on my desk for analysis, I saw that the earliest case had occurred in 1956, the latest a mere two months ago.

Then there's my own case.

I don't know what compelled me to go into the shop on Harbor Boulevard in Santa Ana. The shop itself—Bill's Video and Books—was the last American-owned establishment in that section of Orange County that had turned into Little Saigon. I had been there before and didn't think much of it. So when I walked into Bill's that afternoon on my way home from seeing my daughter and her husband, I knew I wasn't going to spend much time in the shop. The sexually explicit videos and DVDs didn't interest me, nor did the glossy magazines piled on the racks. I went straight to the back of the store where the blowup dolls were stocked and immediately saw it on a high shelf.

With trembling hands, I reached up and brought it down.

I felt such a sense of dread, such a strong emotion of fear, that I almost put the box back where I had found it. But another part of me demanded to follow through with the path I had chosen, to follow my investigative instinct. So I took the box to the counter and asked the clerk what it was and where it had come from.

"Don't remember where this come from," the clerk said. He was Vietnamese and spoke in broken English.

"How much?"

The clerk checked the tag on the side of the box. "Seven hundred dollar."

"What's it called?"

"Dream Girl."

Along with the sense of dread was a feeling of excitement. I wasn't buying this doll to partake in some kinky sex the way those other men had. I had no desire to fuck a blowup doll and pretend it was somebody else. That settled it for me. I pulled out my wallet. "I'll take it."

When I got home, everything that I had learned in the past five years flashed through my mind. I set the box on the living room floor, thinking of all I had learned about this particular novelty: how the doll appeared as the woman of the buyer's sexual fantasy; how it comes with blond hair or black hair, or large breasts or is skinny or fat; how after the initial coupling it turns into a human being, the woman of that particular man's dreams; how the sex with it is fantastic, and that she does everything for the man, everything he desires, further ensnaring him. Most of all I thought of how all the men in question later killed loved ones—girlfriends, wives, families—all claiming they had been told to do so by a woman whom the police could never identify, a woman that was claimed to have once been a blowup doll, now come to life. I thought of all this and told myself I was going to get to the bottom of this. If this thing had power, I was immune to it. I had no intention of using the doll as a proxy lover.

I opened the box with shaky hands.

And heaved a sigh of relief.

The doll inside the box was so generic looking it was almost funny. It was so obviously fake. I think I laughed when I saw it for the first time.

I took it out and laid it on the floor. Sure enough, it was very phony looking. After all, it was only an inflatable blowup doll with the requisite squeeze bulb attached to it.

I did notice that the fake hair that had been affixed to its head was black with streaks of gray, but I didn't pay it any mind at first. I examined the doll's facial features, which were crudely rendered. The doll's mouth was a red "O" for the obvious. I examined the deflated doll and the box it came in, noting that there were no instructions, just the clear decal that was affixed to the box itself saying this was my "dream girl," and that she could be "anybody I desired."

Figuring I had nothing to lose, I found an air compressor and began to pump the doll up.

With the compressor humming, I stepped away briefly for a beer. When I came back, Gloria was waiting for me in the living room.

She was naked.

I stood in the threshold of the living room in shock. My wife, Gloria, was *really* there. She was standing in the center of the living room smiling at me. The black box was where I had left it on the floor.

"Jose . . ." she whispered.

It was her. It was really *her*. I could see her, I could smell her.

I went to her.

She held me, and I'm afraid I wept in her arms.

I was with her that evening, and it was the most erotic sex I had ever had.

Her caresses were gentle and teasing. Her lips were sweet, her skin was warm, her nipples hard. When I entered her she moaned, cradling my face in her hands and kissing me as I moved inside her, crying her name over and over. She stayed hot and wet and excited all night and, surprisingly, I stayed hard. While our sexual relations had exploded in the months following our joint retirement, that evening it was more than explosive; it was orgasmic.

We even tried things we normally wouldn't have tried earlier—different positions, ones I never imagined existed. Each thrust, each caress, each kiss was like touching an electrifying orgasm.

Some time later, we lay together on our king-sized mattress and I tried to catch my breath. My senses were on full alert and my skin tingled. I wasn't imagining things or hallucinating. I had just had incredible sex with my dead wife, Gloria, who wasn't dead. She had returned to me as she had been in the months prior to her getting cancer. When I told you earlier that Gloria was the only woman I had ever desired, I hope you see what I now knew to be the Dream Girl doll's power: It took the mental image of each man's fantasy woman and brought her to life for him. When the men who bought the Dream Girl doll had sex with it, their fantasies brought that woman, the dream girl in their mind, to life. This had happened to me, too. Because Gloria was the only woman whom I had ever fantasized about, the doll brought her back.

I thought about this as we lay in bed. I turned to Gloria and touched her. She was real—my fingers touched sweaty skin. Gloria turned to me, her eyes ablaze with passion and desire. She smiled. "I've missed you."

"I've missed you, too." We kissed. Pleasures of sensation shivered up and down my spine, brought me back to life.

"I want to stay with you forever," Gloria said, settling into my embrace. "I don't ever want to have to be away from you again."

I turned to her. "You want to be with me forever?"

"Of course I do!" Gloria said, turning to me. She kissed my neck. "I've always wanted this—to be together like this, just you and me all the time. Forever."

"You're here now. Why can't you just stay?"

She paused, and I sensed tension. "You know it's not that easy."

She turned to me and I read sorrow in her eyes. Sadness. My heart wept. In all the years of our marriage, I'd only seen Gloria look so saddened once. That was in 1969, when she miscarried our third child. The doctors had told us after that we would be unable to bear any more children, so to avoid further pain and suffering, I had undergone a vasectomy.

Now that beautiful, regal face bore that same look of impending hurt. I immediately wanted to comfort her, to make that hurt go away. "Talk to me," I said.

"I can't stay," she said, her voice trembling. Her eyes brimmed with tears. "I *want* to stay . . . more than anything I want to. I don't want to go back. I don't ever want to go back in that dark hole I just came from. But . . . I can stay if you . . . do something that will help me stay."

"I'll do anything so you can stay," I blurted out before realizing it.

"Will you?" Her eyes lit up and she clutched at me like a drowning woman clinging to a life preserver in treacherous seas. She was like a little girl, defenseless, and hadn't I always vowed to protect her?

"Yes," I said, holding her close and kissing her.

Then she brought her lips to my ear and whispered what I had to do for us to be together.

And that's what has led me to my present predicament. When she whispered those awful words in my ear, I knew that I was damned either way. If I did what she asked I was damned, and if I ignored her I would be even worse off.

I fought her. I tried to get rid of her, but she wouldn't go. Fighting her was useless. She always appealed to my baser emotions and fleshly desires in the end. That weakened me.

I called the shop where I'd bought her, and when I asked to speak to the clerk who had sold me the doll, he claimed not to know what I was talking about. I reminded him that I had spent seven hundred dollars on the doll, and he claimed he didn't remember. Then he hung up on me.

Through it all, Gloria waited for me in our bedroom, calling to me.

And, oh God, I couldn't control myself. I couldn't resist her.

I couldn't help going to her and coupling with her, losing myself inside her.

The sex got better all the time.

And my strength and resolve weakened each and every time.

I'm left here writing this all down as evidence. I have been struggling between following my desire and doing what is right. I know it will be hard for those of you who read this to understand, but think of what I am going through as what heroin addicts feel when they cannot resist the allure of the needle, the sense of calm that pervades their beings when they ride the spike. Their bodies crave it just not to feel sick. This is the way it is with me now regarding Gloria; the more I try to resist her, the sicker I feel. Being with her makes me feel alive and whole, and when I think about the rest of my life with her, it is like glimpsing an oasis of beauty and sensuality in which we can reside together forever.

That is what she is promising me, and on some level I believe this can happen if I go about it the right way and am not caught. I can plan—I have the means and the ability to arrange for a new identification, and can easily slip out of the country, taking all my money with me. I can settle us somewhere down in Mexico, Baja perhaps. I probably have a better chance of evading capture if I plan methodically.

The problem is, I can't do it. I cannot bring myself to do what Gloria asks of me.

If I don't follow through with what she wants, I know what will happen. My children and grandchildren will be tainted forever with the knowledge that their father and grandfather was a madman, a necrophile.

You see, the longer I wait to make my decision and carry out what Gloria wants me to do for us to be together, the more Gloria begins to deteriorate.

Somehow, she manages to change back when we make love. She is lovely, whole, healthy, and beautiful. She'd have to be. I am not a necrophile, have never been attracted to the dead, and the few times I've even thought about the rotting thing I've been seeing the past few days when we aren't making love has been enough to drive the desire right out of me. Gloria always has the antidote to that. She always appeals to my pleasures, pressing the right buttons, and then I'm hers again and she is no longer the wretched thing she turns into. She is the Gloria I knew and loved before the cancer got her.

I know this is happening because I am stalling, and I know that the smell will soon attract the neighbors. I haven't left the house in over a week, and I'm afraid that if I steal outside now for a quick trip to the store for bread and milk that people will look at me funny. Perhaps somebody will grow suspicious and send the police to my house.

What I know will happen, though, is that either my son or daughter will grow worried and stop by. I've already received a few phone calls from them. I've let their calls go straight into voice mail. Jessica left one just this morning, her voice tinged with worry as she said, "Dad, it's Jessie. I called you yesterday and the day before and I'm starting to get a little worried. Um . . . if I don't hear back from you I'm coming over, okay? Please call me. Bye."

One of the calls I let go to voice mail was from a friend of mine still on the force, David Harrison. His voice sounded strained, worried. "Hey Jose, how's it going? Listen, I hate to spring bad news, and I know you're probably off visiting your kids or something, but . . . well . . . some crazy assholes vandalized Forest Green Cemetery last week and dug up a bunch of graves and . . . well . . . Gloria is missing—"

The smell is getting stronger.

The whiskey is almost gone, and I cradle the Colt in my

hands lovingly. I can't do it . . . I can't do what she asked me to do.

Gloria's whispering to me, telling me what to do.

My son's last phone call to me, just an hour ago: "Dad, Carrie is with me, and we have the kids. Are you home? Listen, Jessie's been worried about you. She just called on her way home from picking her kids up, and we're going to meet at your place. We're on our way over now."

I know I can fill the chamber of the Colt with the rest of the .45-caliber shells I have, thus doing what Gloria asked me to do in order for us to be together. On one hand, that could be a very easy way out. My kids will not have to live the rest of their lives knowing their father went mad and dug up their mother.

But I can't do it . . . I can't wipe them all out . . .

I love my grandchildren. I would never hurt them.

Ever.

I hear the sound of car doors slamming shut outside. It's a warm, sunny day. The house reeks.

In the bedroom, Gloria keeps changing, shimmering from the ageless beauty I've always known her to be, to the dripping, rotting thing she really is. Her voice calls to me, caressing me. "We can be together, Jose . . ."

I can't do it.

Footsteps, coming up the walk to the front door.

I look at the Colt with that one bullet already in the chamber, my feelings torn.

Please kids, please know this isn't what you think.

There is a knock on the door. Soon I will hear the rustle of keys as they let themselves in.

I take a quick breath, willing back my tears. Gloria calls to me again. I pick up the gun and make my decision.

The Last Romance

Catherine Dain

She heard her name, not the name others called her, but her true name. Turning slowly, looking up, she saw him waving to her from the hillside, where he stood knee-deep in grass. The afternoon sun shone on his curly golden-brown hair, and his cheeks were ruddy with health. He laughed, and then he called her name again. As she started up the slope, he pulled the loose shirt over his head and dropped his trousers. Naked, already aroused, he waited. She untied her bodice as she climbed, and when she reached him, she barely paused long enough to step out of her skirt.

His flesh was warm under her searching fingers, his body hard. Their open mouths wandered all over each other's face, necks, shoulders. She could taste the sweat, smell his animal gladness that she was with him. They dropped together into the grass, young and in love, and he quickly slid into her.

The orgasm woke her up. It was strong enough, rippling through her body, that her legs jerked, disturbing Aurora, her fluffy orange cat. Aurora looked at a spot above the bed, glared, resettled herself, and went back to sleep.

Diane knew she wouldn't be that lucky. It was five-thirty in the morning, and she would be watching the sunrise. At least she had stayed with the dream until the orgasm. This one was her favorite, the easiest to stay with, and Steve knew that. She hated waking up in the middle and having to reach for the vibrator to finish. And Aurora didn't like the sound of the vibrator.

At first, Aurora had been bothered—or at least startled—when Steve had visited. But now she ignored him unless he was flying around the room. Diane sat up and looked at the spot above the bed, the place where Aurora had seen him.

"That was nice," she said softly. "Not quite as good as it was when we were both in the flesh, but that was nice."

Kill Howard.

She heard the words clearly, although she knew they were only echoing in her head.

"We've been through this before. I won't commit murder," Diane said. Steve was privy to her thoughts unless she shielded them. But words had more weight when they were actually spoken.

Kill Howard.

"No."

She felt him leave, and the loneliness rushed into her so swiftly, boring into her heart, that she almost called him back.

But she resisted the impulse. She didn't want to encourage his presence if all he had to say was "Kill Howard."

She shivered as the loneliness rippled out to her skin, as she became aware of how cold her bedroom was in the predawn stillness. She gently moved Aurora off her pink flannel bathrobe, put it on, and got up. A cup of coffee would help to ground her. Or at least warm her up.

Diane moved slowly from the bedroom to the bathroom and flipped on the light. She gasped and shut her eyes for a moment. The image in the mirror of a gray-haired woman, hollow-eyed, cheeks sagging, a faded pink bathrobe wrapped around her flabby body, wasn't what she wanted to see. They had both been so young in the dream, younger than they had ever been when they had known each other in this life. She wanted that reality. She had forgotten this one.

Coffee. She needed coffee. The kitchen was her next stop. She started the automatic coffeemaker, sat down at the table, and dropped her head into her hands.

A client was coming at nine-thirty. She had to be grounded and focused by then. The dreams, the sleep disturbances, Steve's presence—they were affecting her ability to make a living. Every time she laid out the cards and opened herself up to the images, she would find herself saying, "There is a strong male energy from the other side with an urgent request." So far she had managed to stop herself before she said too much.

Kill Howard.

Diane sighed. She hadn't felt him come back.

"Steve, this has to stop. I'm a year and a half away from Social Security, and I have to make a living. I'm starting to lose clients. They think I'm nuts."

She felt silly even as she said the words. Psychics see things that aren't there, hear things that aren't there, even feel things that aren't there. By definition, that's nuts.

The coffeemaker burbled, and her nose responded as the hot water released the aroma. Diane liked the smell of coffee even better than the taste.

Steve faded away as she poured herself a cup.

The first sip of coffee cleared her head enough that she could start to focus on her options. First option, do nothing. Let Steve float around as he was, an earthbound spirit—popularly known as a ghost—nagging her to kill Howard. No good. Diane was tired of that.

The second option was to call a couple of friends and do an exorcism to send Steve on his way. She didn't want to do that, because releasing him entirely would mean the end of their dream meetings. As tired as she was of the nagging, Diane didn't want to give up sex.

She and Steve had been nearing middle age when they met, and they had each had other lovers in their youth, but this relationship had been an erotic awakening for both of them. They had had fifteen years together, fifteen years in which sex was always fresh and exciting, before she lost him. And she knew, at her age and in her shape, that the dreams with Steve were her last romance.

Of course, there was no guarantee how long Steve would stick around as a ghost in any case. But spirits who died violently tended to be earthbound for a while longer than those who died peacefully, and five years wasn't long from the perspective of eternity.

The third option was to kill Howard. And that was out. Not only did she not like the idea of committing murder, she also didn't like the thought of spending the rest of her life in prison. She was getting older, but she had a lot of years left. And while she might be able to persuade a jury that she was nuts, she couldn't count on being able to convince them that she didn't know right from wrong.

There had to be a fourth option.

She sipped coffee as she thought. But nothing more came to her.

A second cup of coffee didn't help.

Once the caffeine kicked in, Diane decided to clean the apartment and burn some sage. Shifting the energy might keep Steve away for a few hours, at least until her client left. She grabbed the paper towels and the furniture spray and went to work.

Cleaning the apartment felt like an exercise in futility. She lived on the second floor of a dilapidated stucco building around the corner from a gas station, and a film of soot spewed from oil-bearing trucks had floated in through the open windows—she had to keep the windows open; she couldn't stand being there with them closed—and settled onto the few pieces of furniture she had left.

Almost everything had been sold when she lost the house in

the bankruptcy. Diane had saved only a sofa, two chairs, and a coffee table, pieces Steve had contributed to the apartment they moved into when they were first married. And the bed. The mattress was twenty years old, but she wouldn't consider parting with it, not until she was ready to say good-bye to Steve.

The small kitchen table had come from a thrift store, as had all the clothes she had bought for the last five years.

Maybe she ought to kill Howard after all.

Diane felt a flutter of energy in the room and stifled the thought.

She found a stub of white sage in a kitchen drawer, lit it, and placed it in an ashtray on the coffee table. That was all she could do for the moment.

By the time her client arrived, Diane felt capable of setting her own problems aside. And the apartment was as clean and clear as it was going to get.

The woman was middle-aged, slightly overweight, and obviously unhappy. Diane sat her down on the sofa and pulled one of the armchairs around so that she could use the coffee table for the cards.

"I need to know what's going on with my husband. I just can't live like this," the woman said. "How much do you want me to tell you?"

"Nothing before we start," Diane replied. "Then you can ask questions. Shuffle the deck, and then cut it into three stacks."

When the woman had finished her task, Diane picked up the smallest stack and laid out a Celtic cross. She let her vision go slightly out of focus, allowing images to run together, allowing them to reshape into a story.

There is a strong male energy from the other side with an urgent message.

"That's not it," Diane said, annoyed at Steve's intrusion.

"What's not it?" the woman asked.

"A strong male energy from the other side with an urgent message."

The woman gasped. "My father? Is it my father? He never liked my husband. He didn't want us to get married."

"Do you want a message from your father?" Diane was doing her best to focus on the cards, on the images on the table, but Steve's energy was sliding down her body, flicking over her breasts, nuzzling into the warm spot between her thighs.

Her heart began to beat faster, and her skin released a film of perspiration. Her armpits and her crotch were immediately soaked, and she could feel drops forming on her upper lip.

She found herself fighting an almost irresistible urge to masturbate.

"Well, that's not why I came . . ." the woman said. "Are you all right?"

"Just a hot flash," Diane said, faking a smile.

"Oh, God, menopause." The woman shook her head in sympathy.

"Why did you come?" Diane asked, forcing herself to look the woman in the eye, forcing herself to ignore her own body.

But it wasn't enough to ignore her body. The energy between her legs was getting stronger. If she was going to deal with this woman at all, she was going to have to shut down her own psychic energy, shut Steve out.

Sorry, she thought. She didn't hear Steve's reply, if he offered one.

"I think my husband may be interested in another woman."

Diane nodded wisely. "Yes. There are problems in the relationship."

And that was all she needed to say. Fortunately.

Diane kept the woman talking for most of the hour, giving her best therapeutic, if nonpsychic advice, making educated guesses as to what was going on with the husband, since she couldn't tune in to him without letting Steve in as well. The urge to masturbate never totally went away, her shield wasn't that solid, but she never quite lost control, either.

And finally the woman was gone, apparently without realizing that Diane had faked the session.

Diane dropped the shield.

"Damn it, Steve, I keep telling you, I have to make a living. Maybe this woman doesn't know when I'm faking, but others do. This is my only talent, Steve. You have to let me alone when I use it."

Kill Howard.

"Kill him yourself," Diane snapped.

The energy disappeared so quickly that Diane wished she had thought of saying that before.

She heated a cup of leftover coffee in the microwave and sat back down at the kitchen table. Maybe there was a fourth option, one that she hadn't yet seen. If she couldn't kill Howard, she could at least talk to him. Maybe Howard could come up with another option.

Calling him was out. He wouldn't want to talk to her. So that meant going to his office, being there when he was arriving or leaving so that his secretary couldn't put her off.

Diane shut her eyes again and focused on Howard. While she couldn't be certain, her sense of his energy was that he was having a normal day, no trials, and he would be at his office at normal times. For Howard, that meant from nine to five-thirty, with a two-hour lunch starting around noon.

For Diane, that meant another hour before she could leave to see him, which translated into too many cups of coffee, not enough food, and fried nerves.

Nevertheless, at quarter to twelve, she had brushed her hair, put on a little makeup, dressed in her closest approximation of business wear—a jacket and blouse over a long skirt—and she was ready to leave the apartment.

Howard's office, which had once been Steve's office as well, was only a fifteen-minute walk, on the same street as the gas station. Diane knew there was something perverse in living so close to where Howard worked, but after Steve died and she lost so much else in the bankruptcy, proximity to Howard was at least something solid in her life.

The three-story building had been painted a strange shade of stucco, muted peach, sometime in the last century. It sat like an island in the midst of an almost-full parking lot. None of the cars looked new.

Diane walked purposefully across the lot to the front door, went inside, and climbed the stairs to the second floor.

She paused outside the door to an office halfway down the hall and focused on the sign. HOWARD KRELL, ATTORNEY AT LAW. Five years before, it had said KRELL AND MORTON. Howard was inside, she was certain.

She opened the door and caught him standing beside his secretary's desk.

"Diane!" Howard was short, overweight, bald, and bearded. Mouth hanging open, he looked like an albino walrus, but without the tusks.

"I need to talk to you, Howard. It's important. It's about Steve."

"I have a lunch appointment," Howard said, turning to his secretary for confirmation. When she responded with a blank stare, he added, "But I can be a little late. I can give you a few minutes. Come on in my office."

Diane followed him into the inner office, passing the blank-faced secretary.

"Do you want me to lock the door when I leave for lunch?" the young woman asked as Howard shut the connecting door.

"Yeah, that's fine," Howard replied.

Diane sat in one of the smooth leather chairs on the client side of the desk and waited for Howard to sit down on the other side. The office was as messy as ever, papers all over the desk. She wondered what Steve's office looked like now, what Howard used it for.

"Okay, what is it?" Howard asked once he was seated. "Do you need money?"

Diane almost said yes. She shook her head.

"I told you, it's about Steve."

"What about Steve?"

"He keeps asking me to kill you, Howard. I don't want to do that, but his nagging is making me nuts."

Howard's face sagged. He shut his large, dark, walrus eyes, sighed deeply, then opened his eyes again. He leaned forward across the desk.

"Steve is dead. He committed suicide five years ago. I know it was hard for you, Diane, especially when it turned out that he had run up all those gambling debts and left you to face the bankruptcy alone. But he can't be nagging you to do anything. So are you threatening to kill me? Is that it?"

"No. I'm not threatening you. In fact, I'm asking for your help." Diane said it firmly, unblinking, as he stared at her. "Steve says he didn't run up the debts and commit suicide. He says you ran up the debts, murdered him, and made it look like suicide. I've told you that before. You were clever, Howard. You convinced the police. But that doesn't change what really happened. And now Steve wants me to kill you. I don't want to do that, Howard, and I keep telling him I won't. But he keeps nagging. I'm hoping you can help me think of another way to make him happy."

"That whole story is nuts, Diane. Nuts. I've told *you* that before, every time you've come in here saying Steve was talking to you. You just don't want to believe Steve committed suicide. But you can't believe I would have killed him. He was my partner, my friend. And I don't know what more I can say that will help."

Howard looked so sincere, sounded so sincere, that Diane would have wavered if she hadn't been so certain of the truth. But she knew. So she sat and waited.

Howard blinked first. "What do you mean that Steve is nagging you to kill me?"

"You know I'm psychic, Howard." Diane knew Howard

didn't really believe in psychic abilities. Sometimes that annoyed her, but this time she didn't care. "And you know that Steve has been contacting me ever since he left his body, almost always in dreams. But the connection has become stronger, much stronger than it was when he first passed over. Now I don't even need to be asleep to talk with him. In fact, it's the stronger connection that's the problem."

"I don't understand." Howard pulled back a little, as if the perceived threat felt stronger.

Diane hesitated, not certain how much she wanted to tell him.

"We have sex. Steve and I. At first it was only in dreams. We would be young and beautiful, living in all kinds of different places, wearing exotic clothes, like memories of past lives. And the sex was always great, as long as I didn't wake up. I had to be asleep to feel him. But now it's intruding on my waking life—Steve's intruding on my life—arousing me at the wrong moment. And when I respond to him, even to tell him the sex is great, all he says is, 'Kill Howard.'"

"And what do you tell him?" Howard's voice was hoarse.

"That I won't do it. I keep telling him I won't do it. But he's driving me to the edge, Howard. He's driving me to the edge." Diane clasped her hands and leaned forward to punctuate her point.

Howard shrank further into the chair.

"What do you want me to do?"

"I haven't figured that out." Diane felt Steve's presence beginning to slide over her body again. The urge to masturbate was back. "Damn. This isn't working. I have to leave."

"What?" Howard's mouth gaped open.

"Steve wants me to masturbate, and I don't have the energy to shut him out. I hadn't realized how much energy it took to keep him out this morning. I have to go home and take a nap so we can have sex." Diane stood up, but her knees were shaky, so she paused to take a deep breath.

"You don't have to masturbate, Diane. For old time's sake, I could help you with an orgasm. I've always been fond of you. I'd be willing to help with that." Howard's gaping mouth twisted into a smile. "The door is locked. Nobody will intrude."

The soft film of perspiration covered Diane's skin again. She looked at Howard, at his leering face, and knew she had to get out of there quickly. Sex with Howard was not the answer she wanted.

"Think about Steve, Howard, not about me. I'll be in touch."

She had to fumble with the lock, but she made it out of the office with her dignity intact.

The trip home took her barely ten minutes, the fast pace further tiring her out. She hung up her jacket and lay down on the bed, so eager to fall asleep that she ignored Aurora, who curled up quietly at her side.

The dream slipped over her almost at once, and she gave herself to it.

She was seated on a throne, dressed in a long brocade gown, wearing a jeweled tiara on her head. Courtiers surrounded her, and one was kneeling at her feet. She looked down at his curly brown hair. He lifted the edge of her dress, leaned forward, and kissed her ankle. The thrill of his touch ran up her leg. She felt the warmth, the moisture. She was ready to receive him. He removed the slipper from her foot and kissed her toes through the silk stocking that covered them.

"Leave us alone!" she ordered.

The stunned courtiers murmured among themselves, but no one argued. They disappeared, leaving her with this hot-blooded youth. He looked up, smiling, and she knew his face.

He reached up under the heavy skirt, pushing her thighs apart to reach the source of her pulsing desire. She slid forward, helping him lift the cloth, until his mouth replaced his hand, and his tongue searched and teased her pleasure spot. Both hands were under her buttocks, supporting her body, as she gave herself to him.

She heard herself moan with joy.

Unfortunately, the moan woke her up.

"Damn. You want to watch while I finish with the vibrator?"

There was no answer.

"Steve?" Diane sat up.

Aurora adjusted herself to Diane's movement and went back to sleep.

Not even a *Kill Howard*.

Diane's desire for orgasm was replaced by a surge of fear. Steve wasn't around, and she was going to have to think about what that meant and what she could do.

About an hour later, she thought she had it figured out. This wasn't the way she would have planned it, but she could live with it.

The next thing she had to do was buy a gun.

There was a pawn shop within walking distance, just down the street from Howard's office. That was her best bet for an immediate gun.

Diane sighed, got dressed again, and headed out on her errand.

As it turned out, buying the gun was easier than she feared. The young man at the pawn shop was willing to bypass the waiting period in exchange for an extra twenty dollars, once she explained that a neighbor had been attacked and she really felt the need for self-defense.

"This is the same model I sold my mother," he told her, as he showed her how to load, unload, aim, and fire.

She was back in her apartment, sitting at the kitchen table, drinking a cup of coffee that she didn't really need, when the phone rang.

"I've thought about our conversation," Howard said.

"And you think you have the answer," Diane purred.

"Yes, yes, I think I do. How about if I come to you, this evening, say, after I finish up some work here at the office? About ten?"

Diane gave him directions. "I'll be waiting," she said, in her most seductive voice.

She spent the intervening time as she would any other evening, fixing dinner, watching television. A little before ten, she took off her dress and put on her faded pink bathrobe. This had to look right. She slipped the gun into the pocket of the robe.

Howard knocked on her door right at ten.

Diane opened it wide to let him in. He was panting, either from exertion or anticipation, she wasn't sure which. His tie was hanging out of his pocket, and he had unbuttoned his collar.

"How are you feeling now?" he asked, as he plopped his heavy body onto the couch.

"I don't know." Diane sighed and shook her head. "The dream didn't do it. I couldn't have an orgasm." She ran her hands down her body, so that he could see there was nothing under the robe. "But this is about Steve, right? You said you thought of a solution?"

"I have." Howard smiled, showing teeth the color of tusks, reminding Diane again of how much he looked like a walrus. "I think you've been alone too much these last few years, Diane. I think that's what the problem is. So, as your friend, and Steve's friend, I'd like to spend a little more time with you, beginning tonight. I'm hoping we can be close friends. What do you think of that?"

"I think that's kind and generous, Howard. Can I get you something to drink?" Diane took a step toward the small kitchen.

"No, no, I'm fine." Howard bounced up, almost tripping over the coffee table in his haste to reach her.

"Then let me find you a robe," Diane murmured, evading his grasp and backing toward the bedroom, "so that you can slip into something more comfortable."

She didn't actually have a spare robe in the bedroom. But she counted to ten, giving Howard time to shed his clothes, and returned to the living room, gun in hand.

Howard was down to his red-and-white striped boxer shorts. When he saw the gun, he dropped to his knees and grabbed for his pants.

"Stay still, Howard." Diane snapped the words, imagining them as bullets. "I know you have a gun too, and if you don't stop trying to put your hands on it, I'll shoot you right now."

That's what she should do, of course, shoot at once, and she knew it. But shooting Howard was harder than she thought it would be.

Howard stopped wiggling, pants crumpled in his hands.

"How do you know I have a gun?" he gasped.

"I'm psychic, Howard. Steve left this afternoon, and I had to figure out why. I realized it was because he saw a possible future in which you killed me, and he didn't want to be around to watch it happen. That freed me to kill you, which is what he wanted all along. I'm hoping your blood will bring him back. And now I can call it self-defense. You came over with a gun and tried to rape me, and I had to defend myself." Howard was scrambling again. Diane tightened her grip on the gun. "Fortunately, I also knew that you wanted to fuck me before you killed me, so you were going to help me out by taking off your clothes. You're going to die, naked, with the gun in your hands."

Diane saw the flash of metal in Howard's hands and pulled the trigger.

But she pulled it an instant too late. Howard managed to shoot before he fell.

Some good your psychic powers are, Diane. You just got us both killed.

I should have fired sooner, Howard, and I knew that. My psychic powers were right on. The problem was the flesh. I couldn't get myself to move fast enough.

Okay, if you're so psychic, why haven't we moved on? Why are we floating here above our bodies?

Violent death does that. We may be tied to the earth for a while.

Together?

Not on your life! And not on your death, either!

Steve? Steve?

There was a third energy in the room. Diane felt herself gravitating upward, toward Steve's presence, a stronger energy than she had felt from him when she was in flesh.

Howard's energy fluttered, confused.

Steve? What are you doing here?

I came to say good-bye, Howard. Now get out!

A surge in Steve's energy sent Howard reeling to the corner of the room.

Steve! I'm sorry, I was wrong. You have your revenge—I killed you, Diane killed me—can't we forgive and forget?

And who revenges Diane's death?

Another blast of Steve's energy and Howard was gone.

Hi, kid. I'm sorry it happened this way. I didn't want Howard to kill you.

I know, honey. But it's okay. I wasn't doing that well. And I'm glad we're together again.

Yeah. Me too.

They floated for a while in silence. They listened to the sirens that meant the police were coming, watched the police examine the bodies, followed the ambulance that took the bodies to the morgue.

What now? What do we do now?

What do you want to do now?

Diane had to think about that, if she could call the process of shifting energy "thinking."

I want to make love with you, Steve. Can we do that?

I think so. If we find a couple who are open to our energy, I think so.

They didn't find the couple immediately, but time was of no interest to either of them, so it didn't matter. One night they heard the moans and knew where they were going.

The woman had full, firm breasts, and her supple legs went straight back so that her ankles were hooked over the man's muscled shoulders. He was holding himself above her, thrusting slowly, pulling back, thrusting gently again.

"Oh, God, yes!" the woman gasped. "Now, please, now!"

Diane and Steve drifted down into the bedroom, letting their energies settle into the two young bodies, just in time for the orgasmic waves to sweep them up.

"Oh, God, yes!" the man echoed.

That was wonderful, Diane. It's been so long since I've felt anything like that. Do you want to do it again?

Diane felt herself in the body of the young woman with long hair and soft skin. She looked at the man on top of her, with his dark hair and straight features, his strong arms. She felt how hard he was, still inside her. For a fleeting moment, she wondered if this young man and woman would mind the intrusion, but then she didn't care.

Of course, Steve. Let's do it again.

Love Connection

Alan Ormsby

"Let me in," he said.

"I can't," she said.

He pulled her closer, pressing his body hard against hers.

"*Let me in. . . .*"

"No . . ." she whispered, ". . . don't . . ."

He breathed against her neck—light, little breaths—then kissed it up and down. She shivered. He ran his tongue around the inside of her ear. She moaned. He felt her legs begin to buckle.

"I want you," he said. "I know you want me, too."

Yes, she nodded. Yes. *Yes.* Her eyes were shiny in the dim glow from the street lamp; her hair rippled in the cool night breeze.

"Then let's go *in. . . .*" He edged her toward the entrance to her apartment building.

"No," she said. "You don't understand."

He kissed her and put his hand on her breast; her nipple was hard, erect.

"Oh, God." She pulled back. "Please . . ."

"Please what?" he said. "Please what?" He ran his hand

down her body and between her legs. She tried to pull away, but she was too weak. He pressed her back against the wall; her body rocked against his hand.

"Oh," she moaned. "Oh, God . . ."

"Say yes," he said.

"I can't," she said.

"Yes, you can," he said. "Your body's already saying it. . . ."

"Please stop," she said. She could barely speak. "Please . . ."

"No," he said. He kissed her again. Her mouth opened, warm and yielding.

"I need to be inside you," he said.

"Oh, yes," she said, "Oh, God, yes . . . I want that too . . . so much . . . but I'm afraid."

"Afraid?" he said. "Of what? Of me? Why?"

"Because," she said, "I . . . like you."

"I like you, too," he said. "What's there to be afraid of?" He tugged at her belt.

"I don't want to get attached to you," she said.

"Why not?" he said. "What's wrong with that?"

"I don't want to get hurt," she said. "I'll get attached to you and then you'll disappear."

He got the belt unhooked. "I won't," he said.

"That's what every guy says," she said.

"I'm different," he said.

She looked into his eyes. "Are you?" she said.

"Yes," he said, holding her gaze as he reached down again, this time inside her skirt. She closed her eyes and bit her lip. He slid his fingers under her panties and between her legs.

"You're so wet," he said.

She dropped her skirt in the living room while he took off his pants and flung them across the couch. He came up behind her, reaching around to unbutton her blouse. She leaned her head back against him and reached down to stroke him with her hand.

"Oh, my," she said. "What have we here?"

"All for you," he said.

She turned into his arms as he unhooked her bra and kissed her again. She knelt and took him in her mouth and sucked on him, ravenously. He pulled her up and kissed her, tasting himself on her tongue. They fumbled their way into the bedroom and fell on the unmade bed. She apologized for the messiness. He pushed her legs apart and licked her like a dog. She moaned and bucked against him. She had a slightly bitter, salty taste that excited him, made him throb. He rose up on his knees and pulled her toward him by the hips, her arms stretched limp and helpless above her head. She cried out as he plunged into her and whispered his name over and over—or at least, the name he told her—her whisper like the sound of waves and, for a moment, he felt buoyant and weightless, solitary master of an endless sea.

When he awoke, it was still dark. She was asleep, curled up against his back. Maybe he could sneak out without waking her. If he left now, he could drive home, take a shower, have breakfast, and be there for his wife's phone call. She was in Florida visiting her parents and wouldn't be back for another week. But she called every morning to check in before he went to work.

He sat up slowly, hoping not to wake the naked girl beside him, but something held him back: her hair was tangled in his. He tugged at it gently, but it seemed to be in a knot.

Shit, he thought. *How did* that *happen?* If he pulled any harder, it would wake her. He turned to get a better grip, but now his foot was tangled in the covers. He was half-turned toward her, half-turned away, one foot on the floor, the other still in the bed. He tried to gently kick away the covers, but they seemed tightly wrapped around his ankle. He would have to untangle his hair if he wanted to untangle his foot. He tried again to free himself, but the hair seemed more knotted than ever, as if gum had gotten stuck in it. It would have to be cut with scissors. He would have to wake her up; he had no choice.

He turned to her, but couldn't remember the name she had given him in the bar. How awkward. He said, "Hey," and shook her gently by the shoulder. She didn't stir. He shook her harder. She slept on, her breathing steady and slow. Her eyes were slightly open, a sliver of white showing at the bottom.

"Hey," he said, "wake *up.*"

She opened her eyes slowly and looked into his face. Her eyes looked slightly metallic in the powdery, gray light.

"I have to go home now," he said.

"Already?" she said. "Can't you stay the night?" She lifted her head to glance at the clock and felt the tug in her hair. "Oh," she said. "We're stuck."

"That's why I woke you," he said. "My leg, too." He laughed at the absurdity of the situation. "I can't get up," he said.

"I'll get you up," she said. She ran her hand down his stomach to his groin.

"Not now," he said, "I've got to go. I have things to do before work."

"Work, schmurk," she said, fondling him.

He could feel it growing, filling, pulsing in her skilled hand. She leaned over and kissed him, their tangled hair falling across his face. Her mouth covered his; she sucked on his tongue. His nose was clogged; he couldn't breathe; he felt dizzy, claustrophobic, but at the same time filled with desire as her hand continued to stroke him. It took all of his will to push her away.

"I have to *go,*" he said.

"Okay," she said sullenly. "Then it looks like I have to go with you."

"At least for the moment," he said. "Where do you keep your scissors?"

"In the bathroom."

She pulled the covers back and he was surprised to find that they weren't tangled around his feet at all. Instead, what looked like some kind of pink netting had been stretched from her ankle to his.

"What the hell is that?" he said.

"I'm sorry," she said. "But you can't say I didn't warn you."

He sat up, dragging her upright with him, and looked closer at the netting. It had the hard shiny surface of scar tissue and had burrowed, like wormy little veins, into his flesh.

"What *is* that?" he said.

"We're attached," she said. "I told you—you said it was okay."

He couldn't believe it. It had to be a trick. He yanked on it and felt a current of sharp pain travel up his leg.

"Jesus Christ!" he said. "What the hell *is* that?"

She shrugged. "Some kind of defense mechanism. I don't remember the technical term. My mom says it's genetic."

"Jesus Christ!" he said.

"We can get the scissors if you want," she said, "but it won't do any good. I'm already in your bloodstream. If you cut the hooks, you'll bleed to death."

"'Hooks'?" he said. "What are you talking about, 'hooks'?"

"They're sort of like little hooks," she said. "At the beginning, at least. They have a tendency to expand."

"You're insane!" he said. He tried to pull himself to his feet, but found that they were now joined at the hip, the pink netting stretching between them like chewed gum.

"Oh my God," he said.

Panic filled him. He lunged to his feet, dragging her with him, and stumbled toward the bathroom, searing pain reverberating up and down his spine. He screamed and clutched the door frame.

"Sorry," she said calmly. "Unfortunately all the pain centers have now transferred from me to you. It's a sort of protective feature of the condition."

"What do we do?" he gasped. "What do we do?"

"Move carefully," she said.

They inched along the hallway in the dark. When they reached the bathroom, she turned on the light and he saw the two of them in the mirror. The netting had spread across his midsection, a membranous, groping thing, attaching them like Siamese twins.

This can't be happening, he thought. *I'm having a nightmare. If I close my eyes I'll wake up—*

"It's not a nightmare," she said. He tried to look at her, but their hair had grown more knotted and restricted his head to a half-turn. He looked at her reflection in the mirror.

"Thought transference occurs, too," she said. "At least from you to me."

"Meaning what?" he said.

"Meaning I know what you're thinking, so be careful what you think."

"What is this?" he said. "What *are* you?"

"Just a girl with a rare condition." She seemed apologetic. "Unfortunately, you get all of the problems of the syndrome and none of the benefits."

He grabbed her by the throat and squeezed. Instantly, he couldn't breathe, and his neck buzzed with a pain so intense that for a moment he blacked out.

"Don't faint, for God's sake!" she said. "I can't lift you if you fall down!"

The searing pain reawakened him and kept him on his feet. He held the towel rack for support. Tears filled his eyes.

"Now, listen," she said. "Stay focused and listen. If you stay calm, and loving, and retain a positive outlook, the attachment will slow down . . . in some cases, it will even reverse."

"Stay . . . calm . . ." he repeated. "Yes . . . okay . . ."

She smiled. "It won't be easy, because in many ways the condition functions as a kind of aphrodisiac."

He nodded. "Aphro . . . disiac."

"For you. Not so much for me. In fact, as your desire increases, mine will probably decrease. You may notice you're already starting to get an abnormally intense erection."

He felt a painful pressure in his groin.

"It's important," she said, "that you stay attuned to my mood."

"Your . . . mood?" he said.

"Yes," she said. "And it won't be easy, because it changes so rapidly. If you're too passive, I may get bored. If you're too aggressive, my immune system will read it as a threat and . . ."

A scalpel seemed to pierce his testicles. He screamed.

". . . will act defensively."

"Don't . . ." he gasped. "Please . . . don't."

"The good news is," she said, "we can still cuddle."

"Cuddle," he said. The word sounded strange.

"And, yes, we can even have intercourse occasionally, if we're very careful," she said.

"Careful," he said.

"Careful and loving and . . . romantic."

"Careful . . . loving . . . romantic."

"And honest," she said.

". . . honest."

"It's all about consciousness," she said. "That's your best defense against the ingestion process."

"In . . . in*gestion* process?"

"It's been known to happen," she said, pulling him slightly off-balance as she leaned in to the mirror to check a small blemish on her cheek.

"You mean this has happened to . . . other guys?" he said.

"Well, yeah," she said. "I mean . . . I haven't exactly been celibate. Have you?"

For a moment he didn't answer.

"But what . . . what happened to them?" he said. "How did they get . . . unattached?"

She smiled and patted his cheek.

"Don't be naïve," she said.

Her earlier words came back to him with fearsome new clarity: *I'll get attached and then you'll disappear. . . .* A bottomless feeling of terror and regret opened within him, and his wife's face flashed through his mind. A stabbing pain knifed his side.

"This is not the time to think about your wife," she hissed.

"I'm sorry," he groaned. "I'm sorry."

"Yeah, yeah," she said. "Enough of that. Now tell me you love me."

"I love you," he whispered, through gritted teeth.

"I don't believe you," she said.

A lightning bolt exploded in his groin, forking into unbearable branches of pain that coursed up his spine, down his arms and legs, into his fingers, his toes, his skull, his eye sockets, his teeth.

"I love you!" he sobbed, when he could speak again.

"Better," she said. "Now try again. And this time, I want you to *mean it.*"

She stopped brushing her hair and studied her face in the mirror. She hated the way she looked after an outbreak, puffy and full-cheeked, and the way she felt, logy and languid, like a python who's ingested a rat. It would be a month before she felt right. It always took a month to complete the cycle: a week to absorb them, a week to digest them, a week to void the bones and hair, a week to recuperate and make herself presentable again. She plucked some fleshy clots from the bristles on the hairbrush and dropped them into the wastebasket. It was annoying when the residue seeped out through her pores. Ultimately, though, it would be healthful. Her body, having retained the nutrients, would emerge stronger, more glowing, more beautiful than ever. The small knobby growths on her thighs and breasts would keep her confined to the apartment for a while, but gradually these too would retract and disappear. In the meantime, she would take it easy, zone out on the sofa and watch the soaps and have a good cry or two. Sometimes you needed that.

She put the brush on the shelf and padded out of the bathroom into the living room. She would have to clean up the place—his clothes still lay strewn about. She kicked them aside and opened the blinds. The sunlight of a beautiful spring day poured into the apartment. Spring, and here she was, alone again. She flopped down on the sofa and stared blankly at the sky.

Men.

It was too bad. She had liked this one, and had thought after that first night that he was going to come through, open himself up, learn to share, maybe even turn out to be—she smiled ironically—her "soul mate." But in the end, he was like all the others: out for one thing and heedless of love, even when it offered salvation, even when it could have saved his life.

It was sad. Sad to read their boringly predictable thoughts, pathetic to watch their futile struggles, hard to endure their pleading, their sobs and screams, hurtful to withstand their curses and lies, bitter to witness their final paralysis and lumpish dissolution. But what could you do? She supposed they just couldn't help themselves.

Anyway, he hadn't disappeared entirely: he was still inside of her—"mulched," yes, (as her mother humorously put it) and no longer whole, but something of him remained—a kind of residual aura that lingered in her senses, an acute presence that called to her in dreams like the echo of a distant, drowning man, too far from shore to save. He would fade in time, of course. They all did. All things would fade with time, except for love—if you could ever find it.

Strip Search

Elle Frazier

Vanessa Ellis strutted brazenly across the stage, initiating a sultry dance of seduction beneath radiant lights that illuminated her bronzed skin. The brilliance of the light bouncing off glimmers of perspiration emphasized calculated yet acutely effective movements that appeared effortlessly executed. Leigh Rogers beheld the act from mere inches away, then moved intimately close, splaying her fingers across the performer's sleek, moist navel. "Relax and enjoy this," Vanessa urged, moving her hands from her knees to under the hem of her sexy plaid skirt, allowing her fingers to disappear under the soft fabric and keeping her eyes transfixed on her student understudy, gauging Leigh's willingness to submit to the seduction. The ingenue held the look meaningfully; her gaze didn't falter.

Murky darkness filled the gentlemen's club. Only a few of the lights that normally strobed and throbbed illuminated the surroundings, except for those that blasted the stage. Cream—the club's enticing name—was closed and lifeless, the aura of the place decidedly different from the brazen nights when men filled the building chugging drinks, blowing smoke from cigars, and growling out catcalls. Under the bright lights, Leigh could barely see past the edge of the stage. Maybe that's what made it bearable for the girls—they couldn't see the leering faces out there ogling them, so they felt free to parade, strut, let go.

Vanessa flicked a pink tongue across her full lips, wetting them, expertly creating temptation. Leigh's reciprocated desire manifested itself through trembling hands that caressed the rippling flesh of Vanessa's bare belly, inducing a shudder as they explored the dancer's responsive skin. The lightest touch from the student ignited electrical pulses that charged from the contact point on Vanessa's stomach to between her legs.

"You don't have to do or say anything unless you want to," Vanessa encouraged, with a flirtatious wink. "This final experience could make the difference between your research being marginally good and being phenomenal. Think of the respect you'll get when everyone finds out you went the distance to get inside me." Vanessa giggled at her clever phrasing.

Even though it was warm on stage under the glare of the intense spotlights, Leigh's fingers felt frigid against Vanessa's warm skin, indicating she must still be nervous. "My little protégé! Could it really be true that you've only dated two guys in your life? How cute is that?" Vanessa teased, tracing a French-manicured fingertip gently down the skin of Leigh's throat and crooking it in the neckline of her top. "Relax a bit, Leigh. And those bulky clothes have to go if we're going to get anywhere." Vanessa boldly tugged Leigh's arms out of the confining conservative top, revealing a bra-clad chest and the softest looking skin Vanessa had seen. The situation required finesse, but as Vanessa looked into Leigh's trusting eyes, she knew the reward would be worth the effort. She laughed delightedly. "That's a good start, at least."

Leigh took a necessary breath and sighed as she watched Vanessa rumple the sweatshirt that had just been plucked from Leigh's body and discard it, sweeping it away from their feet across the stage floor with her foot. Leigh crossed her arms protectively against her chest. "I don't think I can go through with this," she asserted, but couldn't help being mesmerized by the way Vanessa's beautiful teeth rested on shimmering lips, the liquid gloss contrasting brilliantly with the polished enamel. Or the way her expressive eyes flashed beguilingly under delicately arched eyebrows.

"Sure you can. You're just anxious. It's not like you've got something I've never seen before." Vanessa laughed wildly, flinging her voluminous head of teased hair over her shoulders and letting her gaze savor Leigh's natural beauty. "You've got a gorgeous body, Leigh." She admired the young student's body while sauntering offstage. "Stay right there. I've got an idea."

Vanessa's enrapturing, hypnotic voice and confident demeanor enchanted Leigh, who watched the silhouette of the dancer's body melt into opaque shadows. As Vanessa moved, her sun-lightened hair swayed in sync with her hips. An exotic fragrance lingered in the air in her absence, seductive and alluring, and as the raving beauty reentered the room, a potent blend of vanilla and jasmine, luscious and intoxicating, wafted back inside. Leigh closed her eyes and indulged herself with the scintillating scent, noting that her senses were intriguingly sharpened in Vanessa's presence.

A generously sized crystal cocktail glass filled to the rim with amber liquid balanced in Vanessa's hand. Leigh observed Vanessa's frown of disapproval that she was still clad in jeans, so she dropped her head and hesitantly undid the zipper and popped open the button of her jeans. Slowly, she eased the material over her hips, stopping briefly to adjust her panties so they didn't roll down with the denim, exposing more than she was ready to share. The contrast of the rough, stiff denim against her tender skin elicited a fierce vulnerability similar to removing body armor. Stepping out of the jeans, she folded them neatly, laying them on the floor near the crumpled sweatshirt. Heat rose to her cheeks as she stood face-to-face with little more than a few thin patches of material separating her and the emboldened Vanessa. The all-but-transparent material of her undergarments didn't allow for much modesty, but made Leigh feel as if she retained some modicum of dignity. Shaking her head, she released thick caramel-colored hair that tumbled across her chest, concealing some nakedness. Still, she looked humbly into Vanessa's eyes for a glimpse of approval.

Vanessa nodded with obvious pleasure and took a generous swallow from the glass in her hand. "Stunning! Your body is divine," Vanessa complimented, briefly touching Leigh's taut stomach, causing her abdominal muscles to involuntarily contract. "Here, have a sip of this. It'll help you relax and feel more confident."

Putting her hands in front of her chest to refuse the offered beverage, Leigh declined. "No, thanks, I don't drink."

It was difficult to say no to smoldering Vanessa, but Leigh sensed she should be assertive and remain somewhat in control. It might be different if no one ever found out. She admitted to a definite curiosity, but would be horrifically ashamed if her secret became public knowledge. Her strict Baptist upbringing and the attitudes of her reserved family and community tugged at her conscience.

Vanessa's blue-green eyes flashed. A visible display of harsh anger briefly crossed her lovely exotic face at the refusal of the refreshment. "I can't help you, Leigh, if you don't let me," she berated, crossing her arms over her chest, spilling a few drops of the cocktail in the process, roughly penetrating Leigh's eyes with daggers from her own.

Leigh blinked at the scolding, so uncharacteristic of Vanessa's normally placating manner.

Vanessa softened with an audible breath. "I'll just water it down a little for you. You really need a little something to help you relax. You're far too tense." In the darkness, a few ice cubes clinked and splashed into the glass, and then Vanessa reentered the room, her heels tapping the floor harshly with every step.

"You'll like this, I promise. Drink it, then come dance with me," Vanessa suggested, approaching Leigh with an indulgent smirk, extending the drink in front of her and hooking her free arm around Leigh.

Leigh obediently reached for the glass and allowed a mouthful of its dark, honey-colored contents to empty into her mouth, where she experienced it on her tongue. It burned slightly and made her eyes water. As it flowed down her throat, it radiated heat, potent and scratchy, barely watered down at all. She imagined how strong it must have been to start with. She choked, blinked, then handed the cocktail back to Vanessa.

Alluring girls of Vanessa's caliber often draped themselves over the arms of men like Hugh Heffner, or spent time in the studio with Howard Stern. They didn't just happen to be parading around small towns teaching stripping lessons. The skimpy attire Vanessa wore revealed the outline of perfectly shaped, jaw-dropping breasts and legs from hell, sinfully statuesque. The fabulous breasts enticed Leigh, who secretly fantasized of having similar ones herself, though she would never consider having the required surgery. Her heart palpitated fast and furiously at the forbidden nature of being invited to stare appreciatively at the swollen assets. She and her college friends modestly changed clothes with their backs toward each other or behind doors.

"That's better, baby. Just relax and follow my lead. No one's here except you and me. What's in this room stays in this room," Vanessa encouraged, moving her body intimately against Leigh's, feeling the sensation of chemistry sparking between them.

Leigh began to let go and lose some of the paralyzing rigidity that had plagued her moments ago. The influence of the spirits she consumed seemed to be relaxing her significantly. Vanessa's fingers sensually explored Leigh's responsive skin, and it felt incredible, all apprehension draining from her body, replaced by desire. The assumptions she'd brought with her to this project might be incorrect, premature theories that strippers performed to get attention from men or to feel desirable.

Or that maybe they had been molested as children and still struggled with confidence issues. She'd never guessed that many of them had lesbian inclinations, as she had come to discover. Except for the odd situation, the ladies worked for the money. Period. Not many places a girl could work three or four nights a week and bring home a grand or more tax-free.

Lascivious, engaging Vanessa could have married a doctor or lawyer, or gone to college without the need to strip for a living. It would seem there had to be some dark secret in her past that resulted in her choosing such a risqué and somewhat degrading profession. But everything was not as it seemed in the adult entertainment business. The ladies appeared to be all about the men they danced for. The average night consisted of promises whispered in expectant ears, eyes flashing behind false eyelashes, and crooked fingers that invited men for a closer look. Soft body parts brushed brazenly close to hard, erect ones and set the stage for seduction. Money went from his wallet to her G-string, and the girls went home to share a bed with a steady lover who knew the sexual limits of the business and the benefits of the money and found a way to live with the controversial arrangement.

Cream was the only establishment of its kind of any consequence for forty miles, so it was the only game in town for most of its patrons, who couldn't feasibly drive farther and make it back home to wives and children without facing a firing squad of accusations. It was far enough away to be a discreet place to visit, but close enough that one could blame his tardiness on getting stuck on the wrong side of a highway accident or on a last-minute conference call and still be believable.

"It's a come-and-go business." Vanessa laughed, winking at her play on words. Her management position afforded her the opportunity to bring friends to the bar to hang out after hours, or, as in this case, before hours, whenever she liked.

Vanessa poured herself onto Leigh, melding her body close to Leigh's almost as intimately as any man's had ever been. It felt sinful. Wicked. *Thrilling.* Leigh wanted to keep an open mind to the exploration out of gratitude to the dancer for agreeing to help with her thesis. "My focus," she had explained, "is to get inside the head of someone totally unlike myself and discern what it is that makes that person tick." Some of Leigh's classmates were doing such things as interviewing criminals on death row, and one guy, a confirmed homophobic, was living with a flaming gay theater manager for three months. Ideally, the researcher should find someone who thought and acted almost opposite of him- or herself. Researching the life of a stripper was the obvious choice for conservative, demure Leigh.

Leigh reluctantly took another sip of the cold beverage Vanessa offered, then returned casually into Vanessa's intimate embrace. Vanessa rewarded her with a chaste kiss on the closed, cold lips that had just been moistened with the frosty cocktail. "To do this convincingly, you'll need to think about good sex. What's your boyfriend's name? James, isn't it?"

Leigh nodded. James, her fiancé, had been dead set against this project. She told him she had changed her study to the evaluation of psychiatric patients at the local hospital and used that as an excuse for being away from her apartment so many nights during the week so she could go on with her study of choice. James would be irate if he discovered the truth, since it conflicted so strongly with his beliefs. Of course, those were his supposed beliefs, not his reality. Once, while he was out of town, she revamped his never-used guest room to accommodate new office furniture she was giving him to show support for his impending political career. When she began emptying the room of neglected linens and out-of-date clothing, she stumbled upon two large shipping boxes stashed at the back of the closet. She was aghast to find hard-core porn magazines, kinky videotapes, and vulgar-looking devices whose purposes she could only guess at. She picked through the repulsive contents as if she might contract an incurable disease from touching it. It simply didn't reconcile with the man she knew. Afterward, she'd been too horrified to confront him. He would only claim innocence—say the items belonged to someone else and that he was just storing them.

Sexually, things had not been impressive between them lately either. He claimed a preoccupation with the family's political career was interfering with his ability to become aroused, yet Leigh had to wonder if his lack of interest had anything to do with the foul boxes she'd found. For appearances' sake, she and James seemed the perfect couple. Obviously, appearances could be deceiving.

"Isn't that just like a man, afraid of what he doesn't know anything about? I think he's just afraid he might like it, or worse, *you* might!" Vanessa had teased, winking at Leigh, who had divulged only her fiancé's first name and his aversion to the adult entertainment industry. You could never be too careful what you told people.

"I never let a man get the upper hand. That's my cardinal rule. I'll do whatever it takes to maintain control," stated Vanessa, toying with Leigh's bra strap, then caressing the tender skin just above the thin, elastic band of Leigh's panties and planting a feathery kiss to the side of Leigh's neck.

James and his father both consumed themselves with political affairs, as James's family had done for ages. It would not do for word to get out that the fiancée of such an important family spent two nights a week at a strip club, even if it was only for research for a psychology thesis.

Leigh forced her attention back to the task at hand.

Vanessa brushed her hand across Leigh's stomach lightly, nudging Leigh's hands toward her surgically enhanced breasts. Leigh tentatively began to caress them through the halter top Vanessa wore. Leigh's gentle, curious touches, instead of the raw, vulgar groping Vanessa was used to, sent her spiraling in anticipation. To a purely heterosexual female, this gesture could mean little—like a gay guy dancing for a heterosexual man—but if she could use emotion to appeal to Leigh, she could turn things in her favor.

"I hope you don't think my breasts are vulgar because they're so big," Vanessa said, slowly taking Leigh's hand and pulling it across the tightly stretched fabric, hoping Leigh would lose herself to the forbidden touches.

Leigh smiled drunkenly with a glazed, blurred look on her face. "I think you're very beautiful. Your breasts are awesome," Leigh answered.

Vanessa let go of Leigh's hands, yet they continued to caress and explore the cloth-covered breasts of the performer. Breaking their embrace briefly, Vanessa strutted across stage into the darkness. Music filled the room, a ballad by Prince interrupting the silence. Sexy music. Guys tended to like harder-hitting rock songs while watching her work. Grab-the-girls-by-their-hair-and-fuck-the-shit-out-of-them songs. Women liked the more subtle, erotic music.

When Vanessa reemerged, she brought with her a metal chair and pushed it in front of Leigh. "Watch me dance, baby."

Vanessa moved in front of the cold, metal chair Leigh now inhabited and angrily tugged at the material of the confining halter with her teeth, eyes flashing, tossing her hair, and cursing the restraint of the fabric. Firm, fleshy breasts broke free and bounced from under the halter to command full attention. Large, painfully erect nipples sporting a delicate pink tint begged for stimulation. Her dance featured her tits as the stars of the performance and the rest of her body as best supporting actress. Leigh tentatively reached for a nipple with curious fingers, making Vanessa inhale audibly. Vanessa allowed her protégée to indulge her curiosity, then broke away to torment her more, delayed gratification being essential to the game.

Vanessa extended a long, tanned leg beside Leigh's head, giving her a brief look under her short skirt at the lace panties she wore. With her back to Leigh, Vanessa shook her mane of teased hair across her bare back and pulled up her skirt, exposing a thong-clad, firm, round ass. She squeezed her buttocks and bent over enough to present a lace-covered yet obviously shaved region barely concealed by fabric to her audience of one. Vanessa moved in time with the sensuous music, expertly undulating her hips and legs, while indulgently fondling herself in the process.

"It's okay to like this, Leigh. It doesn't mean you're gay. It's just fun," reassured a heavily breathing Vanessa. "I find you awesomely sexy," she moaned, getting so close to Leigh's face that their lips practically touched. Leigh hesitantly explored Vanessa's panties with two curious fingers and shuddered when she found the stripper welcomed the lewd gesture. Vanessa knew her panties were drenched with her pleasure.

The Prince song ended and another ballad followed, this one by Sade. Provocative and sensuous, Vanessa lowered herself to her knees between Leigh's legs. "Are you scared?" Vanessa whispered.

Leigh nodded slightly.

"Don't be."

Vanessa moved her face toward Leigh's, who accepted the invitation. Vanessa felt the softest lips merge with her own. She felt the texture of Leigh's long hair falling over her bare shoulders.

Leigh remained near Vanessa's face with half-closed eyes and a serene, amazed look on her face.

"Not as bad as you thought, was it?" Vanessa teased, locking her gaze on Leigh, letting her know that the kiss had exceeded her expectations.

Wrapped up in the intensity of the moment, Leigh became consumed with how her body responded to Vanessa's touch. Nothing existed outside the space they encompassed. So when an incongruous noise, seemingly human, alive and guttural, unrestrainable as a sneeze, emanated from outside the perimeter of their lust, it startled Leigh, jostling her abruptly from the drunkenness of her obsessive fixation to terrorized awareness.

Her relaxed body turned rigid, and blurry, unfocused eyes attempted to gauge the imminent danger by surveying the surroundings. "Someone's here!" Leigh warned, desperately whispering her fear into Vanessa's ear.

Vanessa encircled Leigh in a comforting arms-and-chest embrace that enveloped Leigh's alert posture. "No, sweetheart, no one else is here. I've got the only key to the place, and I assure you we're alone, except for a slight rodent problem we haven't managed to rid ourselves of. The sound you heard was just our resident mascot, Bacardi, a common rat, letting me know he's disgusted with what's been left out for dinner in the break room. We get used to it around here. He can sound quite human at times, just like my clients can seem very ratty themselves on occasion."

Leigh strained to hear another sinister sound, but registered only silence beyond her own measured breath. Leigh felt confused. The sound was clearly human, wasn't it? Vanessa seemed so at ease and uncaring, though, that perhaps it wasn't anything to be concerned about. Her heart slowly returned to a moderate beat and her body relaxed. She was being paranoid for sure, but a rat! Disgusting.

Vanessa attempted to draw Leigh's attention back into the vortex of seduction that had been spiraling before the disturbance. She boldly suckled Leigh's nipple, then toyed with her own and led it to Leigh's mouth. The smallest sounds of pleasure escaped Leigh's throat as she discovered the taste of another woman's flesh in her mouth.

"That feels amazing, baby. Go on, do whatever you want," encouraged Vanessa, adjusting her position to make contact between them more convenient. She giggled naughtily, pleased with how easily Leigh succumbed once again to her torrid seduction. "Would it be okay to unhook this?" she asked, reaching behind Leigh and tugging at the confining bra strap.

"Mine are much smaller than yours," Leigh warned, drawing back.

"But natural, full, and beautiful," assured Vanessa, tugging Leigh closer, undoing the clasp, and brushing away the confining material, letting the bra fall to the floor. Round, full, B-cup breasts awaited judgment from the woman who had seen too many others to count, mostly saline-filled. "I've never wanted anyone more," Vanessa stated, taking Leigh's nipple that strained against her tongue and teasing it expertly with warm, slow licks and delicate nibbles. How awesomely provocative it was to experience a woman entering unknown territory for the first time.

Vanessa bit Leigh's small, pink nipple with a touch of pain-inducing hardness for just a fraction of a second, then switched abruptly to the most tender of caresses. "I'm going to remove these," Vanessa announced, tucking her fingers inside the band of Leigh's bikini panties. This time she didn't ask. Inconspicuously as possible, she worked Leigh out of her cotton panties so that the innocent ingenue sat there completely nude on the chair, a patch of kitten-soft hair between her legs. In one swift motion, Vanessa straddled Leigh and kissed her firmly on the mouth.

"Is this good?" Vanessa asked breathlessly, devilishly tossing her head and guiding Leigh's down between her breasts.

"Yes. It's really good." Leigh breathed heavily, her hair edged in sweat, her face flushed. Vanessa eagerly ran her hands over Leigh's chest, aware of the thundering heartbeat beneath the delicate skin. She moved her hips, pressing her warmth, rubbing against Leigh's body intensely.

"Tell me what you're feeling, baby," Vanessa encouraged.

Leigh gasped and arched her back, tossing her head from side to side as if possessed by demons. "It feels intense. Forbidden. Hot."

Vanessa took Leigh's hair and gently brushed it from her pretty face, then began to orchestrate the grand finale, the coup de grace. She passionately kissed Leigh once more, forcing the kiss to linger, then abruptly broke contact. She eased off Leigh's lap, back to the floor, where she sat on the stage between Leigh's legs and nudged them open widely, purposefully burying her head between them.

Leigh twitched and moaned, arching her back so that it and her soft, warm hair fell back against the cold chair. Her naked torso stretched upward as Vanessa worked diligently between her legs.

"Baby, you taste divine. I've never tasted better, and you're beautiful down here. So soft." Vanessa swirled her tongue, licking and kissing so fervently that both women moaned simultaneous pleas that the other continue the dance of seduction. Vanessa knew what felt good to a woman and what it took to get results. She was happy to oblige. She tormented Leigh's clit, tasting her sweetness, savoring her responsive movements against her, using her ring finger to stimulate Leigh internally. Moisture drenched her fingers.

Vanessa took pleasure at the delight on Leigh's face and the wetness she had created in Leigh's body. Burying her face once again in the space between Leigh's tan, young legs, feeling Leigh's thighs against her cheeks, Vanessa sucked and worked her tongue until Leigh squirmed, whimpering in pleasured agony. Vanessa studied Leigh's enraptured profile. It had obviously been a long time since she was last pleased by a lover's touch; her sensitive body responded fiercely to stimulation. That, or James was one lousy, selfish lover. In mere seconds, seven staccato desperate pleas escaped Leigh's throat and ended in one long, fierce scream. Her body fell lifelessly onto the chair.

The Sade song ended and only silence filled the room. Leigh's body relaxed a bit and she opened her eyes dreamily. "That was incredible, Ness," Leigh said. "It's been a long time since anything's felt that good."

Vanessa stood from the floor and now glared at her student, who was just reentering the world, obviously satiated. Vanessa was angry that Leigh would leave this club and go back unscathed to her collegiate, prestigious life and career. She was angry that girls like Leigh judged her and felt superior to her.

Leigh appeared lifeless and limp, eerily similar to the way that bastard in Vegas looked after Vanessa hired someone to "mess him up" after he promised the world and delivered nothing—guaranteeing her a stellar Vegas career—taking her money, betraying her trust, and using her body for his own perverse pleasure to get what he wanted. When it turned out he didn't have the power or connections to make good on his promises, she showed him that he had literally screwed the wrong woman. In her line of work, she had seen and heard it all and knew how to deal with problems to whatever extent necessary. No one fucked her over and got away with it. He would think twice before attempting to take advantage of another "easy" mark. Leigh wasn't going to get away with exploiting Vanessa through a lame research project, either.

Vanessa looked at her spent victim and purposefully began to clap. The sound was a slow, mocking applause that somehow insinuated sinister implications.

Suddenly, the arena all around the stage came alive with light, revealing many empty seats directly in front of the stage, but with three full rows of impeccably dressed men and women beyond it who joined in with Vanessa's perverted applause.

Leigh sat upright in the metal chair and drew her knees to her chest. She wrapped her arms around herself as if to conceal her disturbing nakedness. "What is this?" she shrieked, tears streaming.

Vanessa crossed her arms over her ample nude chest and stood admiring the way she had manipulated Leigh expertly, as she had numerous men every night. The power was such an aphrodisiac; she was ready for a good orgasm herself. Luckily, someone was waiting for her who could drive her insane and actually paid her to make it happen. She normally preferred sex with women, but fucking this man was sublime, and she was quite addicted to his torturous touch.

Everything around Leigh began to swirl and flip. Lights blurred; sounds all around her became unbearably amplified. "How could you do this to me?" she screamed. "I trusted you!" She found the courage to bolt from her chair and quickly threw on her clothes, now scattered about the stage. She glared at the remaining crowd in the back rows of the club. Many of the patrons left after the "show," and only a few remained to gawk at her misfortune and taunt her with vulgar, humiliating comments.

"Great show, baby. You'll be the star of my wet dreams for a long time," one man jeered.

Leigh rubbed her cheek as if the sting of the verbal abuse physically wounded her. She shuddered to think who might have been in the audience and what it could mean for her future.

Vanessa laughed vindictively. "Trusting me was your first mistake, wasn't it? Doesn't appear you're too good at your chosen field of study, baby. Your ability to read people successfully could use some work." Vanessa sneered. "I played you just like I play all the guys who throw their hard-earned money away to get me to make them feel desirable. Didn't you learn anything from your research?"

Leigh wiped streaming tears from her face and steeled herself from running from the room. She needed answers. Between sobs, she vented, "You like women. I thought you wanted *me*. You seemed to care . . ."

Vanessa found her halter top and put in on without haste, slowly stretching herself into it and saving the top, most revealing button closures for last. "*Seemed* is the key word, honey. Just like I *seem* to care about all the drooling, pathetic men who come in here, so I can manipulate them out of their money. Some of them are even aware that strippers find them repulsive, but they still pay," Vanessa raged, slinging her hair behind her shoulders and propping one long leg on the side of the metal chair that Leigh had vacated.

"People see strippers undress all the time. Not such a big attraction, really, but it's rare to see a virginal college chick take off her clothes, have lesbian sex, and reach orgasm without realizing she's being watched, isn't it? You commanded a very high price, Leigh. I knew just which clients to call, which of them would lay out the big money."

"You can't get away with this!" Leigh shrieked, sobbing while her body convulsed. She grabbed the chair from under Vanessa's foot, knocking her leg from it. "I'll have you arrested," she threatened.

Vanessa rubbed her newly bruised thigh absently. "No, you won't. You wouldn't drag your name through the gutter along with that uptight fiancé of yours," Vanessa stated. "You'd live in private shame for the rest of your life before you'd do that."

Leigh flinched. Vanessa was right, of course. She would leave here and not mention a word of this to anyone, in hope that no one ever exposed her shameful secret. The implications haunted her. What if someone from the audience dangled this shame over her indefinitely? Would she live in fear the rest of her life over this one mistake?

"Sorry to cut our party short, baby, but it's time for you to get your uptight virginal ass out of here. I have no further use for you and I have an appointment to get to." Vanessa smiled, glancing at her watch, then pointing a long acrylic nail toward the back door of the club, indicated the direction Leigh should go.

Leigh stood transfixed, wanting to confront Vanessa, craving revenge, but not capable of enduring another moment of this hell she had stumbled into. She reluctantly moved past her nemesis, using all the restraint she possessed not to ball up her fist and slam it squarely into Vanessa's perfect face. As she exited the stage, she was aware of Vanessa's presence behind her from the clicking of stiletto heels. As she passed the bar where Vanessa had created the potent cocktail, she noticed an open drug bottle near the ice bucket and a white residue on the bar's surface. Vanessa had put something in her drink! She remembered Vanessa taking a sip of the beverage after offering it, but felt certain that Vanessa possessed a high tolerance to drugs, and Leigh would be much more susceptible to any effects. She had consumed much more of the beverage than Vanessa, as well. No wonder her guard was down enough to have allowed things to go that far.

At the door, Vanessa pulled her by the hair at the nape of her neck and forced a last, strong kiss on Leigh's closed lips. Leigh angrily wiped the sticky moisture from her mouth with the back of her hand and clenched her jaws.

"It's a shame it didn't work out between us," Vanessa sneered, tossing the keys that Leigh had left on the break table into Leigh's hands. "You're a tight little thing. I don't hook up with girls like that too often." Vanessa shoved Leigh out the door and slammed it behind her, jarring the glass fiercely.

Leigh prayed the nightmare was over. She would have to live with the personal disgust and humiliation of her sinful indiscretion. That was torturous enough, but surely anything that anyone who had been here today threatened her with would be hearsay. There was no proof of this humiliation. That was the only saving grace.

It took several attempts to get her key into the ignition with her trembling hands. Driving home seemed impossible, but she pulled herself together enough somehow to creep out of the parking lot. A car blasted its horn as she narrowly escaped a collision. She slammed on the brakes and gasped for breath, the wailing horn piercing her brain. Navigating with tear-filled eyes and struggling to keep her mind off the horrid events of the day, she proceeded cautiously ahead. At the first red light, she barely made a complete stop before opening the door and vomiting forcefully on the asphalt. Luckily, no one was behind her to witness the purge of devastation.

It occurred to her that she could go to James's cabin. He kept a place outside of town as a getaway when the constant attention of aspiring to a public office got to be too much. He was still out of town, but she knew where he kept a spare key outside his private retreat. She could be alone and not have to explain anything to anyone until she became capable of making it home, still a twenty-five minute drive across town.

In minutes, she rounded the final curve to his cabin. She felt like a determined marathon runner, mustering all her remaining resolve to make that final mile. Her knuckles were virgin-white from the massive grip she had on the steering wheel.

Her heart sank. Something was wrong. James's car sat squarely in the center of his driveway. If that wasn't enough, lights illuminated the inside of the cabin, and curtains billowed from open windows. Music streamed loudly from inside, filling the air. He must have returned early from his trip, or never actually left at all and decided to come to the property to unwind. Odd that he hadn't bothered to call and let her know.

Leigh couldn't face James in such a disheveled state, and couldn't understand why he was there when he said he'd be out of town. The cabin was a retreat yes, but not from her. She couldn't face him under the circumstances, yet didn't have the energy to drive home, either. Instead, she backed her car off the road onto a narrow gravel drive. She put the car in park and turned off the engine. She could still see the cabin, but unless he really looked, he'd be unable to see her. She'd sit here until she felt capable of driving herself home, however long that took.

The words Vanessa had tormented her with blasted over and over in Leigh's ears. Her vision registered nothing but instant replays of what occurred onstage at Cream. She couldn't imagine ever living a normal life again, one that was innocent and expectant, not mired by knowing what evil was possible within others and oneself. She kept wondering who might have been in the audience. Would she pass them on the street and not know? Would she work with one of them in the future? Attend church with someone who had been there? The thought sickened her.

The sound of an approaching car confused Leigh. Only James lived on this road, the rest of the properties being owned by people who didn't live this far out—they just kept it for hunting purposes. Leigh shuddered at the prospect of being confronted by the owner of the property. How would she explain herself? The car came into sight and Leigh recognized it immediately. As the late-model Ford Escort with tinted windows passed, she confirmed her suspicions by reading the license plate—STRPR GRL. Her heart lurched. Fear seized her that Vanessa had stealthily followed her to somehow destroy her further. But the Escort pulled confidently into James's driveway as if it made the drive routinely. Vanessa parked the car and emerged wearing the same getup she'd had on at Cream. She yanked a small piece of luggage and a couple of items on hangers from the backseat, then slammed the car door closed with her butt. Leigh watched her movements numbly, confused and disbelieving.

James appeared on the front deck, bare-chested, clad in faded jeans, and sporting a welcoming smile. He embraced Vanessa, smothering her with his arms. He patted her on the ass and led her inside, shutting the door behind them.

Leigh gaped at the house, wondering if she were dreaming, having a nightmare—imagining every bit of this horror.

She recounted in her mind bits of conversations with Vanessa. She had admitted a tendency toward lesbianism, but also expressed a great affection toward some guy she saw from time to time, when it was convenient for him. She'd said he traveled a lot and was a high-profile customer who paid her well to be especially discreet. Vanessa apparently enjoyed the prestige of being associated with such an eligible bachelor, even in a perverse way.

Leigh managed to extract herself from her car. Adrenaline poured through her system. She reached into the backseat and grabbed the camcorder she kept there for taping segments at the club for her research. The tapes contained footage from interviews with the girls, but she knew the tape in the camera still offered a good deal of available space. She gingerly pushed the door of her car, not even clicking it closed, to preserve silence, and winced at the sound her shoes made as they crossed the gravel drive. Exposed on the main asphalt road that abutted James's property, she knew she must hurry to some form of refuge. If he or Vanessa looked out the window now, they would see her. With his music roaring, James apparently hadn't heard her car approach mere minutes before Vanessa's.

Leigh elected to go to the rear of the cabin with her camcorder so she would be less exposed. Laughter blended with the music that spilled from the window that Leigh knew belonged to James's bedroom. She metamorphosed herself, playing a role, resolving to feel emotionless and uncaring enough so that she could get through the horror of the situation.

Fortunately, the bedroom curtain languidly billowed in the breeze as the front ones had, granting her full visual and auditory access. She now heard James's male voice intertwining with Vanessa's purring chortle.

Stealthily, Leigh pushed her way between two tired-looking shrubs desperately in need of pruning, and ensconced herself in the space between them and the wall. The spindly branches scratched at her face. Up close, visibility into the high window was impossible. She scoped the yard for something to elevate her, but seeing nothing, opted to just punch *record*, stretch on tiptoe to aim the camera toward where she knew his bed was, and hope for the best. She expected to hear shouts of protest the moment the camera appeared in the window, but the intoxicated laughter and cooing continued without ceasing. Apparently, the occupants were so blissfully engaged that they were oblivious to any goings-on around them. The shrubs evidently helped conceal the camcorder as well.

The jovial mood that erupted from beyond the window switched suddenly. James's angered voice spewed erotic obscenities at Vanessa, rough and crude, so unlike the James that Leigh knew. "You like to fuck, don't you, baby? You like my big cock ramming deep inside you. Tell me how you want me to get you off," he roared. Vanessa matched his tone and volume pitch for pitch, seemingly enjoying the roughness that repulsed Leigh, who trembled from the shock she was feeling. The footage she obtained would be nearly unwatchable if she didn't steady herself. She prayed it would be decipherable enough to capture the evidence to get her life back.

Eventually the deed consummated, and Leigh heard Vanessa's protest. "Jimmy, you keep promising me a ring. If you don't do something soon, you'll leave me no choice but to spill your dirty little secrets and ruin that sweet political career you've always dreamt of," Vanessa threatened.

Leigh's arms began to throb under the unaccustomed strain of holding her arms above her head. The room grew silent, and Leigh lowered the camcorder to make her escape before she could be discovered.

As she maneuvered out of the shrubs, she heard Vanessa's scathing warning, "Don't underestimate me, baby. I want to be the kind of girl with the respect that a senator's wife commands, and the way I see it, you can make it happen."

Leigh eased out of the shrubs and turned off the camcorder. She'd seen and heard enough. With great effort, she crept to the car and secured the camcorder. She hoped she'd been able to adequately record the raunchy events. She wouldn't know for sure until she got home and tested it herself. *If* she got home.

Vanessa Ellis served two cups of fragrant espresso to table nine on the verandah. On the way back inside, she stopped to check her reflection in the mirror behind the lavishly stocked bar of Café Indulgence. At first she couldn't find her reflection; instead, she was met with an image of a conservative woman occupying the space where a seductive siren should have been. She dismissed it as being someone else before recognition set in. Her hair, barely skimming the nape of her neck, radiated auburn highlights within a chestnut base. Chic, small-framed glasses lent an intelligent nuance to her bold features, while a crisp, white blouse modestly camouflaged her ample assets. "I need a dirty martini for table eleven," she requested politely of the bartender, a hunky Italian who would wet his pants for a chance to be with the woman she used to be, but barely acknowledged her new incarnation. That suited her fine. And suited Senator Cade, too. He had finally taken office and was openly dating her now that she had her new look and her new job, which he had used his connections to land for her. Indulgence was a sought-out and elegant establishment with a country club clientele. Working here afforded her a respectable identity that didn't have to be concealed. Apparently she had fooled everyone. And since things were going so well, Jimmy had actually conceded that they might get married soon. She giggled, pleased with herself, ecstatic about her future.

As Tony mixed the cocktail in an aluminum shaker, Vanessa absently toyed with a plastic cocktail sword and half watched, half ignored the seven o'clock news. It was a slow night, and the lingering customers were jovial, allowing her a few moments of peace. Usually the news bored her, but she tried to pay attention so she could converse intelligently with Jimmy and his circle of supporters. The volume was turned so low that the anchorwoman was nearly muted, but by the passion on her face, it was clear that she was elucidating something serious, piquing Vanessa's interest. "Tony, give me some volume on that TV, will you?"

Tony shot her an annoyed look as he topped the martini with a single fat olive on the plastic sword he retrieved from Vanessa's fingers, before punching up the volume on the console behind the bar. Vanessa gasped and felt heat crawl up her cheeks as the rest of her body went numb and cold. The report ended, and after a moment of concrete stillness, she ejected herself from the barstool she had slumped onto, knocking over the dripping cocktail that spilled across the bar's surface and flooded the floor. "Hey!" Tony called out angrily. Vanessa didn't register his summons. She grabbed her purse from the waitress station and shot out the door.

* * *

Leigh tied her robe over expensive lingerie. From her pocket she retrieved a thin yellow charge stub from the parcel she mailed two days ago, and used it to fan her face as she studied the picture on the front page of the weekend newspaper. It sported a flamboyant photograph of Senator Cade being inducted into office, his face an exhibition of pride, joy, and self-congratulation. Leigh snarled distastefully at the photo of last week's inauguration and smirked at the yellow stub she held, then shoved it back into her pocket.

James's repulsive face came to mind as she recalled his indifference over her decision to break up with him after the Cream incident. Leigh wadded up the dated newspaper, distorting the face she'd managed to avoid by conducting the breakup over the telephone. She hadn't even given him a good reason for her decision. He had seemed so preoccupied and self-absorbed that her departing words seemed to elicit no emotional response.

Leigh tossed the crumpled paper into a plastic wastebasket. Had the story broken yet in the local media? She'd worked late last night and missed the late news. Unfortunately, David Letterman didn't seem to know or care if there had been any damage to Senator Cade's career. Maybe today would bring the news she waited for. It wasn't a matter of *if* the tape would be released to the public; it was a matter of *when*.

Leigh swallowed a large gulp of coffee and nibbled a few bites of a bagel. She meandered over to open the outside door. Today's newspaper hadn't yet been delivered; it was the second time she'd checked for it this morning. She rubbed her eyes. She'd never gotten used to the new contacts, but they suited her well so she kept them in for vanity's sake.

Leigh switched on the television, flipping through the channels fruitlessly until at last finding what she hoped for. A black news reporter wearing too much makeup and fake hair extensions enthusiastically dramatized her scoop. Leigh reached behind herself to feel for the surface of the coffee table and planted her butt on it without letting her eyes leave the television screen.

". . . the front lawn of Senator Cade's office, where late last night, Vanessa Ellis, a former adult entertainer, marched into Senator Cade's office, pulled out a small revolver, and murdered the senator among horrified onlookers. Because Ms. Ellis had been openly dating the senator for some time, Senator Cade's security staff was caught off guard by the violent assault. Chaos had already engulfed the senator's office just hours before, when a secret video was aired on local news stations that clearly exposed the senator in a compromising position with a confirmed stripper, outraging the public that had just voted him into office. The video was released late last evening, after its authenticity was verified and it was suitably altered for public viewing. In subsequent questioning of Ms. Ellis, she admitted that it was viewing this edited videotape last night that spurred her to commit this horrific act. She claims to have mistakenly believed that the video was of a recent event, and that the senator was being unfaithful to her after she had changed her life for him. She states that it was only after committing the crime that she came to realize that the video was of herself and the senator, recorded months ago without her knowledge or consent when she was still in the adult entertainment business. Ms. Ellis is reported to be both shocked and horrified that she killed the man she loved and intended to marry."

Leigh clicked off the television.

Although it had never been her intention for James to die, she couldn't say she was upset. James had been a manipulator all his life, and she believed his selfish behavior had finally caught up with him. Vanessa's evil character had emerged once again, bringing more demise and destruction. It was a deserving ending for both, Leigh concluded.

Leigh kicked up her feet onto the break table of Cream. She wore exquisite stiletto heels that made her legs look decadent. She reveled in the fact that she made more money in her new profession than she would have had she opened her own psychiatric practice. She'd used everything she learned from her psychology classes to create a successful new career. At this rate, she could retire young and settle down with someone who'd appreciate having a private dancer of his—or her—own.

Maybe one of those leering faces in the darkness on that bleak day months ago was one of her regulars now. She didn't know, and honestly didn't care. She had power over all of them now, not the other way around. She didn't have to live in fear of exposure. Rather, she chose to embrace it.

A knock on the door disturbed her reverie. Leigh reluctantly pulled her robe closed around her body and the red silk corset she wore, then stretched gently before welcoming her visitor. It was early yet for her dancers to show up, so she wondered who it could be.

On the concrete stairs stood a mousy, impossibly young waif dressed in a sweatshirt and jeans holding a copy of the day's newspaper. Leigh made a mental note to tell the paperboy to throw it all the way to the door next time; she couldn't be expected to walk across the lot to fetch it every morning. Leigh took the paper from the girl, but suddenly felt more interested in the young, feminine visitor than in the scandal the paper reported.

The young girl pushed her thick-rimmed glasses farther up her nose and addressed Leigh. "Excuse me. My name is Audrey Lang. I'm a sociology student at USC. I'm wondering if someone here would be willing to help me with a little research?"

The ingenue possessed a superior air, as if she was above coming into a club like Cream, as if she thought she was about to interview a subspecies of humanity and probably turn in a ridiculing report to her professor. Leigh winked at the young girl. "You've come to just the right person. I'll teach you everything you need to know."

As she led the girl inside, she asked, "How about a drink to help you relax?"

Committed

Jeff Gelb

It's true I have commitment problems; always have. What red-blooded heterosexual male doesn't? It's like Jack Nicholson said in *Cuckoo's Nest*: he was great unless he saw pussy, and then he just hadda go for it. Man, can I relate.

I'm George, but of course, you knew that already, didn't you? I live in L.A. and I don't care who calls Las Vegas the "Sin City." I'm here to tell you it doesn't hold a candle to L.A., city of wet dreams. Massage parlors in every neighborhood are thinly disguised as "Oriental Therapy" locations. Yeah, and the therapy begins when the cute little Asian honey gets you behind closed doors and says, "I fuck you very much."

And then there are the strip clubs. I've been going to strip clubs since the days when all the girls did was take their clothes off onstage. Now they take you in a semi-private room and sit on your face.

But why go out at all? The Internet has all the porn the human brain can handle and then some. Thousands of sites where the female human anatomy is reduced to a few square inches of flesh-colored pixels, on display for the erotic entertainment of half the world's population.

Or there are the free L.A. newspapers that carry page after page of ads for hometown honeys who will come to your own house or apartment and give you a "complete nude rubdown," meaning you're both nude, and she promises "total relief." Make that "total release" and you've got truth in advertising.

I should know—I've done all of that stuff and then some. There's only one problem—I'm married. And I'd do anything for Shelly: lie in front of a train, jump off a bridge. She's an angel. But somehow my dick also wants to play devil. Often. Too often. You guys get what I'm saying, right?

Women wouldn't understand that, but women just don't understand the male mind. How can they? They don't have dicks! I swear my dick has a brain of its own. Someone called it the "little brain" but they were wrong—most of the time it's much bigger than my other brain. My dick gets its way more often than I want it to. But I'm not schizo, I promise. Just a normal guy. And that's where my problem started.

One thing I never did was to have an affair—I mean a real affair, where you get to know someone, buy them dinners and presents, get involved with their lives. Ultimately, you make a real commitment to them. Who needs a second "relationship" when he's already got one waiting for him at home? So I never fucked around at work. Until three months ago.

Barbara and Renee. How to describe them? Well, my first impression of them was when I was grabbing a cup of coffee in the company lunchroom. They walked in together, chatting. One was pretty and the other was gorgeous. Barbara was the ultimate girl-next-door who babysat your kids while you spent the evening wondering what she looked like naked. She'd never make the cover of *Glamour* or *Mademoiselle*, but call it pheromones or whatever, she was sexy in a way I couldn't put my hands on, but sure wished I could.

Renee was more exotic, with huge eyes that you could drown in, long brown hair, and great breasts tucked into a white blouse I swore I could see through. But I tried desperately not to notice. She looked wholly unapproachable, so far above my level of experience that I couldn't imagine what I could even say to her to capture her attention. But I decided to try my luck nonetheless.

"Ladies, are you lost? The bank's on the first floor." Barbara laughed, a very pleasant melodic sound, while Renee just looked at me. I've seen friendlier cobras.

"Actually we're new here. We both started today," Barbara explained, offering her warm hand. I shook it and offered my hand to Renee, but she looked at it like it was my dick or something. It figured. What an ice queen. Definitely not my type.

"I'm Barbara," the nice one announced, "and this is Renee."

"George Bennett," I enthused. "Where are your offices, ladies?"

This time Renee took the lead. "Why, George, I think our offices are right next to yours. Aren't you the guy with all the old movie posters on your wall? I saw you this morning when I came in. You were on the phone. What do you do here?"

"Oh, I'm one of the sales reps. You know, the king of snacks and beverages." I shrugged, embarrassed that at age forty-three I had nothing more to show for myself than being another phone sales guy for a company that serviced vending machines in office lunchrooms. A very small cog in a very big wheel. "And you?"

"We work for Brenner."

"The boss? Both of you?"

Barbara again: "Well, you know Marla, his assistant, just left for maternity leave."

Renee: "He told us he plans to expand and needs more help."

"Well, that's . . . great," I forced myself to say, thinking that Brenner had never told me he had any expansion plans. I immediately wondered if those plans included replacing me with a younger sales rep who came with a master's in Business.

Barbara smiled warmly. "I look forward to getting to know you better, George."

"Hey, thanks." I waited a second for Renee to say the same, but she had already stopped paying attention to our conversation and was slipping coins in the soft drink machine. "Well, anyway," I stammered, "I guess I better grab that coffee and get back to work."

"George?" Renee's voice was like honey, and I wanted to lick it off her tongue. I cocked an eyebrow.

"Looks like we need more Diet Cokes here," she said as she eyeballed the soda machine.

"Oh, I don't service our own machines. But I'll get someone on it right away."

"Thanks," she said, a combination of fire and ice in her voice. She was a bitch all right, but the most beautiful one I'd ever met. I wondered what she'd look like naked with my dick in her mouth. Like I'd ever know.

I retreated to my office and spent the rest of the day surfing Internet porn sites, looking for women who looked like Barbara and especially Renee. When I found a woman who actually favored Renee, though with smaller tits, I shut my office door, locked it, and jerked off onto the computer screen. It felt great, too. I wondered why I'd never done that at work before, in fact. Guess I never had the inspiration till Renee and Barbara had been hired.

As I was cleaning up, there was a knock on my office door. After quickly checking to make sure everything was back to normal, I opened the door. Surprisingly, it was Renee. She looked around. "Can I come in?"

"Sure." I let her pass me by and I caught a glimpse of her fine round ass, tight against a short skirt. I couldn't help but notice the lines of thong underwear under that skirt, and my dick trembled.

She sniffed the air. "Something smells . . . odd in here."

Oh shit, she smelled my *cum*, for chrissakes.

I laughed nervously. "Must be the spaghetti I had for lunch at my desk. I gotta empty the wastebasket." I offered her the only guest chair in my office, a threadbare thing that had never in its decades of use hosted an ass like hers. She wrinkled her nose and shook her head.

"Actually, I was wondering if you could help me hang up some paintings in my office. They're a bit heavy for me to lift."

"Oh sure," I said, glad for the chance to get out of my office before she put two and two together about the odor.

We stepped into her office and I looked around. "You know, these offices were empty for months. I should have known someone was coming, though, because I heard some guys working in here the other day. Probably painting." Sure enough, the office looked like it had recently been refurbished. Her carpet was brand new—mine was years old—and so was the massive desk in the center of the room. "They did a nice job, too," I said, feeling jealous of this woman even as I lusted after her.

I grabbed the first painting, which actually was pretty heavy, and ugly, too: some sort of modern art thing that was unidentifiable by subject and did nothing for the room but make it look as if someone had thrown up on the wall. "So where do you want this one?"

She actually touched my shoulder, an electrifying sensation. Maybe it was her perfume, which was musky and yet seductive, or maybe it was just that she was clearly the best-looking woman who had ever laid one well-groomed finger on me. I spun around as she nodded to the wall behind me. "Got it," I said as I hoisted the painting up. "Is this good?"

She looked at the wall, then at me. She took her time. I swear she was looking at my dick through my trousers, and it made me wonder if I'd dripped a bit of semen through my underwear. What in hell was I thinking, jacking off in my office? Finally she spoke. "That looks good, George. Really, really good."

I put the painting down and grabbed for the hammer and nail, but she stopped my hand. "Not just yet," she purred. Then she did a most amazing thing: she stuck her tongue in my ear, and licked it like it was full of sugar. I immediately backed away in shock, and she just laughed, then grabbed my ears and pulled my face to hers. She stuck her tongue down my throat and sucked on my lips, and I thought I'd died and gone to heaven. Finally I came up for air.

"Uh . . . thanks! To what do I owe the pleasure?"

"Are you complaining?" she said as she kicked the door to her office closed with one high heel, then kicked off the heels and went to her knees in front of me. She started unzipping me right there in her office. I looked around in a near panic, wondering if anyone in the office building across the street could see what was transpiring here. This was the stuff of dreams, not of my reality.

I thought of Shelly. I thought of the kids. I thought of Brenner and what would happen to both of us if he walked in the office just then. And I thought of this crazy bitch in front of me, about to give me head. What was I to her, anyway? Just another pushover whom she could laugh about later that night with her girlfriends?

I pulled away. Incredibly, I wriggled out of her groping hands. She gasped in surprise. "What do you think you're doing?" Obviously she wasn't used to guys stopping her when she was on her knees.

"It's just that . . ." I stuttered as I zipped up. "That is, I forgot about a dinner meeting I have for tonight."

"Are you kidding? You're putting pop and chips ahead of head and fucking?"

I edged to the door. This bitch was pressing all my buttons, and I felt like I had to get out of that room or I'd blow a gasket. "I . . . I just don't think I should be doing this with someone I work with." My hand was around the door handle as she pulled me back toward her.

"That sounds like my line, not yours. What, are you queer?"

I was speechless. No woman had ever called me gay before. I might be a lot of things, but that isn't one of them.

"You're going to say no to these?" She unbuttoned her blouse, pulled her lacy bra up, and let me glimpse the two best-looking tits I have ever eyeballed, bar none. They literally took my breath away. From somewhere a million miles away I heard her say, "I can fuck you in five ways you've never even imagined before."

"I . . . just can't," I stuttered as I rushed out of her office.

"You asshole!" she shouted from behind me as I literally ran back into my office, shutting and locking my door. My heart was pumping so fast I felt like it was about to leap through my throat. I stood against the wall facing her office and could hear her swearing. I could not understand what had just happened, but more importantly, I could scarcely believe I had finally said no to a gorgeous woman. Had I finally resolved my commitment issues? Was I actually . . . growing up? Or had she just managed to piss me off enough that my little brain short-circuited for once?

I waited until I hadn't heard a sound from her office for over half an hour before I tiptoed out of the office. I made it out of the building and to my car without seeing her. As I steered toward home, I couldn't stop my hands from shaking.

The next morning, Renee was the invisible woman. The door to her office was shut and I didn't see her in the halls or the lunchroom—thankfully.

I admit I was feeling damned good about myself. I mean, a cover girl offers to fuck me silly and I walk out. Was that really me? Of course, she had pissed me off in a way no woman had in years. Maybe that was the secret of staying committed.

I'd gone home that night and fucked the brains out of my wife; she didn't know what had hit her. I'm usually not forceful in bed, but while I was screwing Shelly, I was imagining I was doing Renee. It made for some bruises and scrapes for Shelly, who looked at me once or twice as if I was a total stranger. But

I honestly think she liked the roughhousing. And it was the only way to get Renee out of my system. I apologized to Shelly the next morning. I told her I'd gotten into a fight at work. She told me not to take it out on her like that ever again.

Shelly aside, I was feeling pretty damned good about myself that day. Thinking that maybe commitment wasn't the big issue I'd made it out to be all those years. That just because the buffet table has a gorgeous dessert doesn't mean you have to eat it, if you know it isn't gonna be good for you.

I actually walked by Renee's office at odd moments throughout the day, hoping to catch her in the hallway or at the watercooler, wanting to rub in the fact that just because she was hot as shit didn't mean she could fuck up my life. That she might be used to getting whatever she wanted, but that she didn't have that kind of control over this man. No, sir. But she wasn't around.

Barbara was, though. I met her late that afternoon on my fifth trip to the coffeemaker. She was lookin' pretty damned good, too. My dick did its little pants dance as I approached her.

"Hey," I offered tentatively.

Her smile lit up the room. "Oh, George! I'm so glad to see you!"

I was immediately suspicious. "Really?"

"It's crazy—Renee quit this morning." My eyebrows rose. "Walked right into Brenner's office and told him she couldn't work here."

My heart was trip-hammering. "Did she say why?"

"I have no idea. He closed the door after she said that. I could hear them talking through the walls, but I couldn't make out anything more. It was all very weird."

"I'll say." I was wondering whether this crazy sexual predator had talked to Brenner, or just fucked him right in his office.

"So anyway," Barbara continued breathlessly, "I'm up to my eyeballs in work, as you might imagine. And I could use a little help. . . ."

"Hanging paintings?" I smirked.

"What? No, I don't have any paintings. What do you mean?"

"Never mind. What can I do for you?"

"Well, I need some help on the invoicing process. The spreadsheets just don't have enough fields. . . ."

Where had Brenner found this girl? I mean, yeah, she was as cute as anyone I'd ever wanted to have as a girlfriend and maybe even bring home to Mom, but she obviously had more looks than brains. Still, she was a charmer. Probably didn't even know it. Some girls just have it, innately. An x-factor that exudes sexiness effortlessly. If the perfume makers could bottle it, they'd be the biggest companies in the world. Except that people would be too busy fucking to buy it.

"I'll be happy to help," I offered. She actually grabbed my hands and wrung them furiously. "Oh thank you, thank you. I want to make a good impression on Brenner. I really need this job."

"Hey, no problem. See you toward the end of the day." She thanked me again, and I went back to my office and called Shelly, told her I'd be home late, that I'd been called in to a project by Brenner. Which wasn't really a lie. Well, not much of one, anyway.

So around 5 P.M., I knocked on Barbara's half-open door. She jumped up from her desk, which I noticed was as massive as Renee's had been. Maybe she'd inherited it that morning. I looked around the sparsely furnished office. "Hey, you lied."

"What?" Her confusion was evident in her lovely green eyes as she led me to the desk.

I pointed to the wall to our left. "You do have a painting."

She rolled her eyes. "Oh, gosh, that thing? That's not mine. One of Brenner's kids did it as a school project. I think it's actually painted on glass. Can you imagine? I mean, how tacky!"

But my attention was no longer on the painting, it was on Barbara. I was reevaluating my initial impression of her. I'd begun to notice that women I wouldn't have thought were stunning in college had become much more appealing to me since then. Maybe I was starting to see their inner beauty more easily. Take Barbara for instance. She had a slight overbite, which some people might have confused for buck teeth. But I was a fan of the old movie stars, and Gene Tierney's overbite had always fascinated me. Whatever it was, I was starting to think that Barbara was, in her own way, as much of a bombshell as Renee had been. And a whole lot nicer, which went a long way in my book.

She closed the door. "I don't want Brenner to walk by and find out I don't know how to do this stuff already."

I nodded. "Shall we start on this spreadsheet problem?" I smiled as I approached her at the desk.

"Do you want to sit?" She started to rise.

"No, I'll just stand and point, and you can do the actual work. I've already put in a full day." We both smiled at that, and I demonstrated how to make the spreadsheet expand to her needs, as she *oohed* and *aahed*. As I stood over her shoulder, I couldn't help but notice the beautiful curve of her breasts under her cashmere sweater. I could even see her boobs rise and fall in time with her soft breathing as she concentrated on the computer screen in front of her pretty face. By this time, her less obvious charms had won me over completely, and I was contemplating how to get her to make the offers Renee had made next door just twenty-four hours earlier.

"So that's it," I came back to earth. "Think you've got it?"

"Yes, George, and thank you so much for your help." She touched my arm and it sent tingles straight to my dick, which started purring again. "I'm sure this is going to impress Brenner." She turned to me. "Thank you so much."

I shrugged. "Just being friendly."

She took my arm again. My dick was doing a rumba by this time. I wondered if she noticed.

"No, really," she purred. "I'd like to do something for you in return . . . buy you a drink . . . or . . ." She lowered her gaze, and

I couldn't say for sure, but it looked like she was zeroed in on my hot spot. I could hardly believe my luck. First Renee and now Barbara. I must have been dreaming—again!

Only this time it was much, much harder to say no. I mean, Barbara was so much nicer than Renee. It was obvious she really liked me. And then too, that comment Renee had made about my manhood had really pissed me off. I had to prove to myself that I was a real man.

So when Barbara reached that hot hand out and actually caressed my dick through my pants, I didn't back away.

"Is this . . . all right?" she whispered, looking up at me with those gorgeous eyes. I couldn't help but notice her face was in exactly the right place to satisfy me. I guess she noticed too, because the very next second, she must have read my mind and started to unzip me—with her teeth!

I groaned as she turned me around and pushed me down on that big desk, which was made for fucking, I realized. I let her hands push my trousers and underwear down, and then she took me into her warm, wet mouth. And took me, and took me deeper, until I was buried to the hilt in her talented mouth.

"Unbelievable," I managed. I could feel that sexy overbite grabbing my shaft, gently nibbling it up and down, up and down, until I thought I would explode. But she pulled me out of her mouth first, a small precoital bubble on her moist lips as she smiled. That had to be the sexiest smile I'd ever seen.

"And that's just for starters," she said. She cleaned off her mouth with the cuff of my shirt. "That is, unless you have to get home . . . for supper?" An eyebrow rose in question.

"Uh, no, that's okay. It's just leftovers, anyway." I didn't even know what I was saying at that point. I doubted I was making a stitch of sense, but then, neither did this entire experience. Somewhere, from about a million miles away, a tiny portion of my brain was saying, *don't go there, Bucko*. But there was way too much static in my brain just then for me to get any other message.

Then it was back to reality as Barbara pulled her soft sweater over her shoulders, and I gasped at the fact that she was not wearing a bra. I mean, I'd seen girls at fancy restaurants who were obviously braless, but I'd never thought about the women at work going braless before. What's more, Barbara's breasts were just damned perfect. It was obvious she'd never nursed a child—they were plump but firm, gravity-defying mounds with distended nipples. My hands reached out to them like magnets to steel. I actually groaned as I squeezed their soft toughness. I suppose Shelly's tits might have felt this good at one time, but it was so far in the past I couldn't recall.

"Oh God, George, that feels good. Do you want to do more?"

"Oh, yeah!" I started to pull her skirt down but she stopped me, pointing to my ring finger, arching an eyebrow.

"You . . . didn't know?" I could feel my dick complaining—I was sending it decidedly mixed messages.

"Well, I guess I assumed, but . . . well, are you sure you're okay with this?"

I started to respond and then bit my tongue. She was asking me if I was committed to my marriage. Just last night the answer had been yes. Just twenty-four hours ago! And now I was ready to pull a Jack Nicholson and just go for that pink pussy thing. Was I totally schizo or just a normal American male?

Maybe to help me decide, Barbara lifted her skirt and pulled aside the corner of her panties so I could catch a flash of things to come. So far as I could tell, she was fully shaved. It figured. And that did it.

"No. No, it's no problem. Believe me."

"I mean, I just don't want to think I talked you into doing something that would make you feel bad later. . . ."

"Hey, I'm a big boy," I said, and swung my dick at her. "Remember?"

"So you're really committed to doing this?"

She was starting to annoy me, to turn me off.

"Yes, of course! Let me prove it to you. . . ."

"Oh-kay," she said, and then she started to put her clothes back on again!

"Hey, wait, wait a minute. What'd I say?" I reached out to Barbara but she pulled away, smirking as she pulled the sweater back over her head. She turned away, facing the ugly wall painting, and said, "So, do I win?"

My dick was going through withdrawal, collapsing on itself so fast I could have been the incredible shrinking man. Suddenly the office door burst open, and in walked Renee, then Brenner, then a small army of strangers.

"What the fuck!" I shouted, as I quickly pulled my pants on. Renee gave Barbara a cool handshake and stood to one side, glowering at me. Brenner's face showed nothing but scorn, while the strangers approached me with video cameras, their tiny red lights announcing that they were capturing this entire scene for some kind of perverse posterity.

"Did you film . . . film us?" I looked again at the glass painting and realized that it was undoubtedly a two-way mirror. I'd been victimized by some crazed porn videographers. "If this is a sexual harassment thing, I've been set up."

Brenner snorted. "Not at all. Fact is, you just won $25,000."

And then Barbara planted a smooch on my cheek. "And I just won $100,000 thanks to you, Georgie Porgie!"

Then a guy with dark glasses and a goatee stepped out from behind one of the cameramen and offered his hand. I ignored it. He looked vaguely familiar, but I couldn't place him.

"Allen Everett," he announced, like I should be proud to meet him.

"I . . . I don't understand." My vision was blurring, my head pounding. I felt like I'd stepped into an insane alternate dimension, a *Twilight Zone* with tits.

"Allen Everett, from the cable TV hit *Are You Committed?* Surely you watch it? Well, George, I want to congratulate you—you win $25,000 for getting to round two of the show."

He turned to Renee. "Sorry, doll, but you didn't make it all the way to the grand prize. But you do get $50,000, and that ain't hay!" He turned back to me. "But tell me, George, just how did you do it? I mean, half of the free world would screw Renee in a second. What's your secret? And why did you pick Barbara? America—and the world—wants to know . . . in fact, needs to know!" The room broke into laughter.

All I could do was shake my head. What in hell was he saying? I felt like I was having a heart attack and a stroke at the same time.

The goatee guy was still yapping. ". . . would you like to say to your wife, George? I'm sure she's watching. In fact, we called her about fifteen minutes ago to tell her to turn on her TV."

"You . . . can't run this on TV. . . . And anyway, I'll sue. . . ."

"You can't sue, George. You weren't coerced into anything. We have it all on camera. Great head, by the way, sweetie," Goatee said as he turned to Barbara, who blushed a royal shade of red. She couldn't look me in the eyes anymore. "Good thing we're on pay-per-view, where people can see all that fine oral action. In fact, that's what they're paying extra for!"

"No," I stammered. "My wife . . . my kids . . . my career . . . you people can't do this to me."

Goatee man smiled. "We can't? George, it's already done. We're live, baby, throughout America and, thanks to our Web site, the entire world. And anyway, are you kidding? George, you're a superstar, baby! Why, right now, millions of folks know just how big your dick is—you're gonna get more pussy than Mel Gibson ever did." Goatee man turned back to face the camera. "Next week, be sure to watch as we travel to another secret city, and choose another lucky bastard like George, who could just be you!" He pointed at the cameras and winked lasciviously.

Then he took my hand and shook it limply. "Thanks, George, for being on the most popular reality TV show ever—*Are You Committed?*"

* * *

And that's how it happened, as best as I can remember. You know the rest. It's a blur to me, but I've seen the same footage you have. How I took Everett by the neck and squeezed till he turned blue, then kicked him in the nuts and tossed him through the window. How a cameraman rushed to lean out the window to catch his entire fall to the concrete, seven floors below. How the girls all screamed and fled the room, and then the other guys either fought me or ran from me for their lives. How I killed another one of them before they were able to subdue me. Just about tore his head off, I hear. How they drugged me, tried me, ultimately brought me here.

The wife split, of course. The kids won't talk to me. Sure, Brenner lost his gig in the process, but I hear he's writing his memoirs. He'll do all right. Probably fucking Barbara on the side, right about now. Or Renee even.

They tell me if I ever get out of here, I'm gonna be a rich man. That $25,000 is still waiting for me. And my lawyers made the TV networks cough up a million to run the footage of me killing Everett and the other guy. You know how it was eventually repackaged on DVD and sold over seven million copies. I really do have the most famous dick in the world now.

Of course, I don't see myself getting out of here anytime soon. People think I'm way too dangerous. I don't know, maybe they're right. Truth is, I'm still kind of in a haze about the whole thing, or maybe it's the drugs they force down my throat every few hours.

Yeah, I've had my troubles with commitment my entire adult life. But I finally have made it past that issue. Now, when I can think straight, when I can talk, when they let me out of this straitjacket so I can get some exercise once a day in this shithole of an asylum, it's true:

I am well and truly, finally, fully committed.

Okay—so did I give you enough for the Special Edition DVD?

The Last Man on Earth

Marv Wolfman

He screamed as the first needle bore through his right index finger, cutting deep until it hit bone. He struggled, trying to pull free from the steel restraining bonds, but all his writhing made the next needle crack his left index finger in half before recalibrating itself for a second try. He fainted long before the final six needles took their positions. Kate smiled.

What can I tell you about my former boss? Let's start with the obvious. Kenneth Diller was handsome, Tom Cruise handsome, when there still was a Tom Cruise, back before The Change. Thick black hair. Chiseled chin. Incredible eyes so blue you wanted to swim in them. Broad shoulders. And an ass that . . . okay, when I saw him that first time, yeah, I would've bedded him in a second, had I been given a chance, which I wasn't, so it's moot.

Ken had been born to wealth; his grandmother was involved with the invention of something that made the catalytic converter work, and her patents made each of her six husbands multimillionaires at a time when a million dollars was more than a down payment for a three bedroom fixer-upper. Ken's father, Josiah, inherited his mother's scientific acumen, and most certainly passed it down to his son, who tripled the family fortune before he turned eighteen.

Way back then, in the days when there was still a choice, you'd bet your life savings that Ken would be pursued by anything with breasts, and not an inconsiderable contingent without. He was handsome. Brilliant. Rich. Everything anyone could ask for. Hell, with a multibillion-dollar empire, he could have been a ninety-nine-year-old incontinent prune and still get every Barbie wanna-be to hike up her skirt and stick his shriveled stem anyplace he wanted it stuck.

Except he had a problem: Ken Diller was a major asshole the likes of which had not been seen before. Ken was cruel to everyone he met, and doubly nasty to women, specifically. He thought of us the way children think of ant farms; we were mindless beings there for his pleasure only.

Women he thought too ugly to sneeze on got off easy. He ignored them.

Ordinary women got the brunt of his tactless behavior. To start off, he'd insult their looks, move on to their intelligence, their behavior and their very reason to exist. If they weren't reduced to tears, he'd continue his relentless assault.

It wasn't as if Ken was purposely being mean—that was a by-product—Ken honestly believed these women, and most of the men he knew, too, were too stupid to live and needed his help to make them better. They weren't supposed to take his criticisms as criticisms, but as guides. If they reacted badly because of something he said, it was their fault, not his. He was simply trying to help them.

Beautiful women, who were the only ones he'd consider dating, got it the worst. Like a Patriot missile, he'd target in on any perceived flaw and go for the kill.

Here are a few examples of the wit and wisdom of His Assholiness.

To Mona M., the stunning trophy wife of a Fortune 500 CEO, who climbed into his bed after seeing his *60 Minutes* interview: "Your nipples are making me nauseous."

To Laurel B., the gorgeous movie star recently cast as the lead in the remake of *10*: "Tighten your muscles, goddammit. You're like the Grand Canyon down there."

To JoAnn W., voted "Sexiest Woman of the Century" by *People* magazine: "Is that cellulite?"

Most recently, to Serena G., a sexoholic so committed to her constitutionally protected pursuit of happiness that she's listed in the travel guidebooks as the number one theme park ride in thirty-seven states. In the oldest cliché of all time, Serena saw him across a crowded room. They were at a charity event for Children with Small Heads, or something equally *who cares*. All eyes watched Serena weave through the crowd, her hair flowing in slow motion. She smiled at him. Ken whispered something in her ear. At first, it didn't register, but five seconds later, her eyes bugged out like a cartoon coyote. She stood shaking, her body spasming as she tried to bring voice to her sudden outrage.

"I wouldn't fuck you if you were the last man on earth!" she finally screamed, slapping him as hard as she could before running from the room. Rumor has it Serena is now living a quiet life in Bolivia, although the sheep she tends occasionally notice her breaking into uncontrollable sobbing.

Despite his angelic looks and bottomless wealth, if you were born with more than a hint of estrogen, Ken would somehow do something that would invariably make you say, "I wouldn't fuck you if you were the last man on earth," usually just before slapping him in the face, kneeing him in the balls, or just screaming at him at the top of your lungs. Never were women more drawn to someone who was able to repel them so quickly and so thoughtlessly.

You'd think the constant rejection, not to mention the bruised balls, would eventually teach him a lesson. You'd think.

If someone told him what a shit he'd been, Ken assumed it was their problem, not his. It's not as if Ken didn't get his rocks buffed; his looks, wealth and intelligence usually distracted his victims for at least one good roll. It's after sex that "Evil Ken" emerged, saying something so revoltingly nasty and personal that any thoughts of being Mrs. Billionaire fled from the mind of even his most avaricious pursuer.

I never had the joy of saying what I thought of him, but only because I didn't fit his paradigm for what he considered fuckable. The first thing he ever told me was that my breasts were too small. Conversely, my ass, he insisted, was too big. My arms were much too flabby, he said, pinching them to prove his point, and my nose was hooked somewhat where, he gleefully pointed out, it should have been little more than a button tip like some demented 1920s Kewpie doll.

I asked him why he was telling me this when I was in his office for a job interview and not a date, and his answer so perfectly summed up his personality that you'll have no question as to why I did what I did, drastic as it may seem. He said, and I quote, "You need to know up front you're not very attractive and therefore I won't be interested in you. If I give you this job, we'll have a working relationship only." That was how our "relationship" began and, had I not desperately needed the job, that was how it should have ended.

I went to Harvard with a major in medical research and graduated near the top of my class with a master's and, less than two years later, a doctorate. I was going to find the cure for cancer. I had reasoned, correctly, that rather than try to kill cancer cells with radiation or chemotherapy, I should instead prevent cancer cells from growing in the first place. The cells leech onto blood vessels and feed off them, gaining strength while they grow and duplicate. If I could kill their ability to feed, the cell would wither and die before it was able to split and multiply. I found a desperate patient who agreed to be my test subject. I focused my lasers into his left ventricle, intending to sever the connection between the offending cell and its food, and instead accidentally severed his heart—into three parts.

Others have since proven my theory, but that didn't give me comfort when the medical review board determined that though I was not financially liable for my patient's death—he had signed all the necessary insurance waivers releasing me from potential lawsuits—I was guilty of gross negligence (their words) and recommended that I be fired from the hospital. Because no other hospital would then hire me, I was put into the position of becoming a lowly, underpaid assistant. I think knowing I had no other possibilities pleased Ken. Power is as power does, after all. Still, as he was to learn, though perhaps not the genius he was, I was not without certain abilities myself.

It took three of them to move him off the ground and into the Plexiglas container that four other women had wheeled into position. The container was built to handle the cables that would be inserted through its predrilled holes. Each cable was attached to a separate sensor that was stuck along the length of his body, starting with the top of his head, which had been crudely shaved and showed the roughness of his impromptu haircut with a dozen or so crisscross cuts that bled from the back of his neck and across the top of his scalp. The sensors in place, the women allowed themselves a moment to take in their handiwork. He'd killed more than three billion men in fewer days than God had taken to create them. Even if this wasn't some sort of biblical retribution, it was a beginning.

"Katherine," he said to me the Friday before The Change, his tone perceptibly more somber than usual, "is it the lower testosterone count that makes women irrational, or are all of you just nuts?" I shot him one of my eye-squinting glances, as I usually did when he started off on another insane rant, but, as usual, said nothing. I was almost out of debt and another six months would give me enough of a cushion to quit.

But Ken didn't continue. He looked at me, as if expecting an answer, and after a few very long moments, the awkward silence became uncomfortably palpable. There was something about his tone and look that made me think he was trying to pose a question but didn't know how to actually engage a woman he didn't want to have sex with in conversation. I finally spoke.

"What do you mean?"

"In science," he started, "when we perform an experiment and our expectations are not realized, we learn from our mistakes and try something different. There are no recriminations, no agonizing over what should have been. We don't personalize our failure. We just move on."

I wondered where this was going. Ken had never asked my opinion on anything personal before. Our discussions were limited to "We need a redesign on the catheter gauge. Get on it," or "The image converter requires recalibration. Handle it." When we talked, or actually, when he decided to spout his views on whatever flitted through his mind, it wasn't so much a conversation as a polemic.

"So?" I said, for once curious.

"Science deals in absolutes. There is nothing personal about the scientific method. You either achieve results or you don't. In pure science, we don't worry about the niceties of language or if we're offending someone by being honest in addressing those absolutes."

"And . . ." I said, trying to force his point.

"Last night, I went out with, what's her name? Shit, what is—? Damn. Oh, fuck it, it doesn't matter."

"Princess Laureline?" I kept his calendar. "From Belgium."

"Laureline. She was acceptably beautiful."

"Of course."

"After an hour or so, I came to believe she was something, I don't know, something else, something more than what I had seen before. Most women I've known have no ability to deal with honesty, being too caught up with who they are to deal with what they could do to improve themselves."

I sat down. This could take a while.

"Women take criticism personally, instead of just dealing with it and moving on. Facts are facts and arguing about them doesn't change them. But, ummm . . ."

"Laureline."

"Right. She laughed. She was funny. She was actually smart. She was . . . different. More like you, you know, intelligent, only beautiful."

He was annoying me again.

"We talked most of the night, and then I said it was time to fuck, and, I don't know, but something changed between us."

"I can't imagine why."

"You, too? I said I'd invested, at that point, about five hours with her and now it was time to—"

"I get it. And she said . . . ?"

"I wouldn't fuck you—"

"—If you were the last man on earth." I knew the drill.

"She suddenly became every other woman I'd ever gone out with."

He paused, searching for the right words.

"They all say the same thing: 'I wouldn't fuck you if you were the last man on earth.' It's hard to admit this, but that's been happening a lot lately. Is there an e-mail chain letter I don't know about that's being sent to women ordering them to tell me that in the possibility that every other man in the world suddenly disappeared, I still wouldn't get lucky?"

I shook my head. "No idea. My cable modem's down."

"Anyway, I couldn't sleep. My mind kept rehashing the problem. What was wrong with them? What? Was? Wrong? With? *Them?* Then, about five this morning, I got it. Testosterone."

Testosterone is produced in the testicles and responsible for reproduction and the development of secondary sex characteristics. Where women have estrogen, also a steroid hormone, men have testosterone. I couldn't wait to see where he was going with this.

"Men are logical. Women obviously are not. Men confront a problem head-on. Women skirt around said problem. Men can be instructed and then move on without feeling inferior. You can't talk to a woman without having them break out in tears. What's the difference between men and women? Testosterone.

"Women," he went on, "want men who are more like them. Weak, emotional and unpredictable. If they could isolate our testosterone, I honestly believe they would find a way to replace it with estrogen and create a new sex, a physical male with female emotions. Hell, those are the only kind of men they want to fuck these days anyway."

"Or," I said, making the fatal mistake of not realizing he was being serious, "you could find a way to target testosterone, yourself excluded, of course, and get rid of the competition."

His eyes glazed over. "They keep saying they wouldn't fuck me if I was the last man on earth. But if I actually *was* . . ."

He stopped talking. For once. He sat quietly in his lab chair for the rest of the afternoon and was still focused somewhere beyond the rainbow when it came time for me to leave for the weekend. I didn't bother saying good-bye.

I met Charles, my boyfriend, for dinner. We went back to his place, watched some TV, had sex, and then went to sleep. We woke up Saturday morning, screwed each other's brains out again, then fell back to sleep. We woke up around eleven, cuddled until noon, and finally dragged ourselves out of bed by one. The rest of the day was a blur. On Sunday, we went to a street festival, ate greasy food that in no way was any good for us, saw a movie, and got a late dessert before heading back to his place. We were both too tired to do anything more than spoon and fell asleep locked together. There'd be time for sex in the morning.

If only I knew then what I know now.

* * *

Kate made an indelicate incision into his balls and inserted the electrodes, one into each. She then attached them to the tube which had been roughly fitted over his dick. He was still unconscious. Lila made certain the wiring was properly connected, as per instructions, while Angel checked the electrocardiograph. Joline and Bethany watched and waited. It wouldn't be long now.

I woke up Monday morning alone in bed. Charles, I assumed, must have gone to work early. So much for sex. I took a long, hot shower, found something to wear in his closet, got into my car, turned on the new Annie Lennox CD and drove to work. Along the way, I saw hundreds of panicking women rushing down streets, shouting for something, but I couldn't make out what. I turned off the CD, which automatically changed my radio to an AM all-news station. Instead of Charles Kurtz, the normal morning news anchor, there was a woman I'd never heard of before giving the news. She sounded confused and agitated.

"Unconfirmed reports, from here in the U.S. and as far away as Asia, Europe, South America, and Africa, are coming in that the male race has somehow disappeared from the face of our planet. . . ."

I rolled down my car window and heard the women outside calling out names: "Peter!" "John!" "Brad!" The women were panicking. I closed the car window and turned up the radio.

". . . Martha Anderson, assistant press secretary for President Darnell, has refused to comment on the rumor that the disappearance also includes the President, Vice President, and most of the Senate and Congress. 'There is no reason to panic,' Anderson said, her voice quivering as she read the press report. 'The situation will be dealt with. If terrorists are behind this, we will respond with the full power of our armed forces.'" Which,

I immediately thought, was probably fewer than ten thousand women, few of whom had had any combat experience.

Ahead of me, three out-of-control cars collided with each other. Within thirty seconds, more than sixty cars were jammed into the intersection, gridlocking traffic in all directions. I could make out only women sitting behind the steering wheels, and for the first time I began to panic as well.

Two thoughts suddenly collided. The first was *I wouldn't fuck you if you were the last man on earth.* The second was *Kenneth Diller.* Somehow, the bastard did it. I got out of the car, pushed my way through the tangle of frightened women, and ran the mile and a half to the office.

I found Ken in his chair, feet up on his desk, his fingers locked behind his head, watching a bank of computer monitors on which were Internet feeds from around the world, each reporting on the male crisis. "What the hell did you do?" I shouted.

As he kept watching the monitors, a crooked smile snaked across his face. "Why do you think I did anything?" he asked, trying to feign innocence.

"Because you're the only goddamn man left on the planet. What the hell did you do?"

"I got rid of the competition."

Ken explained that he spent most of Friday night thinking about what I had jokingly suggested.

On Saturday, in a frenzy of enthusiastic genius, Ken discovered a way to synthesize an airborne genetic bacteria that targeted testosterone above a certain count. He unleashed it Saturday evening. By Sunday night, it had targeted 95 percent of the men in the world.

Within three hours, most of those men quietly disintegrated. By morning, 99 percent of the men and 8 percent of the women—all of whom had a higher than female average testosterone level—also disintegrated. Ken, of course, had taken the antidote.

It was, bizarrely and unexpectedly, as simple as that. Within a week, Ken was The Last Man on Earth.

He awoke to find himself strapped in the Plexiglas tube, wires and sensors rubbing against every uncomfortably naked part of him. He saw what he thought to be several hundred women sitting in bleacher seats, popcorn in hand, waiting for the evening's entertainment to start. Serena was in the second row next to Mona. Audrey was in front, chatting with Cathy and Simone. Ken saw Katherine walk out from behind a large machine. "Good morning, Ken." Kate talked for a few minutes more, her fingers dancing across the overly large red button that was in the center of her remote control. Done, she smiled warmly at him. "You fucked us, and now we're going to fuck you."

The first two weeks after The Change consisted primarily of panic, but I was surprised how quickly the remaining politicians did what was needed to organize what was left of the armed forces to work alongside the smattering of policewomen to keep the peace. Riots were quelled by the end of the first month. Hospitals were still staffed, though operating at reduced efficiency. The biggest problem we had was in the delivery of food and other necessities, but even this was solved by week five, after enough women had been taught how to drive the massive sixteen-wheelers that had been abandoned on highways when their drivers suddenly vanished. We did our best to get back into a routine, knowing full well that if we didn't, the rest of what we now called the world would continue its slide into hell.

Intellectually, we didn't miss the men all that much, but two problems did crop up that should have been expected. The first was we were getting horny. There were alternatives, of course, but most of us weren't willing to go there. Yet. Also, God knows they were always pains in the ass, but, dammit, men answered some manner of emotional need we didn't know we had.

Ken was counting on both these problems to solve his own.

It was at the beginning of month two that he announced himself to the world, actually explaining what he did and why he did it. He figured the basic concept of supply and demand would overwhelm any moral indignation.

"Get over your problems, ladies," he told his TV audience. "Since I'm the only hope the world has to repopulate the species, here's my plan. To create a more beautiful world, I intend to bed only the world's most beautiful women. I know what you're thinking: Is that fair? Probably not, but there's only one of me and four-plus billion of you, so why should I accept anything less than the best of the best? Genes will out."

I have to assume at least half the television sets across the world were turned off that instant, but that still left more than two billion potential listeners. If only one half of one percent of those women fit Ken's requirements, that would mean he still had over one million choices, which was approximately nine hundred thousand more women than even he could service at an average of five a day for the next fifty years.

If he thought you were beautiful, and you cared about the world, and if you were horny enough to do it with him, you couldn't turn him down. Ken was right. Supply and demand. He was going to get everything he wanted.

Ken asked me to come back to work to help keep his schedule straight. I didn't want to, but there's something about a train wreck that fascinates the magpie in me. Also, being in the backseat of history was too great an opportunity to turn down. One way or another, I was going to be there to not only witness the birth of a new world, but also its conception.

For the first few weeks, Ken was almost a gracious paramour. Maybe it's because he got exactly what he wanted. The women he chose were beyond beautiful. I was getting horny helping them fill out their applications. On day one, Ken had sex with twelve different beauties. They must have exhausted him, because on day two he was only able to bed down five. Day three provided him with nine women, including a set of triplets and a mother-daughter team.

Ken wasn't a bigot, which was in his favor and increased the number of women he'd have sex with. The girls could be white, black, Oriental, whatever, and none of it mattered as long as they were flawless. I was astonished at how many perfect bodies there were out there. They'd sit straight up in the waiting room, backs arched, hair thick and flowing, wide-eyed, full-lipped, their pert breasts jutting out, firm and perfectly shaped, waists ridiculously tiny, leading to perfect asses and well-formed legs. They casually chatted with each other, as if waiting for their turn to have sex with someone they didn't even know was something they had done every day of their lives. In some cases, I'm sure that was probably true.

For the majority, however, they felt very alone and wanted to be held for a short while, and, in nine months, have a baby, preferably male, to help repopulate the planet. I wanted to hate them for looking the way they did, but most of them honestly believed what they were doing was the right thing. Unfortunately, I couldn't disagree. I missed Charles a lot, but even knowing him as I did, Ken was almost starting to look like a halfway acceptable substitute, not that I'd ever be invited to share his bed. My breasts were definitely not perfectly pert.

Something happened halfway through month two. According to my figures, Ken had had sex with 212 women in the first six weeks. The novelty was either wearing off or, given his wide choice, he was becoming pickier. By the end of the month, Ken reverted to form. No longer gracious, he'd berate the girls' looks—how that was even possible I couldn't understand; at worst they were absolutely perfect. He'd complain about their personalities, tell them they were lousy in bed, and, in general, reduce them to tears.

"God, you are a pig," he told Felicia K.

"Do something. Don't just lie there," he told Anja W.

"Anyone ever teach you how to fuck?" he asked Marika J.

Even as he ground his way into their loins, he'd tell them there were a million more just like them and if they didn't please him exactly the way he wanted to be pleased, he'd have no problem finding ten more to take their place.

"I'm the goddamn last man on earth!" he screamed at them. "You. Will. Fucking. Do. What. I. Fucking. Say."

By month three, the word on him had gotten out, and only a few women continued to show up for their twenty minutes of emotionless penetration. Most still wanted to save the world, but not this way, and certainly not with him. Still, even a few women out of a million were enough to provide him with two or more girls a day, every day. If he had to do the same one twice, so be it.

By the end of month four, the constant flow of females was reduced to a sporadic trickle. Ken actually had days with no sex at all.

"Find someone with some brains," he ordered me. "I am so goddamn sick of talking to morons." Despite this, most of the women had actually been, surprisingly enough, college graduates, and as I got to know them, almost none were remotely stupid. Needy perhaps, but not dumb. But I diligently poured through my database and found enough women who had gone through grad school to please him, I calculated, to the end of the year.

But, of course, that didn't help. Ken continued to scream at the women, berating them for any imagined slight or nonexistent imperfection. He never cared if any of them ever had an orgasm; he was solely concerned about his own.

It wasn't long before he began to hurt them physically as well as emotionally.

He hit them and humiliated them, all the while knowing they would still have to do everything he told them, or they, not he, would be responsible for the extinction of the human race.

As long as the women had wanted to have sex with him, I may not have approved but I wasn't about to interfere. But not now.

"I quit," I told him.

"You can't. Everything in this world is about me, remember? You will do what I tell you to do."

"Screw you."

"In your dreams."

I stared at him for what seemed forever, growing angrier even as his smile grew broader. Finally, I forced myself to calm down and then, very quietly and matter-of-factly, said to him, "Ken, please listen to me and understand that what I'm about to say I mean with every fiber of my being. Ken, I wouldn't fuck you if you were the last man on earth."

With that, as they say, I turned on my heels and left, and I didn't look back.

But that wasn't the end of it. There were a half-dozen women waiting their turn in the lobby, and I stopped to talk to them. I reminded them what he had done to other women and tried to explain why they shouldn't let him do the same to them, but I was sure I lost them when Ken opened the door, saw me standing there and said, "I'll fuck all you girls together right now. C'mon."

The women started to obey, but they hesitated when they saw me blocking their way.

They looked at him. They looked at me. They looked at him. He was offering to hold them. He would fulfill their needs. He was the hope for the future, and I was just some embittered horny bitch who was standing in their way.

"Move it, you bitches, or I'll call in the next crew of sluts," he threatened.

And that's when they surprised me: They followed me out the door.

Ken screamed at us, "Go ahead. Go, but you'll be back." We kept walking.

"You need me!" he shouted. "Go ahead. Fuck each other if you think that'll get you off, but in a month you'll come crawling back. You need a man, you fucking bitches. I'm the only hope the world has!"

It was the hardest thing we ever did, but we kept walking.

Ken didn't have sex for the next four weeks, but he knew it would only be a matter of time before the women would cave in and rush back to him, pleading with him to do anything he wanted.

Adora Kant was, before The Change, known throughout the world as the supermodel of supermodels. They hung her calendar on walls throughout Europe. The Japanese worshipped her. They thought she was a goddess in Africa and Asia. South America would buy anything that had her picture on it. In America, they paid fortunes for her old underwear on eBay. Men were known to jump out windows to get her attention. Women were known to strip naked in her presence, praying she was secretly gay. Adora Kant was *this close* to being declared a universal goddess.

Adora Kant made her way through the city to Ken Diller's estate. She announced that she could no longer be without a man and that she needed sex now, and lots of it.

For his part, Ken had been prepared to bed down with a pig. There were still plenty of them anxious to do him. But to have sex with Adora Kant would be a double coup. The first was obvious: she was beyond perfection. The second was that sex with her would be telling all the other women that it was useless to resist him. If Adora Kant needed him, how could they pretend otherwise? The line of horny women going to his mansion would stretch from New York to Colorado.

Ken started to undress, but Adora stopped him.

"I want sex," she said, "but I need it to be in public. Public sex is dangerous, and dangerous sex makes me hot. And when

I'm hot, my love, you will never experience anything better. That's a promise."

Ken was torn. His swollen dick was pressing against his pants, hungry for immediate release. But, to have sex with Adora Kant, and to do it while the world watched what they were missing would give him incredible power. "Where do you want to do it?" he stammered. It was getting difficult to talk.

"Yankee Stadium. I always wanted to be fucked on home plate. With the cameras rolling. Will you fuck me there, Ken, dear? On home plate?"

It wasn't as if Ken had any choice.

It had been eight months since anyone had played ball in Yankee Stadium. Eight months since The Change. Ken showed up at six o'clock, as Adora requested. On her side, she had already made certain that the cameras were ready to film the fuck of the century and that it would be broadcast live around the world. Ken could barely contain himself.

Adora, dressed in a filmy robe, her hard nipples clearly visible, stepped onto the field. On first base, she edged her robe off her shoulders, exposing them. On second base, she lowered it some more, revealing her breasts. As she rounded third base, she dropped her robe completely.

Ken had never seen anything like her before. She was the perfection he'd been seeking all his life. Adora Kant was everything he ever wanted, and she was there, demanding to have him.

She made her way to home, hunkered down on the plate and undid his belt. He was afraid he'd blow his wad even before she could lower his pants, but somehow he held himself together. She took off his boxers and for a moment caressed his dick with both hands. He wanted to explode, but he also knew this wasn't the time. "Wait until you're inside her," he kept telling himself.

"I want to be on top," she said. He nodded, no longer able to speak.

He lay down across home plate.

"Stretch your arms out," she told him. He didn't argue. "And now your legs. Stretch them as far apart as possible." He looked at her, confused. She smiled and swept her tongue across her moist lips. He did what she said.

She leaned over him, her breasts barely brushing his chest. She reached out and grabbed both of his wrists and moved them just a bit. They were in place. Her legs pressed against his. They were in place as well.

"Now," she said.

"Now?" he asked.

"Now," she smiled.

Suddenly, she lifted steel clamps from the dirt and locked them around his wrists and then his ankles, pinning him into place. He was surprised, but what the hell, he thought. She said she liked it dangerous. Then she got up off him.

"What are you doing? I'm ready. I can't wait. I'm ready now."

Adora smiled at him. "Are you joking, Ken, dear? I wouldn't fuck you if you were the last man on earth."

He screamed at her, "What the hell are you doing?"

That was pretty much the reaction I expected. I prayed the home audience enjoyed it as much as I did.

As she walked off, Ken saw me, Mona, Laurel, and two hundred or so other women make their way from the dugouts to sit in the bleachers. He struggled, but the steel bonds held firm. I kneeled beside him and checked the clamps. "You're not going anywhere, boss," I said.

"What are you doing? Let me out of here." He was nervous, but not yet afraid. That would come soon enough.

While I drilled insertion holes into his fingers and toes, and placed the wire sensors inside, Angelica shaved his head, nicking him a goodly number of times. Ken had passed out, but his body spasmed with every new cut. He was moved into a Plexiglas chamber, where more wires were attached to him. I attached the sensors which had been fitted in his balls to the tube surrounding his dick. We were nearly ready.

Ken woke to see Joline with a handheld video camera aimed at his genitals. "Ready for your close-up?"

He tried to break free, but the Plexiglas container held him firmly in place. "What are you doing? Let me go."

I patted his head. "Good morning, Ken," I said. Joline turned the camera toward me. This was it. Showtime.

"Women of the world," I began, "the Bible starts with Genesis, and the words 'In the beginning, God created the heaven and the earth,' but that isn't the part of the Holy Book I want to recall now. I prefer a less passive quote. One from Deuteronomy, actually. 'Life for life, eye for eye, tooth for tooth, hand for hand, foot for foot.'"

Ken began to thrash about in the container, desperately trying to break free. I smiled at him. "Don't be a pussy, Ken. Despite the fact that you humiliated nearly all the women here personally, and let's not forget that you murdered three hundred million members of the male sex, we're not here to murder you. 'Life for life, eye for eye.' That's a metaphor. You took life, and yes, we could take yours, but instead, we feel it's more apropos if you now gave life."

Ken calmed down. What was I talking about?

"You had sex with all these women, and, Ken, I checked, but not one of them ever had an orgasm. You didn't care about their pleasure, just yours. We feel it's time that was reversed."

"You want me to have sex with them again?" he asked.

"'Screw me once, shame on you. Screw me twice . . .' No way. But you did take life, Ken, and the Bible demands a life for a life, so we've decided you're going to spend the rest of yours giving life back. You see, you were partially right. Being the last man on earth we, the women of Earth, need you, but, at the same time, we don't need . . . *you.*"

He looked at the tube surrounding his dick. He saw the wires leading into it. He was smart. He suddenly understood what I had done and he tried again to pull himself free. Unconcerned, I continued.

"Bossie here, that's what I call my little milking machine, was designed to stimulate you. As you're stimulated, you will manufacture sperm, which will be ejaculated into that tube. We'll collect the cum even as Bossie forces you to create more and more. It'll take a lot of jizz to rebuild the world.

"There's another thing, Ken. Something else I built into Bossie for my own jollies. She's designed to remove any sense of pleasure you'll get from your release. In other words, you're going to come and come and come and come, but like all those women you screwed, you're never going to enjoy it. And that's where biblical retribution comes into this. You see, you fucked us, and now we're going to fuck you."

I hit the *start* button on the remote. When the first spark of electricity sizzled through Ken's balls and up his dick, he screamed as loud as any man has ever screamed before.

And the women of the world smiled. And we knew that it was good.

HypoErotica

Dana Solomon

Penetration was a single downward thrust. The shaft pierced her like a hot skewer burning through warm butter, and he savored the expression on her face, the wince and flutter of her eyelids, the tension, slight resistance, then acceptance as her body was breached.

Fulfillment followed a moment after. The fluid seeped into her flesh, his ears picked up the tiny sound of a soft, almost inaudible sob, and she turned her head and looked away. They always looked away. Sometimes he wished they would look up and let him stare right into their eyes in the moment of release. He waited, motionless, until the last drop of essence had been forced inside her, then began to pull out in a slow, steady motion.

With his breath controlled and his face impassive, not evidencing the slightest external trace of his internal ecstasy, he reached forward with a cotton ball soaked in alcohol and dabbed her shoulder at the point of impact, then cleared the huskiness from his throat.

"That wasn't too bad, was it, Ms. Garritson?" he asked, allowing only a hint of casual friendliness into his voice.

She shook her head and let down the rolled-up right sleeve of her blouse, shielding from his hungry eyes the slight red dot swelling on her white skin.

"You can make an appointment for your next allergy shot with the receptionist," he told her, reverting to his most professionally neutral tone.

This time she looked directly at him, and he breathed a silent thanks for the long white coat that concealed his arousal. "I guess I'll see you next month," she answered.

"I'll look forward to it."

She left the room and he waited a few discreet seconds before lunging down the hall and into the lavatory, where he ripped his pants down to his ankles and, with a few vigorous strokes, unleashed the tempest that had been growing inside him since his first appointment of the day.

He wiped away the effulgence from his thighs with a tissue and the sweat off his forehead with a towel, then refastened and readjusted his clothes. A few heavy breaths helped him regain his composure and he stepped back out into the hallway just as the receptionist's voice announced over the speaker, "Dr. Carroll, Ms. Rae is waiting for her injection in room four. Dr. Carroll, room four."

Images raced through his mind of the alluring Ms. Rae—her slender arms and the smooth skin of her soft shoulders. Before he could repress it, a smile of delicious anticipation broadened on his face. He forced his features into their accustomed expression of dignified detachment, straightened his tie, and stepped down the hallway toward his next conquest.

Five patients and two sweet releases later, he left his receptionist to lock up the office. He walked out to his car and drove the short distance home to a quiet, solitary dinner, his only emotion a slight fatigue, coupled with annoyed impatience at the empty evening hours and lonely night that lay between him and the next day's injections.

From an early age, he'd felt powerful, almost obsessive attractions to the young girls in grade school and high school, and then the young women in college. Tall, with strong features, thick, dark hair and wiry muscles coiled around a slender frame, he'd found many of them willing and eager to share his bed. But some twisted circuit, some miswired switch of the psyche had thwarted him at every turn. Each attempt to consummate his lusts had ended in abject failure, and by the time he entered medical school, he'd resigned himself to a miserable existence of inner desires with no hope of outward expression.

Then, fifteen years ago, he'd finally found an outlet for his passions. The memory remained with him as vividly as a lucid dream in the first moments of waking. He and his fellow residents were following Dr. Marcus, a squat, elderly internist, through Robert Wood Johnson's antiseptic hallways like a dozen sheep in baggy blue scrubs, when a nurse walked out of a respiratory illness ward and announced that a patient had become critical. Dr. Marcus led his flock to the bed of a young girl, barely out of her teens, who was choking and wheezing in the throes of an acute asthmatic attack.

The nurse drew a syringe of 120 milligrams of methylprednisolone sodium succinate and handed it to Dr. Marcus, who began scouring the ranks of residents like a battalion commander choosing a soldier for a suicide mission, before stopping in front of him and presenting it with a terse, "Dr. Carroll, will you administer the injection?"

He'd felt himself stiffen with a strange, sudden delight the moment his hand closed on the plastic shaft. His passion mounted as he prepped the girl's shoulder with an alcohol swab, then held the needle upright for the tiny pre-cum squirt. Finally, he'd pressed the point into her, and it had taken all his powers of self-control to keep from erupting inside his drawstring pants when he pressed the plunger and shot the fluid into her body. He was still shaking when he withdrew it and handed the syringe back to Dr. Marcus.

"See?" said Dr. Marcus. "Nothing to be nervous about."

He watched the girl respond to the treatment, gasping, her eyes glazing as if in a postcoital daze, until she collapsed back onto her pillows. Then he turned back to the doctor.

"I wasn't nervous," he replied. "Not a bit."

In the years that followed, he'd often tried to explore, in the safety of his own consciousness, the seed of his obsession. He spent hours each day searching his mind for the single epiphany that would cure his deviance and open the way to a normal life, a normal love, marriage, a house in the suburbs, 1.7 children, and the corresponding fraction of a dog. First, he'd wracked his consciousness for some early recollection of arousal at the sight of a woman, hopefully his mother, wincing as a needle pierced her arm. When that failed, he'd consulted psychologists, psychiatrists, even a hypnotherapist, in hopes of recovering some repressed memory, some ancient, hidden image. But after years of treatment and tens of thousands of dollars, the source still remained elusive.

His second clearest memory was the afternoon he'd left the last therapist for the last time and spent a few hours in the medical library, researching which specialties involved the most injections. He immediately switched from surgery to allergy and asthma and set himself on his current course, with practicing medicine his only life and penetrating the bodies of beautiful young women his only pleasure.

The next day proved disappointing. His patient roster comprised an almost unbroken succession of men and children, the only women coming from the ranks of the portly, squat, elderly, or otherwise ill-favored. He always left all those injections to his nurses. He was sulking in his office, reviewing the latest pharmaceutical literature, when the telephone intercom interrupted him with a plaintive buzz.

"Dr. Carroll," it announced, in the receptionist's voice. "You have Ms. Wilder waiting in room three."

He tried to answer, but his breath caught in his throat. Images of his most beautiful patient flooded through his mind, washing away any sense of the moment. A woman in her early twenties, Ms. Wilder had the face and tousled off-blond hair of a film starlet, a slender, supple young body, and skin as soft and smooth as a child's. He brought himself back to the present with a shake of his head and a noisy exhaled breath, then snatched up the receiver.

"Ms. Wilder?" He tried to control a stammer. "She's not due in today. Her next allergy shot isn't for another two weeks." There were certain patients whose schedules he kept committed to memory, and Ms. Wilder was at the top of the list.

"I know, Doctor, but the schedule was a little looser than usual this morning. She called with an emergency, so I squeezed her in. I hope you don't mind."

He answered with a stern, begrudging, "Not at all," then stood up, buttoned his coat just above the belt of his trousers, and walked down the hallway to room three. He kept his body to a purposeful step and his face to a bland, professional expression, while every fiber of his consciousness molded and enfolded the mental image of the woman waiting for him behind the door. He opened it, focused on the figure sitting in a plastic chair beside the examination table, and the picture that met his eyes eclipsed even the fond memory his mind had treasured since her last appointment.

Her face reflected a unique character, far more striking than simple, bland perfection. A slight tawny hue had tinted the creamy, milk-white patina of her arms, visible outside the straps of her simple tank top, and her hair, half a shade lighter than the last time he'd seen her, cascaded onto her bare shoulders like an off-blond waterfall.

"Good afternoon." He softened his curt greeting with a smile, then snatched up the manila folder with her chart and held it over his face before the smile widened to a leer. "What can we do for you today?" He lowered the chart. "I wasn't expecting to see you for a while yet."

"I know I'm not due for my allergy shot, but I had a little accident. Went hiking over the weekend and caught my hand on a bit of barbed wire." She held it up, and he winced at the round red welt that desecrated the pink palm. "It seemed sort of rusty, so I thought I should probably get a tetanus shot—I haven't had a booster in years."

He took her hand and examined the wound, punctuating his poker face with a few purely professional hums. "Yes, that seems in order, and I can certainly have the vaccine drawn up. I share the office with a pediatrician, and his kids are always getting into scrapes." He stopped himself and took a breath.

"But if I may ask, why didn't you call your general practitioner? This sort of injection isn't usually administered by an allergist," he continued, like an alcoholic talking himself out of a century-old bottle of single malt scotch.

"I don't really have one," she answered, a matter-of-fact counterpoint. "Except for the hay fever, I'm really pretty healthy," she added, and he strangled a heartfelt agreement.

He summoned the nurse, then struggled at small talk until she returned with the syringe full of amber liquid. She clicked the door shut behind her, and he turned to Ms. Wilder, staring up at him with the perfect trust some patients still place in their doctors.

At that moment, a delicious, unthinkable plan formed in his mind. The impulse control that had protected him over the years failed completely, and he began to stutter. "The tetanus shot is traditionally administered in the arm or shoulder." His eager tongue wiped the saliva from his lips. "However, given that a few days have passed since the initial puncture wound, a posterior administration might be most effective." Her look of trust turned to confusion.

"In the buttocks," he clarified.

She thought for a moment, then nodded wordless consent. She stood up and smoothed her slacks, and he helped her up onto the examination table. She turned over and stretched out into a prone position, crinkling the white paper as she eased her head down onto the pillow. Together, in a joint effort toward the ultimate goal, they slipped her slacks down below her thighs, revealing the most perfect globes of flesh he had ever seen, pink, pristine, without the slightest hint of blemish.

Controlling both himself and the needle from premature release of the entire contents, he approached the beautiful left hemisphere. Her head was turned toward him, and he could see her eyes mist and lip tremble as the needle entered her flesh. Her back arched in a slight spasm as the needle discharged into her body, and he erupted beneath his white coat at the same moment, then she slumped on the table and closed her eyes.

A second later, it was over. He withdrew, tired, sad, spent. He put the needle into the disposal canister, breaking its tip, like a pathetic, pitiful insect drone that gives its life for one chance to mate with its queen.

Remorse and fear followed a few seconds later. What he'd done had been absurd, ridiculous. Worse, it was his first true transgression. Until now, every part of his obsession had remained purely within the realm of thought. In outward action, he had done nothing but administer proper, professional care. Now, he had passed beyond sins of the heart into an act of overt depravity. He had violated his oath, violated a patient for one moment of ecstasy, and he struggled to mask his thoughts behind his bland exterior as he pondered the crime with self-directed rage, the aftermath with terror. She might report him, she might sue. In either case, loss of his practice, his livelihood, and his life's one delight would surely follow. Merciful self-possession returned. With luck, she would never complain. He would never repeat the crime. In time, it would be forgotten.

He gave a tentative glance down into the face of his victim, expecting, in his most frightened fantasy, a look of fear, anger, betrayal. Instead, she was smiling. Thank God, she was smiling. She leaned up onto her elbows, her slacks still dropped to her knees, and hope battled disbelief so firmly in his mind that he could barely comprehend the words as her smile grew wider and sweeter.

"Doctor," she began, and her voice softened to a pleading whisper, as if barely daring to express her most desperate desire. "Do it again?"

The Next-Best Thing

Michael Garrett

Electrodes firmly in place on his scalp, chest, and penis, Ed James settled his slightly underweight frame against the narrow cot of his small cubicle and focused his vision at the side of the cot. His eyes glazed over into a trancelike state as he watched his deceased wife materialize before him. Her image flickered and faded, then locked in to a solid full-dimensional state. He took a deep breath; it was wonderful being with Leah again. A peaceful calmness settled over Ed as he extended a hand and invited her to join him.

"I've missed you so much," he said.

Leah said nothing. She never did; it was one of the few limitations of the technology that allowed Ed to continue the intimacy they'd shared prior to her untimely death. So lifelike, she smiled and sat on the edge of the mattress. Her brown hair, layered to her shoulders, glistened in the artificial lighting, and her blue eyes sparkled just as they had in life. The image was perfect, all the way down to the tiny scar on her right temple and a few isolated premature gray hairs. She'd been thirty-two when the simulation was recorded; she died at thirty-seven.

Ed ran his fingertips up her arm to her face, lightly outlining the gentle curve of her lips. He could actually feel her—or could he? Regardless, this experience was so close to the real thing that he couldn't complain. Little difference registered in his mind between this prerecorded simulation and the actual presence of Leah. He could even smell the fragrance of her hair, making his heartbeat race as it always did.

"I wish you could talk to me," he said, tears welling in his eyes. "You can't imagine how much I've missed you."

He absorbed her image, overcome by the mere sight of her. "The kids are doing fine," he continued in a vain attempt to prolong the meeting, to make it more than it actually was, but the events to follow were predetermined. As if on cue, Leah ran her fingertips across his balding head and kissed him tenderly once again, then she slowly disrobed while maintaining eye contact, the smile never leaving her pretty face. Ed's breath quickened. Though they'd made love in reality hundreds of times, and scores more in simulation, she still excited him more than any other woman had ever been capable of. She reached for the waistband of his jeans and loosened his belt, unsnapped and unzipped him. Ed marveled once again at how the image of Leah had substance of some kind, fully capable of making physical contact and exerting energy—or so it seemed. The technology was uncanny; she seemed incredibly real.

Leah tugged his jeans down his legs and slowly removed the remainder of his clothing, as she sensually slipped out of her own. Ed marveled at her body, realizing that while the immediate experience was intensely pleasurable, there was also an element of torture in knowing he could never take her home with him, that his time with her was limited to weekly static appointments in this cold scientific environment. Still, the opportunity was priceless.

Leah cuddled beside him. The narrow cot provided barely enough space for the two of them, but Ed didn't mind. The confinement was all the more reason for their bodies to be fused together. He gently stroked her hair as she nibbled at his neck and earlobe, the intensely satisfying sensation surging through his body.

He recalled the first couple of times he'd experienced simulated sex with Leah. It had seemed odd, almost inhuman, but he'd been forewarned by the laboratory personnel. In time, you'll adjust, they'd said, and they'd been exactly right. In fact, Ed no longer thought of Leah as deceased. To him, she was only in a different dimension, and this laboratory provided the portal through which to see her regularly.

The two kissed, long and lingering, and Ed's manhood stiffened. Leah stroked him and he could actually feel her hand pump him gently, could feel her warm breath on his neck and her erect nipples pressing against him. Ed closed his eyes and imagined life as it used to be. Leah had been so perfect for him in every way. They'd been virtually inseparable until leukemia took her from him, and for a brief moment Ed resented the focus of science. Without a matching bone marrow donor, she never had a chance. Had technology concentrated more upon curing cancer than on creating afterlife pleasures, she might still be with him today.

Lying on their sides facing each other, the couple gently massaged each other. Ed ran his fingertips down the length of her back and grabbed and squeezed her ass. Even if he'd done the same a million times before, the pleasure would never diminish. Leah, indeed, had been his "other half." Now he lay on his back, and she resumed the preprogrammed command earlier than he wished; what he wouldn't give to alter her actions just this once for more spontaneous lovemaking. She straddled his waist, bending over to kiss his chest, then inched farther south as she eased to the foot of the cot. The tip of her tongue lingered at his belly button before making its way through his pubic hair to his engorged manhood.

She took him into her mouth and Ed tensed with pleasure. He watched her sensuously tantalize him with her tongue, the sensation making him harder still. Her knees planted on the mattress on both sides of his legs, she faced him as he gazed above her lowered head to the gentle curves of her ass arched high in the air behind her. Then he focused on her face as she maintained steady eye contact. Her eyelashes swept up and down as she took him slowly in and out, deeper and deeper, true adoration and devotion radiating from her expression. She loved giving him pleasure, both in life and even now. The warm, wet friction sent chills of ecstasy through Ed's veins.

"Leah," he moaned. "Leah, I love you, honey."

She stopped when the time was right to mount him. Ed tensed at the feel of his manhood inside her. Slowly she rode him, gradually increasing in speed as Ed's breaths grew heavier. He opened his eyes and watched her breasts gently bounce in rhythm. They were medium in size and perfect in shape, her rosy pink nipples erect and upturned. God, he wished he could taste them again, but that hadn't been recorded in the simulation. Her beautiful blue eyes were like magical pools that lured him farther into the depths of passion.

"Oh, baby, *yes*!" he blurted at orgasm. He imagined nothing else on earth feeling so good and giving him such pleasure. She slowly eased his shrunken manhood from inside her and returned to his side, kissing him once again with mounting passion.

Tears seeped again from Ed's eyes as he held her tightly. "Don't go," he whispered. "Let me please you, too, honey." But slowly, as always, her image began to dissolve; the playback disk had reached its end. "No!" he gasped. "Not again! Please let me make love to you, Leah—*please*." But Ed found himself alone on the tiny mattress, sated but not entirely fulfilled.

He sat on the edge of the cot, head in hands, softly crying as he snatched the electrodes from his body. When he and Leah had decided to preserve their lovemaking in the event of untimely death those many years ago, they'd recorded two separate versions—him making love to her, with settings at the standard female brain frequency, and her making love to him at the standard male brain frequency. If he had been first to die, Leah could have experienced his lovemaking after death. *Why did I not also record myself making love to her at my male brain frequency?* he questioned himself. *How could I have been so selfish to think only of what she could do for me, when giving pleasure to her was also one of the great joys of my life?*

Now it was too late. She would endlessly make love to him, but never the reverse. Never again would he hear her moan at the point of orgasm, a sound so sweet that he still imagined it at odd moments of his life. The memory of her soft moan, slowly increasing in pitch and rhythm, was like music in his mind.

Ed wiped away the tears, dressed, and removed the *Leah* disk from the simulation deck. Moments later, he returned the disk inside its container to the front desk.

"Any news about the price hike?" he asked Carl, the admissions clerk.

Carl, an overweight man in his midthirties, shook his head. "Not a word," he answered.

Ed had launched a verbal assault against the company's announcement of a price increase for its services, but his complaint that a fee hike was like holding his deceased wife for ransom had apparently fallen on deaf ears. Ed frowned and looked away. "No one can understand unless he's lost someone special and depends on her to get through every day."

Carl spoke more seriously. "I gotta tell you, Mr. J. Everybody who uses this service has lost someone special, but nobody else seems as hooked into it as you."

Ed took a deep breath. "Huh!" he snarled. "Nobody else had somebody like Leah. She's incredible. Nobody else knows what they're missing."

Carl took the disk box and inserted it into its storage slot in the vault behind the desk. "Same time next week?" he asked.

"Have I ever missed a session?" Ed answered.

Carl grinned. "You're one of our noisiest clients. She must be one helluva fuck," he said.

Ed stiffened, a hard grimace tightening his face. His pulse increased; he balled his fists till the knuckles turned white. "Don't cheapen my wife like that!" he growled.

Carl was instantly on guard. "Hey, I'm sorry, Mr. James. Guess I just don't know what it's like to miss someone so. I've never been lucky enough to have what you and Leah had."

"I understand," Ed said, softening somewhat. "Just try not to be insensitive, okay?"

"Sure thing, Mr. J."

At home, Ed moped more than usual. Someday in the not-so-distant future, home devices would likely be affordable enough to offer more private simulated sex as often as desired. For now, memories of Leah would have to suffice between sessions. Amazingly, she'd been a virgin when they'd first met. Ed didn't believe her at first, but became convinced when he had to essentially train her how to make love.

What a treasure she'd been. She became a wonderful student of the art of making love, and in time became the best lover he'd ever had. And she'd been incredibly devoted to him. He'd asked her once if, since he had been her only sex partner, would she like to experience it with someone else. Perhaps she had known that his intense jealousy would never allow her another partner anyway, but he'd always allowed himself to believe that her refusal to even consider such an experience was an indication of her love and loyalty to him.

Now, however, Ed felt an increase in nervousness, like he was a ball of string slowly unraveling. Stress grew uncontrollable as his need for Leah increased. The effect of his regular visits with her were losing their impact faster every week. In the beginning, he managed to maintain a semblance of normal life between his visits, but now he needed more—she was like a drug—and for the first time Ed questioned whether it was psychologically healthy to experience after-death sex with her. Was he growing too dependent? How much longer could he mentally handle a loss that grew greater every day despite their simulated conjugal visits? God, it seemed he missed her worse than ever. He'd developed a jitter in his left hand already and a twitch in his right eyebrow.

Days later, an answer came. It wasn't the perfect solution, certainly not a long-term antidote, he knew, and deep inside he realized it wasn't the healthiest recourse, but in the short-term, it should help maintain his sanity. He'd start seeing Leah twice a week. He could afford it, at least until the price increase took effect. He might have to cut out a few extravagances to swing it financially, but what could be more important than time with his wife? He'd simply make a second appointment—Tuesdays sounded good—in addition to his typical Friday trysts.

Memories of Leah consumed Ed's weekend. Everywhere he turned, he was reminded of her. Saturday afternoon, he found himself speaking to her as if she were standing beside him, and he feared he might be losing his mind. Sunday night, he took some of her night wear from a drawer and bundled it around his pillow in hope of feeling some sense of her, but her scent had long faded away from her clothing. He dreamed of her, but of course, that was nothing new. There was seldom a moment, day or night, when she wasn't on his mind.

She'd been gone more than two years, yet her loss seemed to have had a cumulative effect. Due to the simulated immediacy of her in his life, it was as if the grieving process never truly ended. With each visit to the lab, he lost her all over again when the disk reached its end. Would it be possible to ever go on with his life? Perhaps the simulation was a curse rather than a blessing, something to fixate on that would never allow him to leave her in the past to forge a new future.

A quick call to the lab Monday morning brought bitter disappointment. They were booked to full capacity—absolutely no available time slots were open—and the thought of limiting himself to only one visit per week was now maddening.

Ed entered the revolving door of the lab, determined to see the manager. Perhaps a bribe would free up more visitation time. Diane was manning the front desk today, and her cheerful attitude irritated Ed, despite her provocative figure and flowing blond hair.

Ed's pulse raced. He didn't like the person he was becoming, but at the moment he knew only that he *had* to be with Leah again. Nothing else mattered anymore.

"Mr. James!" Diane exclaimed. "It's nice to see you—and it's not even Friday!"

"Look," Ed began, on the verge of stuttering. "Someone in the reservations office says you're all booked up, but you've got to do something. I've *got* to have a second weekly appointment."

Diane smiled and spoke in a soothing tone. "Did they explain our expansion plans to you, Mr. James?"

"No, they didn't."

Diane shook her head sympathetically. "Someone should have," she said. "We plan to open a whole new wing in a few months. The same technology can be used for a number of other services, so we'll be doubling our capacity."

Now Ed shook his head. "No, no, no! That's not good enough. I need extra time now!" he growled.

"Well . . ." Diane began, seemingly at a loss for words, until an idea occurred to her. "How about cancellations? We could call you when openings occur, if you'd like to try that."

A smile slowly spread across Ed's face. "Yes! Of course! I don't live far from here at all! I could be here at a moment's notice!"

"In fact . . ." Diane continued as she tapped a few keys and scanned the appointment screen, "we have a cancellation opening right now. You can have that session if you like."

Ed exhaled in relief. "Thank God!" he exclaimed. "This is wonderful. I never dreamed I'd be able to see her today!"

Ed signed in as Diane pivoted to retrieve the *Leah* disk from the vault. "That's odd," he heard her say. He looked up to peer over her shoulder at the empty slot where the disk should have been stored.

Suddenly Ed froze. Why hadn't he suspected this before? He should have seen it coming. How could he have been so stupid? Anger surged through his body; he felt as if he were about to explode. "Which cubicle was canceled?" he asked. Then, as Diane stood motionless, he voiced his demand even more forcefully. "*Which cubicle is open?*"

Diane swallowed nervously as she checked the screen. "4-C," she answered. Ed burst past the security checkpoint and hurried down the hallway with Diane in pursuit. "Wait!" she called out to him. "You can't go back there without—"

But he had already stormed through the barrier to 4-C and stood in a frozen stance. There, on a cot, rested Carl, the selfish, inconsiderate, nosy jerk who'd been asking way too many questions, fully clothed and breathing heavily, but not entirely conscious. Only a computer nerd like Carl would have the brains to break the system's security codes and commit such an incredible violation of privacy. Ed glanced around the tiny cubicle. Atop the simulation deck was the disk box labeled *Leah James*. Ed checked the nearby monitor screen and gasped. There, on the screen, was Leah positioned on her knees at the lower end of the mattress. She and Carl were both naked. Leah was making eye contact with Carl, smiling, and slowly taking him into her—

"*No*!" Ed screamed. His eyes flared as wide as golf balls; his breath grew rapid and deep. Not this! It couldn't be happening! His pulse pounded inside his eardrums, an intense irreversible rage mushrooming inside. "My *wife*! My *Leah*!"

Carl lay incapacitated, engaged in the simulation experience, completely dazed and unaware of Ed's presence. On the monitor screen, Leah tenderly ministered to her partner's sexual needs, tenderly stroking him, taking him deeper and deeper. With a rush of adrenalin, Ed snatched the monitor and snapped its cables free from their connectors. With the simulation circuit broken, Carl was jarred back to reality just in time to see the monitor come crashing down against his face with bone-crushing force.

"You bastard!" Ed screamed, lifting the monitor from the bloody pulp on the cot and pounding it back into place again. Blood and brain matter sprayed across the snow-white pillow. "You're raping her! You're raping my Leah!"

Months passed. Ed faced a dark future with no Leah at all, not even the imitation to which he'd grown addicted. He'd been convicted of second-degree murder, sentenced to imprisonment of no less than ten years. Handcuffed, he trudged, devoid of expression, toward the site of his detention. A lifetime without Leah, of that there was no doubt. And the worst punishment of all was the torturous image that played endlessly in his mind—Leah unknowingly fucking Carl. It wasn't rape; hell, she wasn't even real. Or was she? It wasn't exactly consensual either, since the simulation had no decision-making capacity. Leah had made love to Carl exactly the same way she'd made love to her own husband, and Ed could barely stand the thought. In his mind he still saw Leah and Carl together, naked, exchanging intimacy.

Ed's hands shook, jingling the handcuffs at his wrists. If only he could erase that moment from his mind. How many times had Carl taken advantage of Leah? Had anyone else done the same? Had the lab he'd grown to love become nothing more than a black market high-tech whorehouse? Tears streamed down Ed's cheeks. How could anyone violate such a loving bond? It was sacrilegious, incomprehensible.

Ed was escorted down the hall of the new simulation lab wing, past the row of small cubicles like those where he'd experienced Leah so many times. Inside a cold, drab new cubicle, he was ordered to remove his shirt and lie on a cot, just as he'd done with Leah so many times before.

A lab tech attached electrodes to his scalp and chest. Trembling, Ed took a deep breath and watched the disk of his imprisonment slide into the simulation drive, the disk labeled *State Penitentiary*. Tears streaming down his cheeks, Ed focused his glazed vision toward the foot of the cot and watched cold steel bars materialize before his very eyes. The image flickered and faded, then locked in to a solid full-dimensional, eternal state.

Camelot

Graham Masterton

Jack was scraping finely chopped garlic into the skillet, when he heard somebody banging at the restaurant door.

"Shit," he breathed. He took the skillet off the gas and wiped his hands on his apron. The banging was repeated, more forcefully this time, and the door handle was rattled. "Okay, okay! I hear you!"

He weaved his way between the circular tables and the bentwood chairs. The yellow linen blinds were drawn right down over the windows, so that all he could see were two shadows. The early morning sun distorted them, hunched them up and gave them pointed ears, so that they looked like wolves.

He shot the bolts and unlocked the door. Two men in putty-colored raincoats were standing outside. One was dark and unshaven, with greased-back hair and a broken nose. The other was sandy and overweight, with clear beads of perspiration on his upper lip.

"Yes?"

The dark man held out a gilded badge. "Sergeant Eli Waxman, San Francisco Police Department. Are you Mr. Jack Keller?"

"That's me. Is anything wrong?"

Sergeant Waxman flipped open his notebook and peered at it as if he couldn't read his own handwriting. "You live at 3663 Heliograph Street, Apartment 2?"

"Yes, I do. For Christ's sake, tell me what's happened."

"Your partner is Ms. Jacqueline Fronsart, twenty-four, a student in Baltic singing at the Institute of Baltic Singing?"

"That's right."

Sergeant Waxman closed his notebook. "I'm sorry to tell you, Mr. Keller, but Ms. Fronsart has been mirrorized."

"What?"

"Your neighbors heard her screaming 'round about nine-thirty this morning. One of them broke into your apartment and found her halfway in and halfway out. They tried to pull her back, but there was nothing they could do."

"Oh, God." Jack couldn't believe what he was hearing. "Which—what—which mirror was it?"

"Big tilting mirror, in the bedroom."

"Oh, God. Where is it now? It didn't get broken, did it?"

"No, it's still intact. We left it where it was. The coroner can remove it for you, if that's what you want. It's entirely up to you."

Jack covered his eyes with his hand and kept them covered. Maybe if he blocked out the world for long enough, the detectives would vanish and this wouldn't have happened. But even in the darkness behind his fingers, he could hear their raincoats rustling and their shoes shifting uncomfortably on the polished wood floor. Eventually he looked up at them and said, "I bought that mirror about six months ago. The owner swore to me that it was docile."

"You want to tell me where you got it?"

"Loculus Antiques, in Sonoma. I have their card someplace."

"Don't worry, we can find it if we need to. I'll be straight with you, though—I don't hold out much hope of any restitution."

"Jesus. I'm not interested in restitution. I just want—"

He thought of Jacqueline, standing on his balcony, naked except for a large straw hat piled ridiculously high with peaches and pears and bananas. He could see her turning her face toward him in slo-mo. Those liquid brown eyes, so wide apart that she looked more like a beautiful salmon than a woman. Those brown shoulders, patterned with henna. Those enormous breasts, with nipples that shone like plums.

"Desire, I can see it in your every looking," she had whispered. She always whispered, to save her larynx for her Baltic singing.

She had pushed him back onto the violently patterned dhurrie and knelt astride his chest. Then she had displayed herself to him, her smooth, hairless vulva, and she had pulled open her lips with her fingers to show him the green canary feather that she had inserted into her urethra.

"The plumage of vanity," she had whispered.

Sergeant Waxman took hold of Jack's upper arm and gave him a comforting squeeze. "I'm real sorry for your loss, Mr. Keller. I saw her myself and—well, she was something, wasn't she?"

"What am I supposed to do?" asked Jack. For the first time in his life, he felt totally detached, adrift, like a man in a rowboat with only one oar, circling around and around, out of reach of anybody.

"Different people make different decisions, sir," said the sandy-haired detective.

"Decisions? Decisions about what?"

"About their mirrors, sir. Some folks store them away in their basements, or their attics, hoping that a time is going to come when we know how to get their loved ones back out of them. Some folks—well, they bury them and have proper funerals."

"They *bury* them? I didn't know that."

"It's unusual, sir, but not unknown. Other folks just cover

up their mirrors with sheets or blankets and leave them where they are, but some doctors think this could amount to cruelty, on account of the person in the mirror still being able to hear what's going on and everything."

"Oh, God," said Jack.

The sandy-haired detective took out a folded handkerchief and dabbed his forehead. "Most folks, though . . ."

"Most folks what?"

"Most folks break their mirrors, sooner or later. I guess it's like taking their loved ones off life support."

Jack stared at him. "But if you break a mirror, what about the person inside it? Are they still trapped in some kind of mirror world? Or do they get broken, too?"

Sergeant Waxman said, solemnly, "We don't know the answer to that, Mr. Keller, and I very much doubt if we ever will."

When the detectives left, Jack locked the restaurant door and stood with his back against it, tears streaming down his cheeks, as warm and sticky as if he had poked his eyes out. "Jacqueline," he moaned. "Jacqueline, why *you*? Why you, of all people? Why you?"

He knelt down on the waxed oak floor, doubled up with the physical pain of losing her, and sobbed between gritted teeth. "Why you, Jacqueline? Why you? You're so beautiful, why you?"

He cried for almost ten minutes, and then he couldn't cry any more. He stood up, wiped his eyes on one of the table napkins and blew his nose. He looked around at all the empty tables. He doubted if he would ever be able to open again. Keller's Far-Flung Food would become a memory, just like Jaqueline.

God, he thought. Every morning you wake up and you climb out of bed, but you never know when life is going to punch you straight in the face.

He went back into the kitchen, turned off all the hobs and

ovens, and hung up his apron. There were half a dozen Inuit moccasins lying on the chopping board, ready for unstitching and marinating, and yew branches for yew-branch soup. He picked up a fresh, furry moose antler. That was supposed to be today's special. He put it down again, his throat so tight that he could hardly breathe.

He was almost ready to leave when the back door was flung open and Punipuni Puusuke appeared, in his black Richard Nixon T-shirt and his floppy white linen pants. Jack didn't know exactly how old Punipuni was, but his crew cut looked like one of those wire brushes you use for getting rust off the fenders of 1963 pickup trucks, and his eyes were so pouchy that Jack could never tell if they were open or not. All the same, he was one of the most experienced bone chefs in San Francisco, as well as being an acknowledged Oriental philosopher. He had written a slim, papery book called *Do Not Ask a Fish the Way Across the Desert.*

Punipuni took off his red leather shoulder bag and then he looked around the kitchen. "Mr. German-cellar?" (He always believed that people should acknowledge the ethnic origins of their names, but translate them into English so that others could share their meaning.) "Mr. German-cellar, is something wrong?"

"I'm sorry, Pu, I didn't have time to call you. I'm not opening today. In fact, I think I'm closing for good. Jacqueline was mirrorized."

Punipuni came across the kitchen and took hold of Jack's hands. "Mr. German-cellar, my heart is inside your chest. When did this tragedy occur?"

"This morning. Just now. The police were here. I have to go home and see what I can do."

"She was so wonderful, Mr. German-cellar. I don't know what I can say to console you."

Jack shook his head. "There's nothing. Not yet. You can go home if you like."

"Maybe I come along too. Sometimes a shoulder to weep on is better than money discovered in a sycamore tree."

"Okay. I'd appreciate it."

He lived up on Russian Hill, in a small pink Victorian house in the English Quarter. It was so steep here that he had to park his Ford Peacock with its front wheels cramped against the curb and its gearbox in *Backward*. It was a sunny day, and far below them the Bay was sparkling like shattered glass, but there was a thin cold breeze blowing that smelled like a fisherman's dying breath.

"Jack!"

A maroon-faced man with white whiskers was trudging up the hill with a bull mastiff on a short choke chain. He was dressed in yellowish brown tweeds, with the cuffs of his pants tucked into his stockings.

"I say, Jack!" he repeated, and raised his arm in salute.

"Major," Jack acknowledged him, and then looked up to his second-story apartment. Somebody had left the windows wide open, Jacqueline probably, and the white drapes were curling in the breeze.

"Dreadfully sorry to hear what happened, old boy! The Nemesis and I are awfully cut up about it. Such a splendid young girl!"

"Thank you," said Jack.

"Buggers, some of these mirrors, aren't they? Can't trust them an inch."

"I thought this one was safe."

"Well, none of them are safe, are they, when it comes down to it? Same as these perishing dogs. They behave themselves perfectly for years, and then suddenly, for no reason that you can think of, *snap*! They bite some kiddie's nose off, or some such. The Nemesis won't have a mirror in the house. Just as well, I suppose. With a dial like hers, she'd crack it as soon as look at it—what?"

Jack tried to smile, but all he could manage was a painful smirk. He let himself in the front door and climbed the narrow stairs, closely followed by Punipuni. Inside, the hallway was very quiet and smelled of overripe melons. Halfway up the stairs, there was a stained-glass window with a picture of a blindfolded woman on it, and a distant castle with thick black smoke pouring out of it, and rooks circling.

Punipuni caught hold of his sleeve. "Your God does not require you to do this, Mr. German-cellar."

"No," said Jack. "But my heart does. Do you think I'm just going to hire some removal guy and have her carted away? I love her, Pu. I always will. Forever."

"Forever is not a straight line," said Punipuni. "Remember that your favorite carpet store may not always be visible from your front doorstep."

They reached the upstairs landing. Jack went across to his front door and took out his key. His heart was thumping like an Irish drum, and he wasn't at all sure that he was going to be able to do this. But there was a brass ankh on the door where Jaqueline had nailed it, and he could see her kissing her fingertips and pressing them against the ankh and saying, "This is the symbol of life everlasting that will never die."

She had been naked at the time, except for a deerstalker hat like Sherlock Holmes. She loved Sherlock Holmes and often called Jack "Watson." Without warning, she would take out her violin and play a few scraping notes of Cajun music on it and proclaim, "The game is afoot!"

He opened the door and pushed it wide. The apartment was silent, except for the noise of the traffic outside. There was a narrow hallway with a coatrack that was cluttered with twenty or thirty hats—skimmers and derbies and shapeless old fedoras—and the floor was heaped with smelly, discarded shoes—brown oxfords and gilded ballet slippers and $350 Guevara trainers.

Jack climbed over the shoes into the living room. It was

furnished with heavy red leather chairs and couches and glass-fronted bookcases crammed with leather-bound books. Over the cast-iron fireplace hung a large colored lithograph. It depicted a voluptuous naked woman riding a bicycle over a hurrying carpet of living mice, crushing them under her tires. Only on very close examination could it be seen that, instead of a saddle, the bicycle was fitted with a thick purple dildo, complete with bulging testicles. The caption read "The Second Most Pleasurable Way to Exterminate Rodents—Pestifex Powder."

The bedroom door was ajar, but he hardly dared to go inside. At last, Punipuni nudged him and said, "Go on, Jack. You have to. You cannot mend a broken ginger jar by refusing to look at it."

"Yes, you're right." Jack crossed the living room and pushed open the bedroom door. The pine four-poster bed was still unmade, with its duvet dragged across it diagonally and its pillows still scattered. On the opposite side of the room, between the two open windows, stood Jacqueline's dressing table, with all of her Debussy perfumes, and her Seurat face powders, and dozens of paintbrushes in a white ceramic jar.

In the corner stood the cheval mirror, oval, and almost six feet high on its swiveling base. It was made out of dark highly polished mahogany, with grapevines carved all around it and the face of a mocking cherub at the crest of the frame. Jack walked around the bed and confronted it. All he could see was himself, and the quilt, and Punipuni standing in the doorway behind him.

He looked terrible. His hair was still disheveled from taking off his apron, and he was wearing a crumpled blue shirt with paint spots on it and a pair of baggy Levi's with ripped-out knees. There were plum-colored circles under his eyes.

He reached out and touched the dusty surface of the mirror with his fingertips. "Jacqueline," he said. "Jacqueline—are you there?"

"Maybe there was mix-up," said Punipuni, trying to sound optimistic. "Maybe she just went out to buy lipstick."

But Jack knew that there had been no mistake. In the mirror, Jacqueline's white silken robe was lying on the floor at the end of the bed. But when he looked around, it wasn't there, not in the real world.

He leaned close to the mirror. "Jacqueline!" he called out, hoarsely. "Jacqueline, sweetheart, it's Jack!"

"Maybe she hides," Punipuni suggested. "Maybe she doesn't want you to see her suffer."

But at that moment, Jacqueline appeared in the mirror and came walking slowly across the room toward him, like a woman in a dream. She was naked, apart from very high black stiletto shoes with black silk chrysanthemums on them and a huge black funeral hat bobbing with ostrich plumes. She was wearing upswept dark glasses and dangly jet earrings, and her lips were painted glossy black.

Jack gripped the frame of the mirror in anguish. "Jacqueline! Oh God, Jacqueline!"

Her mirror-image came up to his mirror-image and wrapped her arms around it. He could see her clearly in the mirror, but he could neither see nor feel her *here*, in the bedroom.

"Jack . . ." she whispered, and even though he couldn't see her eyes behind her dark glasses, her voice was quaking with panic. "You have to get me out of here. Please."

"I don't know how, sweetheart. Nobody knows how."

"All I was doing . . . I was plucking my eyebrows. I leaned forward toward the mirror . . . the next thing I knew I lost my balance. It was like falling through ice. Jack, I hate it here. I'm so frightened. You have to get me out."

Jack didn't know what to say. He could see Jacqueline kissing him and stroking his hair and pressing her breasts against his chest, but it was all an illusion.

Punipuni gave an uncomfortable cough. "Maybe I leave now, Mr. German-cellar. You know my number. You call if you want my help. A real friend waits like a rook on the gatepost."

Jack said, "Thanks, Pu. I'll catch you later." He didn't turn around. He didn't want Punipuni to see the welter of tears in his eyes.

After Punipuni left, Jack knelt in front of the mirror and Jacqueline knelt down inside it, facing him, although he could see himself kneeling behind her.

"You have to find a way to get me out," said Jacqueline. "It's so unfriendly here. . . . the people won't speak to me. I ask them how to get back through the mirror, but all they do is smile. And it's so silent. No traffic. All you can hear is the wind."

"Listen," Jack told her. "I'll go back to Sonoma, where we bought the mirror. Maybe the guy in the antiques store can help us."

Jacqueline lowered her head so that all he could see was the feathery brim of her funeral hat. "I miss you so much, Jack. I just want to be back in bed with you."

Jack didn't know what to say. But Jacqueline lifted her head again, and said, "Take off your clothes."

"What?"

"Please; take off your clothes."

Slowly, like a man with aching knees and elbows, he unbuttoned his shirt and his jeans and pulled them off. He took off his red-and-white striped boxer shorts, too, and stood naked in front of the mirror, his penis half-erect. The early afternoon sun shone in his pubic hairs so that they looked like electric filaments.

"Come to the mirror," said Jacqueline. She approached its surface from the inside, so that her hands were pressed flat against the glass. Her breasts were squashed against the glass, too, so that her nipples looked like large dried fruits.

Jack took his penis in his hand and held the swollen purple glans against the mirror. Jacqueline stuck out her tongue and licked the other side of the glass, again and again. Jack couldn't feel anything, but the sight of her tongue against his glans gave him an extraordinary sensation of frustration and arousal. He began to rub his penis up and down, gripping it tighter and tighter, while Jacqueline licked even faster.

She reached down between her thighs and parted her vulva with her fingers. With her long middle finger she began to flick her clitoris, and the reflected sunlight from the wooden floor showed Jack that she was glistening with juice.

He rubbed himself harder and harder until he knew that he couldn't stop himself from climaxing.

"Oh, God," he said, and sperm shot in loops all over the mirror, all over Jacqueline's reflected tongue, on her reflected nose, even in her reflected hair. She licked at it greedily, even though she could neither touch it nor taste it. Watching her, Jack pressed his forehead against the mirror in utter despair.

He stayed there, feeling drained, while she lay back on the floor, opened her legs wide, and slowly massaged herself, playing with her clitoris and sliding her long black-polished fingernails into her slippery pink hole. After a while, she closed her legs tightly, and shivered. He wasn't sure if she was having an orgasm or not, but she lay on the floor motionless for over a minute, the plumes of her hat stirring in the breeze from the wide-open window.

Mr. Santorini, in the downstairs apartment, was playing "Carry Me to Heaven with Candy-Colored Ribbons" on his windup gramophone. Jack could hear the scratchy tenor voice like a message from long ago and far away.

San Francisco folk wisdom says that for every ten miles you drive away from the city, it grows ten degrees Fahrenheit hotter. It was so hot by the time that Jack reached Sonoma that afternoon that the air was like liquid honey. He turned left off East Spain Street and there was Loculus Antiques, a single-story conservatory shaded by eucalyptus trees. He parked his Peacock and climbed out, but Punipuni stayed where he was, listening to Cambodian jazz on the radio, "That Old Fish Hook Fandango," by Samlor Chapheck and the Southeast Asian Swingers.

Jack opened the door of Loculus Antiques and a bell jangled. Inside, the conservatory was stacked with antique sofas and dining chairs and plaster busts of Aristotle, and it smelled of dried-out horsehair and failed attempts to make money. There was a strange light in there, too, like a mortuary, because the glass roof had been painted-over green. A man appeared from the back of the store wearing what looked like white linen pajamas. He looked about fifty-five, with a skull-like head and fraying white hair and thick-rimmed spectacles. His top front teeth stuck out like a horse.

"May I show you something?" he drawled. His accent wasn't northern California. More like Marblehead, Massachusetts.

"You probably don't remember me, but you sold me a mirror about six months ago. Jack Keller."

"A mirraw, hmm? Well, I sell an awful lot of mirraws. All guaranteed safe, of course."

"This one wasn't. I lost my partner this morning. I was just starting work when the police came around and told me she'd been mirrorized."

The man slowly took off his spectacles and stared at Jack with bulging pale blue eyes. "You're absolutely sure it was one of mine? I don't see how it could have been. I'm very careful, you know. I lost my own pet Pomeranian that way. It was only a little hand mirraw, too. One second she was chasing her squeaky bone. The next . . . gone!"

He put his spectacles back on. "I had to—" and he made a smacking gesture with his hands, to indicate that he'd broken the mirror to put his dog down. "That endless pathetic barking . . . I couldn't bear it."

"The same thing's happened to my partner," said Jack, trying to control his anger. "And it was one of *your* mirrors, I still have the receipt. A cheval mirror, with a mahogany frame, with grapevines carved all around it."

The man's face drained of color. "*That* mirraw. Oh, dear."

"Oh, dear? Is that all you can say? I've lost the only woman I've ever loved. A beautiful, vibrant young woman with all of her life still in front of her."

"I am sorry. My Pom was a pedigree, you know . . . but this is much worse, isn't it?"

Jack went right up to him. "I want to know how to get her out. And if I can't get her out, I'm going to come back here and I'm going to tear your head off with my bare hands."

"Well! There's no need to be so aggressive."

"Believe me, pal, you don't even know the meaning of the word aggressive. But you will, if you don't tell me how to get my partner out of that goddamned mirror."

"Please," said the man, lifting both hands as if he were admitting liability. "I only sold it to you because I thought that it *had* to be a fake."

"What are you talking about?"

"I bought it cheap from a dealer in Sacramento. He wouldn't say why he was selling it at such a knock-down price. It has a story attached to it, but if the story's true . . . well, even if it's only half-true . . ."

"What story?" Jack demanded.

"Believe me, I wouldn't have sold it to you if I thought there was any risk attached, especially after that last outbreak of silver plunge. I'm always so careful with mirraws."

He went over to his desk, which was cluttered with papers and books and a framed photograph of Madame Chiang Kai-shek with the handwritten message *To Timmy, What a Night*!

He pulled open his desk drawers, one after the other. "I put it down to vanity, you know. If people stare into the mirraw long enough, it's bound to set off *some* reaction. I mean, it happens with people, doesn't it? If you stare at somebody long enough, they're bound to say 'who do you think you're looking at?' aren't they?"

He couldn't find what he was looking for in his drawers, so he pulled down a steady shower of pamphlets and invoices and pieces of paper from the shelves behind his desk. At last he said, "Here we are! We're in luck!"

He unfolded a worn-out sheet of typing paper and smoothed it with the edge of his hand. "The Camelot Looking Glass. Made circa 1842, as a gift from an admiring nation to Alfred, Lord Tennyson, on publication of the revised version of his great poem 'The Lady of Shalott.'"

"What does that mean?" said Jack, impatiently. "I don't understand."

"The mirraw was specially commissioned by the Arthurian Society in England as a token of esteem for 'The Lady of Shalott.' You do know about 'The Lady of Shalott'?"

Jack shook his head. "What does this have to do with my getting Jacqueline back?"

"It could have everything to do with it. Or, on the other hand, nothing at all, if the mirraw's a fake."

"Go on."

The man pulled up a bentwood chair and sat down. "Some literary experts think that 'The Lady of Shalott' was a poetic description of silver plunge."

"I think I'm losing my patience here," said Jack.

"No! No! Listen! 'The Lady of Shalott' is about a beautiful woman who is condemned to spend all of her days in a tower, weaving tapestries of whatever she sees through her window. She weaves tapestries of all the passing seasons. She weaves courtships, weddings, funerals. The catch is, though, that she is under a spell. She is only allowed to look at the world by means of her mirraw. Otherwise, she will die. Let's see if I can remember some of it."

There she weaves by night and day
A magic web with colors gay.
She has heard a whisper say,
A curse is on her if she stay
To look down to Camelot . . .
And moving thro' a mirraw clear
That hangs before her all the year,
Shadows of the world appear.
There she sees the highway near
Winding down to Camelot . . .

"Yes, great, very poetic," Jack interrupted. "But I still don't see how this can help Jacqueline."

"Please—just let me finish. One day, Sir Lancelot comes riding past the tower. He looks magnificent. He has a shining saddle and jingling bridle-bells and his helmet feather burns like a flame. The Lady of Shalott sees him in her mirraw, and she can't resist turning around to look at him directly.

She left the web, she left the loom
She made three paces thro' the room
She saw the water lily bloom,
She saw the helmet and the plume
She look'd down to Camelot.
Out flew the web and floated wide;
The mirraw crack'd from side to side;
'The curse is come upon me,' cried
The Lady of Shalott.

"She knows that she is doomed. She leaves the tower. She finds a boat in the river and paints her name on it, 'The Lady of Shalott.' Then she lies down in it and floats to Camelot, singing her last sad song. The reapers in the fields beside the river can hear this lament, as her blood slowly freezes and her eyes grow dark. By the time her boat reaches the jetty at Camelot, she's dead.

"Sir Lancelot comes down to the wharf with the rest of the crowds. He sees her lying in the boat and thinks how beautiful she is, and he asks God to give her grace. That's what Tennyson wrote in the poem, anyhow. But listen to what it says on this piece of paper.

"Several other stories suggest that Sir Lancelot visited the Lady of Shalott in her tower many times and became so entranced by her beauty that he became her lover, even though she could not look at him directly when they made love, because of the curse that was on her. One day, however, he gave her ecstasy so intense that she turned to look at him. She vanished into her mirraw and was never seen again.

"The mirraw presented to Alfred, Lord Tennyson, is reputed to be the original mirraw into which the Lady of Shalott disappeared, with a new decorative frame paid for by public subscription. When Lord Tennyson died in 1892, the mirraw was taken from his house at Aldworth, near Haslemere, in southern England, and sold to a New York company of auctioneers."

Jack snatched the paper out of his hand and read it for himself. "You knew that this mirror had swallowed this Shalott woman and yet you sold it to us without any warning?"

"Because 'The Lady of Shalott' is only a poem, and Sir

Lancelot is only a myth, and Camelot never existed! I never thought that it could happen for real! Even Lord Tennyson thought that the mirraw was a phony, and that some poor idiot from the Arthurian Society had been bamboozled into paying a fortune for an ordinary looking glass!"

"For Christ's sake!" Jack shouted at him. "Even ordinary mirrors can be dangerous, you know that! Look what happened to your dog!"

The man ran his hand through his straggling white hair. "The dealer in Sacramento said that it had never given anybody any trouble, not in thirty years. I inspected for silver plunge, but of course it's not always easy to tell if a mirraw's been infected or not."

Jack took two or three deep breaths to calm himself down. At that moment, Punipuni appeared in the doorway of the antiques store, and the bell jangled.

"Everything is okay, Mr. German-cellar?"

"No, Pu, it isn't."

The man jerked his head toward Punipuni and said, "Who's this?"

"A friend. His name is Punipuni Puusuke."

The man held out his hand. "Pleased to know you. My name's Davis Culbut."

"Pleased to know you, too, Mr. French-somersault."

"I beg your pardon?"

"That is what your name derives from, sir. The French word for head-over-heels. Topsy-turvy maybe."

"I see," said Davis Culbut, plainly mystified. He turned back to Jack and held up the typewritten sheet of paper. "It says here that Sir Lancelot grieved for the Lady of Shalott so much that he consulted Merlin the Magician to see how he might get her back. But Merlin told him that the curse is irreversible. The only way for him to be reunited with her would be for him to pass through the mirraw, too."

"You mean—?"

"Yes, I'm afraid I do. You can have your lady friend back, but only if you join her. Even so . . . this is only a legend, like Camelot, and I can't give you any guarantees."

"Mr. German-cellar!" said Punipuni, emphatically. "You cannot go to live in the world of reflection!"

Jack said nothing. After a lengthy silence, Davis Culbut folded the sheet of paper and handed it to him. "I can only tell you that I'm very sorry for your loss, Mr. Keller. I'm afraid there's nothing else that I can do."

They sat by the window in Steiner's Bar on First Street West and ordered two cold William Randolph Hearsts. Their waitress was a llama, with her hair braided and tied with red-and-white ribbons and a brass bell around her neck.

"You want to see a menu?" she asked them, in a high, rasping voice that came right from the back of the throat. "The special today is saddle of saddle, with maraschinos."

Jack shook his head. "No, thank you. Just the beers."

The waitress stared at him with her slitted golden eyes. "You look kind of down, my friend, if you don't mind my saying so."

"Mirror trouble," said Punpuni.

"Oh, I'm sorry. My nephew had mirror trouble, too. He lost his two daughters."

Jack looked up at her. "Did he ever try to get them back?"

The waitress shook her head so that her bell jangled. "What can you do? Once they're gone, they're gone."

"Did he ever think of going after them?"

"I don't follow you."

"Did he ever think of going into the mirror himself, to see if he could rescue them?"

The waitress shook her head again. "He has five other children, and a wife to take care of."

"So what did he do?"

"He broke the mirror, in the end. He couldn't bear to hear his little girls crying."

When she had gone, Jack and Punipuni sat and drank their beers in silence. At last, though, Punipuni wiped his mouth with the back of his hand and said, "You're thinking of trying it, aren't you?"

"What else can I do, Pu? I love her. I can't just leave her there."

"Even supposing you manage to get into the mirror, what's going to happen if you can't get back out?"

"Then I'll just have to make my life there, instead of here."

Punipuni took hold of Jack's hands and gripped them tight. "If your loved one falls from a high tower, even the flamingos cannot save her, and they can fly."

That night, Jack sat on the end of the bed staring at himself in the cheval mirror, like a fortune-teller confronted by his own mischance. Outside, the city glittered on the ocean's edge, like Camelot.

"Jacqueline?" he said, as quietly as he could, as if he didn't really want to disturb her.

He thought of the day when he first met her. She was riding sidesaddle on a white cow through a field of sunflowers under a sky the color of polished brass. She was wearing a broken wedding cake on her head and a white damask tablecloth wound around and around her and trailing to the ground.

He stopped and shaded his eyes. He had been visiting his friend Osmond at the Mumm's Winery in Napa, and he had drunk two very cold bottles of Cuvée Napa *méthode champenoise*. He had taken the wrong turn while looking for the parking lot and had lost his way.

"Excuse me!" he shouted, even though she was less than ten feet away from him. "Can you direct me to Yountville?"

The cow replied first. "I'm sorry," she sighed, with a distinctive French accent. "I've never been there." She slowly rolled her shining black eyes from side to side, taking in the sunflower field. "To tell you the truth, I've never been anywhere."

But Jacqueline laughed and said, "I can show you, don't worry!" She slithered down from the cow and walked up to him, so that she was disturbingly close. The tablecloth had slipped and he could see that, underneath it, her breasts were bare.

"You're not really interested in going to Yountville, are you?" she asked him. She was wearing a very strong perfume, like a mixture of lilies and vertigo. "Not any more."

"Have I drunk too much wine or is that a wedding cake on your head?"

"Yes . . . I was supposed to get married today, but I decided against it."

Jack swayed, and blinked, and looked around the sunflower field. Sunflowers, as far as the eye could see, nodding like busybodies.

"Hold this," Jacqueline had told him.

Jacqueline had given him one end of the tablecloth, and then she proceeded to turn around and around, both arms uplifted, unwinding herself. Soon she was completely naked, except for the wedding cake on her head and tiny white stiletto-heeled boots with white laces. Jack was sure that he must be hallucinating. Too much heat, too much *méthode champenoise*.

Jacqueline had an extraordinary figure, almost distorted, like a fantasy. Wide shoulders, enormous breasts, the narrowest of waists, and narrow hips, too. Her skin had been tanned the color of melted caramel, and it was shiny with lotion. The warm breeze that made the sunflowers nod had made her nipples knurl and stiffen.

"I was supposed to consummate my marriage today," she told him. "But since I don't have a groom any longer . . ."

"Who were you supposed to be marrying?"

"A Frenchman. But I decided against it."

Jack licked his lips. They were rough from sunburn and too much alcohol. Jacqueline rested one hand lightly on his shoulder and said, "You don't mind doing the honors, though?"

"The honors?"

She turned around and bent over, reaching behind her with both hands and pulling apart the cheeks of her bottom. He found himself staring at her tightly wrinkled anus and her bare, pouting vulva. Her labia were open so that he could see right inside her, pink and glistening.

"Well?" she asked him, after a moment. "What are you waiting for?"

"I, ah—"

The cow stopped munching sunflowers for a moment. "*Si vous ne trouvez pas agréables, monsieur, vous trouverez de moins des choses nouvelles,*" she quoted, with yellow petals falling from her mottled lips. "If you do not find anything you like, sir, at least you will find something new."

Jack stripped off his shirt and unbuckled his belt, undressing as rapidly as he used to when he was a boy on the banks of his grandpa's swimming hole. His penis was already hard, and when he tugged off his white boxer shorts it bobbed up eagerly.

He approached Jacqueline from behind, his penis in his hand, and moistened his glans against her shining labia.

"With this cock, you consummate our union," Jacqueline recited.

He pushed himself into her, as slowly as he could. She was very wet inside, and hot, as if she were running a temperature. His penis disappeared into her vagina as far as it would go, and for a long, long moment he stood in the sunflower field, buried inside her, his eyes closed, feeling the sun and the wind on his naked body. He felt as if a moment as perfect as this was beyond sin, beyond morality, beyond all explanation.

With his eyes still closed, he heard a light buzzing noise. He felt something settle on his shoulder, and when he opened his eyes he saw that it was a small honeybee. He tried to flick it off, but it stayed where it was, crawling toward his neck. He twitched his shoulder, and then he blew on it, but the honeybee kept its footing.

He heard another buzzing noise, and then another. Two more honeybees spiraled out of the breeze and settled on his back. Jacqueline groped between her legs until she found his scrotum, and she dug her fingernails into his tightly wrinkled skin and pulled at it. "Harder!" she demanded. "Harder! I want this union to be thoroughly consummated! Harder!"

Jack withdrew his penis a little way and then pushed it into her deeper. She let out a high ululation of pleasure: *tirra-lirra-lirra*! He pushed his penis in again, and again, but each time he did so, more and more honeybees settled on his shoulders. They seemed to come from all directions, pattering out of the wind like hailstones. Soon his whole back was covered in a black glittering cape of honeybees. They crawled into his hair, too, and onto his face. They even tried to crawl into his nostrils and into his mouth.

"Harder, sir knight!" Jacqueline screamed at him. He gripped her hips in both hands and began to ram his penis into her so hard that he tugged her two or three inches into the air with every thrust. But now the honeybees were gathering between his legs, covering his balls and crawling up the crack of his buttocks. One of them stung him, and then another. He felt a burning sensation in his scrotum, and all around the base of his penis. His balls began to swell up until he was sure that they were twice their normal size.

A honeybee crept into his anus, and stung him two or three inches inside his rectum. This explorer was followed by another, and another, and then by dozens more, until he felt as if a blazing thornbush had been forced deep into his bottom. Yet Jacqueline kept screaming at him, her breasts jiggling like two huge Jell-Os with every thrust, and in spite of the pain he felt a rising ecstasy that made him feel that his penis was a volcano, and that his sperm was molten lava, and that he was right on the brink of eruption.

Jacqueline began to quake. "Oh con-sume-AAAAAAAAa-tion!" she cried out, as if she were singing the last verse in a tragic opera. She dropped onto her knees on the dry, baked earth, between the sunflower stalks, and as she did so, Jack, in his suit of living bees, spurted semen onto her lower back, and her anus, and her gaping cunt.

He pitched sideways onto the earth beside her, stunned by his ejaculation, and as he did so, the bees rose up from him, almost as one, and buzzed away. Only a few remained, dazedly crawling out of his asshole, as if they were potholers who had survived a whole week underground. They preened their wings for a while, and then they flew away, too.

"You've been stung," said Jacqueline, touching Jack's swollen lips. His body was covered all over with red lumps, and his eyes were so puffy he was almost blind. His penis was gigantic, even now that his erection had died away.

Jack stroked the line of her finely drawn cheekbones. He had never seen a girl with eyes this color. They were so green that they shone like traffic signals on a wet August night in Savannah.

"Who are you?" he asked her.

"Jacqueline Fronsart. I live in Yountville. I can show you the way."

They lay amongst the sunflowers for almost half an hour, naked. Jacqueline stretched out the skin of Jack's scrotum so that it glowed scarlet against the sunlight, like a medieval parchment, and then she licked it with her tongue to cool the swelling. In return, he sucked her nipples against the roof of his mouth until she moaned at him in Mandarin to stop.

Eventually the cow coughed and said, "They'll be wondering where I am. And anyway, my udder's beginning to feel full."

"You shouldn't eat sunflowers," Jacqueline admonished her.

"You shouldn't eat forbidden fruit," the cow retorted.

* * *

But now Jacqueline was gone and the mirror showed nothing but his own reversed image, and the bed, and the dying sunlight inching down the bedroom wall. Dimly, far away, he heard a boat hooting in the Bay and it reminded him of the old dentist from Graham Greene's *The Power and the Glory*. Still there waiting, last boat whistling in the last harbor.

"What's going to happen if you can't get back out?" Punipuni had asked him.

He didn't know. He couldn't see much of the world in the mirror. Only the bedroom, and part of the hallway, and it all looked the same as this world, except that it was horizontally transversed. Medieval painters invented a device with three mirrors that enabled you to see your face the way it really was. Frightening, in a way. Your own face, staring at you, as if your head had been cut off.

He stood up and pulled his dark blue cotton sweater over his head. He had never felt so alone. He unfastened his belt and stepped out of his stone-colored chinos. He folded his chinos and laid them on the bed. At last he took off his shorts and stood naked in front of the mirror.

"Jacqueline?" he called. Even if he couldn't penetrate the mirror, he needed to see her, to know that she was still there. "Who hath seen her wave her hand? Or at the casement seen her stand? The Lady of Shalott."

"Jacqueline?" he repeated. "Jacqueline, I'll come join you. I don't care what it's like in the mirror-world. I just can't stand to live without you."

The phone rang, beside the bed. He ignored it to begin with, but it rang on and on and in the end he had to pick it up.

"Mr. German-cellar? It is I, Punipuni Puusuke."

"What do you want, Pu?"

"I have decided that it is in the interests of both of us for me to open the restaurant this evening. I will be serving boiled pens in their own ink."

Jack didn't take his eyes off the mirror. He was sure that he had seen the mirror-curtains stir, even though the windows were closed.

"Pu . . . if that's what you want to do."

"We cannot afford to be closed, Mr. German-cellar. The fierceness of the competition does not allow us." He paused for a moment, and then he said, "What are you contemplating, Mr. German-cellar?"

"Nothing. Nothing at all."

"You are not reconsidering a plunge into the mirror, sir? You know that it is better to rub margarine on your head than to run after a wig in a hurricane."

"Pu—"

"Mr. German-cellar, I do not wish for throat-constricting good-byes. I wish for you to remain on this side of the reflective divide."

"Pu, I'll be fine. Just open the restaurant."

"You must promise me, Mr. German-cellar, that you will not do anything maniacal."

Jack put the phone down. He couldn't make any promises to anyone. You can only make a promise if you understand how the world works, and after Jacqueline's disappearance he had discovered that life is not arranged in any kind of pattern, but incomprehensible. Nothing follows. Nothing fits together.

He returned to the mirror and stood facing it. As he did so, the door in the reflection slowly swung open and Jacqueline slowly walked in. Her face was very pale, and her hair was elaborately curled and braided. She was wearing a royal blue military jacket, with gold epaulets and frogging, and black riding boots that came right up over her knees, but nothing else. Her heels rapped on the bedroom floor as she approached him.

Jack pressed the palms of his hands against the mirror. "Jacqueline, what's going on? Why are you dressed like that?"

She pressed her palms against his, although all he could feel was cold glass. Her eyes looked unfocused, as if she were very tired, or drugged.

"It's a parade," she told him, as if that explained everything.

"Parade? What parade? You're practically naked."

She gave him a blurred and regretful smile. "It's all different here, Jack."

He felt a tear creeping down his left cheek. "I've decided to join you. I've thought about it, and there isn't any other way."

"You can't. Not unless the mirror wants you."

"Then tell me how."

"You can't, Jack. It doesn't work that way. It's all to do with vanity."

"I don't understand. I just want us to be together, it doesn't matter where."

Jacqueline said, "I walked down to the Embarcadero yesterday afternoon. The band was playing. The bears were dancing. And there it was, waiting for me. A rowboat, with my name on it."

"What?"

She looked at him dreamily. "Jack, there's always a boat waiting for all of us. Still there, last boat whistling in the last harbor. One day, we all have to close the book and close the door behind us and walk down the hill."

"Tell me how I can get into the mirror!"

"You can't, Jack."

Jack took a step back. He was breathing so heavily that his heart was thumping and his head was swimming. Jacqueline was less than three feet away from him, with those salmon eyes and those enormous breasts and that vulva like a brimming peach. All of the days and nights they had spent together flickered through his head like pictures in a zoetrope.

Jacqueline said, "Jack, you have to understand. It's not that everything changes. Don't you get it? *Everything was back-to-front to begin with.*"

He took another step back, and then another, and then another. When he reached the bed, he stepped to one side. Jacqueline stood with her hands pressed flat against the mirror, like a child staring into a toy-store window.

"Jack, whatever you're thinking, don't."

He didn't hesitate. He ran toward the mirror, and on his last step he stretched out both of his hands ahead of him like a diver and plunged straight into the glass. It burst apart, with a crack like lightning, and he hurtled through the mahogany frame and onto the floor, with Jacqueline lying underneath him.

But this wasn't the soft, warm Jacqueline who had wriggled next to him in bed. This was a brilliant, sharp, shining Jacqueline—a woman made out of thousands of shards of dazzling glass. Her face was made of broken facets in which he could see his own face reflected again and again. Her breasts were nothing more than crushed and crackling heaps of splinters, and her legs were like scimitars.

But Jack was overwhelmed with grief and lust and he wanted her still, however broken she was. He pushed his stiffened penis into her shattered vagina, and he thrust, and thrust, and grunted, and thrust, even though the glass cut slices from his glans and stripped his skin to bloody ribbons. With each thrust, the glass sliced deeper and deeper, into the spongy blood-filled tissue of his penile shaft, into his veins, into his nerve endings. Yet he could no longer distinguish between agony and pleasure, between need and self-mutilation.

He held Jacqueline as tightly as he could and kissed her. The tip of his tongue was sliced off, and his face was crisscrossed with gaping cuts.

"We're together," he panted, with blood bubbling out of his mouth. "We're together!"

He squeezed her breasts with both hands and three of his fingers were cut down to the bone. His left index finger flapped loosely on a thread of skin and nothing else. But he kept on pushing his hips against her, even though his penis was in tatters and his scrotum was sliced open so that his bloodied testicles hung out on tubes.

"We're together . . . we're together. I don't mind where I live, so long as I have you."

At last, he had lost so much blood that he had to stop pushing, and lie on top of her, panting. He was beginning to feel cold, but he didn't mind, because he had Jacqueline. He tried to shift himself a little, to make himself more comfortable, but Jacqueline crackled underneath him, as if she were made of nothing but broken glass.

The afternoon seemed to pass like a dream, or a poem. The sun reached the floor and sparkled on the fragments of bloodied mirror. Jack could see his own reflection in a piece of Jacqueline's cheek, and he thought, *now I know what she means about the last boat whistling in the last harbor.*

Eventually it began to grow dark, and the bedroom filled with shadows.

For often thro' the silent nights
A funeral, with plumes and lights
And music, went to Camelot.
Or when the moon was overhead
Came two young lovers lately wed;
"I am half-sick of shadows," said
The Lady of Shalott.

Punipuni knocked on Jack's door at midnight. He made three paces through the room; then stopped.

"Oh, Mr. German-cellar," he said. He pressed his hand over his mouth to stop himself from sobbing out loud, although nobody would have heard him. "Oh, Mr. German-cellar."

He wrapped Jack's body in the multicolored duvet from the bed and carried him down to the street. He stowed him in the trunk of his aging brown Kamikaze and drove him to the Embarcadero. The night was very clear, and the stars were so bright that it was difficult to tell which was city and which was sky.

He found a leaky abandoned rowboat beside one of the piers. He lifted Jack into it and laid him on his back, so that his bloodied face was looking up at Cassiopeia. Then he untied the rope and gave the rowboat a push, so that it slowly circled away. The reflected lights of Camelot glittered all around it, red and yellow and green.

Punipuni stood and watched it with his hands in his pockets. "Men should never go looking for darkness, Mr. German-cellar. You can only find darkness in a closed cupboard."

During the night, as the tide ebbed, the rowboat drifted out toward the ocean, under the Golden Gate Bridge.

As the tide began to turn, another rowboat appeared from the opposite direction, and in this rowboat lay a naked woman in sunglasses, lying on a bed of dried brown chrysanthemums. The two rowboats knocked against each other with a hollow sound, like coffins, and then they drifted away, their prows locked together as if there were only one rowboat, reflected in a mirror.

About the Authors

ABBIE BERNSTEIN

The California resident is director/producer of *The Making of "Robin of Sherwood"* and has acted as director/writer/producer for several short films. She has written several screenplays, and as a journalist, she works for *Fangoria*, *Dreamwatch*, *Buffy the Vampire Slayer* magazine, *Angel* magazine, *The Audio Revolution*, *Revolution Home Theater*, *Cinescape*, *Star Trek Monthly* and *Backstage West*. She is working on a novel.

ILSA BICK

Bick is a child, adolescent, and forensic psychiatrist. Her story "A Ribbon for Rosie" won the grand prize in *Star Trek: Strange New Worlds II*, and "Shadows, in the Dark" took second prize in *Star Trek: Strange New Worlds IV*. Her work has appeared, among other places, in *Writers of the Future Vol. XVI, SCIFI.COM, Challenging Destiny, Talebones,* and *Beyond the Last Star*. She is also the author of the fourth novel in the Star Trek: The Lost Era series, *Well of Souls.* Forthcoming are stories in *Be Mine, Hauntings*, and elsewhere.

MICHAEL BRACKEN

Bracken is the editor of *Fedora, Fedora 2, Hardboiled*, and *Small Crimes* and the author of *All White Girls, Bad Girls, Canvas Bleeding, Deadly Campaign, Even Roses Bleed, Psi Cops, Tequila Sunrise,* and nearly eight hundred shorter works. His horror fiction has appeared in *Aberrations, Black Rose, Decadence 3, Delirium, Fantasy Macabre, Midnight, Night Voyages, Northern Horror, Score, Thin Ice, Weirdbook*, and many other publications. He has earned numerous awards for advertising copywriting and a Derringer Award nomination for his short story "Cuts Like a Knife." He lives with his family in Waco, Texas.

CATHERINE DAIN

Dain is the author of twelve mysteries, including *Death of the Party* and *Follow the Murder*, two books starring actress-turned-therapist-turned-amateur sleuth Faith Cassidy. Dain also wrote the Freddie O'Neal series, for which she was twice nominated for a Shamus award by the Private Eye Writers of America. She lives in Ojai, where she is an active member of the Art Center Theater Company and the Ojai Shakespeare Festival, and works as a professional tarot reader, as does the protagonist of her two New Age mysteries, Mariana Morgan. A collection of Dain's short stories, *Dreams of Jeannie and Other Stories*, was released in 2003.

CHRISTA FAUST

Christa Faust has published two novels, including *Control Freak*, recently reissued, and a new novel-length version of her apocalyptic novella "Triads," co-authored with Poppy Z. Brite and set for release in 2004. Faust is a Hot Blood veteran who lives and writes in Los Angeles.

ELLE FRAZIER

Elle Frazier resides on a South Carolina lake where she finds inspiration in the scenery and people of the area to create imaginative stories. Tae Kwon Do, scuba diving, being a band groupie, weightlifting, and riding on the back of Harley Davidson motorcycles through the mountains are just a few of her indulgences. This is her first published work.

LONN FRIEND

Friend is a veteran rock journalist and multimedia personality. He was editor-in-chief of the iconoclastic hard rock *RIP* magazine, hosted the "Friend at Large" segment of MTV's "Headbanger's Ball" and the weekly syndicated radio program, "Pirate Radio Saturday Night." He recently composed the liner notes for Bon Jovi's "One Wild Night" and Ronnie James Dio's "Dio: Stand Up and Shout, The Anthology." He is frequently seen in VH1 documentaries. Friend was born and raised in Los Angeles but has recently relocated to Las Vegas to, as he puts it, "compose twixt the sinful neon of the Strip and the spiritual shadow of Red Rock Canyon." He co-edited the debut Hot Blood collection with Jeff Gelb and Michael Garrett in 1989.

MICHAEL GARRETT

Garrett is an internationally published author and fiction editor. He's the co-creator and co-editor of the *Hot Blood* series and author of a nonfiction guide for beginning writers, *The Prose Professional: Your Career as a Fiction Writer*. A new edition of his movie-optioned sold-out novel *Keeper* has been issued. He's a Writer's Digest School instructor and also teaches writing workshops for colleges and as fund-raisers for writers' groups. Serving as a "book doctor," he's an editor-for-hire to help writers improve the quality of their manuscripts. His Web site is www.writing2sell.com.

JEFF GELB

This edition of *Hot Blood* marks Gelb's nineteenth published book as editor, co-editor, or author. And he's not tired yet! In 2005, he'll co-edit a new anthology series called *Dark Delicacies* with Del Howison and hopes to continue further volumes of Hot Blood with lifelong best pal Michael Garrett.

J. F. GONZALEZ

Gonzalez is the author of the novels *Clickers* (with Mark Williams), *Shapeshifter, Conversion, Maternal Instinct, Fetish*, and *Survivor*. Over fifty of his short stories have appeared in various magazines and anthologies ranging from *Penthouse Letters* to *Shivers II*. *Old Ghosts and Other Revenants* collects a dozen of his short stories, and he shares editorial credit with Garrett Peck on the two-volume *Tooth and Claw* anthologies. A former resident of Los Angeles, he recently escaped life in the big city to live in the Pennsylvania country with his family. For more information, visit his Web site at http://www.jfgonzalez.com.

STEPHEN GRESHAM

Gresham teaches and writes in Auburn, Alabama. He has published eighteen novels and several dozen short stories. His latest novel, *Haunted Ground*, was published by Pinnacle Books in January 2003, and an untitled vampire novel is scheduled for publication by Pinnacle. He has a Web site at www.stephengresham.com.

DEL HOWISON

Howison, with wife Sue, created America's only all-horror book and gift store, Dark Delicacies, as fans and for fans, and they remain horror's biggest aficionados. Del has been the frequent guest of horror conventions and is a respected horror historian for numerous DVD features. He regularly advises writers, directors and studios on the directions in which horror is headed. He's been an actor in several horror films and has written blurbs for many horror novels. Their Web site can be found at www.darkdel.com.

GREG KIHN

After a successful run as a rock star that included several international hit records (including "The Breakup Song" and "Jeopardy") Kihn reinvented himself in the late '80s and now hosts the top-rated morning radio show on 98.5 KFOX in San Jose, California. He has published four novels and numerous short stories over the past decade. In addition, Greg recently edited an anthology of short stories by musicans, *Carved in Rock*. Greg is nearing completion of a two-novel set based on his rock and roll experiences, *The Memory Maker* and *Rubber Soul*. "Abomination" is his third contribution to the Hot Blood series.

MICHAEL LAIMO

Laimo's first novel, *Atmosphere*, published in 2002, was nominated by the Horror Writers Association for the prestigious Bram Stoker Award. His second novel, *Deep in the Darkness*, was published in 2004. His short fiction has been published in a variety of anthologies and magazines and has been collected in *Demons, Freaks and Other Abnormalities*, and *Dregs of Society*.

GRAHAM MASTERTON

Masterton lived in Cork, Ireland, for four years, where he wrote *Trauma*, the story of a crime-scene cleaner, which was shortlisted in 2003 for an Edgar Award; *A Terrible Beauty*, a horror-crime novel set in Cork; *Unspeakable*, the story of a deaf woman who reads lips to assist in police investigations; a children's dark fantasy called *The Hidden World*; and *The Devil in Gray*, a horror novel with a spooky Civil War setting. Now back in Britain, he has written *Outrage*, a Hollywood-based chiller, and a sixth book in his series featuring Jim Rook, the psychic college teacher, *Darkroom*. His thriller *Genius* was published in November 2003, and will be followed in 2004 by another thriller, *Holy Terror*. He has been commissioned to write three new horror novels featuring characters from some of his best-known works, including *The Manitou* and *Night Warriors.* His latest nonfiction book of sexual advice for men, *Up All Night*, was published in April 2004. His story in this collection, "Camelot," reflects a lifelong interest in Victorian romantic poetry and pre-Raphaelite art. His Web site is www.grahammasterton.co.uk, where he encourages discussion on a wide range of subjects. He and his wife, Wiescka, live in Leafy Suburg, England.

ALAN ORMSBY

Ormsby has been an actor, director, screenwriter, makeup man, toy designer, playwright, caricaturist, and teacher. He wrote the screenplay for *My Bodyguard* and *Cat People* and for the cult movies *Deranged* and *Dead of Night*. He is finishing a novel for publication next year.

DANA SOLOMON

Solomon began writing in Edgar Doctorow's narrative literature class at Sarah Lawrence College and has since sold short stories to numerous dark fantasy and horror magazines, starting with Galaxy Magazine some years ago. Her fiction has appeared more recently in the *Bucks County Writer*, *Pegasus Review*, *Horror Garage*, and most recently the *Amazing Heroes* anthology. A one-act play, *Prolonged Interval*, was produced off-Broadway. Her fiction has won several writers' competitions.

MARV WOLFMAN

As executive producer of Pocket Dragon Adventures, Wolfman oversaw storyboards, voice recordings, and all designs as well as scripts. As founding comics editor of *Disney Adventures* magazine, editor-in-chief of Marvel Comics and senior editor of DC Comics, he supervised a large staff and was involved with all creative and business decisions. As a writer/editor, he created numerous characters which have been translated into TV, movies, animation, and toys, including Blade the Vampire Hunter, Bullseye, and Teen Titans. Wolfman is also a novelist, animation writer, and prolific comic book scribe.

DAVE ZELTSERMAN

Zeltserman works as a software engineer in the Boston area and, along with running the Hardluck Stories Web-zine, writes crime fiction in a futile attempt to keep his sanity. He has had stories published in *New Mystery* magazine, *Hard-boiled* magazine, *Futures,* and a number of Web-zines. His first crime novel, *In His Shadow*, is scheduled to be published soon in Italy.